THEM OR US

ALSO BY DAVID MOODY

Hater

Dog Blood

Autumn

Autumn: The City

Autumn: Purification

Autumn: Disintegration

Autumn: Aftermath

DAVID MOODY

THOMAS DUNNE BOOKS
ST. MARTIN'S PRESS NEW YORK

THOMAS DUNNE BOOKS.
An imprint of St. Martin's Press.

THEM OR US. Copyright © 2011 by David Moody. All rights reserved. Printed in the United States of America. For information, address St. Martin's Press, 175 Fifth Avenue, New York, N.Y. 10010.

www.thomasdunnebooks.com
www.stmartins.com

Design by Gregory Collins.

Library of Congress Cataloging-in-Publication Data

Moody, David, 1970–
    Them or us / David Moody.—1st ed.
        p. cm.
    ISBN 978-0-312-53583-4
    1. Regression (Civilization)—Fiction.   2. Survival—Fiction.   3. Life change events—Fiction.   I. Title.
    PR6113.O5447T47 2011
    823'.92—dc23

                                                        2011025878

First Edition: November 2011

10 9 8 7 6 5 4 3 2 1

For Mum, Dad, and Pete

ACKNOWLEDGMENTS

Sincere thanks to all those who've helped make the *Hater* series what it has become: Both those who've read and enjoyed the books (okay, maybe *enjoyed* isn't the right word), and those involved with the publication of the series (particularly Brendan Deneen and all at Thomas Dunne Books in New York, and all at Gollancz in London).

Particular thanks to John Schoenfelder and Jo Fletcher, without whom I. these books might never have happened, and 2. the overall story wouldn't have been half the story it eventually became.

Thanks to my friends and family, especially Lisa and the girls. Ladies, without you all I'd probably have plenty of cash and loads of spare time, but I'd also be bored, lonely, and completely uninspired. I may be becoming a grumpy old man, and I might not say it often enough, but you are my world and I love you all.

Finally, thanks to my late father-in-law, John Tipper, and my mother-in-law, Betty, for introducing me to Lowestoft and the surrounding area. Thanks also to whoever it was who once casually said to me, "I bet it's easy thinking about the end of the world when you're staying with the mother-in-law," and set me on the path to writing *Them or Us!*

THEM OR US

The Last English Summer

AT THE HEIGHT OF the last English summer, the skies turned black as coal and never cleared. Backed into an inevitable corner by an enemy that had remained elusive and invisible until the last possible moment, the Unchanged military was left with only one remaining card to deal. And they dealt it, unleashing hell and killing millions. Or had they? Had that final, decisive strike been delivered by those who coordinated the so-called Haters? Had they pushed the button? Whoever was ultimately responsible, the end result was the same. As the vast city-center refugee camps all imploded, over the space of a few short days virtually every major city in the country was destroyed in a white-hot nuclear haze.

"A limited nuclear exchange" was an overused misnomer: limited in duration, perhaps, but not in effect. Although the weapons that had been used (mainly tactical, field-based missiles) had relatively low yields in the overall scheme of things, their combined aftereffects proved to be immense and catastrophic. Many thousands of people, predominantly the tightly packed, panicking Unchanged, perished immediately in the initial blasts (collateral damage, they used to call it). Those who had survived the maelstrom were forced out into the wastelands where their enemies waited for them impatiently: relentless, determined, and with an insatiable bloodlust.

The numerical advantage at first believed to have been held by the Unchanged proved to be another crucial miscalculation based on misguided and outdated assumptions. There may well have originally been an average of three Unchanged for each one of *the others*, but when the typical Unchanged was too slow and afraid to kill even one Hater, and yet a single Hater was so full of brutal hostility that even the weakest of them was capable of killing literally hundreds, that initial statistical advantage was swiftly canceled out, then reversed.

The Unchanged became a vanishing breed. Millions were slashed to thousands by the war. Thousands were reduced to hundreds by radiation sickness and starvation. The remaining hundreds were steadily hunted out and killed.

*Five Months,
Four Days Ago*

BEFORE THE BURNS ON his back and his busted right leg had even begun to heal, they made Danny McCoyne fight again.

He waited deep in the forest of yellow-leaved trees, one of a group of more than forty fighters, sheltering in twos and threes from the dirty black rain, waiting for the next kill. Johannson, the hard bitch who'd ousted the last leader of this pack when she'd hacked him down in the middle of another battle a week ago, knew exactly how to hunt the enemy out. That was why so many people stayed with her now. The hunt and the kill was all they had left.

McCoyne sat with his back against a rock next to a man whose name he didn't know, sheltering under a limp canopy of bracken and drooping branches. He stared deep into the forest, eyes struggling to stay focused, looking for signs of the movement he knew would inevitably come. In times past he would have been desperate to fight and tear those fuckers apart, but not anymore. Those days were gone, and now he didn't give a damn. He did it because he had to. The war had taken its toll and left him a hollow man; little more than a shell, just a shadow of who and what he'd once been. Body broken, spirit crushed.

There was a time not long ago when Danny McCoyne fought without question. *When all the Unchanged have been hunted out and destroyed,* he used to tell himself again and again, *then things will start to change. When the enemy is extinct, the rebuilding will begin.* The longer the war continued and the more intense the fighting became, however, the less likely that seemed. The level of damage inflicted on everyone and everything was severe, the scars indelible. So why did he bother? Why not just turn his back on the rest of them and walk away? The answer was disappointingly simple: His body had been badly damaged, and the reality was that, right now, he couldn't survive on his own. For the moment, McCoyne's options were stark: If he wanted to stay alive, he'd have to stay with these people, and if he wanted to stay with these people, he'd have to keep fighting and killing.

They'd been waiting out here in the dying forest since before dawn. It was lighter now, but McCoyne struggled to estimate the time or even how long they'd been here in the undergrowth. The heavy, smoke-filled sky was dark and had been that way since the bombs. He'd barely seen the sun since the morning he'd lost the last thing that mattered to him, his final tangible connection with the man he used to be.

Johannson's tactics were uncomplicated and effective. Faced with little alternative, many of the Unchanged who had survived the blast had gradually returned to the outskirts of the city the fighters were now camped close to, taking cover in those few buildings that had remained standing after the shock wave and firestorm, figuring that an inevitable slow death from starvation and radiation poisoning would somehow be preferable to an equally inevitable yet immeasurably more violent death at the hands of their enemy. Johannson, however, had other plans. She had at her disposal a core of dedicated fighters, desperate for action and almost Brute-like in their passion for Unchanged blood, who'd do anything she demanded just to kill again. She sent a squad of them into the city to flush the enemy into the open, rounding them up and herding them toward the waiting Hater hordes.

Was this it? McCoyne sensed a sudden murmur of activity around him and caught a glimpse of movement up ahead. His heart began to pound hard, beating too fast, making him feel dizzy with nervous anticipation. He remembered the excitement and exhilaration he used to feel at moments like this, but now he just felt sickness and dread. *Can't do it*, he told himself, trying to picture the moment when the Unchanged finally came into view and he had to attack, *I can't fight anymore*.

Then they came.

Rustling undergrowth and snapping branches heralded the arrival of the fittest. Two relatively strong Unchanged stumbled through the forest, too terrified of what they were running from to think about what they might be running toward. They zigzagged through the trees, looking behind them twice as often as they looked ahead. Johansson's fighters waited, fighting against their basic instincts, swallowing down the Hate and desire to kill until their leader gave the signal. They'd learned to obey her, safe in the knowledge that if they didn't, they'd be dead, too. Do what she says and you'll get to kill. Fuck with Johannson and she'll break you in two.

Johannson stood up and revealed herself just a few yards ahead of the farthest forward Unchanged, who, unable to stop in time, ran into her suddenly outstretched arm at full speed. It caught him across the windpipe and he dropped hard onto his back, too stunned to react.

"Kill 'em!" she screamed, her deep, hoarse voice echoing through the trees.

There were eight Unchanged in view now and still more following, all of them splitting off in random directions like a herd of panicked deer. They were attacked from all sides as fighters emerged from their various hiding places, dragging their enemy down and tearing each one of them apart, anything between three and ten focusing on each individual Unchanged.

As usual, McCoyne lagged behind. In spite of the sudden frenzy of the ambush and the chaos all around, his reticence hadn't gone unnoticed. There were others with worse injuries who moved faster.

"You don't kill, you don't eat," a ruthless and far stronger fighter called Bennett said as he shoved McCoyne out of the way to get to another Unchanged. It was a young woman, directly up ahead now, creeping back through the trees, thinking she hadn't been noticed and trying to get away again before it was too late. McCoyne forced himself to follow, legs heavy as lead, body aching, head pounding. Then, before Bennett had got anywhere near the lone woman, a Brute appeared, charging through the undergrowth. McCoyne pressed himself back up against a tree to get out of the way, terrified as the powerful, barely human killer approached. He shot a quick glance at the Unchanged the three of them were converging upon. Christ, she looked bad: so pitifully weak he knew that even in his own miserable state he'd have no problem killing her. Badly burned in the bombings, her skin was blackened, her face a haunted mask of scar tissue with the whites of her eyes the only remaining visible features. She dragged herself along, aware of the danger ahead now but resigned to her fate and unable to do anything about it. She glanced back over her shoulder—every additional movement requiring massive effort—then seemed to shrug and falter. McCoyne could see more killers approaching now, at least another three.

Before any of the fighters could react, the Brute struck. It leaped through the air with a grace that belied its stature, its powerful body naked and lean, still manlike in appearance but its movements more animal than human now. The creature covered the girl's entire face with one large hand, then slammed her head against a rock, caving in the back of her skull. With a flash of awe-inspiring violence and speed, it stamped on her chest, crushing her ribs, then yanked her right arm from its socket with a single powerful tug. It ran deeper into the woods, carrying the spindly, blood-soaked limb like a trophy and leaving its dying enemy spurting blood into the leaf litter. One of the fighters booted the woman's disfigured face. Then the rest of the fighters moved on, each of them desperate to be the one who made the next kill.

McCoyne stopped and waited for them to disappear. Johannson was close; he could see her beginning to move toward him as she finished killing another. She stumbled momentarily, tripping over the trailing legs of her victim, then steadied herself as she crashed through a brittle-branched bush into the clearing where McCoyne was hiding. He quickly grabbed the collar of the Brute-kill, lifted the woman's head inches off the ground, then punched her jaw and dropped her back down, making sure the leader had seen him, hoping to give the impression that he was the one who'd struck the killer blow. Johannson made momentary eye contact with him, and he relaxed, relieved that the boss had seen him at work, satisfied that she'd fallen for his pathetic, improvised deception.

"Keep fighting," she grunted. "More coming."

She grabbed his shoulder, hauled him up onto his feet, and dragged him back into battle.

Many hours later, in an empty warehouse on a hillside near a long-deserted factory, the group took shelter from the heavy, polluted rain that had been driving down all day and all night. It was cold, more like February than August. Some heat and light came from a pyre of Unchanged corpses, but ringside seats were reserved for Johannson and her most prized fighters. McCoyne and the rest of the hangers-on—the weak, the injured, the old, the indifferent—sat on the edges and took what they could, begging scraps and trading anything they'd managed to scavenge during the course of the day for a few meager mouthfuls of food.

Soaked through, shivering with cold, and unable to sleep, McCoyne stared into the darkness outside. Another endless night. The fear of being attacked kept him awake, but when he did manage to lose consciousness, nightmares would inevitably wake him again. He dreamed about the bombs every night, remembering the heat and the light and the impossibly huge mushroom cloud of smoke and ash rising up over the vaporized city; horrific images forever burned into his mind. For a few days immediately after the attack, the bombs had given him a misplaced sense of relief, comfort almost. He'd sought solace in the fact that such unspeakable horror had been unleashed and he'd survived. The bombs were the ultimate symbol of the Hate—how could things possibly get any worse?

As the night dragged on, McCoyne remembered a conversation he'd had many weeks ago with a friend. They'd talked about vampires and werewolves and other fictional creatures from the past, and had come to the conclusion that although they were still alive, the monsters he and the rest of his kind had come to resemble most of all were zombies. Back then he'd tried to imagine what would happen to the undead once the last of their prey had been hunted down and destroyed. Today he decided he'd found the answer. *This* was all that remained: this constant, never-ending purgatory. Dragging themselves through what was left of their world until their physical bodies finally failed them, all of them desperate to satisfy an insatiable craving that would never be silenced. Nothing else mattered anymore. Their lives were empty but for the hunt and the kill. It was an inescapable paradox: By destroying their enemy they were also removing their own reason to live.

He curled up in the darkness on the outside edge of the group and tried to rest, knowing that he somehow had to build up his strength for tomorrow. The hunting and fighting would begin again at daybreak. *Who I used to be and everything I've done before today counts for nothing,* he thought to himself as he tried to shut out the noise of the animals around the fire. *If I don't kill tomorrow, I'm dead.*

Three Months, Three Weeks Ago

JOHANNSON WAS GONE, KILLED in a battle over hunting grounds several weeks back. In the days preceding her death, her growing army had slowly drifted east toward the coast, ultimately reaching the edge of territory controlled by a man called Thacker. Although nowhere near as ruthless a warrior as Johannson, Thacker had other qualities that inspired hordes of fighters to follow him, and their numbers ultimately gave him a crucial edge. In contrast to much of the now nomadic population, he ran his operations from an established and easily defendable location that provided shelter and a place to store food, weapons, and other supplies. When Johannson had challenged him, her own people had turned against her, realizing they'd be better off with this new lord and master. Thacker was different. As well as being aware of the importance of finding the next Unchanged to kill, he was already thinking about what might happen tomorrow and the next day and the day after that. Unlike just about everyone else, he had started to plan ahead.

Thacker, his fighters, and an ever-increasing horde of accompanying scavengers had occupied the coastal town of Lowestoft. The most easterly point on the map, before the war it had been a curious mix of industrial port and seaside resort, and its relative remoteness seemed to have shielded it from the worst of the fighting. Sure, it was a mere shadow of the place it had once been and it had been stripped of pretty much everything of value, but unlike most of the rest of the country's towns and cities, it remained remarkably intact. Unbroken windows, secure doors, and the like were still few and far between, but most buildings remained standing, and its basic physical infrastructure was sound.

A sensible man (in his prewar life he'd been national operations manager for a large and successful chain of hotels), Thacker immediately recognized the potential value of a place like Lowestoft in this new, postwar world. Its coastal location was important and easy to defend. Furthermore, its size was ideal: large and established enough to cope with a decent-sized population, but sufficiently compact to be managed effectively by him and his small army.

First light.

McCoyne reported for duty and joined the back of the line of volunteers as he did every morning. The hunting parties he'd been forced to be a part of since being picked up off the road after the bombs exploded had begun to gradually change in purpose over the last few weeks. The Unchanged were becoming harder to find each day, and the competition to be the one who actually made the kills when they found them was intensifying. Like an increasing number of other people (Switchbacks, Thacker liked to call them—Christ, McCoyne thought, why does everyone have to have a label these days?), McCoyne volunteered daily to head out into the wilderness alongside the hunting parties to scavenge. Other people, those who weren't particularly capable fighters but who had retained useful skills from their prewar vocations—builders, mechanics, medics, and the like—found some useful employment in the town and were paid by Thacker with scraps of food to repair and rebuild as best they could with limited resources. There was no call, though, for a useless, second-rate desk jockey like the man McCoyne used to be. His career options had been reduced almost overnight to a simple choice: scavenge or beg. At least scavenging sometimes enabled him to find the odd extra scrap, which he'd shove in his pocket when no one was looking to either eat himself or trade with later.

Lowestoft was as good as it was going to get. McCoyne knew what he needed to do to survive, and he knew the town was his best chance. He wasn't stupid. Tired, apathetic, and sick of fighting constantly perhaps, but not stupid.

A fleet of battered vans left Lowestoft each morning at daybreak: a couple of fighters in each sitting up front, a handful of scavengers crammed into the back behind them. Thacker's generals (as the few fighters who exerted sufficient influence over the rest of them had come to be known) dispatched the vehicles out toward villages and towns in a steadily widening arc. Once they'd arrived at their predetermined locations, the teams were under orders to split up and search, looking for Unchanged first of all, then food, water, and fuel. Then anything else they could find.

McCoyne stood behind the van in the middle of a dead village he didn't even know the name of and looked around dejectedly. The hissing gray rain had stopped momentarily, and now all he could hear was the water dripping off roofs and trees and trickling down drains. It was already obvious that this was a lifeless place, and he silently cursed whoever it was who had decided to send them out this way. There were clear signs that numerous other scouting parties had been here before them. It probably wouldn't have made any difference where they went, he thought to himself: Everywhere was like this now.

Hook, the lead fighter who'd driven the van this morning, shoved McCoyne toward a row of buildings on the other side of the road, grunting at him to check them out. McCoyne stumbled forward but managed to keep his balance and didn't protest for fear of provoking a reaction. A momentary scowl over his shoulder was as defiant as he dared to be. Grumbling under his breath, he wrapped his arms around himself and limped toward the buildings, chest rattling with the cold.

He peered through a grubby, cobweb-covered window into the first of five narrow row houses. He couldn't see anything inside and moved on, more interested in the takeout place next door and the newsagent's next to that. The newsagent's seemed the most sensible place to start. The door was stuck, but he managed to shove it open, the unexpected noise of an old-fashioned entrance bell ringing out and announcing his success at gaining entry. He stood still in the middle of the shop and waited for a moment, wondering if anyone was going to come to the counter. It was a dumb, instinctive reaction. The owners of this place were almost certainly long gone or dead, and judging by the stench in this gloomy, icy-cold building, he was betting on the latter.

Once his eyes had become accustomed to the low light, he swung his empty backpack off his shoulders and started picking his way through the waste scattered all around the musty, enclosed space. He took everything he could find, no matter how insignificant: newspapers and magazines to help light fires, a couple of paperback books, some string, scissors, bits of stationery . . . Around the back of the counter he found some sweets—several bars of chocolate and a handful of lollipops, which he split unequally between Thacker and himself, shoving his personal hoard into the pockets of the trousers he wore under his baggy overtrousers, where Hook and the others wouldn't find them. He checked the rest of the building but found little: some garden tools in an outhouse, some bedding, and a few pieces of cutlery. He briefly checked inside a half-empty storeroom but didn't waste much time there. He could tell from the droppings that covered the floor and the holes that had been gnawed in the sides of the few cardboard boxes that remained on the shelves that he wasn't the first scavenger to have been there. There was a body slumped against the back wall, and he could see the flesh of the corpse had been picked clean by rodents' teeth. Yellow bone was visible beneath flaps of heavily stained clothing.

McCoyne returned to the road outside to dump his stash. The rest of the party had busied themselves clearing out a service station and hotel, and by the looks of things they'd already found a damn sight more than he had. Hook, who just happened to be looking up at the wrong moment, stormed out to meet him and snatched his backpack. "This it?"

"There's nothing left. What am I supposed to do if there's nothing left? I can't magic stuff out of thin air."

Hook angrily shoved McCoyne in the chest. He tripped back and fell on his backside in the gutter at the side of the road, getting soaked with dirty rainwater. Hook grabbed another empty bag from the back of the van and threw it at him.

"Keep looking," he ordered. "Find more."

McCoyne wearily picked himself up again and trudged toward the takeout restaurant, praying he'd find enough stuff inside to avoid the inevitable beating that fucker Hook would give him if he came back empty-handed. His body ached and he felt permanently tired these days. He didn't know how much more of this he could take.

Inside the shop, a waist-high counter separated the public area from the rest of the building. He fumbled with an awkward brass latch, then lifted up a hinged section of counter and went through. *Please let me find food*, he thought to himself. He started making desperate contingency plans just in case, for a while even considering trying to creep back to the van, steal some of what the others had already found, then hand it back in again as his own and try to make it look like it was newly discovered stash.

The kitchen was disappointingly—but not unexpectedly—empty. It had obviously been ransacked like the shop next door, and subject to the same ferocious vermin infestation. McCoyne checked every cupboard and shelf, desperate to find something that might appease Hook, but there was nothing. He walked along a hallway into a small and compact living area behind the kitchen and stared out into the overgrown back garden. He was trying to decide whether he had enough strength (or desire) to try to get back to Lowestoft by himself, and avoid facing that bastard Hook altogether, when he heard something. It was directly above his head—footsteps in a room upstairs.

McCoyne quietly laid down his bag, unsheathed one of his knives, then crept slowly toward the bottom of the staircase. Whoever or whatever was up there, he knew it might be enough to help him avoid a battering. There was silence now, but he hadn't imagined it. With his pulse racing and his mouth dry, he climbed the steep steps to the second floor. It was dark, but he didn't need to see to know that there was someone up here with him. The smell gave it away—a pungent, inescapable whiff of sweat and fresh human waste. He needed to take his time and not screw this up. It was either someone like him who'd turned their back on what was left of society (and he'd come across several people like that before now), or it was one of *them*.

The room above the kitchen was empty. There was a bed that looked like it had been recently slept in, and a pathetically small store of supplies. Whoever had been staying here had shown some initiative and had been living off the vermin who were living off the food downstairs and next door. Three dead rats were hung by their tails from a clothes drier, and next to them was the deflated husk of something that had been either a cat or a small dog, he couldn't tell. Regardless of what else turned out to be here, this pathetic stock of meat meant that McCoyne did at least now have *something* to give to Hook. He opened a pair of threadbare curtains, filling the room with dull morning light, and looked around for something to put his booty into.

As McCoyne walked back toward the top of the stairs to check the other rooms, he noticed that a wooden chest of drawers he'd just passed was in an unusual position. There was a gap of a couple of inches between the back of the unit and the wall. Curious, he leaned over the top of it, looked down, and saw that there was a small hole in the wall between this building and the next, just wide enough for someone to crawl through. Clever little fucker, he thought to himself as he carefully pushed the chest of drawers out of the way. Whoever he'd disturbed in here had got their escape route planned, and that was no doubt how they'd survived undetected for so long. By now they'd probably either have disappeared out through the back of the building next door or locked themselves away in some other equally devious hidden hideaway. He crouched down and looked through the gap but couldn't see anything other than complete darkness on the other side. He leaned farther in and was about to crawl right through when he heard scurrying footsteps running up fast behind him. He tried to back out and turn around but couldn't move quickly enough in the confined space. He heard someone give a grunt of effort, then felt sudden, intense pain as he was cracked across the back with a plank of wood. He screamed out in agony and managed to roll over in time to see a scrawny figure sprinting out through the bedroom door.

"Up here!" he yelled, hoping that someone outside would hear him and help. "Unchanged!"

He limped out of the room, legs weak and back throbbing, then staggered downstairs. By the time he got outside, Hook and another fighter had already caught and killed the Unchanged man. His body was spread around the front of the restaurant, bright bloodred splashes of dribbling color among the dust-covered gray. Hook was standing on the sidewalk, the euphoria on his face clear even from a distance.

"Bastard was hiding," McCoyne said, groaning and stretching for effect. "Came up behind me and—"

Hook grabbed him by the scruff of the neck and threw him against the side of the van. McCoyne, stunned, couldn't move.

"You're fucking useless, McCoyne," Hook sneered. "Couldn't even kill one starving Unchanged. You need to watch yourself, pal. Fuck up like that again on my watch and you'll be the next one I kill."

"I won't," McCoyne tried to say, his strangled voice barely audible.

"That Unchanged," Hook continued, pointing at the man's remains smeared up the window, "he had more backbone than you, you prick. At least he made an effort. You, you're just a waste of oxygen. Completely fucking useless."

Seven Weeks Ago

MCCOYNE STOOD OUTSIDE THE recently built cordon that had been erected around the very center of Lowestoft, jostling for position in the middle of a crowd of some fifty others. None of them wanted to be there, but had to. They kept themselves to themselves and barely spoke or acknowledged each other, but, given the unseasonably low temperature and biting wind, the shelter and warmth provided by having other people in close proximity was welcome.

In the days immediately after the bombs, if anyone had asked Mc-Coyne if he thought things could possibly get any harder, he'd have said no. How could life get any worse? But that was before he'd reached Lowestoft. Sick and malnourished, he'd spent every day since then hunting and scavenging for little return, only to have the scraps he did manage to find immediately taken and added to Thacker's "central store." That was then, and Thacker was no more now. He'd been usurped and disposed of in a very public manner by one of his prize fighters, an evil fucker by the name of Hinchcliffe. The people on the streets called him KC. King Cunt. McCoyne had always harbored doubts that Thacker, and before him Johannson, had been bloody-minded and ruthless enough to cling to power in this screwed-up new world disorder. There were no such questions over Hinchcliffe's suitability for the role. In the short time since he'd assumed power, Lowestoft had been transformed and McCoyne's position (like that of every other nonfighter) had deteriorated rapidly. Now used to attacking first and talking second, those with the most strength ruled the place with their fists. The strongest fighters had, by default, assumed positions of authority, which they weren't about to give up.

Hinchcliffe's first move had been to blockade an area around the very heart of town where he and his army of several hundred fighters based themselves. Just half a mile square in size, it was more than large enough to house Hinchcliffe, his people, and all the supplies, vehicles, and everything else of any value that had been scavenged since Thacker and the others had first moved in. On one side was the ocean and on the other the main A12 road, which ran through the center of Lowestoft and was barricaded at either end of the compound. Two large metal gates had been erected across both the A12 and the A1144 at the northern edge of the town, with a single blockade-cum-checkpoint positioned across the full width of the road bridge that spanned the narrow channel of water at the mouth of Lake Lothing to the south. All other access points were sealed with row upon row of empty houses being boarded up along the remaining edges of the compound, and every minor road rendered impassable with piles of rubble, abandoned cars, and the like. The area was completely sealed off from the rest of the town, and no one came in or out without the KC's approval. Many of the so-called Switchbacks were allowed inside if they were useful or could fulfill a particular function, but the rest of them could go to hell as far as Hinchcliffe was concerned. McCoyne, with no discernible talent or incentive, had become one of a thousand-strong underclass, living in the ruins.

The outskirts of Lowestoft had come to resemble a shanty town. Many of the underclass occupied abandoned houses; many more camped out on the streets or in the gaps between buildings in makeshift shelters, reminding McCoyne of what he'd seen in the squalid Unchanged refugee camps before they'd been nuked. The people here were different, but many of the problems they experienced were the same. Disease was increasingly becoming an issue, and violence frequently erupted in the outlying regions. Food was in desperately short measure, with Hinchcliffe occasionally deigning to provide essential rations to a fortunate few. A briefly burgeoning black market collapsed quickly. The commodities became the currency, and there was never going to be a good enough supply to satisfy the population's constant demands.

Those who were in the best position outside Hinchcliffe's compound were those who continued to volunteer to scavenge the wastelands. They were paid for their efforts with a meager cut of whatever they found. The terms were grossly unfair, but that was tough. For the most part, with nowhere else to go (and no means of going anyway), the ever-growing underclass population remained in and around the town, building up on street corners like drifting snow. Hinchcliffe tolerated them and used them when it suited him. He controlled the food supplies (carefully coordinating storage across numerous sites so that he was the only one who knew where everything was), and he controlled the fighters. Far more than his predecessor, Hinchcliffe had wormed himself into an apparently unassailable position. His foot soldiers were rewarded for their loyalty with a life that was more comfortable than many would have ever thought possible again when the war had been at its bloody peak. On the right side of the compound wall there was a supply of fairly clean water, enough food for all, and, occasionally, heat and power. On the other side: nothing.

The crowd McCoyne had joined this morning was gathered in front of the larger of the two gates at the northern edge of the compound. Word had spread that a scavenging party was heading out west today into an area that had, until now, remained relatively untouched. Over the last couple of months it had been established that at least six cities (more precisely, six refugee camps) had been destroyed by the nuclear strikes last summer: London to the south, Edinburgh to the north, and several others, including Manchester and Birmingham. Without the means to measure pollution and radiation levels, it had been assumed that the bottom third of the country and a wide strip running the length of the land from the south coast right up into Scotland was most probably uninhabitable. Now, however, almost six months after the bombs, necessity had forced the foragers to start looking farther afield for supplies. A Switchback who'd once been a high school science teacher had done some basic research for Hinchcliffe in what was left of the Lowestoft library. She'd used reference works and other, less scientifically accurate books documenting what had happened in Hiroshima and Nagasaki, and had eventually come to the unsupported conclusion that although the bomb sites were nowhere near completely safe, the risks involved in scavenging a little closer to them had probably reduced enough by now to be worthwhile. Hinchcliffe didn't care. He wasn't the one going out there.

The metal gate across the road was pushed open. Two trucks drove out of the compound, the nose of the first gently nudging through the crowd, which quickly parted. Once they'd driven out and the gate had been closed behind them, the trucks stopped again. A shaven-headed fighter jumped down from the cab of the second truck. People scurried out of his way, leaving a bubble of empty space around him, their sudden distance a mark of fear, not respect. This nasty bastard was Llewellyn, and he was one of the few fighters known by name to virtually everyone left in and around Lowestoft. With a military background and undoubted strength and aggression, he was Hinchcliffe's right-hand man. His reputation was second only to that of his boss. He was older and quieter, but no less deadly.

"I'm looking for about fifteen of you," he said. McCoyne squirmed forward, trying to squeeze through a gap that wasn't there. The person on his right reacted and pushed him back the other way. He tripped over someone's boot and landed on all fours at Llewellyn's feet. Llewellyn grabbed his collar and pulled him up.

"What the fuck are you doing?"

"Volunteering," McCoyne said quickly. Llewellyn screwed up his face and looked him up and down.

"Suppose you'll do," Llewellyn said, throwing him toward the back of his truck before reaching out and grabbing someone else, "and you, and you . . ."

McCoyne climbed into the empty truck and found himself a dark spot at the very back of the vehicle, where he could watch the others and keep all his options open. He pulled his knees up tight to his chest to try to get warm. *Get out there*, he told himself, *get what you can, then get back.*

The drive away from town was long, slow, and disorienting. Conversation in the back of the windowless truck was sparse, and the time dragged painfully. It reminded McCoyne of another journey he'd taken like this, many months ago now, almost a year. Back then his eventual destination had been a gas chamber, from which he'd barely managed to escape with his life. What the hell was he going to see when they opened up the back of the truck today? He felt bad—an uncomfortable mix of travel sickness and nerves. Or was it more than that? He knew that every mile they drove in this direction took them deeper into the deadlands with its poisoned, radiation-filled air.

The journey ended abruptly. There were sudden murmurs from the people all around McCoyne, some of whom he could hear getting up and moving about. He stayed where he was, fingering the hilt of one of the knives he always carried attached to his belt, just in case.

The roller-shutter at the back of the truck was thrown open, flooding the inside of the vehicle with unexpectedly bright light.

"Out," one of the fighters ordered, and the volunteers did exactly as they were told. McCoyne was the last to move. He jumped down onto gravel, then looked around and grinned, caught off guard by his unexpectedly bizarre surroundings.

"What the hell's this?"

In front of him was a picnic area and an iced-over, duck-free duck pond, to his right a children's playground.

"I came here with the family once," a stooping, painfully thin man next to him whispered, grinning wryly. "Place has gone downhill since then . . ."

The group of volunteers and their fighter escort were stood in the first of several immense, interconnected, fieldlike parking lots. Mc-Coyne shielded his eyes from the hazy sun and looked around. Behind him was a huge billboard covered with faded pictures of smiling kids' faces, cartoon characters, roller coasters and rides, and other things he'd hadn't thought about in what felt like an eternity. A theme park. He'd heard of this one. He'd even talked about bringing the kids here once with Lizzie, but he'd managed to get out of it because, as he'd told her at the time, it was too far from home, and the entrance prices were obscene, and then he'd have had to pay to feed them all, then the kids would have wanted to go to the gift shop and . . .

"Hey, you!" an angry voice shouted in his direction. McCoyne spun around and realized he was on his own. The others were already shuffling away along an overgrown path that led through a copse of bare trees, deeper into the park. "Stop fucking daydreaming," the fighter yelled at him. "You're here to hunt, not fucking sightsee."

McCoyne ran after the others, legs already aching, struggling to catch up. He tried to focus on the job at hand, but it was all but impossible in these unexpectedly surreal surroundings. He crossed an artificially rickety wooden bridge over a murky stream, then caught his breath with surprise when he looked down and saw a frozen figure standing ankle deep in the water. It was a mannequin—a caricature of an old-time gold prospector with fading paint and exaggerated, cartoonlike features—but the plastic man still looked in better shape than he felt.

Ahead of the group, the silent heart of the theme park began to appear through the trees. Initially all they could see was the tops of the tallest, long-since-silent rides, the occasional scaffolding tower or the curving arc of a stretch of roller-coaster track. Being in a place like this was unexpectedly painful. It wasn't so much that it made McCoyne think about who and what he'd lost; rather, it made him realize what he'd never get back again. When finding the basic necessities to survive each day was such a struggle, would there ever be a time when places like this fulfilled a useful function again? Playing, laughing, time-wasting . . . it had been a long time since anyone had done anything even remotely pleasurable, and he thought it would be another age before any of them did again.

The group stopped in an open courtyard at the edge of the theme park proper, crowding dutifully around Llewellyn as if he were their tour guide. There were numerous buildings around, small and insignificant beneath the erstwhile attractions, all done up in a mock gold-rush style. The prospecting theme felt strangely appropriate. Directly in front of them was a large, odd-shaped concrete building with a faux-rock fascia and a large sign hung across its frontage announcing simply THE MINE. Its door had been roughly boarded up, like the windows of the house in a zombie movie where survivors were hiding, gaps between the overlapping planks for undead arms to reach through. McCoyne couldn't tell whether the boards were real or just there for effect.

Llewellyn, wearing a face mask and with a rifle now slung over his shoulder, flanked by similarly masked fighters on either side, addressed the volunteers.

"Hinchcliffe figures we'll find good pickings here," he announced, voice muffled. "Places like this have been overlooked, not looted over and over like the towns. If you don't bring me back as much stuff as you can carry, then you will be officially designated as being fucking useless and I will leave you here to rot. Understand?" No response, but no arguments either. Llewellyn continued. "And the quicker you move, the less chance there is you'll get sick. There's probably all kinds of nasty shit still hanging around in the air here."

Llewellyn's second comment got more of a reaction than the first. Even the vaguest mention of radiation and poisoning was enough to cause concern in the underclass ranks. McCoyne couldn't understand it. Why were they so stupid? He knew from what he'd seen and heard that Hinchcliffe certainly was no fool, so would he really have sent them here to collect poisoned food from a poisoned place? It was just scare tactics, designed to increase the tightness of the stranglehold grip he already had on the rest of the population. Was Danny the only one who could see him for what he was? Maybe they all realized but, like him, had chosen to keep their mouths shut rather than risk incurring Llewellyn's wrath?

The group split up. McCoyne kept his distance from everyone else, deliberately keeping to himself. If he didn't collect enough stuff today, he was a dead man.

"One hour maximum," Llewellyn shouted, his voice echoing eerily across the empty theme park. "Tear this place apart, then let's get out of here."

More than three-quarters of the allotted hour gone and McCoyne knew he was in trouble. His bag was only slightly less empty than when he'd started hunting. He'd wasted time mooching around an abandoned zoo, trying to work out what each of the various piles of odd-shaped, oversized bones and mangy scraps of fur had once been. For a place Hinchcliffe had assumed would have provided rich pickings, there was hardly anything here. He had been right in one respect; the theme park hadn't been trashed and torn apart like everywhere else. It was as if the food and supplies here had simply disappeared.

Use your brain, he told himself, trying to stay calm and not panic. *Think logically.* He walked under a dried-up log flume, heading for a long and narrow wooden hut that spanned the space between where people would have lined up to get on the ride and where they would have gotten off—the place they'd have been slowly channeled through to buy low-quality, overpriced souvenir photographs of themselves screaming, and presented in tacky cardboard frames or printed onto mouse mats, key rings, hats, and mugs. None of this was helping. *Put yourself in their shoes,* he thought. *Try to remember what it used to be like. I'd have gotten off this ride and I'd have been cold and wet and hungry . . .* He looked around and noticed the side wall of another shack facing out onto a lake with dark green, almost black water, which, he presumed, would have supplied the flume. Was this a café or something similar? There was no one else scavenging around here. This was his last chance. Christ, he hoped he'd open the door and find a previously undiscovered stock of food in this hut. Anything would do. Just something for him to hand in to Llewellyn . . .

McCoyne was about to force the door of the building when he stopped. He could smell something. It stank like raw sewage. Was it just the stagnant lake? He leaned over an ornamental wall and peered down. On the muddy bank below him he could see (and smell) a glistening heap of shit being slowly washed away by the lapping water. It made his sensitive stomach turn, but he managed to keep control and not throw up. This didn't make any sense. It looked like human waste, and there was far too much of it to be from just one person, so was this from an emptied-out slop bucket? Judging by the height it had been dropped from and the splatter pattern, that was the only logical explanation. Would one person have repeatedly used the same bucket? Wouldn't they have just come here to shit and saved themselves the hassle? *So, he decided, unless Llewellyn has passed around a communal bucket for everyone to crap in while I've been out here alone, this is probably from another group of people—and if they're hiding in a place like this, then there's every chance they're Unchanged.*

"Ten minutes," Llewellyn bellowed from the courtyard. McCoyne had to move fast.

"Found anything?" a voice asked, startling him. He turned around and saw it was the stooping man he'd spoken to earlier.

"Nothing," he answered.

"Anything in there?" the man asked, gesturing at the shack Mc-Coyne had been about to investigate.

"Empty," he answered quickly, lying to protect his potential find. "Look, do me a favor, will you. Go tell Llewellyn that I think there have been Unchanged here."

"Unchanged? Are you out of your fucking mind? Don't you think we'd have found them by now?"

"Don't bother, then. Suit yourself."

The other man turned his back on McCoyne and walked away, shaking his head and mumbling under his breath. "Fucking idiot . . ."

Whether he told Llewellyn or not wasn't important. As soon as he'd gone, McCoyne opened the door of the small wooden building and disappeared inside. He'd been right: It was some sort of café, as empty as everywhere else. It had been stripped clean. A deep-fat fryer in the small kitchen was filled with rancid, congealed oil, but the cooler cabinets and vending machines were empty. Even the packets of sauce and other condiments had been taken. He found one small packet of mustard, which he ripped open and sucked clean while he continued to investigate. There was another door at the back of the kitchen. It opened outward six inches, but no farther. It was chained shut from the other side. He quickly took off his pack, then dropped to his hands and knees, lay on his side, and squeezed through the gap. It was tight, but he was desperately thin now, and once his shoulders were through, the rest of him followed easily. On the other side he pulled his backpack through, then picked himself up and looked around. He was in a triangular-shaped patch of open space with the shack behind him and another similar-sized building adjacent. On the third side was a wire-mesh fence and, beyond that, another part of the forest they'd walked through to get here. He headed for the other hut but paused before going inside, sure he could hear movement. Probably another one of the scavengers, he told himself. He lifted his hand to pull the door but then staggered back with surprise as it was kicked open from the other side. An emaciated man came at him with a knife. Similar in height and age to McCoyne, clothes flapping around his wiry frame, McCoyne knew immediately that he was Unchanged. He felt himself tensing up inside and reached for the knife in his belt but then stopped at the last possible second. *Hold the Hate*, he silently ordered himself, *there might be more of them*. He lifted his hands in mock surrender. The Unchanged man, obviously terrified, took a couple of steps back. It occurred to McCoyne that the longer this unexpected standoff continued, the less obvious it would be that he was going to rip the fucker's head from his shoulders any second now. He could almost see the man's mind working behind his frightened, constantly moving eyes. *If he hasn't killed me yet*, he was thinking, *then he can't be one of them*.

Turn this around, McCoyne told himself. *Play the victim.*

"Help me," he said quietly. "They're here. If we don't get out of sight they'll kill us."

"Who are you?" the man croaked, his voice barely audible. "How did you get here?"

McCoyne was struggling to come up with a plausible response when he heard Llewellyn shouting again, calling them back to the trucks. He didn't have long.

"They're coming," he said. "Loads of them. Two trucks full. They followed me here. We need to get under cover."

The man stood his ground for what felt like an eternity, eyeing McCoyne up and down and trying to make sense of the situation. McCoyne forced himself to stay still and not react, all the time knowing that he should finish this Unchanged bastard now and that if anyone found out he'd been standing here talking to one of them like this, they'd probably kill him as fast as they'd kill them.

"This way," the man said suddenly, turning around and gesturing for McCoyne to follow him inside. He led him into the hut (a gift shop with shelves still well stocked with teddy bears, toys, and other assorted rubbish), through an interconnecting door and into yet another similar building, then out through another rear exit and across a narrow strip of asphalt. Hidden behind garbage cans and a mud-streaked golf cart emblazoned with the theme park's logo was a door in the side of a large brick building. McCoyne followed him through, making sure to shut the door again behind him and block it to prevent the Unchanged from doubling back and getting away. They tripped down a tight and steep staircase, then squeezed down a narrow, twisting corridor before emerging into a huge, dimly lit space. McCoyne struggled to make sense of what he was seeing for a moment. The room was a vast and clearly artificial cavelike structure, with fake stalagmites and stalactites bolted to the floor and ceiling, and pools of foul-smelling, dripping water. Light came from a number of lanterns dotted around the room, just enough illumination for him to see at least another eight Unchanged, wide-eyed and mole-like. He shuffled back until he reached the nearest wall, eager to stay out of sight, and his foot kicked against a heap of dummies like the one he'd seen standing in the stream. Then it dawned on him, this was the Mine—the huge building he'd stood outside earlier.

He could hear the man who'd led him down here talking.

"He was outside by the kitchens," he explained.

"For Christ's sake, Jeff, *they're* outside. Are you fucking stupid? He's with *them!*"

"He's not, I swear. He's like us. Would I be standing here now if he was one of them?"

McCoyne slid along the wall, watching the small group beginning to splinter, listening to the arguments develop and the volume of their voices increase.

No time for this. Got to act.

He ran forward and splashed through an unexpectedly deep puddle, his boots sinking into several inches of silt. Off balance and running almost blind, he tripped over a rocky mound and fell, then picked himself up again and carried on. The Unchanged panicked in response to the sudden movement and noise. Several of them ran after him. They were close behind, and he could hear their footsteps echoing off the walls and low ceiling. He kept moving, unable to see much more than just the occasional shadow, focusing more on the fact that Llewellyn and the others were about to leave than anything else. The ground beneath his feet began to slope upward. He ran up a long access ramp, then hit a wall, bounced off, and glanced over to his right, where he saw the faintest chink of light. It had to be the way out. One of the Unchanged dived for his legs and caught hold of one of his boots. McCoyne kicked out at him and managed to get free and keep moving, running now with arms outstretched. Another sharp bend and up ahead he could see the boards across the entrance that he'd seen earlier, shards of brightness pouring through the gaps between them. He slammed against the wood and peered through. The others were leaving, walking back to the trucks dragging their semifilled bags of supplies behind them.

"Llewellyn!" McCoyne yelled. "Back here!"

Someone lagging behind turned around and looked for him, but when he couldn't see anything he turned back again and carried on. One of the Unchanged reached McCoyne and tried to pull him away from the door. He managed to force one of the smaller boards free. He shoved his arm through and grabbed hold of another piece of wood so they couldn't pull him back.

"Unchanged!" he screamed.

McCoyne didn't know if the others had heard him. With two Unchanged now trying to drag him away from the entrance, he closed his eyes and clung on. The Unchanged, desperate but, incredibly, even weaker than him in their pitiful, malnourished state, couldn't break his grip. He could feel a third one hanging on to the back of him, tugging at his shoulders, and now the fingers on his right hand were starting to slip off the wood. He tried to stand his ground, but it was impossible. With a barely coordinated yank, he was wrenched from the entrance and dragged down onto his back. One of the Unchanged came at him with a knife, its blade glinting momentarily in a narrow shaft of light. As the terrified man dropped down and lunged for him, McCoyne managed to roll over to one side. Another one rolled him back, then another grabbed his kicking feet while others grabbed his thrashing arms.

The wooden boards across the door began to splinter as someone outside struck at them repeatedly with a heavy axe. The Unchanged scattered, and as soon as a big enough gap had been forced open, fighters and scavengers alike began to pour through. Suddenly free, McCoyne scrambled up onto his feet and pressed himself flat against the wall until the flash flood of bodies coming in had dried up, then got down on his hands and knees to avoid the fighting and crawled out into the open. He sat on his backside in the dust, panting hard, listening to the screams coming from the Mine, and waited.

All talk of radiation levels and other such threats had been forgotten in the euphoria of the kill. Three-quarters of an hour later and the theme park courtyard was still a hive of activity. Scavengers searched the den and collected piles of supplies the Unchanged had hoarded. Fighters dragged the bodies of their enemy out into the open and stripped the corpses of anything of value. Eleven kills. More than the last ten days combined.

Llewellyn marched over to where McCoyne was working, piling food into the back of one of the trucks that had been driven in from the parking lot.

"What's your name?"

"Danny McCoyne."

"Lucky find, McCoyne."

"Suppose."

"So what happened? Did you just stumble into their nest? Take a wrong turn and find yourself surrounded?"

"Something like that."

"Talk me through it."

"Why?"

"Because if you don't I'll break your fucking legs."

McCoyne sighed and threw the bag of food he'd been carrying into the truck.

"I found one of them while I was scavenging, I made him think I was like him and that you others were looking for me, then I got him to take me to the rest of them."

"And it was that easy?"

"Yep, that easy."

"So how'd you manage that, then?"

"Just something I picked up."

"Is that right?"

"Yep."

Llewellyn grinned at him. "You devious little bastard, you can hold the Hate, can't you?"

McCoyne looked away and picked up another bag. Did he really want anyone to know?

"So what if I can," he said nonchalantly. "Not a lot of call for it these days, is there? Hardly any of them left."

"When we get back to Lowestoft," Llewellyn said, leaning over him until their faces were just inches apart, "you're coming with me to see Hinchcliffe. He'll be interested to know we've got a freak like you in town."

Today

THE TWO MEN SKULKED silently through the filthy streets like starving rats, skin deathly pale, eyes blinking wide, both of them looking from side to side in constant, never-ending fear of attack. They ran frantically through the collapsed ruins at the edge of the town, arms overloaded with the food they'd unexpectedly managed to scavenge, fear and adrenaline driving them on, temporarily masking their physical pain. Their bodies were wrecked: exhausted and underfed. It was the first time either of them had been out in the open in more than two weeks, but, weak as they were, as the physically strongest members of the last remaining group of Unchanged in the area, this was something Fisher and Winston had had no choice but to do. Including the straggler who'd found them a few days back, there were only thirteen of them left now. They both knew that none of them would last much longer if they didn't have food.

Fisher froze. "Up ahead. Top of the road. Two hundred yards."

Winston grabbed his arm and pulled him back against the wall of the nearest building. He watched the Hater in the distance. Was it alone or part of a pack? His eyes were failing and it was hard to tell anything from here, but it looked like a young boy, probably one of those feral kids like the one that had killed his dad last summer. It paused on the dotted white line in the middle of the road, sniffing at the air like a hunting animal trying to catch a scent. Winston forced himself to remain completely motionless and prayed that Fisher would do the same. Even the slightest movement or noise might give them away and that'd be it—months of constantly struggling to survive ended in a heartbeat (maybe that wouldn't be such a bad thing, he thought). He watched the figure up ahead as it began to move again, very slowly at first, then sprinting away swiftly when something in the distance caught its eye. Winston didn't move until he was completely sure it had gone. In those unbearably long moments, he asked himself again (as he did at least once every hour) why he was even bothering to try to stay alive. Why not just give up and get it over with? A few seconds of agony and it would all be over and he could stop at last. The fear of death had always been enough to keep driving him on until now, but life was rapidly losing its appeal. Imagine the relief, he thought. No more running. No more hiding. No more crying. No more sitting in silence in the dark with the others, freezing cold, doubled up with hunger pains, feeling himself draining away, just waiting for the inevitable. . .

"We're clear," Fisher said, his voice just a whisper against the icy wind. Winston pushed himself away from the wall and ran forward again, just managing to keep his balance as he tripped down the curb, narrowly avoiding the crumbling edge of a huge, egg-shaped crater in the road where the skeletal body of someone who had once been like him lay facedown in several inches of dirty rainwater.

Another few minutes of breathless, stop-start running and hiding, and they were almost there. Winston dropped the supplies he'd been carrying in front of the wooden fence, then quickly lifted up the third panel along from the right, his fingers numb with cold. Fisher hurriedly climbed through the gap, then reached back for the tins and boxes they'd collected. He stood up again and took the weight of the panel so the other man could follow him through. Winston paused to snatch up a can of fruit that Fisher had missed, and to check they hadn't been seen. Behind them, everything appeared reassuringly silent and still. A flurry of gray, ashlike snow drifted down, each flake settling on the ground for just a fraction of a second before melting away to nothing. The remains of the town where he used to live looked as lifeless as Winston felt. The gaping doors and broken windows of battle-damaged houses offered unwanted glimpses into a world he used to belong to but which he was no longer a part of. A dead world. *Their* world.

"Get a goddamn move on," Fisher said anxiously, his teeth chattering. Winston pulled his head back, and Fisher quickly dropped the panel down with a welcome thud, blocking his view. Between them they snatched up their food, then scrambled down a steep, grassy bank toward what once used to be a permanently busy road but was now just a desolate, wide gray scar lined with rusting wrecks.

In their pitiful condition, the two men both struggled to control their descent down the muddy incline. Wearing dead man's shoes two sizes too big, Fisher fell near the bottom of the slope, dropping most of the tins and packets he'd been carrying and filling the silent world with ugly, unwanted noise. He frantically scooped everything back up again, still constantly checking his surroundings for movement, before racing after Winston, who'd been too scared to stop.

Beneath a bridge, midway along an otherwise featureless concrete wall, was a corrugated steel roller-shutter and, another couple of yards farther along, a metal door. Dirty gray, and with once important warning signs now obscured by a layer of black-speckled grime, the door was well camouflaged. Several freshly smudged handprints around the handle and the edges of the frame were the only faint indications that it had recently been used. Precariously balancing his supplies with one arm, Winston hammered on the door to be let inside. Several seconds passed—several seconds too long for his liking—before it finally swung open inward. An emaciated, skeleton-thin man appeared, brandishing a nail-spiked baseball bat. He frantically ushered Winston and Fisher indoors, then peered down the road in either direction before shutting the door again.

Stumbling in the sudden darkness, Fisher and Winston followed the short access corridor down toward a pool of dull yellow light around the main storeroom, where the others were waiting. They dumped their hoard in the middle of the room. The other survivors hiding in this dank highway department storage depot—those who were conscious and still sane—all looked on in disbelief. Sally Marks said what everyone else was thinking. "Where the fuck did you get all that?"

Fisher dropped to his knees and began examining the treasure they'd found outside. He grabbed can after can, holding each of them in turn up to the weak light from the single battery-powered lantern, struggling to read the labels. Around him, stomachs growled with hunger and mouths began to water at the prospect of food. Corned beef, canned vegetables, soup . . . how long had it been?

"Where did you find it?" Sally asked again.

"Where he said," Winston answered, pointing at the man in the corner who'd recently arrived. Thank God he'd found them. He said he'd been following the road for days since his last hiding place had been discovered by the enemy, and he'd tried to take shelter in their hideout, not realizing it was already occupied.

"And how did you find it?" Sally asked him, unable to make out his face in the shadows.

"I already told you," he answered. "I saw it just before I found you all. Couldn't carry it all myself."

"Does it really matter?" Winston sighed.

"Yes, it does."

"Remember that corner store by where the bus station used to be?" Fisher volunteered.

"On Marlbrook Road?" Sally asked.

"That's the one."

"But we've been there before," she said. "Christ, we've been there hundreds of times before."

"So?"

"Well, did we just walk past this stuff all those other times? Did you find a hidden storeroom we hadn't found before? Open a door you hadn't seen? Someone put this stuff there for us to find, you dumb bastards. It was one of them. It's a trap, you fucking idiots, and you walked right into it."

"What the hell does it matter?" Winston spat angrily, struggling with the ring pull on a can of fruit chunks, his fingers numb with cold. "No one followed us back. We only saw one of them in all the time we were out there, and that was just a kid from a distance. If this was a trap, then it didn't work. This place is dead. Even *they* don't come here anymore."

"*He* found us," she said, pointing at the man in the corner again.

"That was just luck," Winston argued. "He's like us, Sally. He found this place the same way we did."

Sally shook her head in despair and walked far enough away into the shadows that no one could see her. She leaned against the wall and massaged her temples. Maybe Winston was right. She'd overreacted, and not for the first time, either. Every day the pressure of being cooped up in here was getting harder and harder to handle. A year ago, all she'd had to worry about was getting the kids to and from school and getting to work on time. Hiding in a disused highway storage depot with strangers, eating cold food from a can, shitting in a bucket in full view of the others, fearing for her safety every second of every minute of every hour of every day . . . if she'd known what her life was going to become, she'd probably have ended it when the troubles first began.

They tried to make the food last, but they were starving and much of it was gone within an hour, empty stomachs finally satisfied after weeks of being drip-fed scraps. It didn't matter. Eating was a distraction that helped reduce the tension in the shelter for a precious few minutes. Sally looked around at the few faces she could see in the low light. Eight-year-old Charlotte stared back at her from the corner where she always sat, surrounded by a barricade of traffic cones she'd built around herself, her face as pale as ever. The two other children sat close by, Chloe fast asleep, eleven-year-old Jake dutifully sitting beside her, drawing shapes in the dirt with a stick. On the opposite side of the room, Jean Walker and Kerry Hayes spoke together in hushed whispers about nothing of any importance. Sally had thought Kerry beautiful when she'd first met her, but her young body had been ravaged by hunger since they'd had to lock themselves away in here. Her full figure had wasted away to nothing. She looked anorexic now: all protruding bones, stretched skin, and strawlike hair. In the opposite corner, Brian Greene did his best to disguise the fact that he was crying again . . .

A packet of stale cookies (what luxury, Sally thought to herself dejectedly) was being passed around. She took one, but stopped before she ate it, distracted suddenly by a low rumbling in the distance.

"Did anyone hear that?"

"Hear what?" Kerry asked, immediately concerned, yellow eyes bulging in the light.

"Thought I heard something," she said, already beginning to doubt herself. "Sounded like an engine."

"There's nothing," Fisher said quickly, scowling at her. "Just *them* moving around up there. Either that or your imagination . . ."

He was probably right. She couldn't hear anything now. Sally passed the packet on to the man sitting next to her—the new arrival. He'd hardly spoken since he'd gotten here, but it was obvious he was as desperate as the rest of them: a scrawny bag of skin and bones, a haunted expression etched permanently onto his weary face. He took the cookies from Sally, then passed them on without saying a word.

He waited for a few minutes longer before quietly getting up and slipping farther back into the shadows. He stepped over a couple of bodies—one sleeping, one dying—then made his way to the part of the cramped storage depot they used as a toilet.

Sally tried to block out the foul noise of the man pissing from a height into a metal bucket, and was relieved when it finally stopped. She waited for him to come back, but became concerned when he didn't immediately return. The rest of the shelter was almost pitch black, but she got up and felt her way along the cold, damp walls until she found him by almost falling over him. He was lying on the ground on his back, trying to force open the roller-shutter. A chink of light spilled across the floor where he'd managed to get his fingers under the shutter. With a grunt of effort he lifted it up another six inches.

"What the hell are you doing?" Sally asked, standing directly behind him. He didn't answer. Didn't even look at her. Instead he kept working, shoving his hands farther under the shutter and forcing it up another couple of inches at a time. He rolled over onto his front and was about to try to slide through the gap when she grabbed the heel of his boot and yanked him back.

"Don't panic," she pleaded with him, keeping her voice low so the others didn't hear. "Please don't do anything stupid. I know it's hard being trapped in here, but don't—"

He scrambled back and stood up fast. Catching Sally off guard, in a single sudden movement he spun around and reversed their positions, pushing her up against the wall. He covered her mouth with his left hand, barely needing to use any force, then sank a knife deep into her belly.

"I'm sorry," Danny McCoyne said, keeping her mouth covered to stifle any noise. "It's better for all of us this way. Trust me."

He laid Sally's body down, waited until he was sure she was dead, then wiped his bloodied hand clean on her jacket and slid out under the roller-shutter.

In stark contrast to the desolate silence an hour or so earlier, the road outside was now full of movement. Several battered vehicles and a group of eight armed figures had gathered a short distance from the storage depot doors. McCoyne picked himself up, brushed himself down, and wearily walked over to talk to Llewellyn, who marshaled the movements of the fighters from the back of a pickup truck.

"Had fun in there, McCoyne?"

"They're fucked," he grunted. "They won't give you any trouble."

"How many?"

"Eleven of them left. Three kids. Few basic weapons. All of them are pretty weak. A couple of them are virtually dead already."

Llewellyn nodded, then gestured for his soldiers to take up their positions. Five men armed with blades, bludgeons, and the occasional gun stood on either side at the doorway and waited. A van reversed back into the gap. The driver got out and moved around to the back.

"Wilson," Llewellyn bellowed at him, "let them go."

On his command, Kevin Wilson, chief kid-wrangler, yanked the van doors open and dragged two small children out on leashes. Naked and covered with grime, they struggled to escape, one of them trying to bite through the lead. When a terrified Unchanged face appeared under the roller-shutter for a split second, the children both lunged forward and threw themselves at the gap with furious speed. It was all Wilson could do to untangle himself from the leather straps and let go before he was dragged inside with them.

Exhausted, McCoyne leaned back against Llewellyn's pickup and waited for the inevitable. Barely half a minute passed before the other door into the shelter flew open and a crowd of terrified Unchanged was flushed out, running straight into the arms of the waiting Haters. He looked on as fighters starved of enemy kills for too long vented all their anger and frustrations on the helpless refugees now flooding out into the open. One of them—Kerry, he'd heard her called—managed somehow to escape, weaving around two fighters who both threw themselves at her at the same time. She'd barely made it another twenty yards before they caught her. One tackled her halfway up the grassy bank, grabbing hold of her spindly legs and thrashing feet. The other thumped an axe into the small of her back, brutally severing her spine. She was already dead, but they continued to fight, overcome with the euphoria of the kill and not wanting it to end, slicing and hacking at the woman until what remained of her body had been spread across an area several yards wide; a bloody swathe of violent red in the wet yellow grass.

THE BONFIRE OUTSIDE THE ransacked Unchanged shelter is burning out of control. The morons who were supposed to be watching it have been distracted, squabbling over food. There's a momentary flash of flame and a sudden loud explosion and they scatter, running for cover like frightened kids on Bonfire Night. Probably just an aerosol can or something similar lying too close to the heat, but whatever it was, Llewellyn's not happy. He grabs hold of one of them and kicks his legs out from under him, then he drags the scrawny little bastard nearer to the fire and pushes his face into it, screaming and shouting at him. Sobbing, the little man reaches into the embers and attempts to salvage some of the meat that's been roasting to pacify Llewellyn, who yells at him again, then kicks him in the side of the head, knocking him out cold. The way the fighters treat the others makes me feel sick to my stomach. I look at the man lying flat on his back and I think, *That used to be me.*

I'd rather keep my distance, but my feet and hands are numb with cold, so I walk toward the bonfire to try to warm up. In a year that's so far been filled with hundreds of fucking miserable days, this must be the worst yet. The gusting wind cuts through me like a knife, making the already subzero temperature sink further still, and the air is filled with sleet, which blows into my face like a constant hail of tiny needles. I'm less than a yard from the fire now, but I can still hardly feel it.

Wilson, the kid-wrangler, is still struggling. He's managed to get one of them back into the van, but the other one's causing him problems. The kid doesn't want to go back inside. He's constantly straining on his leash, desperate to break free and escape out into the wild where he belongs. Three men have got him cornered, but he refuses to give up. He drops to the ground and scuttles away quickly, crawling under the legs of one particularly slow and clumsy bastard. It'd be laughable if it wasn't so pathetic. The feral boy gets up and bolts for freedom, but he's still on the lead. His sudden movement catches Wilson by surprise and almost yanks him over, but he manages to stand his ground. By chance the kid starts running in my direction and, between me and the bonfire, finds his way through suddenly blocked. He stares up at me, and that moment of hesitation is time enough for Wilson and two others to grab hold of him and manhandle him to the ground. They wrap the long leash around him several times, binding his arms and legs tight to his body, then carry him over to the van and throw him in the back, screaming with frustration and rage.

I feel increasingly disconnected from all this bullshit. In some ways it was easier when I was just another face in the crowd. I guess I should feel something—pity for the kid, or the guy Llewellyn knocked out, or the Unchanged even—but I don't. I feel hollow, like every nerve in my body has been cauterized, and I don't give a shit about anyone or anything. I watched Llewellyn's men clear out the Unchanged hideout with ferocious speed and brutality just now and I didn't give a damn. Some bodies were dragged out and thrown on the fire still screaming, others just left on the ground where they'd been killed.

It's been a long time since we found an Unchanged nest like this, and the effect it's had on these fighters is frightening. It's been a release for them—a chance to get rid of some of the pent-up anger and aggression they've been forced to keep swallowed down since the rest of the Unchanged were wiped out. There's an empty void in these miserable people's miserable lives now. Before, when the war was at its height, the hunt and the kill kept them occupied, but now there's nothing. Infighting, bickering, and abusing the nonfighters alleviate some of their frustrations, but they're no substitute. Oh for the days when there were still plenty of Unchanged to kill, I've even heard them say, those who are able to construct such considered sentences, that is. Frequently their conversations are nothing more than a series of increasingly aggressive nods and grunts.

"Food," someone next to me says, jabbing me in the gut with a bony finger. It's a woman my height with dirty, pockmarked skin and clumps of lank yellow-white hair missing where her scalp is scarred. I take the chunk of greasy meat from her—half a leg of something or other, not sure what—then take a deep breath and force myself to bite down and chew. It tastes as bad as I expect, tough and barely cooked. I feel warm blood and grease dribbling down my chin and running down the insides of my throat, but I force myself to swallow, then bite again. And again. And again until the whole damn thing is finished. I throw the bone onto the fire, and it's only then that I allow myself to look at what it is I've just eaten. I'm not surprised when I see the rest of Llewellyn's men tearing strips of flesh off what's left of a dog's carcass. Dog is one of the easiest meats to find these days, along with rats and birds. They all feed off the scraps of the world, and we feed off them. Three of the fighters argue over what's left of the food. The woman who just gave me mine hangs back dejectedly, waiting for scraps and licking grease off her fingers. She sits on the ground next to the guy Llewellyn laid into. He still hasn't moved.

My stomach's already churning, reacting to what I've just forced down into it. I don't have the same capacity for food I used to, but I don't refuse it. I guess I'm fortunate that Hinchcliffe likes to make sure I'm well fed (being in with the man in charge has its advantages), but eating isn't something I derive any enjoyment from anymore. It's a necessity now, a chore. How food looks and tastes isn't important. All that matters is making sure you get enough nutrition whenever you can.

I've learned not to ask questions—you eat what you're given and you deal with the consequences afterward. And after what I've just swallowed, I know there will be consequences . . .

I help myself to a mug of coffee (is it coffee, or just lukewarm dirty water?), which helps take the slightest edge off the overpowering aftertaste of dead dog. The bitter liquid provides some welcome heat for a couple of seconds, but it fades quickly and leaves me feeling twice as cold. Doesn't matter how many layers of clothing I wear these days, I never seem to get any warmer. I'm so thin I sometimes think I might snap. Sometimes, when I look down at my body or catch sight of myself in a window or mirror, I have to look twice to be sure it's me. There was more meat on that dog leg I just ate than there is on my whole body. If they shoved a skewer up my ass and roasted me over the fire, there'd be a lot of disappointed people going hungry.

It's suddenly quieter out on the street, with most of the fighters either busy eating or clearing out the Unchanged hideout. Apart from the "cook" (who's now trying unsuccessfully to pick a rogue scrap of burned dog flesh out of the embers of the fire) and her unconscious mate, there's an ocean of space between me and everyone else. It doesn't bother me. I'm used to it. If it wasn't for Hinchcliffe, they'd have probably gotten rid of me by now. Fact is, I've been damn useful to him and he knows it. I can't match the anger and aggression of most of the people he surrounds himself with, but I can do things they can't, and that, he regularly tells me, makes me valuable.

I guess he's right. Days like today help me secure my place in Hinchcliffe's empire. If it wasn't for me, they'd never have found this nest of Unchanged. He'd had people out here looking for supplies, and the dumb fuckers couldn't work out why the stuff they'd been stockpiling kept disappearing. It was me who set the traps and left the bait and tracked the Unchanged back to this place. It was me who told Hinchcliffe and Llewellyn where this shelter was and how best to attack it. I'm the one who spent the last couple of days underground with those foul fuckers, sitting on my hands, swallowing down the Hate like bile and forcing myself not to kill them until Hinchcliffe's men were ready and in place. If it wasn't for me, none of this would have happened. My own self-preservation is all that matters now, and I have to stay focused on that. If that means playing Hinchcliffe's games for a while longer and keeping him on my side, then so be it. The sooner every single last Unchanged is completely dead and buried, the sooner the war will be over.

There's a sudden flurry of activity around the entrance to the Unchanged hideout again. The door flies open and Patterson, an enormously powerful man, drags a small Unchanged kid out by its long blond hair. The kid is only five or six years old, and she screams with panic and pain. Patterson is visibly struggling to stay calm and not kill her. He could snap her neck in an instant, but he's under orders not to. His fear of Hinchcliffe and Llewellyn is even greater than his desire to kill this kid. Instead he simply picks the girl up and throws her into the back of another van. Hinchcliffe says that Unchanged kids are important. He says we need to understand them.

"Good result," Llewellyn says, startling me. "I was starting to think this holding the Hate business was just bullshit you were using to get out of work and get yourself more food. I've just spoken to Hinchcliffe. He's pleased."

"Good."

"How long's it been since we last found any of them?"

"More than three weeks," I tell him. "Three of them in the basement of that church, remember?"

"Whatever," he grunts, obviously not really interested. "Anyway, get your stuff together. We're heading back."

He walks away, and I watch as the last Unchanged bodies are dragged out of the shelter and dumped on the fire beside me, the noise and smell of crackling, burning flesh making my stomach churn again. Scavengers are rifling through what's left of the Unchangeds' already ransacked possessions, emptying backpacks, crates, and boxes, looking for anything of value but finding next to nothing.

All that time those miserable bastards spent hiding in that godforsaken shelter . . . all those hours and all that effort, and for what? Why did they bother? Did they really think they'd be able to survive here indefinitely? They might have stayed hidden for another couple of days or as long as a few months, but they must have known that some-one like Hinchcliffe or Llewellyn would have been waiting for them. It was inevitable. I guess that's the one thing we all still have in common: We just keep going. Them or us, even when common sense says it's time to stop struggling and roll over and play dead, we all still keep fighting to survive, whatever the cost. It would have been easier if these people had just given up a long time back. Same result, much less pain and effort.

2

NONE OF THE BASTARDS I'm out here with today trust me, and the feeling's entirely mutual. Typically, the only space left in the convoy of vehicles returning to town is in the back of the van with the captured Unchanged kids. There are three of them being held in a padlocked wire-mesh cage that's bolted to the inside wall of the van, and the only other thing in here with them is me. They cower away from me even though there's an ocean of space and the metal barrier between us. They huddle together in the farthest corner of the cage, backs pressed against the wall, a lad in front and two younger girls behind him. He watches my every move, flinching whenever I change position, occasionally spitting and swearing at me when I get too close, too scared to look away. One of the girls is completely motionless, staring vacantly into space over the boy's shoulder. I do all I can not to look at any of them, partly because I don't know what Hinchcliffe's planning to do with them, but also because looking at the children makes me remember the things I try hardest to forget.

The van driver treats me with as much contempt as he does the children. I'm literally stuck in the middle here, not belonging on either side, and at times like this I can't help wondering what's going to happen to me when the Unchanged have finally been eradicated and I've served my purpose. Until we found the group we just killed, there hadn't been any sightings in weeks. For all I know these kids might well be the last three left alive and my "talent" for holding the Hate could soon be worthless. I've no doubt Hinchcliffe will chuck me back onto the underclass scrap heap just as quickly as he plucked me from it.

The van slows unexpectedly, the engine sounding like it's on its last legs, and I'm immediately on guard. I get up fast, and my sudden movements are met with another volley of spit and swear words from the boy in the cage. I look out of the windows but I can't see anything. The days are short and the nights long now, and the light's fading rapidly. I'm guessing we're well into January by now, but the days, weeks, and months seem to have all melted into one another and become a single dragging blur. No one even mentioned Christmas or New Year. I didn't think about them until long after they'd gone.

The tired engine threatens to stall, but, with much cursing, the driver just about manages to keep it ticking over. He overaccelerates and steers up the curb, and I brace myself as the van lurches from side to side. There's a body in the middle of the road behind us. Looks like it was a Brute. Haven't seen any of them in a while. They're a dying breed. The war was all they had, and they hunted for kills at all costs. My guess is most of them ended up back in and around the irradiated remains of the refugee camps, and those that survived are now just roaming what's left of the countryside, looking for Unchanged that are long gone. This guy I know, Rufus, says the Brutes are a warning, that there's a lesson to be learned from what's happened to them. For what it's worth, I think he's right. I'm not sure what the lesson is though.

We've almost made it back to Lowestoft. It's an almost bearable place to live (in comparison to everywhere else), but conditions have steadily worsened. I'm sure there are other places like this around the country, and I often wonder if I'd be better off elsewhere. I can't bring myself to call this a community, because that word conjures up all kinds of nostalgic, old-fashioned images of people actually getting along and working together for a common good. Lowestoft is just a place where people with nowhere else to go have drifted together. The most aggressive fighters rule the roost now like some kind of prehistoric elite, propped up by the subservient underclasses who live off the scraps they discard. Lowestoft limps along from day to day for now, but the bottom line remains; those who can hit the hardest are the ones who benefit most, and these days no one has bigger fists than Hinchcliffe.

There's definitely a problem with this van. No doubt it'll be dumped as soon as we get back to town. The rest of the convoy has long since left us behind, and the driver constantly curses and overrevs the engine to keep it from dying. We swerve again, weaving between the wreck of a car and a pile of crumbling masonry from a battle-damaged building like we're on a racetrack chicane. The Unchanged kids are safe in their cage, but I'm thrown around the back with every sudden change of direction. Eventually I wedge myself into position between the side of the van and the cage and stare out of the window, trying to stay focused on the barely visible glow of the moon behind the dense cloud layer. My guts feel like someone's mixing them in a blender. If I don't get out of here soon we'll all be seeing more of the dog I ate earlier.

We reach the gate across the bridge spanning the A12 at the bottom end of town, little more than a pair of tall metal doors removed from a building, their hinges welded to the back of two trucks parked facing away from each other. These gates don't need to be particularly strong— there are enough guards around to prevent anyone getting inside Hinchcliffe's compound. Pity the poor fuckers who are stationed out here in the cold. Having visible guards positioned at these key points helps the population to remember who's in charge here, and the underclass maintain a cautious distance. Even if any of them did get inside, they wouldn't last long.

We have a delivery of Unchanged kids to make. We're through the gate now, and I can see the drop-off point looming up ahead. Silhouetted against the purple-black sky is the distinctive angular outline of a group of industrial buildings that Hinchcliffe simply refers to as "the factory." It's an ugly, sprawling mess of a place—a redundant relic of the past. Protected from the ocean on one side by a strong seawall, this used to be a seafood processing plant and was probably a major local employer churning out tons of food every day to be shipped around the world. Even now after it's lain dormant and useless for the best part of a year, the stench of rotting fish still hangs over it like a poisonous cloud.

I've heard rumors about what happens here. This is where Unchanged kids like the ones in the back of this van end up. I don't know what they do to them, and I don't want to know, either. A long time back I heard that they could be "turned" to be like us, but I don't know if that's true. More to the point, does it even matter, now the Unchanged are all but extinct? I look at the children in the cage—still cowering, still crying—and I wonder whether I should do them a favor and kill them now. Put them out of our misery. I must be getting soft. I don't think I'd be able to do it.

We come to an abrupt halt in the middle of the road that runs parallel with the seawall, well short of the factory. The wind is fierce tonight, and immense waves batter against the sides of the wall, sending huge plumes of spray shooting up into the air, then crashing back down again. The noise and the water and the constant rocking of the van in the swirling breeze make me feel like I'm trapped in the eye of a hurricane, the full might of which is, for some reason, focused on me alone.

"Out," the driver shouts, and it takes a couple of seconds before I realize he's talking to me. I get up and move toward the back of the van. The kids panic again because they think I'm coming for them, but I'm the least of their problems tonight.

I jump out of the van and land hard on my weak right leg. My feet have barely touched the ground before the driver accelerates away again, the back door still swinging open. He swerves around to the right onto a narrow access road, then disappears away into the bowels of the factory complex.

Suddenly I'm alone: soaking wet and freezing cold, just me and the sea and no one else. I haul my backpack up onto my shoulders and start walking along the seawall back out of town, welcoming the isolation.

An enormous, motionless wind turbine towers above everything in this part of Lowestoft, and I gaze up at it as I pass. Hinchcliffe thinks he's going to get it operational again one day soon, so the town will have a steady power supply rather than having to rely on generators and the like. I hope he's right. For now it just stands here useless: one of its massive blades broken, its internal mechanics and wiring no doubt completely fucked. It's a huge white elephant: a constant reminder of what this place used to be.

I pull my coat tight around me, put my head down, and walk. The house is still more than a mile away. I could live with the chosen few in Hinchcliffe's compound if I wanted to, but I'd rather not. I prefer to remain at a cautious distance on the very outskirts of town, well away from everyone else. Out there I'm close enough to Lowestoft to be able to get in and take what I need, but still far enough away to stay out of sight and out of mind of everyone else.

OUT OF HABIT I follow the same route each day, using the footbridge to cross the empty road from town and get into the housing development. I'm out of shape. The steep steps are always that much steeper than I remember, and I have to stop halfway across to catch my breath.

The world is dark tonight—no streetlamps, house lights, or lines of traffic producing the ambient glow of old—and the center of Lowestoft behind me is easy to make out. In the midst of the darkness of everything else is a clutch of blinking lights and burning fires, their brightness concentrated around Hinchcliffe's compound. It's hard to believe that this is what passes for a major center of population now. The same thing has no doubt happened around the country: minor towns becoming major towns by default because they're the only habitable places left. It reminds me of a medieval settlement. I remember watching TV documentaries when I was a kid about social experiments where people stepped back in time and tried to live in anything from Iron Age settlements to Tudor houses. This place feels like that but in reverse. Today it's as if people from the past have moved in and taken over the ruins of the present. Hard to believe that all those towns and cities I remember are gone, either abandoned or destroyed. All those places I used to know . . . London, Birmingham, Manchester, Cardiff . . . all reduced to piles of toxic ash. I only have hearsay, unsubstantiated rumor, and common sense to go on, but if what I'm hearing is true and all those places really are dead, then out here on the east coast is probably as safe a place as any to be. I'm guessing that it's only areas like Wales, Scotland, Cornwall, and here—the extremities of this small, odd-shaped island—that are still livable.

Down off the bridge again and within a couple of minutes I've been swallowed up by the darkness of the deserted housing development where I've based myself this last month or so. This place feels like a shadow-filled tomb at the best of times, little more than a maze of twisting, interconnecting roads, avenues, and cul-de-sacs. It was probably a perfectly decent, comfortable, relatively affluent, middle-class area before the shit hit the fan and everything went to hell last year, the kind of place Lizzie said she always wanted us to end up in. Now it's just like everywhere else, and the ruins are welcome camouflage.

I use landmarks to guide myself through to the very center of the development, things that no one else would give a second glance. I walk across a deserted children's playground, catching my breath when the wind rattles the chains of an empty swing, turn left at the road where three of the houses have collapsed on each other like dominoes, then turn right and right again to reach the roadblock. I often wonder who built this. Whoever it was, they were obviously determined to defend themselves. There are four cars wedged across the full width of the mouth of a cul-de-sac, nose to tail, almost like they were picked up and dropped into place. When I'm on foot like this I have to climb over the cars to get through, and I always cringe at the noise I make even though there's never anyone else here. Was this the site of a group of Unchanged survivors' desperate last stand? A family like the one I used to be a part of, perhaps? Were they cowering here together in terror like the Unchanged I helped drive out of their hideout today, doomed to inevitable failure but unable to do anything else but keep trying to survive? I've freaked myself out before now, convincing myself that they might still be here, watching me from an upstairs window just like I watched the military advancing ever closer toward my home all those months ago.

At the other end of the cul-de-sac I slip through a narrow alleyway between two large, empty houses. I cross another road, go through the side gate of yet another house, straight down a well-worn path I've trampled along the full length of its overgrown garden, then duck down through a hole in the back fence and I'm there. Home sweet fucking home.

I check around, making sure I haven't been followed or seen. I could have gone for something bigger and more secure, but I deliberately chose the smallest, most inconspicuous house I could find so I wouldn't draw attention to myself.

It hasn't always worked. Something's not right tonight.

I can see from here that the side door of the house is open slightly. I draw my favorite knife from its sheath and creep across the road. It's bound to be scavengers again. Thieving bastards. I really can't be bothered with this. I feel sick and I just want to sleep. I hope they've already gone. I'm not in the mood to fight, but I don't have any choice.

It's hard keeping the house secure without blatantly advertising the fact I've got stuff inside worth taking, so I keep most of my things hidden and locked away. I need to take my time and be careful here. If the thieves are still here and they've found anything worth having, then I need to try to deal with them before they can get out with any of my stuff. I can afford to lose the house, but not what's in it.

Keeping low, I limp across the driveway, then press myself up against the wall beside the partially open side door. The lock's been forced, but it's nothing I can't fix. Someone's moving around in the kitchen. There are no voices, so there's probably only one of them, and chances are they're only looking for food. I peer through the gap and see a single squat figure trying to pry open a cupboard door with a bent bread knife. Whoever it is, they're so desperate and preoccupied that they don't notice me creeping up behind them. I can see that it's a woman now, small and unimposing, wrapped up in so many layers of grubby clothing to keep warm that her movements are restricted. When I'm close enough I reach out, wrap my arm around her neck, hold my blade up to her face where she can see it, and drag her back. She drops her knife with surprise and I spin her around and slam her back, feeling every bone in her ancient body rattle as she thumps against the wall. She tries to fight me off but gives up quickly, knowing that even in my miserable condition I still have the weight and strength advantage.

"Don't hurt me," she begs, her voice a pathetic, strangled moan. I pull her forward, then slam her back again. Her skull cracks, and she whimpers with pain. Lowestoft is full of useless fuckers like this: definitely not Unchanged, but nowhere near strong enough to fight or be of any use to anyone. People like this are only one step up from our defeated enemy. There are far too many of them out there . . . old, crippled, unskilled, those who are naturally just shysters and cowards . . . people who would previously have been protected and propped up by the welfare state. They'll take the place of the Unchanged if they're not careful. I think I've seen this particular one hanging around here before, and she'll probably come back again if I don't do something to deter her. I push the blade of my knife into her wrinkled cheek, deep enough to prick her skin and draw blood. She starts sobbing with fear. Her neck is scrawny and turkeylike, and she must be in her late sixties if she's a day. Just a little old lady. She reminds me of an old bird who used to live down the road from me and Lizzie. She yelps, and for a fraction of a second I almost pity her. She's not Unchanged, just desperate.

"What the fuck do you think you're doing here?"

"Need some food. Starving . . ."

"Nothing here for you. Fuck off back to town."

"But I—"

She starts struggling again. Bitch should count herself lucky she chose my house to break into; anyone else would have killed her by now. I should hurt her, but I can't bring myself to do it. She doesn't need to know that. I lift the tip of my knife up until it's just a fraction of an inch from her right eye, and she freezes with fear.

"If I see you back here again I'll kill you, understand?"

She nods and mumbles something indistinct. I throw her out of the door and she collapses in a heap on the drive. I take a single step forward and she backs away from me, then gets up and runs, slowing down after just a few steps because her body's too weak to keep moving with any speed. I keep watching her until I'm sure she's gone.

I bolt and bar the damaged door, using a padlock and chain to replace the broken lock for now. Once the house is secure I take my bunch of keys from my pocket and unlock the cupboard the woman was trying to break into. She'd have been disappointed if she'd managed to get the door open. All I keep in here is my gas burner, no food. It's tedious having to be so careful with everything, but it's important. The value of pretty much everything has changed immeasurably in the last year. I could leave a fucking Rolex watch in the middle of the street and it would probably still be there days later. Drop a scrap of food, though, and there'll be a crowd fighting for it before the fastest of the few remaining seagulls have had a chance to swoop.

I double-check that the vagrant woman really has gone before unlocking another cupboard and getting out my kettle, a mug, and a spoon. Then I peel back the linoleum in the corner of the kitchen and lift up one of the loose floorboards underneath. Using a torch, I look around for a jar of coffee powder. I know I've got at least two down here somewhere . . . Christ, there's enough food stored under my kitchen floorboards to feed half of Lowestoft. I've been stashing small amounts away for as long as I've been working for Hinchcliffe. I hold on to every scrap I'm given and I'm not eating much, so my stocks are building up. I could open a store and make a fortune selling everything I've got hoarded away in here, except there's no one left who could afford my prices, and food's probably the only viable currency left now, so there'd be no point. Even if I don't eat it or sell it, I figure I'll be able to bargain with some of it if I need to. There's a cruel irony about many aspects of life these days. All that woman wanted was a little bit of food. I've got all this and I don't want any of it. There's nothing I can do about the situation, though, and, ultimately, it's not my problem. If I'd fed her, then she'd only be back again tomorrow, begging for more and bringing others like her to my door. Things don't work like they used to anymore. You have to be ruthless if you want to survive. There's no room for compassion here.

I fetch water from the bathtub upstairs (I collect it in buckets, pots, and jars out back), then block the window to hide the light from the flame and start it boiling on the little stove. The constant hiss of the burning gas is welcome, taking the faintest edge off the otherwise all-consuming silence. I try to warm my hands around the light blue flame, but it doesn't have any effect tonight.

The kettle boils, and I make my coffee. I'm about to start locking everything away again when I have to stop, my stomach suddenly cramping and my mouth watering. I unlock the door again, struggling to free the chains and get it open in time, then run outside, lean over next-door's low fence, and finally say good-bye to a gut-full of the semi-cooked dog from earlier. Vomit splatters noisily over the drive of the house next to mine and steam rises from the puddle. For a couple of minutes I just stand still and breathe the ice-cold air in deeply. Soaked with sweat and feeling worryingly unsteady on my feet, I wipe my mouth on my sleeve and stagger back indoors.

My coffee's gone cold by the time I've pulled myself together again and locked everything away, but it's still strong and bitter enough to disguise the bilious aftertaste of puke. I take my drink through to the living room, put it on the little table I use, and then, still standing up, I zip myself into my sleeping bag. I jump and shuffle around to get to my chair, then collapse into it, pathetically out of breath.

I keep a pile of books by the side of the chair, taller than the table my coffee's resting on. Books are one of the few things that can still be found relatively easily, although they're used to fuel fires more than to fuel minds these days. I have a light on an elastic headband like a miner's lamp (I found it on a body in an Unchanged shelter a while back). I switch it on and pick up the book on top of the pile. I study the cover, and I can't help laughing to myself when I think how my tastes have changed. I'd never have read anything like this in the days before the war—not that I ever used to read much anyway, but this . . . this is the kind of book bored pensioners used to read, the kind of book that used to sell by the bucketload and appealed to lonely, dowdy, middle-aged spinsters, dreaming of the moment they knew would probably never come, when their knight in shining armor would arrive to whisk them away from their dull, mundane, and loveless lives. It's a trashy thriller-cum-romance novel, probably written by a machine that just slotted character names and other variables into a predefined template, but I don't care. As clichéd and far-fetched as it seems, these books have become something of a release. Reading them is all I want to do when I'm alone like this. It's how I escape from the pressures of this increasingly fucked-up world. These books help me to forget where I am and who I am and what I have to deal with each day. They help me forget the things I've done. They almost make me feel human again. I revel in the insignificant details. The far-fetched action set pieces leave me cold. It's little things that get to me: descriptions of people eating, talking, traveling . . . living together. Those fleeting moments of normality we never used to think about. Those banal moments of calm during which we caught our breath as our lives lurched from one trivial problem to the next pointless crisis.

I start reading from where I got to last night, pausing only to look again at the beautiful woman on the painted front cover. Something about the shape of her face reminds me of the Unchanged woman I killed in the shelter earlier today. She was my first kill in weeks. I didn't want to do it, didn't have the same burning desire I used to, but I knew I didn't have any choice, either. It was for the best. She'd have suffered more if I'd let her live.

I've just got to the part in the book where the female lead first meets the guy who'll no doubt go on to change her life forever on his way to saving the world. Christ, what's wrong with me? I can already feel myself welling up. By the time they inevitably end up in bed together, I'll be crying like a fucking baby.

4

SOME FUCKER'S BANGING ON the door. I keep my eyes screwed shut, nowhere near ready to start another day just yet. If I stay still long enough and don't react, maybe whoever it is will give up and go away. I half open one eye and look around. It's light outside, not long after dawn. My book's on the floor. My tired body aches more than it did when I went to sleep.

The hammering on the door continues. I know who it is now. He lifts the flap of the mail slot and shouts at me, but I don't react. I know he's not going anywhere, but I can't be bothered to move. I make him wait a little longer.

"Come on, Danny, I know you're in there."

"Piss off, Rufus."

He starts knocking on the window, rapping on the glass with his knuckles, and the sound hurts my head. I'll go and see what he wants, then get rid of him. Rufus has an annoying habit of coming here when he's got nowhere else to go, wanting to talk for hours about nothing in particular. Sometimes I can tolerate him, but I don't feel so good this morning and I'm not in the mood. Sometimes he stays all day and we play cards together and put the world to rights (although that particular problem's bigger than both of us), but not today. Most of the time I've forgotten everything he's said by the time I've managed to push him back out the door.

He's not going anywhere. Admitting defeat, I start to get up but then fall back down again when the morning cough hits me. I've probably smoked less than a handful of cigarettes in my whole life, but these days I sound like a chain-smoker who's had a fifty a day habit for the last twenty years. The cough comes in wrenching waves, and I know there's nothing I can do to fight it. I manage to stand up and steady myself on the back of the chair as another hacking burst overtakes me. My sleeping bag drops down around my feet like a used condom, leaving me freezing cold and exposed. One more painful, tearing retch, strong enough to make me feel like I'm being turned inside out, and the coughing finally starts to subside. I spit out a lump of sticky red-green phlegm into my empty coffee cup, step out of the sleeping bag, and stagger over to open the door.

"What?"

"You took your time," he says, not impressed.

"What do you want?"

Rufus glares up at me (he's a good few inches shorter than I am), then ducks under my outstretched arm and pushes his way into the house.

"You're a pain in the backside, Danny. Why didn't you just let me in?"

"*I'm* a pain in the backside? You're the one banging on the window like a goddamn idiot."

"Didn't you hear me knocking? Fucking hell, I've been out there for ages. It's freezing outside."

"It's winter, what do you expect? Anyway, it's no better in here."

I climb back into my sleeping bag, pull it up, and sit down again. He stands in front of me in the middle of the living room, flapping his arms around himself to try and get warm.

"You should light a fire or something," he says, blowing into his hands.

"Can't be bothered. Too much effort."

"You need to start taking more care of yourself. You're not looking so good."

"Thanks."

"You know what I mean."

He shakes his head in despair, then picks my book up off the floor and starts flicking through the pages. He has to hold it right up to his face to be able to read anything. Poor bugger's eyesight is bad. He was a voracious reader, but he's been reduced to reading children's editions because the print's larger. He used to wear strong glasses, but the lenses got broken a few weeks back when he got caught up in the middle of a fight he had nothing to do with. Rufus doesn't handle conflict well. Makes me wonder how he's lasted this long. He has another fresh bruise on his face this morning. He's probably pissed somebody off again. Doesn't even realize he's doing it.

"Don't know how you can read this crap."

"It's simple, shallow, and predictable. Just what I need."

"Yes, but there's a whole load of literature out there, Dan. Read some classics. Broaden your horizons."

"I don't want to broaden my horizons. In fact, I want to start limiting my horizons to the four walls of this house, screw everything else."

"Don't be so narrow. Listen, have you read *1984*? I managed to salvage a pile of postapocalyptic books from the library before Hinchcliffe's morons burned them. You should read it. And *Earth Abides*, that's another. It's really interesting to see how people thought things were going to pan out. I mean, they were all miles off the mark, but don't let that—"

"Rufus," I interrupt, "what is it you want? You didn't come here this early just to make reading recommendations."

"Come on, Danny," he sighs, dropping the book down again. "You know I only disturb you when I absolutely have to."

I know he's right, but I'm not going to make it easy for him. He always does exactly what he's told (he's too scared not to), and he wouldn't be here at this hour if he had any choice. Rufus is an ex–civil servant, working as a gopher for Hinchcliffe and his cronies, running errands and carrying messages. His intelligence and natural ability to talk rings around everyone else elevate him above the rest of the underclass, but he's not a natural fighter by any means, and every day is a struggle for him to survive. Rufus calls me his friend, although I think he needs me far more than I need him. I spit into my cup again and wipe my mouth on my sleeve.

"You really do need to start taking more care of yourself, Dan," he says again, looking me up and down.

"I'm tired, that's all. Spent the last few days hunting."

"I heard. Most of the people in the compound heard. The beer was certainly flowing last night. They were toasting your success. Hate to think what's going to happen when they run out of booze."

"Whatever. So why exactly are you here? Is that all you came to tell me?"

Rufus doesn't answer right away. He's distracted by the picture on the cover of another of my trashy novels. I whistle at him to get his attention, and he finally looks up.

"He wants to see you. Says he's got another job for you."

My heart sinks. "He" is Hinchcliffe, and I don't need any more detail. If he wants to see me, then I don't have any choice but to go and find him. When I get there and he tells me what it is he wants me to do, I'll have no choice but to do it.

"Christ, Rufus, what is it this time?"

"I'm just the messenger, Danny, you know he doesn't tell me anything."

"Shit. I swear, it's like being back at work sometimes, the amount of stuff he has me doing. Is it more Unchanged or—"

"I told you, I don't know. He's not a happy bunny, though."

"Great."

Despite the fact that Hinchcliffe genuinely seems to value me (as much as anyone values anyone else these days), and the fact that whatever he asks me to do, I've probably already had to do much worse, I immediately feel nervous. I can try to hide it, and I can bullshit and make light of the situation until I'm blue in the face, but the fact remains: Hinchcliffe scares the shit out of me. Sometimes I think our collective fear of good old KC is the glue that holds this fragile place together.

RUFUS IS ON HIS pushbike, riding alongside me as I walk into town. Truth be told, I'm glad of the company, even though he never shuts up.

"Of course, I saw all this coming before the Hate."

"All what coming?"

"This chaos. We've been on a slippery slope for years. We were over-reliant on technology. There was an irony to that, wasn't there? The easier it was for people to communicate, the worse at communicating they became."

"I don't have a clue what you're talking about."

"Did you ever try phoning a teenager's cell?"

"Not that often, why?"

"I did. Fuckers would never answer. I worked with a lot of students, and they always had their phones in their hands, so how come they never answered?"

"You tell me," I mumble, knowing full well that he's about to.

"Either they were being selective and only talking to who they wanted to, or they were too busy using the phones for something else. All that social networking and stuff. Antisocial networking, I used to call it."

"I wouldn't know about that. We didn't even have a computer at home. Couldn't afford the Internet."

He gives me a sideways glance, then continues. "People started using technology instead of thinking, letting machines do all the work, and now where are we?"

"Lowestoft," I answer glibly.

"You know what I mean," he says. "I knew this lad once, he had one of those SAT NAVs, remember them? Fucking thing stopped working when he was driving up for a meeting, and you know what happened?"

"He got lost?"

"Worse than that. Fucking idiot just kept driving in a straight line until he got a signal again. Didn't think to look at road signs or get himself a map, did he? Took him almost fifty miles to get back on track. There was another time I had a girl in tears because she couldn't unlock her car because the battery had gone and the key wouldn't work. For Christ's sake! I had to march her down to the parking lot and put the key in the fucking door for her myself!"

Rufus continues to chatter tirelessly as we approach the center of town. I say little. I know this is his therapy: his chance to vent his many frustrations without fear of taking a beating. Me, I'm too nervous to give a damn.

"The other day I saw that Curtis fellow, and do you know what he was doing? He was kicking in the door of one of the buildings next to the courthouse and using it for firewood. Where's the sense in that when there's so much they could use outside the compound? They're just too blinkered. They don't look any further than—"

"Rufus, shut up."

I stop walking, and he stops pedalling. We're deep among the underclass now, and something's happening up ahead. I gesture for him to hold back and we wait by the side of a partially collapsed garage. There are other people all around us, most of them doing the same, keeping their distance. There's a truck waiting at the barricade, just back from a scavenging mission by the looks of things, and it's surrounded. One of the fighters in the front gets out and starts swinging a bludgeon at the people who are closest, forcing them back, but the crowd is large and volatile, and when he lunges for one section, people elsewhere surge forward. A couple of them manage to scramble up onto the back of the truck and help themselves, only to be kicked back down by another savage bastard hidden under the canopy. No sooner have they hit the ground than other vagrants are swarming around them, trying to "resteal" what they've just stolen. The situation deteriorates with frightening speed until two more fighters appear from the back and wade into the crowd. One of them brandishes a submachine gun that he fires into the air, and the people scatter. As soon as there's sufficient space around the truck, the gate opens and it drives through.

"Lovely," Rufus says. "I think this is where I'll leave you."

He pushes off and pedals away. I don't know where he's going, but I do know he has as little desire to head into Hinchcliffe's compound as I do. At least he has a choice.

The closer I get to the gate around the compound, the more human detritus there is to wade through. This so-called society has divided itself into its own bizarre class structure. It's like a pyramid now with Hinchcliffe perched alone at the top. Below him are his generals, Llewellyn and a couple of others—those fighters who first, understand how this new world order works, second, have enough brains to know how to deal with Hinchcliffe and keep on his good side, and third, are strong and ruthless enough to hold their own in any conflict. Beneath them are the rest of the fighters, their position in the overall scheme of things depending entirely on their individual strength and aggression, and beneath them are the Switchbacks: people who've desperately tried to regain something resembling their old lives, finding new routines and responsibilities to fill the void where now-defunct jobs, families, and relationships used to be. At the bottom of the heap are the hundreds of useless vagrants like the woman who broke into the house last night. Hinchcliffe has a simple way of evaluating each person's worth: Does he need them? If they weren't there, he asks, would it matter? With resources so limited, he's not about to waste time and effort on those useless people who are only going to take. Those poor bastards are lost without a purpose.

As I pick my way through the crowds of underclass—some begging for food they know I won't give them, some scavenging, some picking through a huge mountain of waste like a landfill site, some hunting rats that others have disturbed, many others just sitting and staring into space—I try to work out where I fit into the hierarchy today. I quickly come to the same conclusion I reach whenever I think about it: I don't. Sometimes, I don't know if I want to. Even before the war I felt out of step with everyone else. Now I struggle to believe we're all part of the same species.

I reach the cordon and hammer on the gate with my fist.

"Who is it?" someone shouts.

"Danny McCoyne," I answer back. "Hinchcliffe wants to see me."

A narrow hatch is opened and a fighter stares out at me, checking I'm who I say I am. There's never any delay when I mention the big man's name. The hatch closes again; then the gate immediately starts to open, and I'm pulled through as soon as the gap's wide enough. It's slammed the moment I'm inside.

I head up what used to be Lowestoft's main shopping street toward the courthouse building, where Hinchcliffe bases himself, avoiding the foul-smelling piles of rubbish that are steadily encroaching on either side of the narrowing road. The atmosphere is different on this side of the barriers. Here there are fewer people out in the open, and those I can see are moving with more purpose than those stuck on the wrong side of the blockade. Here the Switchbacks compete to stay in favor with the fighters. They remind me of the little birds that used to risk their lives to clean crocodiles' razor-sharp teeth or the parasitic fish that lived off sharks. This is a more symbiotic relationship, though, because they all need each other. The fighters are a uniformly foul breed—a mix of the physically strong, the instinctively aggressive, and those who are both. They're a deadly combination of hard, experienced bastards who look like they've been fighting all their lives, and younger vigilantes on the cusp of adulthood, always ready for battle. They float like pond scum on top of everyone else, relying on the subservient Switchbacks to fix their cars, fetch their food, and do most other menial tasks in return for water and scraps of food. It all feels precariously balanced.

I reach Hinchcliffe's place too quickly for my liking. I should go straight inside, but I pace up and down the pavement for a couple of minutes to compose myself first, breathing in slowly to settle my nerves and trying to stop myself from coughing again. The hazy sun peeks unexpectedly through a gap in the heavy clouds, and I cover my eyes. It's probably my imagination, but even the sun seems to have changed since the bombs. It's never as clear as it used to be. The light looks and feels different, like a layer of color and strength has been stripped away. Then again, maybe it's just my eyes.

I feel sick, and the smell here's not helping. Sanitation is pretty basic around town, and the stench is inescapable. People have taken to crapping in the gutters to get their waste into the drains and sewers. If we carry on at this rate it won't be long before we're slopping out again: people emptying buckets of shit into the street from upstairs windows.

A sudden gust of wind clears the air momentarily, and I stop and breathe in the odd breeze. No one pays me any attention, and that's the way I like it. I can see a crowd around the entrance to the small shopping mall that Hinchcliffe uses as a food store and, occasionally, a distribution point. The same thing's happening again a couple of hundred yards away, where a street-corner hamburger stand is being used for a similar purpose. These lines never completely disappear. There are always more people than there is food, but no one dares to steal. Just a little way up the road is what's left of Hook, the last thief Hinchcliffe caught. Once the bane of my life, his corpse now hangs from a lamppost by its feet like a grotesque piece of street decoration. When he found out what he'd been up to, Hinchcliffe strung him up and gutted him like a pig. The rumor was that someone else had been pulling his strings . . .

The courthouse looks squat and small from street level, but its size is deceptive. Hinchcliffe has occupied a large part of the surrounding area, and most of the neighboring buildings have been taken by his small army of fighters. There's usually power and water in this part of town. Huge fuel-fired generators thump away continually in the background like a monotonous, mechanical call to the faithful. Hinchcliffe is no fool. This place is a less than subtle symbol of his unquestioned authority here. He's aligned himself with what used to be the traditional centers of power in Lowestoft, and no matter how the people here behave now and what they've become, everyone is still conditioned to a certain extent. They still look at places like this and, whether they'd admit it or not, they see people in charge. I certainly do.

The sooner I get this over with, the sooner I can head back home again. I take a deep breath and go inside.

I enter the courthouse building unchallenged and head straight for Hinchcliffe's room. Much of the space in here is filled with boxes of supplies, piled so high that in places they've spilled out of rooms and have blocked corridors. It's not that there's a vast amount of stuff here, more that it's just incredibly disorganized. Dirty, too. Cleanliness is the very least of anyone's concerns today. The windows are opaque, and every surface I touch is either covered in dust or sticky with a layer of grime.

Hinchcliffe's empire is based on a few core principles. Central to his control (of both the fighters and the underclass) is the provision (or at least the promise) of food and water, backed up with the threat of brutal force if anyone steps out of line. He drip-feeds the people here to keep them sweet: Do what I say and you might get what you need, he tells them, fuck with me and I'll kill you. It really is as simple as that. Today he hoards whatever scraps he can find and stockpiles everything at various locations within the compound. I know where one stash is kept and I have an idea about two others, but I don't know any more than that. No one knows where everything is except for Hinchcliffe. He manipulates the situation to consciously generate an air of mutual distrust between his fighters when it comes to the supplies, rewarding loyalty with increased rations and at the same time encouraging them to rat on anyone who doesn't play ball.

Hinchcliffe is the worst of the worst. He is physically *and* mentally stronger than anyone else, the closest thing I've ever seen to a Brute with a brain.

I pause outside the tall double doors to his office to compose myself, trying to make myself appear more confident than I feel. I go through and, thankfully, my entrance goes largely unnoticed. The heat in here literally stops me in my tracks. There are electric and oil-fired heaters placed around the edges of the room, probably more here than in the rest of the town combined. Recycling, energy efficiency . . . all consigned to history now. The amount of waste in here alone is astonishing. Hinchcliffe and his posse seem to go through supplies as if there's no tomorrow, as if they're expecting fresh supplies to turn up any day now in a goddamn supermarket truck.

This used to be the main county courtroom, but it's barely recognizable as such today. It's been stripped of all gravitas by yet more boxes and crates stacked around in haphazard piles, and the floor and desks are covered with a layer of rubbish. Most of it is clearly just general litter, food wrappers and the like, but there's a lot of discarded, office-type paperwork lying around, too. Considering this is supposed to be the administrative hub of the town—the beating heart of Hinchcliffe's empire—it doesn't look like anyone's doing very much. I pick up a map that's been left open on the desk next to where I'm standing. Black crosses have been scrawled over every town and village within thirty miles of this place. There's a sudden noise behind me, and I spin around to see Llewellyn hurtling toward me. I try to put the map down without him seeing I've been looking at it, but it's too late. He snatches it from my hand and pushes me back against the wall. He hits me harder than I was expecting and my skull cracks against the plaster.

"What the fuck are you doing?"

"Hinchcliffe wants to see me."

"Does he? And did he say you could come in here and start looking through my stuff?"

"No, I—"

"You nosy fucker. I'll break your fucking legs if I catch you at it again. He shouldn't let a freak like you just wander around."

"You tell him, then," I stupidly say, and Llewellyn wraps his hand around my neck.

"You wiseass bastard. Watch yourself, McCoyne, I'm going to—"

"He's coming," another fighter says as he bursts into the room. "I've just seen him. He'll be here in a sec."

Llewellyn lets me go. The other man is Curtis, his deputy. He's half Llewellyn's age but just as vicious. He always wears full body armor, taken from his first-ever kill, he'll regularly tell anyone who'll listen. Llewellyn grunts at him, then snarls at me, and they walk away together to study the crumpled map, finally leaving me alone. I rub the back of my head and sit down on the edge of the nearest desk. Llewellyn's got a real problem with me, but I don't care. If he touches me, Hinchcliffe will kill him, and he knows it. Maybe that's why he hates me. He doesn't like the fact that Hinchcliffe seems to trust me, if trust is the right word. It's a thinly veiled, childlike jealousy, and it's pitiful.

As I wait for Hinchcliffe to arrive, I watch three other fighters I don't recognize crowding around a thin slip of a man who's trying to repair a radio with shaking hands. Sitting at a desk facing me, keeping to himself and working on a battered old laptop, is Anderson, Hinchcliffe's "stock-keeper." He's another gopher, like Rufus. I'm told he used to be an accountant, but now he's the man charged with keeping a tally of everything that Hinchcliffe owns and controls: the land, food, weapons, vehicles, people . . . I walk farther into the room and pass him, but he doesn't even look up. I glance back and see that he's playing cards on the computer, not working at all.

The man trying to fix the radio makes a mistake. There's a bright spark, accompanied by a sudden loud cracking noise, a wisp of smoke, and the smell of burning, and he yelps with surprise and pain. Obviously not impressed, one of the fighters watching cuffs him around the back of the head, then shoves him into the wall, face-first. Dazed, he reels away with blood dripping from his nose. He wipes his face clean and immediately tries to work on the radio again and avoid another slap, hands trembling, barely even able to focus, frequently stopping to wipe away more drips of blood.

Hinchcliffe appears through another set of doors, which swing shut into the face of a woman I don't immediately recognize who's following behind him. She's straightening her clothes as she walks, and the reason she's been here is obvious. It's unusual to see anyone female around here unless she's been brought in for sex. It's another sad indictment of the backward direction this new "society" is taking. The days of women's lib and equality are long gone. Women fighters are easily as aggressive as men, but generally they're less physically strong. As a result, fewer of them rise up through the ranks. It's ironic; the arrival of the Hate temporarily wiped out all the divisions and prejudices that used to split society, but now the war's ending, they're flooding back and are even more divisive than before. Hinchcliffe and I talked about it a while back. He told me it's tough shit, because that's just the way it is now. There are no human rights groups to help you anymore, he said, we're all on our own. I don't care if you're a black lesbian Jew with one leg, I remember him saying, enjoying belaboring the point, if it comes down to a straight choice between you and me surviving, you're fucked.

When he finally notices I'm here, Hinchcliffe says something to the woman and she slopes away.

"Danny," he grins, his voice full of obviously false enthusiasm, "how are you this morning?"

My head aches, my body aches, and my guts are still in turmoil from last night's dinner of dog, but I spare him the details.

"Shit."

"Excellent!" he says sarcastically. "Come through. I need to talk to you."

He turns, and I follow him down a short corridor, up a flight of stairs, and into the first of his private rooms. I've been in here a couple of times before, but it still takes me by surprise. It's more like a teenager's bedroom than anything else. There's a flat-screen TV on one wall—possibly the last unbroken TV left in the whole town—and numerous game consoles lying around. There's a recently vacated, unmade double bed opposite, and the air is heavy with cigarette smoke and other stale and equally unpleasant smells. We continue through to his office, a slightly more businesslike room. There's a large oval wooden table, covered in as much shit as everywhere else. The grubby cream-colored carpet is stained heavily with blood in several places, no doubt left by those unfortunate people who managed to piss the KC off.

Hinchcliffe sits at the head of the table on a tall-backed leather swivel chair that's bigger than the rest. He gestures for me to sit next to him, and I do as he says, still doing all I can to disguise my nerves. Despite his inner circle of fighters, his is the only seat that really matters. He is the lawmaker, judge, prosecutor, defense lawyer, jury, and executioner, all rolled into one, and I try not to let him see how much he intimidates me. I act casual and do my best to maintain eye contact, but the fucker just grins and I'm the one who looks away first. Is he really such a threat, or am I blowing things out of proportion? He reminds me of the senior managers I used to work for at the council, but far, far more intense, and, unlike them, he has a personality. He's no stronger than many of the people he surrounds himself with, but he's clever and witty and smart, and that's the real danger. When he looks at me like this it's like he's trying to work out exactly what I'm thinking, trying to get into my head and take me apart so he can understand what makes me tick. The war has made most people shed absolutely every aspect of their former selves. Hinchcliffe, though, is different. He used to be an investment banker who'd probably have sold his own mother to turn a profit. He still has the same arrogance and swagger, but now he trades in lower-value currencies for much higher stakes. The rumor according to Rufus (and I really don't want to know whether it's true or not) is that when the Change took him, Hinchcliffe wiped out virtually an entire floor of more than forty City traders single-handed.

Take it easy. Don't let him see you're nervous.

"You really don't look so good," he says, looking me up and down.

"You're the second person who's said that to me today."

"How many people have you seen?"

"Just two."

"Well, we both must be right, then," he says, continuing to stare at me, his face an unreadable mix of fascination and disgust. Then his expression suddenly changes. He ducks down, reaches under the table, and pulls out a four-pack of beer, which he slides over to me.

"For helping us get rid of those Unchanged fuckers yesterday. Good job."

"Thanks."

I take the beers and quickly remove them from the plastic rings holding them together. I shove the individual cans into different pockets of my long coat. I might drink one later, but the rest will be going under the floorboards when I get back to the house.

"I was really pleased with what you did. Biggest Unchanged haul in ages."

"Six weeks."

"I thought we'd seen the last of them. Thought we'd finally got rid of them all."

"Me, too. Maybe we have now."

"And we got a few kids, too. Bonus! Wasn't expecting that."

"Neither were they."

There's another long, awkward (for me, anyway), and uneasy silence.

"I've got another job for you," he finally announces. "Ever heard of a place called Southwold?"

Southwold is a village a few miles farther down the east coast. I've never been there, and I know very little about it other than its name. I shake my head. The more Hinchcliffe thinks I know, the more he'll expect from me.

"It's about ten miles from here," he explains. "Used to be a nice little spot. Couple of people I knew in the City had second homes down there back in the day."

Ten miles. Doesn't sound far, but distances aren't what they used to be. People tend to stay put in Lowestoft now and, unless they're out scavenging, rarely venture more than a couple of miles in any direction. Fuel's in short supply, so most traveling's now done on foot, and that puts Southwold the best part of a day away.

Hinchcliffe lights up a cigarette and leans back, taking a long draw and slowly blowing out a cloud of blue-gray smoke up toward the ceiling. Now there's an expression of status if ever I saw one. Smoking these days says to anyone who's watching that you've got the means and the connections to be able to get your hands on a steady supply of cigarettes to fuel your pointless habit. Most people struggle to find food, never mind anything else. Hinchcliffe knows I'm watching him. Cocky bastard.

"Want one?"

"No thanks. Don't smoke. Bad for you."

He laughs and lifts the cigarette box up in front of me, shaking it.

"You sure? These are the real thing," he says. "Word to the wise, if you do decide to start, come and see me first. There are some dirty fuckers making their own smokes from scrag ends and dried leaves and whatever else they can get their hands on. Bit of a black market starting to spring up around here . . ."

"You were talking about Southwold," I remind him, eager to get the conversation back on track and get this over with. He leans forward secretively.

"I might have a problem," he whispers.

"Unchanged?"

"Not this time."

"What, then?"

"Settlers. I need you to check them out for me."

"Why me?"

"Christ, Danny, why do you always ask the same damn questions? You know why. You're forgettable. No one notices you. No one even gives you a second glance."

"Thanks."

"You know what I mean. You can handle yourself. Doesn't matter who or what you come across, you treat them all the same. You don't rush in there with your fists flying like everyone else I've got who could go."

Bit of a backhanded compliment, but that's as good as it gets with Hinchcliffe.

"So what's your problem?"

"Little issue with the neighbors," he says, grinning again. "There's something going on down there, I'm sure of it. I've been talking to them for a while, trying to get them to pack up and come up here. Thing is, they wanted to stay where they were, so I figured I'd keep them with us and let them get the place organized for me, then get in there and annex them."

"I take it things aren't going to plan?"

He screws up his face and takes another drag on his cigarette.

"It's not that," he explains, "I'm just starting to get a little uneasy. There are about thirty of them, and they're not being as cooperative as I'd like. I think they're stockpiling and digging in, and I need to get a handle on things."

"Before someone else does?" I suggest. He pauses, and for a fraction of a second I think I might have overstepped the mark. Then he grins again and points at me.

"You got it! See, you don't miss a trick, Dan. That's why I like you!"

He doesn't like me and we both know it. Fucking idiot.

"So what do you want me to do?"

"There's a guy called Warner running things down there. John Warner. He's a local. Came with the territory."

"You don't trust him?"

"I don't trust anyone," he answers quickly. "Do you know Neil Casey?"

I struggle for a few seconds to place the name. I know he's one of Hinchcliffe's top cronies, but, truth be told, they're all the same to me. Their personalities have become diluted. Rufus says they've been de-individualized, and I know what he means. I can only tell them apart by comparing their scars and their level of aggression. I lose track of which one's which, but I think I know who Casey is.

"Tall guy, nasty scar on the back of his head?"

"That's him. I sent him down there a few days ago, and he hasn't reported back to me yet. You know the routine, Dan, if you're working for me and I send you outside Lowestoft, you make contact at least once every twenty-four hours. That's the deal."

"You think they've got rid of him?"

"I don't know what I think, and that's why I want you to go there.

Try to get a feel for what's going on and let me know if there's anything I should be worried about, OK?"

I don't want to go anywhere, but what else can I say? Hinchcliffe doesn't ask, he tells.

"OK."

"Good man. Take a car from the pool, pick yourself up a radio, and get down there as soon as you can."

"Now?"

"Why? You got something better to do?"

"No, it's just that I don't feel—"

"Get down there now and report back to me tonight. The sooner you go, the sooner you get back, and the happier I'll be."

Bastard. I can't stand being used like this, but what choice do I have? It's do the job or risk a beating, maybe worse. I get up to leave, but I'm not even halfway across the room when the coughing starts again, worsened no doubt by Hinchcliffe's smoking and the arid, dry heat in here. I'm doubled over before I know what's happening.

"You've got to start taking better care of yourself, Danny," Hinchcliffe shouts after me, "you're a key member of my team." I glance back at him but I don't react. Is he being genuine or sarcastic? I can't tell the difference anymore.

6

HINCHCLIFFE HAS BUILT UP a vast collection of cars in varying states of disrepair. He has several mechanics working for him, but their skills are seriously lacking, as are their resources. Crude body-work repairs are generally managed, but if their engines don't run the cars are stripped down for spare parts, then dumped, much the same as everything else. Hinchcliffe's car pools are starting to look more like scrapyards with heaps of discarded body parts building up and fewer complete vehicles. Some cars have been increasingly cannibalized to keep them running. They look like something out of a third-rate rip-off Mad Max movie but without the performance; sheets of metal welded over missing doors, mismatched tires, wire-mesh windows . . .

Hinchcliffe keeps most of the better vehicles in a parking lot behind what used to be the police station, and the rest on a guarded patch of wasteland adjacent to the railway station. I always try to take the same car. The guards and mechanics look at me as if I'm crazy because I never go for the one with the biggest engine, the strongest body, or the most space inside. Instead I choose the same little silver, box-shaped car every time—a safe, reliable, old man's car. Hardly the Road Warrior, but the reason I use this one is simple: I know it's got a working CD player.

For a long time at the height of the fighting, driving wasn't such a great idea. In the weeks leading up to the nuclear bombings, when the Unchanged still outnumbered us and before they squandered their last remaining military advantage in desperation, it was generally too dangerous to risk traveling anywhere by road. Now, though, it's the lack of people and fuel that makes the roads—what's left of them anyway—quieter than ever. For me, getting in a car today is a relief, a way of shutting out everything and everyone else for as long as the journey lasts—and when you have music, the effect is so much more complete . . .

I leave the railway station with music blasting out, ignoring the bemused stares I get from fighter guards who look at me like I've gone insane. I never used to listen to this kind of music, but I don't care anymore. The name of the piece, the composer, the conductor, the orchestra—none of that matters now. All that's important is the effect. The sound takes me back to a time when people sang and laughed and played instruments and made CDs and listened to the radio and went to gigs. A time when people didn't kill each other (that often), and when having a bad day meant you'd missed something on TV or you'd had a run-in with someone at work.

Checkpoint.

There are two guards on duty here at the gate that spans the bridge. The stretch of water below is called Lake Lothing, although it's less of a lake at this point, more a narrow channel that runs into the sea. One of the guards mans the gate in the cordon; the other stands at the side of the road and flags me down. This guy's always around here. He lost the bottom part of his left leg in the war, but he still keeps fighting. His stump is wrapped up with layers of old, crusted brown dressings, and he rests it on a pile of sandbags level with his other knee so he can stay standing upright. That pile of ballast is probably the closest he's ever going to get to a false leg. I stop a short distance away (far enough so he can't hit me without hopping over first) and wind down the window. I refuse to turn off the music.

"This one of Hinchcliffe's cars?" he asks, shouting to make himself heard.

"I'm doing a job for him," I shout back. "Check with him if you want."

"What?"

"I said check with him."

He still can't hear me. "Turn that shit down, you fucking idiot."

"What?" I yell, feigning deafness. He starts to repeat his request, but I'm just playing with him. I hold up the radio—one of Hinchcliffe's standard-issue handsets—and he immediately nods his head, signals to the other man, and waves me through. Having a radio is almost as good as having an ID card. There's no access to these things without Hinchcliffe's express permission, and he controls them himself. It's not the danger of having communications interrupted that makes him so anal about this radio equipment, it's the fact that he's rapidly running out of batteries and spares.

The other fighter opens the gate, and as soon as the gap's wide enough, I accelerate through it, past the underclass crowds, and on toward Southwold, trying not to think too much about what I might find there.

THE EMPTY ROADS ARE desolate, and I keep driving along the A12 until I reach the village of Wrentham, a strangely skeletal place. Everything of value has long since been removed and taken back to Lowestoft. In the silent center of the village there's a junction. The road sign directly opposite is bent over double like a drunk throwing up against a wall and it's hard to make out what it says. I think it's around a mile and a half to Southwold. Fortunately the road names here are pretty self-explanatory: Lowestoft Road, London Road (note to self—don't go down that one), and Southwold Road. I follow the Southwold Road, looking out for somewhere safe to leave the car so I can finish the last mile or so of the journey on foot. I'll draw less attention to myself and have more chance of avoiding any trouble that way. Damn Hinchcliffe, I really don't want to do this. If there was more fuel in this car I could make a break for it and try to find another place like Lowestoft. Then again, what's the point? Every surviving town will probably have its own KC.

Another mile or so and I reach a business park, which seems as quiet as everywhere else. I drive as deep into the property as I dare, then park the car inside a large warehouse, out of sight. I quickly check the building out, but it doesn't look like anyone's been here for months. There's an undisturbed layer of dust everywhere, and that's reassuring. I need to be careful with the car. Not only will Hinchcliffe hit the roof if I don't get it back to him in one piece, but it's also my ticket out of here. I take my CD with me, just in case, shoving it into my backpack along with some clothes, weapons, two books, scraps of food to trade, and Hinchcliffe's radio.

I skirt around the edge of another village first, Reydon, then follow a dog-eared tourist's street map that Hinchcliffe gave me to get deeper into Southwold. I check the map repeatedly as I follow the main road, which runs right through the center of the town. I don't feel like a tourist today. I'm nervous as hell.

There's not much to this place, and I'm assuming that here, as in Lowestoft, any settlers will have gravitated toward the center, where the shops, pubs, offices, and everything else used to be. If there are only thirty or so people here, they probably haven't spread out that far. I don't know anything about this guy John Warner, but it's safe to assume he's probably a nasty bastard. He must be pretty sure of himself to have turned down an "invitation" to relocate to Lowestoft. Either he's dumb, or he's got balls of steel.

This place is like a ghost town. Perhaps because of its relatively remote location and small size, Southwold seems to have escaped much of the recent fighting. There's plenty of surface damage, but most of the buildings still appear structurally sound. The once carefully tended shoulders and lawns are overgrown and wild now, although the grass is yellow and limp. Weeds are beginning to sprout through the cracks in the pavements. I stare through a dust-covered window into the deceptively normal living room of an abandoned house, then catch my breath when I hear voices nearby, carried on the winter wind. *Focus!* I tell myself. I can't afford to take chances. There's a reason these people are defying Hinchcliffe, and if they're prepared to piss him off, they'll have no qualms about getting rid of me.

There's a lighthouse up ahead. I didn't pay it much attention when I first saw it marked on the map, but now that it's actually looming up right in front of me I can't help but notice it. Unlike most lighthouses I've come across before, this one is nestled deep in the center of the town rather than out on the rocks or at the edge of the water. I edge closer to try to get a better view, peering around the corner of a row of modest-looking houses. Circling the very top of the lighthouse is a metal gantry, and there's someone pacing around it on watch. I can't see much from this distance, but it looks like he's armed. There's no sense taking any unnecessary chances. I decide to work my way around the center of the town in a wide circle rather than risk getting too close too soon and being shot at.

Through a narrow gap between two oddly spaced rows of houses I see a small group of people working in a field near a church. I can't see what it is they're doing from here, but I change direction again to avoid any confrontation. Still staying tucked in close to the fronts of the buildings I pass to minimize the chance of being seen by the lighthouse lookout, I find myself walking down toward the ocean. The steadily increasing noise of the waves crashing against the shingle shore is reassuring and welcome. The morning sun that was briefly visible in Lowestoft has disappeared now, and the sky is again clogged with heavy, dirty gray cloud. The wind coming up off the water is bracing, almost too cold to stand. It's raining—either sea-spray or sleet—and I ask myself again, *What the hell am I doing here?*

A long, uninterrupted, and empty roadway runs parallel with the shingle beach below, appearing to stretch right along the full length of the town, all the way out toward a crumbling pier that reaches into the sea. The promenade is a relatively straight, hardly overlooked strip of asphalt, and I'm suddenly struck by the fact that there's something very different about this place in comparison with everywhere else I've been since I arrived in the area. The deeper I've gone into Southwold, the more obvious it's become. The roads here in this part of town have been cleared. There are the usual burned-out cars and occasional piles of rubble lying around, but here, unlike in Lowestoft, they appear to have been moved out of the way. This is weird. No one cleans anything anymore, there's no point. There's barely anything left to clean *with*. The whole country is covered in a layer of radioactive grime that never gets touched. People usually climb over and around obstructions such as these, very rarely ever doing anything about them.

A sudden gust of wind catches a loose window in a run-down house behind me, slamming it shut. My heart's in my mouth and my body immediately tenses up, ready for confrontation. I grab my knife and look around in all directions, but I can't see anyone, and I curse myself again for getting so easily distracted. Next to the house is a small corner store with a real estate agent's FOR RENT sign hanging above the door. Its bare shelves have long since been stripped of anything of value, but, feeling exposed, I go inside.

The store's as empty as it looked from the street, probably cleared out just before the fighting began in earnest. Again, if this had been Lowestoft or anywhere else, the floor would be covered in crap, the furniture broken into pieces for firewood, the windows smashed, a couple of bodies left rotting in the corner... There's a pile of papers on the end of a counter, neatly stacked next to an empty display unit as if the outgoing owners just left them there on their way out. There's a local newspaper on top of the pile, dated last February, and I casually flick through it, this time happy to be distracted. The yellowed pages immediately take me back to a world that's long gone. There are a few vague mentions of the beginning of the troubles that eventually consumed everything and everyone, but generally the paper's filled with the kind of empty stories that used to be so typical and that used to matter in places like this: local merchants protesting about increased parking charges, the proposed merger of two secondary schools, an amateur dramatics group desperately trying to hawk tickets for their latest production, a new car dealership opening... For a while I'm hypnotized as I read through the TV and local movie listings, looking at program titles I thought I'd forgotten and the names of films I never got to see, but then I remember where I am and what I'm supposed to be doing and I make myself move.

On the floor by my feet, wedged under the counter, is a postcard lying facedown. I pick it up and flip it over. On the front is a picture of Southwold beach and the pier taken on a gloriously sunny summer's day, way back when. The colors of the postcard are still remarkably bright and vivid. GREETINGS FROM SOUTHWOLD it says at the bottom, in large orange and yellow text. Maybe I should send it to Hinchcliffe? I don't think he'd appreciate the joke.

I take the postcard outside with me and compare it to the real world. The original photograph must have been taken from somewhere very near to this exact spot, because the view of the pier is pretty much the same. I cross the promenade and a strip of muddy grass, then lean against the metal railings and look down toward the sea. Holding the postcard up, I can clearly see the contrast between the past and the present. Apart from the weather and the lack of color (everything today is disappointingly monochrome), the other major difference is the pier itself. There's now a large chasm about two-thirds of the way along its length where part of the structure has collapsed and fallen into the sea. Bent girders hang down like tumbling weeds, and several supporting metal struts have buckled. It looks like something impossibly heavy crashed down into the pier from on high. A plane perhaps? Aware that I'm wasting time but not giving a damn, I start to walk down toward it, curious as to how it came to be so badly damaged. Was there a bomb? Did something hit it from below? Was there a fire or a battle here at some point? At the entrance to the pier is a large pale-yellow-painted art deco building that looks like it used to house the usual seaside distractions: an amusement arcade, cafés, and gift shops. Running along the length of the pier, straight up its center, is a line of what look like wooden shacks—yet more cafés and shops, I presume. I resist the temptation to get any closer, and instead I turn around and look back along the beach toward the town, knowing that I have to stop putting it off and start doing what Hinchcliffe sent me here to do. The normality of what I see takes me by surprise—the waves crashing against the shore, the breakwaters jutting up through the surf and spray, a long line of small wooden beach huts ... it all fills me with unexpected nostalgia as I remember long-gone family holidays. The economy of pretty much this whole town, I imagine, would have been based on tourism. Summer vacations, ice creams, buckets, and spades ... all gone forever now. Christ, the very idea of a holiday seems bizarre and out of—

"What the fuck are you doing here?"

The unexpected voice catches me by surprise. I spin around and find myself face-to-face with a tall man carrying a rifle. Dressed in ragged, mud-splattered fatigues with his head wrapped up in a bizarre checked hat–scarf combination, he looks like a cross between a farmer and a freedom fighter, like he should divide his time between milking cows and hiding in Middle Eastern cave systems. A bushy gray beard hides his mouth and makes his expression frustratingly hard to read. Christ, I'm a dumb prick. He could have killed me ten times over and I don't even have my knife ready to defend myself. All I've got in my hand is a fucking picture postcard. I drop it fast, hoping he hasn't noticed.

"Sorry ... I was just looking. I didn't know if—"

"I don't know you. Where you from?" he interrupts. He doesn't sound like he's going to stand for any bullshit. Whether he'd use his rifle on me or not is debatable, but I'm not about to take any chances. I try to clear my head and remember the back story I'd thought up for myself on the way here from Lowestoft. *Act dumb. Pretend you're lost. You're not here to fight*, I make myself remember, *just to observe.*

"I've been working my way up the coast," I lie.

"Doing what?" he sneers. "Taking in the sights?"

"Scavenging. Honest, man, I didn't know anyone was here. Thought the place was dead like everywhere else. Just let me go and I'll get out of your way."

"Found much?"

"What?"

"On your travels ... have you found much?"

"Not a lot. Not a lot left anywhere, to be honest."

"You on your own?"

"Best way to be. What about you?"

"Nope. Plenty more of us in the village."

"You live here?"

"Yep, if you call this living."

He seems reasonably calm, although appearances can be deceptive. I don't get the impression he's looking for trouble, but I can't risk making assumptions. For all I know, he could be head honcho of a family of cannibals or something equally unpleasant. Stranger things have happened.

"Listen, I'm starving. You got any food? I'll trade for it."

"You'll need to talk to Warner," he says, using the end of his rifle to gesture back toward the town. "He makes the decisions around here."

HE TAKES ME BACK toward the center of town without saying another word, leading me all the way back along the beachfront promenade, passing level with the lighthouse, until we reach a pub. There we turn right and walk up a narrow road lined with odd-shaped, brightly painted cottages packed tightly together. The blues and yellows might have faded, but they still stand out amid the muted grays and browns of everything else. This place is in such relatively good condition that I still keep getting distracted, and I don't realize we've reached the boss's place until we're there. It's a large, grubby, white-fronted hotel, right in the very center of the town, overlooking a junction where one road merges with another and forms an open arrowhead-shaped space. The roads are completely devoid of any moving traffic, and this place has become a kind of makeshift village square, with several vehicles parked and other stacks of equipment left lying around. The frontages of some of the buildings have been fortified with wooden barriers and spools of barbed wire. There are two men standing next to a glowing brazier a short distance away, but it's otherwise quiet and there's no one else about. It's still relatively early. No doubt I'll see more activity later, providing I survive my meeting with Warner, that is.

"Is this it?"

The man disappears inside the hotel, both avoiding my question and answering it at the same time. I stand and wait in the middle of the street, feeling vulnerable but doing all I can to keep up the illusion that I'm a scavenger who just happens to have stumbled across this place, not a spy sent here by the local neighborhood despot. I can see movement through the ground-floor windows of the hotel, but I can't make out who it is or what's happening inside. I check my pockets and the leather holster on my belt, feeling for the reassuring shapes of my knives, and I try to prepare myself mentally for the inevitable quick getaway I'll have to make if things turn nasty. I try not to look too conspicuous as a group of people emerges from around the side of a building behind me, dragging a trailer between them. Thankfully they pass by quickly, barely even giving me a second glance. I haven't seen a lot, but I know already that this place is a world apart from Lowestoft. There you often can't move along the pavement for swarms of useless underclass, loitering, begging, and squabbling. But their numbers can be useful, and I can disappear into the crowds when I don't want to be found. Here I have no cover or protection whatsoever.

The tall man appears from a passageway that runs down the side of the hotel, between this building and the next. He beckons me toward him, and I have little option but to follow. The short passageway almost immediately opens out into a large cobblestone courtyard, and he gestures for me to go through a doorway into the building adjacent to the hotel. I'm reluctant; am I walking into a trap? But why should he be trying to trap me, unless he really does want to kill and eat me? Apart from turning up here unannounced, I don't think I've done anything to arouse suspicions.

Judging from the decoration and the almost undamaged oak paneling inside, I think this must have been some kind of town hall, although if it is, it's the smallest town hall I've ever seen. I'm ushered through another door into a large, high-ceilinged room, which is empty save for a gaunt, white-haired man sitting at a table writing figures in a book. He doesn't even look up when we enter. He looks like a country gent, how I imagine a squire might look from history lessons long gone. Appearances can be deceptive, I keep reminding myself. First impressions don't count like they used to.

"You Warner?" I ask. He doesn't react at first. Instead he finishes writing, then puts down his pen, takes off his glasses, and carefully lays them on the desk. Then he looks up at me.

"Yep," he answers, "and who might you be?"

"My name's Rufus," I tell him, picking the first name that comes into my head, then immediately wishing I'd chosen something less conspicuous.

"And what can I do for you, Rufus?"

His simple question is stupidly hard to answer, probably because of the ominous way he asks it, staring straight at me. Is he trying to trip me up?

"Says he's been scavenging down south," the man who brought me here says from the doorway behind me.

"Has he now?"

"That's right," I tell him, mouth dry with nerves.

"Not been too close to what's left of London, I hope," Warner says, grinning knowingly at the other man. "Don't want our little town contaminated."

I shake my head. "Nowhere near it. Look, I don't want any trouble. I swear I didn't know there was anyone here. I'm just looking for something to eat and somewhere to shelter. I'll be gone again tomorrow."

"You look like you need feeding up. The road not been kind to you?"

I shrug my shoulders. "No harder on me than anyone else."

"Why are you here so early, then? Couldn't you sleep?"

Warner's strange question throws me, so much so that I instinctively slide my hand into my pocket and feel for the hilt of my knife again.

"What?"

"You been walking through the night?"

"I don't understand."

"Common sense says," he begins, leaning across the table, eyes burning into me, "that most people rest at night and move during daylight hours when it's safer. Especially with it being the middle of winter and all, and with the world being such a fucking horrible place all of a sudden. So why are you turning up in front of me now, before we've even got to midmorning?"

Stay calm, I tell myself, feeling my body tensing in anticipation of an attack. There could be any one of a hundred plausible explanations why someone might have chosen to walk through the night. *Just don't panic* . . . I grip the handle of the blade in my pocket.

"Go for that knife and I'll have you killed before you've even drawn it," he says calmly. I let it go and lift my hands.

"I set out at sunrise," I tell him, swallowing hard, plumping for the most simple and logical explanation I can come up with. "I knew I wasn't far from this place, but I must have lost my bearings somewhere along the way. I was a few hours farther down the road than I thought. I'd got it into my head I had another half a day's walk ahead of me."

He nods slowly. Is he deciding whether he believes my story or working out how he's going to get rid of me? Warner's obviously no fool. I see flashes of the arrogance of a fighter in his eyes, but there's clearly much more to him than that. I stand my ground, hold my nerve, and keep quiet.

"But I found him up by the pier," the man behind me says.

"So?" Warner asks.

"So that's north of town, John. He said he came here from the south."

Warner's silence demands an answer.

"I did come from the south," I tell them both, trying not to be noticed as I reach for a different knife inside my long coat. "I didn't see anyone when I first got here. I just kept walking out along the seafront, and that's where you found me."

"I'm not sure about this. There are enough people out in the fields. Surely he'd have—"

"I saw them. By the church . . ."

"So why didn't you ask them for food? You said you didn't know there was anyone here."

Warner raises his hand to silence the other man and shakes his head. He sits in front of me impassive, like a judge about to pass sentence. I keep waiting for him to give the order and for a pack of previously hidden fighters to emerge from the woodwork and take me out. I'm woefully out of shape and I haven't fought seriously for weeks. I'd struggle to defend myself against these two today, never mind anyone else they might call in to help them. Fucking Hinchcliffe and his stupid fucking empire building. Why do I let him maneuver me into situations like this? The answer's disappointingly obvious: He'd kill me if I didn't do what he said.

"Let it go, Ben," Warner says, still surprisingly calm. "Does it really matter? Fact is, he's here now and he's got a simple choice to make. He can play ball and follow our rules, or he can fuck off and keep walking. If he's as cold, hungry, and miserable as he looks, I think he'll do what he's told."

"I will," I say quickly, sounding deliberately pathetic. "I don't want any trouble."

"Fair enough, then," Warner says, picking up his pen again and chewing thoughtfully on the end of it. "The first rule you need to know is that it's one day's work here for one meal and one night's shelter. You work hard and you keep working until you're told to stop and you'll get fed. Any slacking and you'll get fuck all."

"Sounds fair."

"I wouldn't go that far, but you get the idea."

"Okay."

"Second rule: Any problems here, you come and see me. Understand?"

"Understand."

"You don't try to sort things out yourself, right?"

"Right."

Warner leans back in his chair and continues to watch me for a few uncomfortable seconds longer.

"You don't look like you'll last the day," he says. Insolent bastard. "I'm fine."

"Right, then," he announces. "Get him out to the others, Ben, and find him something to do."

9

FUCKING HINCHCLIFFE. THIS WAS never part of the deal. The light's poor and I have no way of telling the time, but I feel like I've been working here for hours now. The time is dragging and I'm fucked—completely exhausted—but I don't dare stop and show it. I'm not interested in the promise of a meal (I'll take their food, but I'm not hungry—I'll end up adding it to my stocks back at the house), but I need to keep up the illusion and find out as much as possible about what's happening here. I just want an easy life, and that means putting up with a day's hard work to try to keep Hinchcliffe happy.

He's got good reason to be suspicious. Something's not right here. All this "one meal for one day's work" bullshit doesn't ring true. They're definitely starting to play from a different rule book here in Southwold, but I don't know what they're hoping to achieve. Maybe John Warner's got Lowestoft in his sights and he's trying to build a platform here, a stepping-stone to taking over? Whatever's going on, he must be personally benefiting from it somehow. No one does things "for the greater good" anymore. I need to find out what's going on, and I need to be quick. Hinchcliffe will expect a report from me before nightfall.

Days like today confirm that Hinchcliffe's faith in me is badly misplaced. I'm not cut out for this subterfuge and bullshit. He sent me here to uncover what's happening in Southwold, but so far all I've done is help dig a pit in a field well away from everything and everyone else. I'm working with a handful of other people—some look like fighters, others more underclass in their demeanor—but generally conversation is sparse and everyone keeps to themselves. From what I understand, this is just one of several work parties operating today. There are more people working just outside the town, trying to prepare fields for planting crops next year. They're stupidly optimistic. There's been so much smoke, radiation, and Christ knows what else thrown up into the atmosphere that I doubt anything will grow again for a long time. A while ago, before Hinchcliffe plucked me from the crowds, back when I was just another member of his scavenging pack, I saw the full extent of the damage the war has done: huge swathes of countryside that were completely dead, forests full of bleached, bare-branched trees, the corpses of thousands of birds littering the ground . . .

"You asleep?"

I shake my head and look around quickly. Not asleep, just daydreaming.

"Sorry," I say to the short, nervous-looking man who's standing next to me with a shovel. He's just finished filling a wheelbarrow with soil, and I'm supposed to be emptying it. He stares at me through glasses held together with tape. Long strands of greasy black hair blow wildly in the wind—the comb-over from hell whipping back and forth across his otherwise bald pate like a lid.

"Focus on the job," he whispers to me. "They won't feed you otherwise."

He makes it sound like they're fattening us up so they can eat us. I've got to get this sudden cannibal fixation out of my head, but where else is Warner getting all this food I keep hearing about, and why is he so eager to share it? I push the wheelbarrow over to the mound of earth that's already been dug up and empty it out. The distance I've covered is short, but I'm exhausted and I take my time so I can get my breath back. I pause and look out over a low stone wall. I can see another working party in a field in the distance, and I decide I'm glad I ended up over here. Looks like the people there really drew the short straw. They're plowing a huge, odd-shaped field by hand. There is a single horse, but it's painfully thin, its ribs exposed like it's swallowed a xylophone. It hardly seems able to support its own weight, let alone do anything else. It's the first time I've seen a horse in as long as I can remember. I watch as it bends down, tired legs shaking, and begins nibbling at the weeds on the edge of a sandy pit. There are other pits dotted around, and I realize that I'm looking at what's left of a golf course. The people working there don't appear to have made much progress, and I'm not surprised. Even though it's approaching the warmest part of the day, the soil here is still frozen hard.

When I return to the others, almost everyone else is taking a break. As I was late to the party (and also because my dawdling and lack of effort have been noticed), I've been told in no uncertain terms to keep working. One other man is left working with me. He's a strong, thickset fighter who continues digging at the bottom of the pit. His head glistens with sweat, his thinning silver hair slicked back. He looks like the type of man who's done this kind of work all his life: solid and muscular but not particularly athletic. He's hardly said two words since I've been here, but as the others are a safe distance away and I've got my back to them, I risk trying to make conversation. It's not easy. He's buried chest deep in the large, six-foot-square pit, and he digs constantly, only pausing to either swap his shovel for a pick or pass up another bucket of soil for me to dump into the wheelbarrow.

"You been here long?"

"Couple of weeks," he says, barely acknowledging me. I try offering information to get him to talk.

"I just got in this morning. Looks like a pretty well organized place."

"Warner does okay," he says, grunting with effort as he shifts another bucketful of dirt.

"You get much trouble here?"

"Only from people who ask too many questions."

"Sorry."

A handful of sheep have wandered into the field and are milling around, as hungry looking as the horse. Their fleeces are patchy and mangy looking. They drop their heads and try to graze, but the grass is thin and unsatisfying. They barely look up when I push the wheelbarrow past them to empty it, too weak to run away. When I return to the pit I take a chance and try again.

"Look, I heard what you said about asking questions, but what exactly are we doing out here?"

"Digging a fucking big hole," he answers, no hint of sarcasm in his voice.

"I know that, but what's it for?"

He stops working momentarily and looks over the lip of the pit, back across the field. No one's looking at us. They're far enough away for him to feel comfortable enough to talk.

"You won't do yourself any favors if you keep asking questions like that, I already told you."

"I know. I'm sorry."

He glances around again.

"We lost a few people over the last couple of weeks," he finally explains. "We would have burned them like usual, but Warner's got this idea that things here have gone too far the wrong way. He said he wants them buried like we used to. Says if someone doesn't start making a stand, we'll be living like savages again before we know it. We'll end up going the way of the Brutes."

"So what happened?"

"A few of them got sick . . ."

"And the others?"

"An accident," he tells me reluctantly. "A handful of people got hurt, two were killed."

"What kind of accident?"

I know instantly from the expression on his face that I'm pushing too hard.

"You really need to stop talking and get working. I've told you all I'm going to."

10

THE SUN HAS SET by the time I'm finally allowed to stop. I'm exhausted; weak with effort and numb with cold.

The pit was finished a while back. Warner, his right-hand man Ben, and a crowd of others pulled a trailer loaded with corpses into the field. I tried to watch from a safe distance and I counted at least five bodies. They were wrapped up in blankets and black plastic, so it was impossible to tell who they were or how they'd died. I'm sure one of them must have been Casey, Hinchcliffe's missing soldier. I even volunteered to help fill in the grave so I could get a better look. That was a mistake. A load more unnecessary effort and I couldn't see a damn thing.

Something's definitely not right here. Warner and several others stood silently around the edge of the pit, watching the dead being buried and muttering and whispering to each other. I can't make up my mind whether Warner is genuinely hankering back to prewar values of respect and dignity, or whether this was a mock burial to throw people off the scent. Is all of Southwold just an elaborate facade? Were they burying evidence and trying to hide their crimes?

After they'd buried the bodies, a couple of us were sent into a copse of trees to fetch firewood, which we loaded onto the back of the trailer. Virtually everything's dead, so it took less time than expected to gather up a large enough load. Other people arrived from the center of the village a while back to take the firewood away, and I've been called over into a nearby house with the rest of the group I was working with.

The house is just a shell. There are a couple of faded photographs hanging on the walls, but those are the only traces I can see of the people who used to live here. Everything else—the furniture and all their belongings—has gone. A fire has been built in the hearth, and most of the others are already sitting around in its orange glow, trying to get warm, staring silently into the flames and waiting for a dented pot of water to boil. I find myself a space on the muddy, threadbare carpet and lean back against the wall. The floor's cold but I'm too tired to care. What heat the fire provides is negated by icy drafts sneaking in through broken windows and the gaps beneath doors. I wrap my arms around myself to try to keep warm and look around at the six other people here with me.

A large, straw-haired woman (Jill, I think, one of the work gang leaders) eventually gets up and makes hot drinks, which she hands around in chipped mugs. The wood on the fire crackles and pops as it burns. The chimney's blocked, and the house is filling with smoke.

"There'll be food in the square outside the hotel later," she says. "It won't be much, but it should help keep the cold out."

"What about tomorrow?" the man with the tape-repaired specs and the comb-over asks, sitting opposite, leaning back against the wall.

"No work here," she answers, "but Warner will find you something. There's always the fields."

"This place is well organized," I say to her, taking advantage of a natural gap in the conversation to try to push for information again.

"You just arrived?"

"Got here this morning."

"Then you might want to think about staying. You'll not find any-thing better around here. You'll probably not find anything better *anywhere.*"

"Why's that?"

"Because John Warner's a good man. Because the things he's plan-ning are going to give people like us our lives back."

"People like us?"

"People who don't want to keep fighting for everything," she ex-plains. "The war's over, and it's time to start picking up the pieces. Time to stop all the killing and start remembering what it's like to be human again."

She's obviously never been to Lowestoft, I think to myself, trying not to smirk at the thought. I suddenly feel like I've wandered into a hippie commune from the sixties. Thing is, peace and love and all that bullshit never really counted for much, and as far as I can see, they count for absolutely nothing now. Remorse, compassion, regret . . . publicly demonstrate any of those emotions and you're likely to get torn apart. Give someone an inch, and they'll take ten miles. Hold your hand out to help someone, and some nasty bastard will tear your arm off and beat you to death with the bloody limb. That's how it is in the rest of the world outside Southwold, anyway. Everyone I've so far seen is stuck in a rut—no one wants to go back to the lives they had before, but there are no new roles or routines for people to move into. The violence that brought us all to this point has become the norm.

"So how's Warner planning to change things, then?" I ask, genu-inely curious. "By making you bury bodies? By getting people to plow fields where nothing's ever gonna grow?"

She shakes her head angrily. "If you don't like it, just fuck off."

"It's not that," the silver-haired pit digger I spoke to earlier says from another corner of the room. "Warner's just trying to pick the pieces up again and restore some order. It's not so much *what* we're do-ing, the important thing is the fact we're doing it at all."

"Sorry," I say quickly, backpedaling fast and realizing that publicly bad-mouthing Warner was a stupid move, "I didn't mean to sound so critical. It's just that it's been a long time since I've seen anything like this. This is the first place I've been in weeks where people aren't constantly at each other's throats."

"We've all done more than our fair share of that," Jill says quietly, swirling the dregs of her drink around in the bottom of her mug, then knocking it back, "and chances are we'll all have to fight again someday."

"You don't always have a choice," someone else says, his face hidden by the darkness.

"There's *always* a choice," Jill says. "That's what John'll tell you."

There's an underlying tension and emotion in this woman's voice that I didn't expect. Am I the only one who's picking up on it? She sounds like she genuinely supports Warner and believes in what he's doing, whatever that might be. I guess the fact she's here at all is proof that Warner's chosen not to echo Hinchcliffe's "management model." Were she in Lowestoft, unless she was a particularly strong fighter or had a particular skill that Hinchcliffe needed, she'd most likely have been swallowed up with the rest of the underclass, not assuming any position of authority or worth. Could this place and its leader actually be for real? I'm still not convinced. How can Warner find enough food to feed around thirty people regularly when most people can't even feed themselves?

"Someone I passed on the road said something about another settlement? A little farther up the coast from here?"

"That'll be Lowestoft."

"What's it like there?"

"Don't rightly know," she answers quickly, "and I don't want to know, either. Warner talks to the people in charge up there when he has to, but he ain't got a lot of time for them. We keep our distance. He says they're going about things the wrong way."

"How so?"

"What's your name, friend?"

"Rufus," I reply, remembering at the last second that I used a false name when I arrived this morning.

"You ask a lot of questions," she says. That's the second time I've been warned today. I need to make it the last time, too.

"Sorry. I've been on my own for too long. I'm just looking for somewhere to stop for a while, and if I'll get a better deal here than in Lowestoft, then—"

"It's not about deals," she interrupts angrily. "That's the difference between us here and them up there. We're small enough and sensible enough to work together. Up in Lowestoft Hinchcliffe keeps people dangling on pieces of string. He uses them. Tempts them with promises and stuff, then gets rid of them when they don't do what he says. He's the only one who benefits. It might work for him, but he's a bastard, and we don't want that here."

"Sounds bad."

"It is bad. Fighting has replaced thinking, if you hadn't already noticed—and until people start thinking again, we're all in trouble."

I drink more coffee to stop myself from speaking, sensing that I've pushed as far as I dare. She's absolutely right about Hinchcliffe, and I'm precisely the kind of person she was talking about, sitting here in the cold and being manipulated by him from a distance while he sits in the relative comfort of his courthouse throne room. What choice do I have? Are things really any better here? Is Warner as honest and decent as she's making him out to be? I doubt he is. I don't think anyone really gives a damn about anyone else anymore. I certainly don't. My gut feeling is still that Warner must be profiting from this somehow. Whatever he's doing, he's playing with fire. I wouldn't want to risk doing anything that might piss Hinchcliffe off unless I had a foolproof contingency plan and an untraceable escape route mapped out first.

"I'm off," Jill says suddenly, getting up and walking toward the door. "Got things to do. See you all later."

Now my paranoia is going into overdrive. Have I said too much and is she going to see Warner to rat on me? Is it time to get out of here? I wait for a moment longer, staring into the embers of the fire, then glance up and see that the man with the comb-over and broken glasses is watching me from across the room. He looks away as soon as we make eye contact, and I know that I've aroused suspicions. I'll shut up and keep to myself from now on. They'll be watching me now. Despite all the bullshit I've just heard, I know that like everywhere else, no one here trusts anyone else.

THE WOMAN JILL WAS right about the food—it was warm and it was limited, both in taste and volume. I forced myself to eat, knowing that I needed to build up my energy after the unexpected exertion of the day. I never expected to have to do a full day's physical labor here. Every muscle in my body hurts now and I feel half dead, even worse than usual.

I've been trying to walk off the food lying heavy on my stomach, determined not to spend another night throwing up. I walk slowly around the perimeter of the village square, trying to observe as much as I can without drawing attention to myself. There's a very different atmosphere here, much less immediate tension in the air. Back in Lowestoft, you constantly feel that everyone's on edge, that a fight might break out at any moment for any reason, often for no reason at all. Here there seems to be more tolerance and cooperation, and I'm surprised, if not wholly convinced. They must know something about Warner and his regime that I don't, either that or this place *is* genuine and these people are trying to rebuild.

I do my best to avoid the crowds. Considering there are only around thirty people here (according to Hinchcliffe), it's harder than I expected. Back in the center of Lowestoft, people often cram together in the same buildings. Here, though, they're much more spread out. There are candles and lamps visible in many of the buildings around the square, and I feel like there are eyes watching me constantly. I know that's just paranoia, because no one gives a shit about me, and that's one of the reasons Hinchcliffe sent me here. If anyone asks I'll just lie my way out of trouble and tell them I was looking for a place to sleep.

There's a truck parked across the full width of a road up ahead, blocking it off. It's an ex-army vehicle, I think—painted matte green save for some kind of crude emblem that's been daubed on one side and on the hood. It looks like a target, red and white concentric circles with more red at the bull's-eye. As I get closer, I realize I can hear voices in the street behind it. I walk right past the mouth of the road and try to glance around the back of the truck, but I can't see much. There's a small crowd of people there, but I can't tell how many or what they're doing. I keep moving, then take the next right turn, hoping that the side street I've just entered will somehow connect with the road that runs parallel. It doesn't, but the houses I'm walking past now back on to those on the other road. I carry on a little farther, then stop, check again that there's no one else around, then climb over the gate at the side of the house nearest to me. It's quiet, and I can hear the voices in the blocked-off street as I walk the length of the overgrown back garden. There's a hole in the end fence. I duck through it, squeezing through a gap I'd never have got through if I wasn't so thin, and continue toward the house up ahead, which, to my relief, appears empty and dark. The back door is missing, its frame badly damaged. I go inside, checking yet again that no one's there, then slowly creep up the stairs. From an echoing room at the front of the house, I look down onto the street below.

There are five figures waiting in the road. I can't tell who any of them are from this distance, but I can see that they're armed, although their weapons are held casually and they don't seem to be expecting trouble. One of them sits down on the curb; another takes a swig from a hip flask.

It's a few minutes before anything happens. I'm leaning against the wall, eyes starting to go, almost falling asleep, when the man sitting down gets up quickly and the posture of the others suddenly changes. They stand ready as a group in the middle of the street. Then I hear an approaching engine, and I see headlights coming closer. It's another ex-army truck—similar in size and condition to the one that's been left blocking the other end of the road. It stops a short distance away with a sudden hissing of brakes. The driver, along with two more men, gets out.

They move fast. The driver opens the back of the truck and climbs up into it, then starts passing stuff down to the others, who carry the heavy boxes and crates away toward another house and a storage shed near the blocked mouth of the road. They're working steadily for a good few minutes, unloading a stack of food, some weapons, and other, less easily identifiable, supplies. It's a decent-sized hoard. Suspiciously large, in fact. They won't have got their hands on that much stuff anywhere around here. Within a couple of minutes the unloading is complete, and as quickly and unexpectedly as they arrived, the second truck, its driver, and the passengers all disappear. I catch a glimpse of that same circular red and white insignia as the truck reverses back down the street.

Smugglers. Christ, that's it. No wonder Warner's so cocky. The wily bastard is stealing to keep Southwold running the way he wants it, and he's obviously building up a decent and well-connected support structure, too. So the next question is, where's he getting it all from? This all looks surprisingly well organized, and whoever he's stealing from must have enough stuff in storage not to notice the occasional truckload disappearing. There's only one person who's likely to control enough around here to be in that position, and that's Hinchcliffe. By the looks of things, though, these aren't opportunistic raids. Everything I saw just now looked carefully planned, so that means Warner had help. He must have people on the inside. Maybe Neil Casey wasn't killed? Perhaps he'd been working for Warner all along? Fuck me, this is getting complicated. I feel a strange sense of relief that I've actually found something to go back to Hinchcliffe with. It means I should be able to get out of here before long.

The road outside is completely empty now. I leave the house the way I came, slipping back through the hole in the fence, then going down the side of the adjacent house and out onto the other street.

"So where d'you think that bunch came from?" a voice asks suddenly from somewhere behind me. I spin around anxiously. I go to grab my knife but clumsily drop it. The owner of the voice switches on a flashlight and shines it at me. Shit. I try to rush him, but he steps out of the way, then angles the light directly into my face, blinding me. "Don't panic," he says, "I don't want any trouble."

The man shines the light back at himself for a second, and it reflects off his thick glasses. I recognize him immediately. It's the guy from the working party this afternoon, the one with the bad hair who was watching me so closely in the house. Is he onto me? What am I supposed to do now, kill him? I pick up my knife just in case.

"I don't know what you're talking about."

"The delivery," he says. "I heard it, so you must have seen it. Same thing happens every few days around this time."

"I saw nothing," I tell him.

"So why are you here?"

"I was just looking for somewhere to sleep," I lie.

"Bullshit. I've been watching you. You've walked past more than two dozen empty buildings."

"You've been watching me? Why?"

"Because I want to talk to you. Look, can we go somewhere less public . . . ?"

"The middle of the street's fine. Anyway, why would you need to talk to me? Are you some kind of stalker?"

He ignores my jibe.

"It's Rufus, isn't it?"

"Yes," I answer after a brief but noticeable delay.

"So what do you think?"

"About what?"

"About what they're doing here? About the truck you just saw? About the way Warner's trying to get these people organized?"

"Did he send you to find me?"

"Not at all. I'm just trying to work out what's happening here, same as you are. So I'll ask you again, what do you think?"

"I think I'm bloody tired after working all day and I really don't care about Warner or any mysterious trucks," I answer. "I'm grateful for the food, and now I just want to find somewhere I can crash for the night like I told you. I took a wrong turn, and that's why I'm here. I'm really not interested in anything else."

"I don't buy that."

"I don't care."

It's clear this guy is just some deluded little idiot. Maybe he gets a kick out of causing trouble—some kind of masochist looking for a beating, perhaps? Whoever he is and whatever he wants, I'm not getting involved. Things are complicated enough already. I try to side-step him and head back toward the center of town, but he stands his ground and blocks my way through.

"I'm sorry," he says, "but I don't get it. You've just seen a truck full of supplies being unloaded, and you're telling me you don't want to know where it came from?"

"I'm not telling you anything."

"Why are you really here?"

"What's it to you?"

"I know you're lying to me, Rufus," he says. "I can read you like a book. My name's Peter Sutton, and I want answers, same as you."

MY MIND'S RACING, AND I do all I can not to show it. Who is this person? I need to be damn careful here and keep up my act. If he's working for Warner, then I could be in real trouble. Likewise, if he's discovered I'm here spying for Hinchcliffe, there's every chance I won't get out of Southwold alive. I need to find out which it is.

"So talk."

He looks around anxiously, despite the fact he already knows the street's clear, then speaks.

"I don't think we're seeing the full picture here."

"Tell me something I don't know."

"We're only seeing what Warner wants us to see."

"Isn't that usually the way with leaders?"

"Yes, but this is different."

"How?"

"Can't quite put my finger on it yet, but those trucks are the key. If we knew where they were coming from then things might start making sense."

"Nothing's made sense for the best part of the last twelve months. Anyway, why are you so interested in Warner? As long as he provides food, does it matter where it comes from?"

"Yes, but—"

"You make it sound like you think he has an ulterior motive."

"Maybe he does. Someone's supporting him, that much is obvious."

What's equally obvious is that Peter Sutton doesn't seem to have any information. He sounds as unsure about what's happening here as I am. I start to walk back toward town. I'm tired, and I'm desperate not to screw up my "mission" by saying something I'll regret or getting caught talking out on the street so close to Warner's food and weapons cache. I need to find somewhere quiet where I can report back to Hinchcliffe, then get some rest in case I end up working another full day tomorrow.

"I should go . . ."

"Just wait. Just give me a few more minutes."

"Why?"

"Because I need your help."

"You need my help?"

Now alarm bells are beginning to sound.

"Just stop and listen to me, Rufus. I'm like you."

"The only thing we have in common is that we're both still alive."

He stands in front of me, blocking my way past.

"I know what you can do," he says. "I know you can hold the Hate."

For a second I'm floored, although I try not to show it. I push past him and keep moving. How the hell did he know that? Someone must have told him—although I don't know who, because no one here knows anything about me. Maybe he came here from Lowestoft too? Oh fuck—is that sick bastard Hinchcliffe playing mind games?

"You know nothing about me."

"Yes I do," he says. "I know what you can do because I'm the same. I can hold it too—"

Do I believe him? Does it even matter any more? The Unchanged are extinct, so holding the Hate has become as irrelevant a skill as being able to speak Russian. I'm gripping my knife tightly and psyching myself up to use it if Sutton doesn't leave. Could I kill him? He might not look like much, but I don't know what he's capable of, and it's all about aggression levels now, not size. The screwiest are often the most unpredictable. I've seen people half his height kill others twice their weight. Nope, whatever trouble he's got himself into, I'm not getting involved. I've already got enough on my plate—correction, I've got *nothing* on my plate—and that's how I intend keeping it. I'm about to tell him as much when he starts talking again.

"When I found out what I could do," he explains, "I tried to stop fighting, tried to pull away from the war. But there was nowhere to go, and I got tangled up in things I couldn't get out of. When I learned how to hold the Hate, I started to look at things differently again, started to question what I'd been told and why things were happening. All they wanted me to do was hunt and kill and . . ."

"Wait, who is 'they'?" I ask cautiously.

"Simon Penkridge, Selena, Chris Ankin . . ."

Two of the three names mean nothing to me. I try not to react, but it's impossible when he mentions Chris Ankin.

"Ankin?"

"I never saw him, but the others said they were working for him. They were sending people into refugee camps to kill like bloody suicide bombers."

"You refused?"

"You don't say no to people like that. I went along with it for a time, then managed to get lost in the crowds and got away from them."

"Wise move," I'm forced to admit, reflecting for a second on my own experiences. The things he says add some weight to his story, but the fact remains, why should I care? All of that is history now, and I need to focus on today. Does this guy know anything that might be useful to Hinchcliffe? Against my better judgment I decide to ask. "So what's your connection with this place?"

"Just passing through, same as you."

"About these trucks. You've been watching them for a while?"

"I've seen them coming and going, but I don't know anything about them."

"So you don't know where this stuff's coming in from?"

"No idea, but I'm trying to find out. Fact is, I need all the food I can get my hands on right now, so I'll take whatever's going."

"You don't look like a big eater."

"I'm not. Look, where are you heading?"

"How many times do I have to tell you? To find somewhere to crash for the night."

"I know a place. Come with me, there's something I want to show you."

Now alarm bells are really beginning to sound. This guy doesn't know anything. He's completely out of his tree. What the hell could he possibly want to show me?

"No thanks. I think you've got the wrong man."

"No I haven't," he insists, walking alongside me again. "You're the only one who can help. I can't do this on my own anymore."

"Do what exactly?"

"Not here," he says, looking around nervously. There's a small crowd up ahead gathered around the area the food was distributed from earlier. This guy's a liability and the best way of getting rid of him, I decide, is to get deeper into the crowd, then give him the slip. I'll keep him talking for a few seconds longer so he doesn't suspect I'm about to do a disappearing act.

"We're not the only ones who can hold the Hate, Sutton. I've met plenty of others."

"Yeah? Where are they now?"

"Dead," I'm forced to admit, remembering the misguided, kamikaze freedom fighters I managed to get myself mixed up with.

"Exactly. See, I knew you'd say that. You're the first person like me I've come across since the bombs."

"I'm not like you. Stop saying that. I'm not like anyone."

"Yes you are. I knew it as soon as I saw you out in the field earlier. The questions you were asking just confirmed it. You're no scavenger. That's not why you're here."

Shit, is he onto me? Has my cover been blown?

"So how could you tell? I didn't sense that you were any different. For all I know you could be lying to me, feeding me bullshit so you can—"

"No bullshit, I swear. You didn't see that we're the same because you weren't looking for it. It's not about what you do, it's what you *don't* do that really gives you away."

"What?"

"I don't know what really brought you here to Southwold today, but I'm damn sure it wasn't the promise of a meal and a bed. You didn't pick up on me because you were preoccupied thinking about something else. It was obvious—the way you asked so many questions to different people, the way you avoided eye contact. We're not like the rest of them . . ."

Just keep the conversation going for a few more seconds, I tell myself. I'm close to the edge of the crowd now.

"I ask questions because I don't want to fuck up. I've been on the road for weeks, and this is the best place I've found in a long time."

"You've no more been on the road than I have. I know you're lying, Rufus, but I understand. You don't need to. We all have things we need to keep hidden. I'm on your side."

"On my side? You don't know what you're talking about. Who said anything about taking sides?"

"It's all about taking sides now."

"Is that right?"

"Okay, then, tell me the name of the last place you passed through before this one. How long were you there for? And the place before that . . . ?"

I don't bother answering. This guy's a fucking crank. Probably had one too many bangs on the head on the battlefield and now he's finally lost it. No matter. Not my problem. We've reached the crowd, and when Jill, the woman from the working party earlier, appears in front of me, I take the opportunity to use her as a distraction.

"Jill," I say, grabbing hold of her arm and pulling her closer. "This guy wants to talk to you."

I push her and Peter Sutton together, and before either of them can react I shove my way through the rest of the bodies and slip away into the darkness.

I SPENT ANOTHER HALF hour walking the streets in the late-evening subzero gloom, checking buildings and looking for somewhere where I could report back to Hinchcliffe and then sleep. I eventually found an upstairs room in an empty bank, and from there I looked down onto the square below through a window covered with strong iron bars like a prison cell. From my position up high I could see the entire square down below. By then the place was virtually deserted, just a couple of people left standing guard, warming their hands over a fire burning in a metal trash can near the hotel, and nothing else happened for as long as I watched. A while ago my curiosity was over-taken by my exhaustion. I tried to read my book for a while and forget where I was, but I was too tired. I lay back on the hard floor, made a pillow from a pile of papers and spare clothes from my backpack, cov-ered myself with my coat, then closed my eyes and tried to get a little rest before reporting back to Lowestoft.

That little rest turned itself into a lot of sleep. I've been completely out of it for hours, and I sit up quickly when I realize it's late and I still haven't called in. Hinchcliffe's going to be fucking furious. I grab the radio from my bag.

"Hinchcliffe, it's me," I whisper, keeping my voice low. I cringe and fumble for the volume control when a sudden burst of loud static deafens me and fills the entire building.

"Jesus Christ, Danny," his distorted but distinctive voice immediately answers back. "Where the hell have you been? I was starting to think they'd done you in. Either that or you'd defected."

Defected? Is he serious or just trying to be funny? His voice sounds slurred, like he's been drinking. He probably has.

"Nothing like that," I tell him, wiping the sleep from my eyes and trying to sound more awake and alert than I actually am. "I was just biding my time. Wanted to find out as much as I could before I got back to you."

"And . . . ?" he asks.

I hesitate. "And I don't know what's going on here. Warner's got these people well and truly on his side. He makes it look like all he's trying to do is organize them according to his rules and to get them to—"

"That's half the problem," Hinchcliffe angrily interrupts. I'm surprised by the strength of the alcohol-fueled venom in his voice.

"What is?"

"*His* rules. Don't you see, Danny? Warner's rules aren't my rules."

"Suppose not," I quietly agree, suddenly feeling like I'm walking on eggshells and wishing I hadn't bothered calling in.

"You've heard the old story about two boats in the harbor, haven't you?"

I don't have a clue what he's talking about. "Remind me."

"They start next to each other and they're both supposed to be following the same course. One gets it wrong by just a fraction of a degree. They set off together, but the longer they're at sea . . ."

"The bigger the gap between them."

"Exactly. You see what I'm saying? I can't afford for that to happen, Danny. Not when Southwold is so close."

"Well, if it's any consolation, I can't speak for Warner, but I don't think the people here are looking to pick a fight. They think he's just—"

"Don't get me wrong, that's not what I'm looking for, either," he continues, not listening, "but everybody there needs to understand that things run the way I want them to around here. You play ball or you fuck off, that's your choice."

"Have you tried telling them?" I ask, only feeling brave enough to confront Hinchcliffe because he's ten miles farther up the coast. "You could come down here, try a little diplomacy first and then—"

"Yeah, yeah, yeah . . . Fuck, Danny, it seems to me there's only two options these days, full-on or fuck all. Why can't these people just do what I tell them?"

"I know, but—"

"What happens in Southwold is important," he interrupts again, his voice sounding even angrier now. "I can't risk having a rebellion on my doorstep, you know what I mean?"

"But are you sure Warner's a threat?"

"*Everyone* is a potential threat. I thought you'd have worked that out by now."

"I still think you should talk to him. Try to find out why—"

"What's the state of the place like?" he interrupts.

"What?"

"What kind of condition is Southwold in?"

"I don't know. It's pretty much like everywhere else. A little less damaged than most places, but—"

"And what about supplies?"

"Now that's the thing. Warner's got them getting the fields around here ready for planting. On the face of it he seems to be planning for the future. I've been working all goddamned day digging goddamned holes . . ."

"Nothing's going to grow. Everything's fucked."

"We don't know that for sure. It might be that—"

"I asked you about supplies, Danny. I'm not interested in next year, what are they eating *today?*"

I pause, knowing that Hinchcliffe will hit the roof when I tell him about the delivery.

"I saw a truck arrive."

"A truck?"

"Great big army thing. It wasn't one I'd seen before. They unloaded a stack of stuff out of the back."

"What kind of stuff?"

"Couldn't tell. Food, weapons . . . I couldn't see what they—"

"Fuckers. That will have come from my stores. Fucking Neil Casey, I bet he's got something to do with this. Bastard's told them where I keep my supplies. Cunt's sold me out."

"I haven't seen Casey. He wasn't with the truck. They buried a few bodies this afternoon, and I thought he might have been one of them, but I don't know if—"

"You said weapons?"

"A few rifles, that's all, nothing any bigger than that. Look, Hinchcliffe, I really don't think that—"

"I'm not interested in what you think. All I want to know is what you've seen."

"And I've told you everything. I'll find work again tomorrow and see what else I can find out."

"I don't think you understand the importance of this, Danny. There are implications for all of us if Warner starts getting support and if people here start hearing what he's doing. The grass is always greener on the other side, remember that expression?"

"The grass is yellow everywhere now," I tell him. "What's happening here is on a very small scale, Hinchcliffe. If Warner's stealing from you that's one thing, but I don't think it's worth . . ."

I stop talking when I realize he's not there anymore. The radio's dead.

14

THE SOUND OF ENGINES wakes me up. The top floor of the bank is icy cold as I scramble across the room to the window and look down onto the square. All around the edges of the large triangle-shaped area, people are emerging from buildings and spilling out onto the street. Several of them dive for cover as a fleet of vehicles powers into the center of Southwold, filling the air with black fumes and noise. I recognize some of these trucks and vans, they're from Lowestoft. Hinchcliffe's obviously thought about our conversation last night and has decided to flex his muscles and remind everyone who's boss. So much for diplomacy and negotiation, not that I ever expected anything different from him.

The convoy stops, filling almost the entire square now. An army of fighters flood out into the open and begin rounding people up. For the most part they do exactly what they're told, shuffling toward the center of the square. One woman refuses and runs the other way, but she's chased down by one of Hinchcliffe's thugs and clubbed to the ground.

She lies on the asphalt screaming, blood pouring down her face, everyone else too scared to help. The fighter drags her over to the others. Christ, I need to get out of here.

The arrival of Hinchcliffe's troops means my time here is up. I quickly gather my stuff and pack everything into my backpack, but I start coughing as soon as I stand upright, and for a few seconds it's like I've lost control of my body. I try to drink from a bottle of stale water, but the first gulp I take ends up sprayed across the floor before I can swallow it down. Eventually the coughs subside. Panting with effort, I spit a lump of sticky, foul-tasting muck into the corner of the room, then lean against the window.

Down on the street below, directly outside the hotel, there's an uncomfortable-looking standoff taking place. Several of Hinchcliffe's vehicles have been parked in an arc around the entrance to the building, and his fighters are advancing. I recognize a couple of the more notorious faces. Patterson is moving closer, and Llewellyn is loitering ominously toward the back of the assembled troops, no doubt there to coordinate them and to keep Hinchcliffe updated. Getting out of the lead truck now is his protégé, Curtis, wearing his usual uniform of full body armor. He's a vile, nasty bastard, not known for his negotiation skills. These discussions won't last long.

I finish collecting my gear, then swing my pack onto my shoulders, eager to get out of Southwold fast. I glance out of the window again and see that John Warner has emerged from the hotel now. Barely dressed, he's walking toward Curtis with arms outstretched to demonstrate that he's unarmed and ready to talk, gesturing for him to follow him into the hotel. Curtis marches toward him. Fuck. What the hell's he doing? He doesn't even try talking to Warner. The bastard just lifts up a machete and takes a vicious swipe at the white-haired leader of Southwold. Warner tries to get out of the way, but he's taken by surprise. Curtis chops down into his neck, hitting him with such violent force that he drops to his knees, the blade wedged deep into his flesh. Curtis grips the older man's shoulder and yanks him up, then wrenches his machete free. Still holding him, he sinks the tip of the blade deep into Warner's chest, then pulls it out again, swiping it through the air to get rid of the excess blood before pushing Warner away. He staggers back, his body soaked with glistening red, then his legs give way and he crumbles to the ground like a marionette with severed strings.

There's a brief moment of silent, stunned disbelief, then all hell breaks loose.

The powerful pit digger from yesterday is the first person to react. He charges at Curtis but is killed as quickly and as easily as Warner. Another fighter comes up behind him and cracks him around the side of the head with a baseball bat, almost decapitating him. Perhaps it's because I wasn't expecting it, but even after all I've seen and done myself, this sudden brutal violence shocks me to such an extent that I can hardly move.

"Round them up," Curtis yells to the rest of the fighters. "Take anything worth having and burn the rest. Kill anyone who gets in the way."

Is this my fault? Even though I'm starting to think that Hinchcliffe sent me here just to find an excuse for him to demonstrate his obvious strength and superiority, I can't help wondering if it could have been avoided if I'd handled him differently. If I'd told him everything was okay and that Warner was one hundred percent on his side, would he have let Southwold be? Who the hell am I kidding? The more I think about it, the more I realize that, yet again, I've been Hinchcliffe's patsy and he's played me like a pawn on a chessboard. *Screw the fucking lot of them*, I tell myself as I run downstairs and look for a way out of the bank. *Not my problem.*

I head for the back of the bank, squeezing down a narrow corridor past the open door of an unlocked vault, and I curse myself for picking such an impregnable hiding place. It seemed sensible last night, and the security was welcome, but every window here is either barred or shuttered, and the only other exit is a solid-looking, metal-clad fire door that I'll never be able to get open. I have no choice but to go back out onto the street.

I slip out through the front door and press myself tight against the outside wall, doing all I can to fade into the background. The village square is in utter chaos now, the remaining population of Southwold scattering in panic as Hinchcliffe's troops turn on them. I see Jill, the work party leader from yesterday, struggling to load and fire a rifle with trembling hands. She lifts it up, but before she can even get her finger on the trigger, a fighter chops into her side with an axe. Dumbstruck, I stand there like an idiot as Hinchcliffe's men grapple the locals to the ground, then force those still alive into the trucks that will ferry them back to Lowestoft. Our inglorious leader has obviously decided that having people living here outside his direct jurisdiction is an unacceptable risk. But Christ, did he really need to react like this? A woman is hit with a riot baton when she won't cooperate, winded first, then bludgeoned around the side of the head. Semiconscious, she's left on the ground close to Warner's body, blood pooling around her face, cheekbone shattered and skin split, her eyes moving but nothing else. She looks straight at me . . .

Spencer, one of Hinchcliffe's men, comes at me with a crowbar. I see him coming, but I'm stunned, too slow to move. A tall, sinewy black kid in his early twenties, the sick bastard grins with excitement as he sprints toward me, high on the thrill of the fight. He swings out wildly, and at the last possible second I manage to react. I lean over to one side and the crowbar misses me. I feel the rush of wind and hear it whoosh through the air as it whistles just inches past my ear. He lunges at me again, fired up with the adrenaline rush of battle, intoxicated by the sudden release of long-suppressed frustrations.

"Wait!" I shout at him. "Spencer, don't. I'm on your side. Hinchcliffe sent me here."

He doesn't recognize me, probably doesn't even hear me, and he swings the crowbar through the air again, this time catching me hard on my right shoulder. My padded backpack strap absorbs some of the impact, and I drop to my knees, landing close to the dismembered remains of yet another dead Southwold resident. I scramble back up and run for cover, the fighter still in close pursuit. I weave around the hood of a reversing truck with him gaining fast. I break right, desperate to shake him but knowing I can't keep this speed up for long, then run straight into another one of them who blocks my path. Now I'm really fucked. I drop to the ground and cover my head, anticipating a barrage of strikes.

"Not this one," a familiar voice says. I cautiously look up, still expecting to be clubbed, and see that it's Llewellyn. He reaches down and pulls me up onto my feet like I'm a half-stuffed rag doll.

"What's going on?" I ask him, gasping for breath and desperately trying not to start coughing again.

"What do you think's going on? Just carrying out the boss's orders," he answers abruptly.

"But this is fucking madness."

"You tell him," Llewellyn says, looking me straight in the eye. "I'm just doing what I'm told," he says again. "Now get in the truck or I'll personally beat seven shades of shit out of you."

Relieved, I start to do as he says but then stop.

"Wait, Hinchcliffe's car. I left it just outside town. He'll want it back."

Llewellyn looks at me for a second, then nods his head. "Go and get it, then get yourself straight back to Lowestoft. Any fucking around and you'll have me to answer to. Right?"

I don't need to be told twice. I start running, though I'm not sure which direction I need to take, just desperate to get away. I glance back as I run and see that the center of Southwold has quickly degenerated into a depressingly familiar sight. Broken bodies are scattered across the pavement, the dead and dying side by side, and there are people fighting and running in all directions like a scene from any one of a hundred battles I've seen before. Except this battle is different because there are no Unchanged here. It makes me feel ashamed, responsible almost. I'm ashamed because of my connection with the man behind this bloodshed, and equally ashamed because all they're doing is the same thing I've done countless times before. A different class of target, that's all.

I hear the smashing of glass and see a sudden flash of flame, brilliant yellow lighting up the early morning gloom. It's the hotel. Hinchcliffe's men are firebombing it. So that's his tactic this morning—

eliminate the figurehead in charge of Southwold, take anything and anyone of value, then do enough damage to render the village uninhabitable. That will leave the survivors of the massacre with only one remaining option: It's Lowestoft or nothing.

15

I MOVE QUIETLY THROUGH the courthouse, determined to get in and out quick and without being seen. Hardly anyone's here. There's an unexpected but very welcome lack of fighters in the building. Most of them are still in Southwold, I guess, reveling in the chaos. I can picture them all in the middle of the carnage like a fucking lower-league rugby team on tour; drunk on violence, smashing the place up, stealing food and weapons, bragging to each other about their best kills . . . fucking morons.

I leave the radio on a desk in the courtroom. It should be okay there. Anderson's bound to be around here somewhere, and he'll know what to do with it. I've left radios here before and—

"You okay, Danny?"

Startled, I turn around and see Hinchcliffe standing right behind me. My heart sinks with disappointment and my stomach knots with nerves. I was hoping I'd gotten away with it, but this sly bastard never misses a trick. This was the exact situation I was hoping to avoid—me alone with Hinchcliffe. Much as I want to bolt for the door and disappear, I know I can't. He beckons me through to his room, and I have no choice but to follow.

"You did good in Southwold," he says as we walk.

"Thanks," I answer, not sure what else I'm supposed to say. It didn't feel good.

"We need to keep showing these people who's in charge, you know?"

"If you say so."

I don't want to risk disagreeing with Hinchcliffe, but what happened in Southwold earlier has really gotten under my skin. I never expected him to let John Warner have carte blanche to run the place, but his reaction today was extreme. Hinchcliffe sits down on the corner of his unmade bed and looks up at me, and the silence in here is immediately tense and unbearable. He may be many things, but he's certainly not stupid. He's probably already worked out what I'm thinking. I want to run, but he keeps staring at me and I can't move.

"You still look sick."

"I am sick. Haven't felt well for days, weeks maybe."

"Are you eating enough? Want me to get you some more food?"

"I'm not eating anything."

He shakes his head. "You have to eat, Danny. Look, if you're really that bad, get yourself over to the factory and have a word with Rona Scott."

"Thanks, I will," I answer, although I know I probably won't. The last thing I want to do is to submit myself to an examination by Rona Scott. She's the closest thing Hinchcliffe has to a doctor. When she's not working on the Unchanged kids in the factory, it's her job to keep his fighters patched up and ready for battle. She's not interested in people like me.

"You've had a rough week, what with the Unchanged and now Southwold," Hinchcliffe says suddenly, taking me by surprise, the tone of his voice now different. "I know I ask a lot of you sometimes. It can't have been easy with those Unchanged. I don't know how you do it. Christ, just the thought of them makes my skin crawl, even after all this time. That last catch, Danny . . . you tracked them, trapped them, stayed with them until we were ready to move in. Now that takes guts."

"Just doing what you asked me to," I say quietly. Truth is, I didn't have any choice.

"Listen, I don't think I'll need you for the next couple of days. Get some rest. Straighten yourself out."

I hate it when Hinchcliffe's pleasant to me. This isn't like him. He never gives, only takes. I pause and wait for the catch. When he doesn't say anything, I begrudgingly acknowledge him. "Thanks."

I still don't feel able to move. His piercing gaze makes me feel like my feet are nailed to the floor, and he knows it. The fucker probably enjoys it.

"Something on your mind?"

I want to tell him, but I can't.

"Nothing."

"Come on, I know you better than that. Tell me what you're thinking."

How honest am I prepared to be? I sense he wants me to talk openly, but if I'm too critical he's likely to react badly, and I don't think I can take a beating today. On the other hand, he's not going to let me go until I tell him what's wrong.

"Honest answer?"

"Honest answer."

"I don't understand why you did what you did in Southwold. Fair enough if you've got a problem with Warner, but the rest of them . . . ?"

"It needed doing."

"Did it need to be so brutal?"

"I think so. They needed to know what's what."

"There's a world of difference between sending a message and what your fighters did today."

"I knew that was what was bothering you."

"So why did you ask?"

"Just wanted to see if you had the guts to tell me," he says. "I thought you would. Not many people would have the balls. You and me, Danny, we've got a lot in common."

"Have we?"

"When it comes down to it," he continues, "we both want the same thing. We both want an end to all the bullshit and fighting and we want an easy life. We're just going about it in very different ways."

"You want an end to the fighting? Really? That's not what I saw. The Unchanged are gone, and all you're doing is looking for someone else to batter instead. We don't *have* to fight anymore. I think you want to."

"That's not how it is."

"Well, that's how it looks."

"I know you're happy to bury your head in the sand and keep to yourself, but I'm not prepared to do that. In this world you can either sit back and wait for events to overtake you, or you can go out there and make things happen now and on your terms."

"Is that what you're doing?"

"Yes."

"That's what you're doing when you're ordering the people in Southwold to be beaten and killed? When you've got your fighters burning buildings to the ground?"

"Yes. The people in Southwold had a choice. The ones who didn't resist are on their way here now, and if they're useful, they'll be okay. The rest are dead. You've got to remember, everything is built on aggression now, Dan. We're all fighters, whether we like it or not. The only thing that separates us is our individual strength and determination. If you don't stake your claim, someone else will."

"So where does it end? Last man standing?"

"Possibly."

"I don't buy it."

"I know you don't, and I understand that—but we'll have to agree to disagree because I'm in charge. Anyway, even if you don't like the way I do things, you're smart enough to know you'll be okay as long as you stay in line and don't piss me off, aren't you?"

"Suppose. But did it really need to be so harsh in Southwold? Couldn't you just have dealt with Warner and left the rest of them be?"

"I had to send a message. If I hadn't I'd have just been heading back in a few weeks to straighten them out again. Someone would have taken Warner's place."

"But Warner's people were cooperating with each other. Surely if you—"

"I like you, Danny," he interrupts, obviously no longer interested. "You're way off the mark sometimes, but you're good to have around. You're not like all those sycophants and asslickers. You keep me grounded. You make me laugh."

"You're welcome," I mumble quietly, not sure if that was a compliment or not. There's no arguing with Hinchcliffe. Today he reminds me of all those long-gone world leaders who used to start wars in far-off places to *maintain the peace*. It's the same kind of flawed logic as the government's Ministry of *Defense* that only ever seemed to attack. Feeling a fraction more confident now, and as he's clearly in the mood to talk, I decide to take the bull by the horns and ask a question that's been troubling me recently. "So now the Unchanged are gone, what happens next?"

"What do you mean?"

"Those fighters of yours this morning . . . all they wanted to do was kill. They were like kids at Christmas. So what happens to them now the enemy's been defeated? Do you think they'll just stop? They're not going to want to go back to being bricklayers or teachers or pub owners . . ."

"I know that, and they won't have to. There's a new class structure emerging here, and we're at the top. Have you looked outside this compound, Danny? Seen how many people are waiting out there? They're the ones who'll eventually do the work. They'll do anything I tell them, and you know why?"

"Why?"

"The two *f*'s."

"The two *f*'s? What's that supposed to mean?"

"Come on, keep up! We've talked about this. Food and fear. They'll do what I tell them. When I need bricklayers and teachers and the like, they'll be fighting with each other to help."

His vision of the future seems ridiculously simplistic.

"So what happens when the food runs out?"

"That's not going to happen for a long time," he answers quickly. "We'll see it coming and start planning for it when we need to."

"How?"

"By the time it's become a problem I'll have enough of a workforce to start producing food again, and they'll be hungry enough to keep doing exactly what I tell them. There's no point making people work for food yet, while there's still stuff to be scavenged; they're not desperate enough."

"John Warner was trying to get people farming," I tell him.

"Was it working?"

"No, but—"

"Well, there you go, then. It's too soon."

I could ask him how he ever plans to farm when all the livestock for miles around Lowestoft is either dead, dying, or running wild, and when the soil has been poisoned by radiation . . . but I'm sure he knows that anyway and so I don't bother. Instead I try another tack.

"The batteries in my reading lamp are almost gone," I start to say before he interrupts, laughing.

"Your reading lamp! Fuck me, Danny, you're turning into an old woman!"

I ignore him and carry on.

"The batteries are going in my reading lamp," I say again. "What do I do when they die?"

"You come and see me and I get you some more," he answers quickly. "Same as always."

"So what happens when *you* run out?"

"I send people out to find more."

"And when they can't find any? When we really have used them all up?"

"You have to stop reading at night," he smirks. I'm serious, and his grin disappears. "I know what you're saying, Danny, and you do have a valid point. What *do* we do? I don't know how to make batteries, and even if I did, I couldn't get my hands on the right chemicals and equipment. But the information's out there somewhere."

"It's just that the way you talk about things makes everything sound a lot easier than it's actually going to be. It's not just reading, it's making food, keeping warm, staying alive . . . Once everything's gone we'll struggle to get any of it back again."

"I never said it was going to be easy. Thing is, if I'm too honest with people too soon, I'll lose their support. I can't risk that. I need the numbers right now. It's still early. When we're more established here, we'll start planning ahead. All that matters today is today."

Hinchcliffe slips all too easily into spouting bullshit and spin. Politics never changes, even after everything we've all been through. I guess it doesn't matter how high the stakes are, to people like him, position and self-preservation are everything.

"The trick right now," he continues to explain, clearly mistaking me for someone who gives a damn, "is to let the people who matter think *they're* in control. I give my best fighters everything they want, and the Switchbacks who work hard, they get most of what they need, too. Compared to the pathetic lives they used to lead, this is something much better. They're free, uninhibited . . ."

"For now, maybe."

"Lighten up," he says.

"I don't want to lighten up."

"Things *will* improve, Danny."

"Will they?"

"Of course they will. We'll get that wind turbine working after the winter. Imagine that, constant power for the whole town again."

"It'll never happen."

"Yes it will."

"No it won't. One of its blades is broken, for Christ's sake. Where are you going to get a replacement from? And how are you going to get it up there? Have you got anyone who knows anything about engineering and mechanics? Got a crane tucked away anywhere? Christ, you've just said you'll be screwed when you run out of batteries."

"It's all out there somewhere," he says, starting to sound annoyed, "and there are bound to be people who used to know about these things. They'll help if I give them food and—"

"And if you hold a gun to their heads."

"If that's what it takes."

"I think you've got to get the fundamentals right before you start talking about electricity and stuff like that."

"Is that what John Warner was doing?"

"Maybe," I admit, wondering if I've gone too far.

"You're wrong," he says. "Warner was a thieving bastard who was trying to undermine what I've got here."

"All due respect, I don't think Warner gave a shit what you were doing here."

"The fucker was interested enough to want to steal from me," Hinch-cliffe snaps, a hit of barely suppressed anger in his voice. He gets up and pours himself a drink but doesn't offer me one. I think I've outstayed my welcome. That's a sure sign I've pissed him off. Not a good idea.

"Sorry, Hinchcliffe. I didn't mean to talk out of turn."

He shakes his head and leans against a dusty window, looking out over the divided streets of Lowestoft.

"You're okay. Like I said, Danny, you're not like the others. You're always questioning, and I need that from time to time. Just don't let me catch you talking like this to anyone else."

In for a penny, in for a pound. I'm taking a hell of a risk, but this seems as good a time as any to ask him something that's been on my mind for a while.

"So what about me?"

"What about you?"

"I don't have any special skills. I can't fight anymore. You've kept me onside to hunt out the Unchanged, but now they're gone, what happens to me?"

He thinks carefully before answering.

"You're not going anywhere, my friend. You underestimate yourself. You've proved your worth to me again and again over the last few weeks. There's a lot of work still to be done to get this place how I want it, and I'm gonna need people like you."

I make a mental note to start fucking up more often.

"You really think you'll be able to do that?"

"Do what?"

"Get this place straightened out? Keep people in line? You think they're just going to keep doing what you tell them to?"

"Yes," he answers without hesitation. "They won't have any choice."

I stand there and stare at him, still unable to move, and now unable to speak either. This guy's out of his fucking mind, but I'm not going to be the one who tells him. The whole conversation leaves me feeling empty and hollow. What chance has anyone got if people like Hinchcliffe are left in charge?

Hinchcliffe wraps his arm around my shoulder and walks me back toward the exit.

"I know what you need," he says. "You're too tense. You need to relax. Go home, get some rest, then come back here. Meet me outside the front at dusk."

He shoves me out of the door and I walk back through the courthouse building, relieved to be away from him but nervous about why he wants me to come back. The last thing I want is to spend any more time with Hinchcliffe, but I don't have any choice.

16

HINCHCLIFFE TOLD ME TO meet him outside the courthouse, but I think he's stood me up. He's not inside, and I've been out here waiting in the freezing cold for ages now. The wind is biting, and I thrust my hands deep into my pockets, wishing I was anywhere but here. I would go back to the house, but I don't want to risk pissing him off any more than I think I already have today. He'll kill me if I'm not here when he's ready.

The contrast between Lowestoft and what I saw happening in Southwold is stark. Across the way from where I'm standing, a group of Switchbacks are unloading supplies from a cart and taking them into the police station barracks, where most of the fighters live. Others are collecting waste and dumping it over the compound walls for vagrants to plunder. Elsewhere, more of them are working on setting up a rudimentary water supply outside what used to be the library, to replace the previous one, which fell apart. They've lined up a series of drainpipes and water barrels to collect water from the gutters of buildings, black plastic taps hanging over the lip of a low brick wall for people to take water from. Lizzie's dad used to have one of those barrels in his garden. I remember how the kids used to mess with it, and how they used to complain about the stagnant stench and the flies and the algae . . . and is this the best we can manage now? Still, if it's bad here by Hinchcliffe's courthouse, it's much worse on the other side of the barricades.

Just outside the south gate, on the approach to the bridge, there's an old man who lives in an ambulance. I pass him often when I go to or from the house, and I saw him on my way here today. He's clearly not a fighter—he can barely stand—but he seems able to switch on an angry, violent facade at will, using it as a deterrent to anyone who approaches him. He's well known, and Hinchcliffe's fighters often taunt him for sport, trying to get him to react and bite back. He collects rocks and chucks them at anyone who gets too close. Fucker almost got me today. His ambulance is useless—just a battered wreck with a blown engine and only a single wheel remaining—but it seems to symbolize everything that's wrong here. All around this place, people have taken things that used to matter and turned them into nothing. I've stayed here because this place looked like my best option, but maybe it's time to reconsider. The longer the violence here continues, the further we seem to regress.

"What d'you want?" Curtis asks as he thunders out through the courthouse door, knocking into me.

"I'm supposed to be meeting Hinchcliffe."

"He's not here."

"I know that, I—"

"Factory," he says, shoving me out of the way.

Typical. I immediately start walking, hobbling the first few steps, my legs stiff and painful. It's a relief at last to be moving. My body aches and my face is frozen, completely numb with cold.

It's not far from the courthouse to the factory, but I always get distracted when I walk this route. I always end up imagining what this place was like before the war . . . seaside shops selling worthless junk and kitsch, pandering to the hordes of vacationers who used to come here (hard to believe this was a destination of choice once). There are the usual main street chain stores, supermarkets, banks, real estate agents, doctors' and lawyers' offices—all just shells now, their unlit signs the only indication of what they used to be. Now these wildly different buildings, those which are still safe enough to be used, all look the same. They're dark and uninviting, stripped of anything of worth and occupied by squatters who stare out from the shadows. I just put my head down and keep moving.

"You seen Hinchcliffe?" I ask a remarkably fresh-faced fighter who's on guard duty at the checkpoint at the end of the road into the factory. He's slumped down on a chair inside what looks like half a garden shed, buried under blankets, hardly guarding, and hardly threatening. It's no surprise, really. No one in their right mind would want to come here. Apart from some of the more vicious kids (who'd kill you as soon as look at you), there's nothing here worth taking.

"He's up with Wilson," the guard answers. "He said you'd probably turn up."

The fact that Hinchcliffe's with Wilson, his chief kid-wrangler, is a relief. That means he's at the opposite end of the factory complex from where Rona Scott does whatever she does to the Unchanged kids. I can see a handful of flickering lights in the distance up ahead, and I wrap my coat around me even tighter as the wind whips up off the sea and blasts through the gaps between buildings. Eventually I reach a set of metal gates behind which the useful kids are kept. There's another guard here—an irritating little shit who takes himself too seriously and blocks my way through. When I tell him I'm supposed to be meeting Hinchcliffe he disappears. He's gone for a couple of minutes before eventually returning and begrudgingly letting me pass.

I find Hinchcliffe waiting for me in a small courtyard, surrounded on three sides by a series of squat, metal-walled, box-shaped buildings which probably used to be industrial units, storage sheds or something similar. The roofs of the buildings are covered with curls of razor wire.

"Forgot about you, Danny," Hinchcliffe says, and that's as good an apology as I'm going to get. "I was just checking the stock."

"The stock?"

"The kids," he explains. "I've been thinking more about what we were saying earlier."

"And?" I press hopefully.

"And maybe you're right. Maybe I'm not looking as far forward as I should be."

"So what's that got to do with the kids?"

"Everything, you dumb fuck! No kids, no future."

"That doesn't bode well, does it? All the kids I've seen since the war started have either been Unchanged or are wild animals."

"You lost kids in the fighting, didn't you?"

"Three," I answer.

"One like us?"

"My little girl."

"Where is she now?"

"Dead, I expect. Last time I saw her she was running toward the base of a fucking mushroom cloud, looking for an Unchanged to kill."

He thinks for a moment. "Look at this," he says, gesturing to a narrow window in the front of the nearest metal building. I notice something's been written in chalk on the door. It's hard to make out, but I think it says BOY 5–7. Is that a serial number or an age range? I bend down to look through the window. It takes my eyes a couple of seconds to adjust to the negligible light levels inside. Can't see anything . . .

"What am I supposed to be looking at—"

Something smashes against the glass. It's a young boy, and he hits the strengthened window so hard that he bounces off and crashes back down onto the floor. He immediately picks himself up again and starts hammering on the window, scratching at it with his fingers, trying to claw his way out and get to me. He moves with the same speed and animal-like agility that Ellis had before I lost her. He's feral. Wild. His blue eyes lock onto mine, and after a few seconds he stops struggling. As soon as he realizes I'm not Unchanged he slopes back into the corner, dejected. I keep watching him, unable to look away.

Hinchcliffe shines a flashlight around. Christ, the room the kid's being held in is like an animal's cage. There are yellow-tinged puddles of piss on the floor, chunks of half-chewed food lying around, smears of shit like tire tracks . . .

"This one like your daughter?"

"Just the same."

"Thought so. Now come over here."

I follow him across the square patch of asphalt toward a similar-sized building, almost directly opposite the first. There's writing on the door of this unit, too. It says BOY 10–12. I'm hesitant to get too close to the glass this time, but Hinchcliffe shoves me forward. I tense up, expecting another kid to hurl itself at me. When it doesn't happen I start to relax. I can't see any movement at all through the window.

"Is there anything in here?"

"Over there in the corner," Hinchcliffe says, shining his flashlight toward the far end of the squalid rectangular space. Then I see it: a figure slumped up against the wall. It's another boy, older than the first. He stands perfectly still, staring back at me but not reacting. "The older ones are starting to show more control," Hinchcliffe explains. "Show them one of the Unchanged and they'll still pull its fucking arms out of its sockets, but when they're not fighting, they're more lucid than they were. The older they get, the more control over their urges they seem to have."

"What point are you making?" I ask, not taking my eyes off the child.

"That maybe the kids can be rehabilitated. That there might still be hope for them. Pure instinct made them fight the Unchanged with as much ferocity as they did. Now the Unchanged are gone, we might be able to straighten them out again."

"You think so?"

He leads me away from the cells.

"I'm convinced these kids are as wild as they are because they've just lived through the worst of the war. When things calm down again, so will they. We'll teach them how to be human again, how to control themselves."

"Be human?" I laugh. "What, human like your fighters? Christ, Hinchcliffe, hardly the best role models for them. Anyway, these children have spent the last year killing. Do you really think you're going to be able to make them stop?"

"What use are they to us if we can't?"

"So what are you suggesting? Are you going to keep all newborns locked up until they've grown out of their viciousness?"

I think he's confused being controlled with being catatonic, but I don't want to risk antagonizing him. It says something when his idea of progress is producing a kid that doesn't immediately want to kill everything in the immediate vicinity. These children are hardwired to fight now. They've had a year of running wild, and their immature, prepubescent brains either don't know or don't want to know anything else.

"It's been less than twelve months," he continues. "We'll keep studying the ones we've got here. My guess is that newborns won't be like this, because they won't have lived through the fighting that these kids have. It might be that we end up with a missed generation or two, but there's nothing anyone can do about that."

The guard lets us back out through the gate, and we walk on down the road.

"So what about the other end of the factory?" I ask, stupidly prolonging a conversation I never actually wanted to have, realizing I still don't know why Hinchcliffe wanted to see me.

"What about it?"

"What have you got going on there? Is it the reverse of all this? Have you got Rona Scott provoking Unchanged kids until they fight back?"

"Something like that. It's not so much about making them fight as it is getting them to be like us."

"I don't understand."

"They've got to be able to survive and hold their own."

Hinchcliffe increases his speed. Heading north, I follow him past the farthest end of the complex and then continue along a wide footpath which runs parallel with the seawall. The last light of day is beginning to fade. I don't think I've been out here before. To my left is a sheer drop of several yards down onto another walkway, beyond it the remains of a long-since-abandoned RV park. There are numerous equally spaced rectangular slabs of concrete visible through the overgrowth and weeds where RVs used to stand, looking like oversized graves. It's an eerie place, silent but for our footsteps and the sea battering the rocks on the other side of the wall to my right.

"There's so much I need to know the answers to, Danny," he explains as I catch up with him, "things you probably haven't even considered. For a start, what do we do if any of the women give birth to Unchanged kids? A kid's just a kid, that's got to be the position we get to. It'll get easier over time."

"Will it?"

"Rona Scott thinks so. She says when there's absolutely nothing left but us, they won't know any different. We still don't know why we are like we are, and we probably never will. We don't know if what happened was because of some physical change or a virus or germ or just something we saw on TV. Thing is, kids who are inherently Unchanged are going to have to adapt and become like us to survive. Either that or they'll be killed."

I deliberately don't respond because this *is* something I've thought about already. I've thought about it too much, if anything. Months ago, back when I was looking for Ellis, I saw a pregnant woman. Since then I've often wondered what would happen to a newborn child. What if the kid's born and its mother's gut instinct—the same raw, undeniable gut instinct that made me kill hundreds of Unchanged—tells her to kill her own child? I've had nightmare visions of people crowding around the birth, trying to work out if the baby's like us or like them, trying to decide whether they should keep it alive or drown it in the river. Or worse still, people fighting with each other to be the one who kills an Unchanged child. I've even imagined delivery rooms with a dividing line drawn down the middle—medical equipment on one side, weapons on the other.

I try to bite my lip and stop myself, but I can't help speaking out again. I wish I could ignore what's happening and switch off, but the memory of what happened to all three of my own children keeps me asking questions and searching for answers I know I'll probably never find.

"It's a paradox, isn't it?"

"What is?"

"What you're talking about. You're saying we have to straighten out our kids and corrupt the Unchanged. Isn't there a danger you'll just end up breaking all of them? Aren't you just going to end up with generation after generation of fuckups? Kids that can't fight, can't think, can't even function?"

Hinchcliffe just looks at me and grunts, and I think I've gone too far again.

"Sorry," I apologize quickly, remembering who I'm talking to. "I shouldn't have said anything."

"Yes you should," he says, surprising me. "You should keep challenging like this. I told you, no one else has got the balls to do it. You see things differently than the rest of them."

"I'm not trying to be difficult, I'm just—"

"You're just saying what you think, and that's a good thing. You might turn out to be right about everything, but for the record, I don't think you are. Thing is, there's no way of knowing yet. The world these kids will end up inheriting will be completely different from anything we've experienced, different from what we're seeing now, even. Until then, the only thing we can do is explore every possibility and cover all eventualities."

"That's a tall order. How are you planning to do that?" I ask. I'm really struggling to keep up with Hinchcliffe's fast pace now and I'm relieved when he finally stops walking. He turns around and grins. It scares the shit out of me when he looks at me like that.

"Now we're getting somewhere," he says. "It's like everything else. It all boils down to supply and demand."

17

MY EVENING WITH HINCHCLIFFE is clearly far from over. His speed increases again as we continue farther along the seawall. I'm left dragging behind, panting hard and drenched with sweat, and there's absolutely no one else around. I look back the way we just came and see that we've traveled a surprising distance away from the center of town. The walk back to the house is going to take forever.

"You're far too tense, Danny," he says, waiting for me to catch up again. "I know exactly what you need. Help you get rid of some of that pent-up frustration."

"All I need is some sleep. I'll be okay in the morning."

"You've been saying that for weeks."

I notice there are several buildings up ahead, barely visible in the increasing darkness until now. Hinchcliffe pauses to light a cigarette. He blows out smoke, flicks the match over the wall, then moves on, leading me away from the ocean now and up a steep climb along a muddy pathway. As we get closer, I see that there are dull lights flickering in the windows of one of the buildings. It's hard to make out much detail, but it looks like one of those dime-a-dozen seafront hotels you always used to find in places like this. We cross a road to get closer, and I see that its frontage is painted a grubby powdery blue. There's a lopsided signpost at this end of the short front yard, two truncated lengths of chain hanging down where the building's name would once have hung. There's a guard standing just inside the door. I recognize him right away. It's Joe Chandra, one of Hinchcliffe's most prized fighters. He's a distinctive, ugly-looking bastard. He looks like a comic-book villain with burns covering almost exactly half of his face. I haven't seen him around in a while. Just assumed he was dead. So what's Hinchcliffe got him posted all the way out here for? My heart's pounding suddenly, and this time it's not because of the effort of the walk.

"What is this place, Hinchcliffe?"

"The solution to a couple of problems," he replies, giving little away.

"What problems?"

"Regardless of what they turn out to be, we need people to keep having kids. Also, people need food and they have a need to procreate. So here they can fuck and be fucked for food. Sounds like some kind of screwed-up charity drive, eh?"

I'm so taken aback by what I'm hearing that I don't realize I've followed him into the building until we've already passed Chandra at the door and gone right inside. The air indoors smells stale. It's quiet, and Hinchcliffe's voice echoes off the walls.

"Like it or not, my friend, kids are going to become a valuable commodity. I'm just trying to cover all the bases and keep control of the stock. All that most people are interested in today is staying alive, and they'll do whatever it takes to achieve that. The women I've got here are willing to get pregnant for food, the men are more than willing to try to get them pregnant."

"So which is it? A brothel or a sperm bank?"

"Both, I suppose!" He laughs, filling the building with his noise. "It's hardly the love boat, if that's what you mean, but it does the trick."

"There are no lines at the door. You'd have thought—"

"Times have changed, mate. *We've changed.* Romance and relationships have gone right out of fashion since we all started killing each other, but people still need to fuck."

"But where is everyone?"

"I'm being selective. You didn't know about this place until now, and I tell you more than I tell most people. You have to detach yourself from what used to matter now, Danny. These are business decisions. Doesn't mean you can't enjoy your work, though!"

"How far have we fallen if sex has just become a business decision?" I ask as we climb a twisting staircase that smells damp. Thin curtains have been draped over the windows, and the faint yellow light comes from infrequently spaced oil lamps.

"Oh come on, don't get all soft on me," he groans. "People have been selling sex since year one. You have to face facts, we all do. This is how things have to be for now, and that's why I've been selective with the people I've allowed to get involved in this so far. Better that a woman gets pregnant by someone who can still fight than by one of the losers drifting around out there outside the compound. If I started advertising this place there'd be a line of underclass men outside the door twenty-four/seven, desperate to sow their pathetic seed for a quick thrill and a half-decent meal. It's tough and it's not fair, but for now this is how it has to be."

"I don't think it's right."

"To be honest, pal," he says, stopping at the end of a gloomy landing, "I don't care. I didn't bring you here because I wanted your blessing."

"So why did you bring me?"

"Christ, why do you think?"

"I don't know . . . I . . ."

"You're not the strongest, Danny, but you've got brains, and I know you can fight when you have to. You've already fathered one kid like us."

He grabs my arm and pulls me farther down the corridor.

"But I—"

"You can come here anytime you want," he tells me, pushing me toward an open door. Light spills across the landing. "The women leave their doors open when they're ready. Everyone's a winner here, you know. I give them double rations if they get pregnant, or I would if any of the useless cows had actually managed it."

My brain's spinning, struggling to catch up with what's happening, and my body is numb and unresponsive. I just stand there, staring into the hotel room, remembering the last time I was in a place like this. I remember looking for Lizzie, and I wish she was here today. The memory of her face fills me with pain. Despite everything that happened between us and what we both became, there's a part of me that still clings to what we used to have and the family we made together. Hinchcliffe shoves me forward again, and I make a desperate, instinctive grab for either side of the door frame, not wanting to go through.

"I'll see you later, Danny," he says, taking a few steps back, then standing and watching me. "Enjoy yourself, son."

I know I've got no choice but to do what he says, and I step into the light.

1.8

INSIDE THE ROOM THERE'S a woman sitting on a double bed with her back to me. I'm fucking terrified. I'd turn and run if it wasn't for the fact Hinchcliffe's bound to be waiting around outside. He'll want to be sure I've done what he told me to do.

I can't do this. I can't remember the last time I had a sexual thought or desire or felt anything even remotely erotic. I can't remember masturbating since the war began, or even wanting to. Apart from the occasional, infrequent, involuntary early morning hard-on, the last time I had an erection was probably when I last shared a bed with Liz, just before the Change split us. Does everyone feel like this, or is it just me? I don't want to share my body with anyone now, much less with someone I don't know. I don't want to do this . . .

The woman on the bed wearily looks back over her shoulder. How many times has she already done this today? Am I the first or the twenty-first?

"You coming in?" she grunts, her voice flat and unemotional. I take another hesitant step forward. "Shut the frigging door, then."

"Sorry," I mumble as I turn and push it closed. I lean my head against the door and try to relax or at least hide my nerves. When I finally turn back around I see that the woman has stood up. What does she look like? It's just an unexpected, instinctive thought. Does it matter? The light's behind her and I can't actually see her face from here, can't make out any details at all, and maybe that's for the best. I sense her looking me up and down. What's she thinking? Is she deciding whether or not I'm good enough stock? I start hoping she's going to reject me, suddenly acutely aware of how I must look to her. Like most people, I rarely wash anymore. I hack at my hair and my beard with scissors and blunt razor blades when I have to. Can't remember the last time I brushed my teeth . . . No matter, this isn't a mating ritual. Like Hinchcliffe said, this is purely functional, and how I look and feel is unimportant—but I still don't know if I can go through with it . . .

This horrible, silent standoff continues for what feels like forever, and I'm on the brink of backing out and running when she finally speaks.

"You healthy?"

"Pretty much."

"What's that supposed to mean?"

What should I tell her? That I cough my guts up first thing every morning? That the skin on my back and neck is burned from the bombs? That sometimes there's blood when I piss? I want to go into graphic detail and do all I can to put her off me, but I don't.

"I'm okay."

"You had kids before?"

"Three. You?"

"This isn't a date. Your kids, what were they?"

"Two boys and a girl."

"No, *what* were they?"

"My girl was like us," I answer, realizing what she was actually asking and forcing myself to block out the faces of my dead children. "The boys were Unchanged."

She nods and thinks carefully about what I've just told her, as if it's going to make a difference. Then, with a weary sigh of resignation, she undoes the zipper of her baggy trousers and lets them drop down to her ankles in an incredibly unfeminine and asexual movement. She kicks them away, then lies back down on the bed, psyching herself up. The fine detail of her face is still hidden by the shadows, but I can see her a little more clearly now. She seems strangely expressionless, and it's hard to place her age. Her limbs are bony and long, her muscles taut. Her skin is covered in scratches, cuts, and bruises, and I think for a second about how long Liz used to spend pampering herself each day to look good—using countless creams and lotions, waxing her legs, hunting down every rogue hair with tweezers, razors, or wax . . . My eyes are involuntarily drawn to the top of this woman's legs and her unkempt bush of wiry pubic hair. Since everything changed, everybody—male and female, young and old—has become strangely sexless. How we look is unimportant; keeping warm and staying alive is all that matters. Everything's different now. Back then, before all of this happened, men and women had frustratingly different sexual drives and desires that rarely coincided. Now no one's bothered. I sense this is as much an ordeal for this woman as it is for me.

"Get on with it," she says, looking up at the ceiling, not at me. I nervously start to undress, kicking off my boots, taking off my coat, and pulling down my trousers. Without thinking, I start to remove some of the layers of clothing I'm wearing on top, but she stops me. "No need for that. Just get it done."

Feeling increasingly awkward and embarrassed and now half naked, I climb onto the bed and kneel next to her on the mattress, heart racing, barely able to think straight, too nervous even to reach across and touch her. My pathetic, flaccid cock hangs down between my legs, shriveled up to virtually nothing by the bitter cold. Can't get hard. Starting to panic. Maybe erectile dysfunction will save me tonight? I try to remember all the things I used to think about to get myself aroused, but they're hard to remember and they all have the opposite effect. Each image I dredge up from the past, each buried memory that slowly returns, they all hurt too much. It's obviously not the first time this woman has been faced with someone like me. She reaches up and cups my balls with her hand. She doesn't speak, she barely even moves, but just the touch of her skin against mine is enough, and my cock finally starts to stiffen. She gently runs her fingertips down the length of my shaft, touching me more tenderly than anyone's touched me in almost a year.

My head's clear now, empty of all thoughts but one. I look straight at the woman but I don't even see her face. There's a sudden burning, insatiable need low in my gut and I sit astride her and force myself into her. Hard and dry, then warm. It hurts for a second as my foreskin snags, but then it gets easier as I start to move. I don't think about what I'm doing, I just do it. Again and again, harder and harder, faster now, not giving a damn about what she thinks or feels . . . harder still, balls banging against the inside of her thighs, hands gripping the headboard.

Then it happens.

A split-second pause filled with something that used to matter, then I feel myself empty into her.

I groan with effort and drop down, our bodies finally close, head next to hers, panting hard. She shoves her hands up under my chest and pushes me away. I roll over onto my back as she slides out from under me. We lie there in silence, side by side for several seconds until, without warning, the most brutal and unforgiving wave of postejaculation regret I've ever experienced comes crashing over me. I turn my head to one side and finally look into the woman's face, and I'm filled with shame and remorse. She just stares up at the ceiling, waiting for me to leave.

"Go," she says, and I do it without a word. I can't wait to get away from her. I virtually fall off the bed and scoop up my clothes and my boots from the floor in haste. I have to get out of this room. My cock is still dribbling thick, sticky strings of warm fluid down the inside of my leg as I struggle to hold on to everything and get the door open. I crash out onto the landing and slump back against the wall, freezing cold and still only half dressed but not giving a damn, content to let the darkness of the musty hotel swallow me up, happy to disappear. I look around, half expecting Hinchcliffe to be there, nodding his approval and giving me points out of ten.

I sit down on the ice-cold, threadbare carpet and dress myself. I feel humiliated; empty and defiled. If I could stay in these shadows forever, I think I would.

The shame and regret mutate into anger, then the anger turns to guilt. I can't understand how I'm feeling but every new thought just adds to the confusion. I think about Lizzie and the pain increases massively. Do I feel so bad because I've been unfaithful to her? Am I really feeling remorse because I've just fucked someone other than my dead, Unchanged ex-partner? *Fucked.* Wrong word. That wasn't even fucking. It wasn't anything like that. As Hinchcliffe made clear, it was a business transaction: a way to keep him happy and for that woman in there—Christ, I don't even know her name—to earn herself some extra rations. Have things really come to this? Is this the pinnacle of Hinchcliffe's vision for the future? Is this what we've been reduced to?

I start trying to justify and rationalize what I've just done, making excuses and looking for reasons why it doesn't matter. My irradiated sperm's probably useless, I decide. Even if it isn't, maybe that woman's body has been damaged by the war. I remember hearing about kids born after the nuclear bombings in Japan—increased numbers of stillborns, cancers, and deformities . . .

Who the hell am I trying to fool? I pick myself up and slowly stagger back down the stairs, my mind now filled with memories of sex before the war that I'd tried to keep buried deep down. I remember the last time Lizzie and I made love. We were both terrified that night, but being together was spontaneous and instinctive, powerful and reassuring. We did it to make ourselves and each other feel wanted and protected. In spite of everything that was happening right outside our door, the feelings we shared that night were as intense as they had ever been.

Now, as I push my way out into the dark, freezing-cold night, I'm left thinking about the kids, about Ellis, Josh, and Ed, remembering when each of them was born and the good times we had together before the bad . . .

What have I become?

Sex used to be something that dragged us out of the daily grind and took us somewhere else. Something that transcended all the bullshit and connected Lizzie and me on every level imaginable. How could I have just allowed something as precious as that to become as brutal and insensitive as everything else?

I feel like I've just lost something I'll never get back, like Hinchcliffe's just taken what was left of my soul.

I'M FINALLY BACK AT the house, but all I want to do is head back into Lowestoft and kill Hinchcliffe. Fucking bastard. I kick my pile of books across the living room and they hit the wall with a momentarily satisfying noise, but then all I'm left with is silence.

What the fuck have I become?

Since Hinchcliffe found out what I can do, I've been allowed to stand on the outskirts of this vile, fucked-up ruin of a world and observe. I've just about managed to cope with what I've seen because of the distance I've been able to put between me and everything else, but what I did today with that woman—what Hinchcliffe made me do—has dragged me down to the lowest possible level, and it hurts. He's stripped away everything and now there's nothing left.

Fuck this. I can't take any more. I'm getting out. First thing in the morning I'll leave and I'll take my chances on my own. I'll pack my stuff tonight, then help myself to one of the cars by the railroad station at first light. I'll load it up with the supplies I've hoarded away here, then get as far away from Lowestoft as I can and leave everything and everyone that's here way behind me. I don't need anyone else. More to the point, I don't *want* anyone else. I'll go somewhere I can be alone and I'll never come back. Maybe I'll head straight for the deadlands around the bombed cities. Even a slow death from the pollution and radiation will probably be better than this.

I tried to make myself eat something in readiness for leaving, but tonight, more than ever, the thought of food is making my stomach churn. I managed a few mouthfuls, but that was all. Fortunately, the beer Hinchcliffe gave me was easier to swallow. The gas made me retch, but the alcohol has taken the slightest edge off my anger. I forced myself to finish the first can, then immediately started another. Halfway through the second can I ran out of the side door and threw up on the driveway.

I slump back into my chair and struggle with cold, unresponsive fingers to open the ring pull on my third can. I put it down on the table, the beer frothing and fizzing over the rim, then strap on my miner's lamp reading light and pick up the first book I can find. My eyes are tired and hard to focus, but I stare at the cover. It's a picture of a man and a woman, locked together in a passionate embrace that's a million miles from what I had to endure earlier today. Even though the figures on the cover are airbrushed, overly perfect caricatures of how people used to be, I can't stop staring at them and remembering. The man is rugged, strong and powerful, clean-shaven with short, black, slicked-back hair . . . Then I look at the woman he's holding: her full figure, tight clothing, painted lips . . . when the light starts to flicker and fade (didn't get those damn batteries from Hinchcliffe), I throw the book across the room in frustration, and I'm left staring at my own reflection in the cracked screen of the useless flat-screen TV that sits in the corner of this room. I look like a fucking prisoner of war—spine curved, eyes bulging, arms and legs spindly and thin, skin scarred . . .

The beer makes me belch, but I keep drinking. It must be having an effect, because now I can't stop thinking about my kids. Usually I try to stop myself from remembering, but tonight I'm desperate not to forget.

It's been a long, long time since I've drunk like this. I feel like I'm floating above my chair now, looking back down and watching myself below, and I don't like what I see. In the darkness and quiet there are too few distractions. I keep looking around, half expecting to see Ellis standing there like she used to appear at the side of Lizzie's and my bed when she couldn't sleep, all wide-eyed and vulnerable. I keep waiting to hear Ed arguing with Josh, or playing his crappy music too loud, or switching the TV in his room on again after I'd told him to turn it off. My kids were annoying little fuckers at times, but that didn't matter. I miss them.

Hinchcliffe's vision of the future is terrifying me. I don't want to be responsible for bringing another life into this world. I imagine a child like the kids I fathered before, trying to survive in this foul and hostile place. What if they were born Unchanged? I picture Hinchcliffe backing them into a corner, leering over them and either screaming at them to fight if they won't, or locking them away in isolation and trying to break them if they're too feral and wild to control. What if it's twins? One Unchanged and one like us? Would they fight in the womb . . . that's more ridiculous than it sounds. Now I know I'm drunk.

I force down more beer, but I'm starting to feel really sick. My mouth's watering like I'm going to throw up again. I'll stay still in this chair for a while until the nausea has passed, then start packing my stuff. Whatever happens, I'm leaving this godforsaken place tomorrow.

20

MY HEAD IS FUCKING killing me. Feels like someone's split my skull in two with an axe.

Rufus is pounding on the door again. Why can't he just leave me alone? I'm sure no one else has to put up with this much bullshit. I moved out from the center of town to put some distance between me and the rest of the population of Lowestoft, but certain people seem to spend most of their time out here hassling me. Fuckers. Jesus, it's not even light yet. Couldn't he have at least waited until morning? He can fuck off and leave me be. Whatever he wants, I'm not interested. I'll wait until he goes, then pack up and get out of here. I'd have gone already if I hadn't let the booze get the better of me.

He's not going anywhere.

The knocking has moved now. Persistent little shit. Now he's banging on the living room window. I screw my eyes shut and stifle a cough, doing all I can to swallow it down so the noise doesn't give me away. Jesus, I feel bad. My guts are more sensitive than ever, and my head's about to explode. There's a welcome moment of silence; then the noise changes again. That's the side door this time. He's shaking the handle, rattling the chains I used to secure it after the vagrant woman broke in. Maybe it's another one of those useless underclass fuckers, trying to get in and steal from me. Bastards.

Got to move.

I reluctantly get up from my chair and immediately lurch over to the right, reeling from the aftereffects of the booze. Feeling faint, I stoop down and grab a heavy wrench I keep by the front door for dealing with unwelcome visitors like this. I've just about managed to stand upright again when another coughing fit hits me hard. Whoever's outside must know I'm here now, and they're still not going anywhere. When the coughing subsides for a second I angrily yank the front door open and run along the side of the house, wrench held high, ready to attack or defend myself. A combination of sudden surprise and the ice-cold temperature outside immediately sobers me up and stops me in my tracks. Standing in front of me is Peter Sutton, the bastard who stalked me around Southwold.

"How in hell's name did you find me?"

He walks toward me, and, hands raised, I lift the wrench again and block his way. Fucker's not going anywhere.

"I guessed you had some connection with those fighters who turned up in Southwold yesterday morning."

"They were nothing to do with me."

"I didn't say they were. But you turned up, then they did. It seemed a pretty safe bet that it was more than just coincidence."

"So what's this? Revenge?"

"No, nothing like that."

"That still doesn't explain how you found me."

"I just went into town and asked for Rufus."

"But I'm not—"

"I know who you are now, Danny McCoyne. Here's a tip for you: If you're going to use a false name, never use the name of someone who actually exists. I asked for Rufus at the barricades and ended up being introduced to your friend. He seems like a decent enough guy, but you might want to have a word with him about his loose tongue. I described you to him, and he says, 'Ah . . . you're looking for Danny McCoyne.' So here I am, Danny, and here you are, too."

"Rufus told you where I was just like that?"

"Pretty much," he answers. "He didn't need to say a lot. He told me about this place and he said you were the only one here. I just started knocking on windows and doors until I found you. Wasn't that hard, really."

"How come? There are hundreds of houses—"

"I know, and I've been here for fucking ages. However, yours is the only house with a fresh puddle of vomit on the drive. I thought there was a good chance you might have something to do with it."

Sutton's breath billows in clouds around his face. We're both shaking with cold. There's been a heavy frost overnight, and everything glistens with ice, white-blue in the first light of dawn.

"Okay," I say, still shivering but still not letting him in, "you found me. Now what do you want?"

"Can we talk inside?"

"Why?"

"Because I'm fucking cold and this is fucking important."

He's insistent if nothing else, but the fact he won't talk outside the house just increases my unease. Either what he's got to say is genuinely important or he's trying to trick me.

"It's out here or nothing."

He thinks for a minute, shaking with cold. My hand starts to feel like it's freezing to the wrench.

"Remember that truck? The one you said you didn't see?"

"What about it?"

"Want to know where it came from?"

"Not really."

"That's what I figured, but I'm sure your boss will."

"My boss?"

"Whoever sent you to Southwold. Hinchcliffe, is it? Come on, Danny, stop playing games. Let's talk. This is important."

I need a piss, and the bitter cold out here is making it worse. Oh, what the hell . . . he's obviously no fighter. One step out of line and I'll finish him off with a smack on the head with the wrench. That'll solve all our problems. Against my better judgment, I decide to let him in.

"You've got five minutes," I warn him.

"Thank you," he says, scurrying past me to get into the warmth. I gesture for him to go through to the living room, making sure he gets another eyeful of the wrench as I use it to point the way.

"Try anything and I'll kill you."

"I won't, I swear. I don't want any trouble."

I follow him into the house, watching his every move. "Okay then, talk."

He paces the room, taking his time and choosing his words carefully.

"I guess your boss assumed those supplies came from him. Did he find out who was supplying Warner?"

"Hinchcliffe's not the investigative type. So do you know?"

"Not yet, but I need to find out."

"Why?"

"Look, you're the only other person like me I've found in months," he says, teeth still chattering, "the only person I think I can trust."

"You're not making any sense. For fuck's sake, Sutton, stop beating around the bush and just tell me."

He pauses ominously.

"Those supplies you saw weren't from Lowestoft."

"Where, then?"

"Come with me and I'll show you."

21

SUTTON HAS A CAR with a quarter tank of fuel, which he says he took from the aftermath of the fighting in Southwold. He told me he got out of the center of the town as soon as he heard the first of Hinchcliffe's fighters arrive, then hid on the outskirts until they'd cleared out again. If that's true then he's been a damn sight more alert than I have recently. He drove up to within a couple of streets of the house this morning, and in my alcoholic daze I didn't hear a bloody thing. He could have been anyone.

This car was once a fairly decent and spacious high-end model, but, like most everything else, it's seen better days. It's full of trash, and the upholstery is slashed and torn. Outside it's snowing, but it's not quite cold enough to settle.

No matter how smooth the ride might once have been, today the surface of the road we're traveling over is rough and uneven. Sutton drives straight over a pothole that's full of water and deeper than expected. He doesn't even bother to try to steer around it, and the sudden lurching downward movement makes the liquid in my stomach swirl and wash around again. I swallow down bile and try to concentrate on the music he's playing. He tells me it helps calm his nerves, but it's doing nothing for mine. The fact he still listens to music like me is a good sign, I guess, but this morning the uncomfortably loud noise just makes me feel even more unwell.

"It must be because of the smoke from the bombs," he says suddenly. He's talked nervously for most of the journey without saying anything of any substance. I still don't fully know why I'm here, but I keep telling myself it was worth agreeing because there's the slightest chance he'll show me something worth seeing before I leave Lowestoft forever. Another place like Southwold, or John Warner's mysterious benefactor perhaps? Fact is, I need a way out.

"What's because of the smoke?"

"The drop in temperature. All the snow and ice."

"It's the middle of winter."

"I know, but it's not usually this bad, is it?"

"There are fewer people around than this time last year, fewer cars and no factories, hospitals, or schools. No emissions or exhausts. Think of all the fumes that aren't being belched up into the atmosphere anymore."

Sutton glances across at me and nods enthusiastically, and something about the expression on his face makes alarm bells start to ring again. I'd put his sudden change of mood down to relief that I'd agreed to come with him, but I'm wondering now if I've made a huge mistake and he really is the psycho I'd first feared. I start silently plotting my escape. When he next slows the car down I'll try to get out. I'll roll away along the ground like they used to in action movies, then I'll work out where the hell I am and try to get back to Lowestoft. If Sutton dares turn up on my doorstep again, I'll introduce his face to my wrench, then dump his useless body. No one will miss him.

"Be interesting to see what happens to the environment now, won't it?" he says.

"Will it?"

"I think so. You've got all that pollution and contamination on one hand, and the fact that a huge number of people are dead on the other. Will they cancel each other out? Who knows, McCoyne, maybe genocide will turn out to have been a blessing in disguise!"

He laughs manically, loud enough to drown out the music for a moment, and I want out of here. We pass through Wrentham and turn right at the junction I turned left at for Southwold yesterday. After another mile or so I see something at the side of the road that distracts me temporarily. I've been here before. It's the site of a vicious battle that Llewellyn bragged about once. He said it was like something out of the movies. He was with a group of ex-soldiers that had been cornered by some Unchanged military. They were massively outnumbered, he'd said (although I'm sure he was exaggerating), and yet twenty or so of them had dug in and held off their attackers for hours on end. In frustration the Unchanged commander had requested air cover. Hearing bombers approaching, Llewellyn had ordered his fighters to attack, and then, as the bombs began to fall, they fled. The Unchanged, or so he told me, bore the brunt of their own side's munitions; then Llewellyn's people returned to finish them off. I'm sure he embellished the story with more than a liberal sprinkling of bullshit, but there's no disputing the fact that something huge did happen here. When I first saw this place, the cratered ground was blackened by fire and still covered with the remains of the dead, the tangled blades of a downed helicopter sticking up into the air like the legs of a dead spider. Today it looks almost completely different—overgrown and wild. In a couple of years, no one will know that anything ever happened here. It'll just look like part of the natural landscape.

"Not far now," Sutton says suddenly. I curse myself for allowing myself to become distracted, but I don't respond. Instead I go over the route we've followed again so that I can get back to Lowestoft on my own if need be: Take the coast road out of town to Wrentham, then right at the junction and head farther inland. Out of the corner of my eye I notice Sutton is watching me. "You've got to believe me, McCoyne," he says, his voice now serious again, no doubt picking up on my unease, "what I'm going to show you is important."

"You keep telling me that," I reply, sliding my left hand down into my inside jacket pocket until the tips of my outstretched fingers rest on the hilt of one of my fighting knives, checking it's still there, "but you still haven't given me any details. I'm starting to think this was a bad idea."

"It's hard to explain."

"Try."

"It's difficult. I'm not sure how you'll react or what you'll think."

What's he hiding? Is *he* behind the stolen supplies? Is it worse than that?

"You're not making me feel any better about this."

"I swear, when we're finished you can just walk away if you want, and you'll never see me again—but I don't think you will."

"What makes you so sure?"

"Because you're like me," he says again, starting to sound like a broken record. Sutton takes a sudden hard right turn off the road, driving through an open metal gate and out along a narrow gravel track. The front of the car clatters through a deep water- and ice-filled dip, then rattles over a cattle grid, and I have to concentrate again just to stop myself from throwing up.

"We're here," he says, slowing down and steering around the curve of the track toward a motley collection of ramshackle farm buildings. The farmhouse and its outbuildings appear deserted, black smoke damage visible around the edges of some of the windows and doors. We drive through a large yard full of furrows and puddles, most of them filled with ice. Bizarrely, Sutton has to slow down to allow a lone cow to wander across in front of us. It's as starved and thin as every other animal I've seen recently. When it looks around and sees us it panics. Its hooves skid in the slippery mud as it tries to change direction, and it looks like it's got that "mad cow" disease they used to talk about on the TV news. First cow I've seen in months.

"Don't see many of them here anymore," Sutton says, watching me watching the animal. "Quite a few survived, but I doubt they'll last the winter. Brutes drove most of them away."

"Brutes? I thought the Brutes were all dead."

"As good as."

"Why would Brutes be here?"

"Because they knew."

"Knew what?"

Sutton doesn't answer. He drives the car into a dark, open-ended barn and stops it deep in the shadows, parking next to a filthy, beaten-up delivery truck with a faded picture of a woman's face on its side, advertising something you can't get anymore, which probably wasn't that important anyway. I look up and stare into the face; still as beautiful and perfect as the women on the covers of the books I read. Sutton switches off the engine, and the sudden silence is unsettling.

"The Brutes knew what we were doing here," he explains as he opens his door and gets out. "Don't ask me how, but they did."

Now I really am starting to get worried.

"So what are we here for? Is this where the trucks are from or—"

"Nothing like that," he says, leaning back into the car. "This isn't about John Warner's supplies. Sorry, Danny, I haven't been completely honest with you."

"Fuck it," I shout at him, refusing to move. "I knew I shouldn't have come here. Either give me the keys or take me back to Lowestoft."

"You've come this far," he replies, obviously having no intention of doing either, "might as well see now. This is important, I swear. What I'm going to show you changes everything."

With that he walks away, moving with suddenly revitalized energy and speed. Shit. What are my options? *Kill him?* I don't know if I could. *Make a run for it?* The hungover state I'm in this morning, I wouldn't get far. Oh, what the hell . . . even though I'm sick, I'm armed, and I'm still probably stronger than he is.

Sutton turns back and beckons me to follow him along another track, this one leading away from the farm buildings. The dirt track climbs steeply and snakes away across uneven grassland that's bleached yellow and brown. He's not that much faster than me, but I'm happy to let him build up a decent lead, figuring that putting a little distance between us will make the situation easier for me to control and give me more of a chance of getting away if I need to. I'm distracted by a sudden noise and movement way over to my left. I grab one of my knives, ready to defend myself against an attack, then freeze. Jesus, it's a Brute. My heart starts thumping at the prospect of having to fight. Months ago I'd have relished any conflict, but not today, and definitely not with one of our own. Most of these poor bastards lost all sense and perspective during the war, driven out of their minds by the intensity of their Hate, and killing's all they know now. It's all they have left. Now that there are no Unchanged, apart from the occasional emaciated cow, it seems we've suddenly become an obvious target.

This Brute is old and female. She swaggers slowly toward me like a drunk, unable to move in a straight line, still several hundred yards away. Far removed from the strong and vicious fighter she probably once was, this woman is now a grotesque physical wreck. She's completely naked and blue with cold; her bare flesh is a mottled gray-brown and is covered with dirt and countless cuts and abrasions. There are traces of blood around her mouth. Her heavy, pendulous breasts swing from side to side with every clumsy, lumbering movement. Loose flesh hangs down from her arms and her gut like she's wearing a dirty, oversized skin-colored coat. Poor bitch. She's probably starving.

"Sorry," Sutton says, scrambling back down the rise. "Should have warned you about that one. She's usually wandering around here somewhere. Damn strong, she is, but slow. You'll easily outrun her if she gives you any trouble. Don't know how she keeps going after all this time. Sheer contrariness, I guess."

He stands and looks at the barely human woman in the distance with an expression on his face that seems to almost approximate pity. I'm surprised by his reaction. Most people, me included, wouldn't give a dying Brute a second thought. Christ, I've seen people carve up their carcasses and spit-roast them before now. It's all meat, they say as they shove them on the fire.

Concentrate, I tell myself. *You're getting distracted. This could still be a trap.*

The Brute's speed is negligible, but she's still a very real threat. Sutton nudges me to start moving again, then scampers back up the steep bank, following the meandering track. Still holding my knife (and telling myself repeatedly that I *will* use it if he crosses me), I follow him. The gradient's steeper than it looks, and the ground beneath my feet is increasingly uneven. I climb the hill like an old man, bent over double and pushing down on my knees to keep myself moving forward. Sutton has to wait for me at the top. I stop to catch my breath and look down over the other side. There's a crumbling, low-roofed redbrick building at the edge of the track a little farther ahead. Looks like a bungalow. What is this? His fucking holiday cottage?

"Almost there now," Sutton says, and before he can move away again, I grab his arm.

"You'd better not be fucking with me," I warn him. He shakes his head, then pulls himself free and walks on. "I'll kill you if you try anything," I shout after him.

"No you won't," he shouts back as he disappears into the ruin of the building up ahead. Is this safe? I'm not convinced. The exterior walls might still be standing at the moment, but they look like they'd fall down if anyone leaned hard enough against them. The mortar between the damp, moss-covered bricks is powdery and fine. The farthest corner of the cramped, rectangular-shaped house has been overwhelmed by ivy, brambles, and other crawling weeds.

Sutton leans back out of the building. "This is it, McCoyne. In here."

22

ARE YOU SURE THIS is safe?" I ask as I tentatively follow him inside. It's surprisingly light in here. There's still some semblance of a roof overhead, but it's patchy. In places the remains of rotten rafters stretch up into the air, leaving nothing but empty sky above us. Sutton kicks his way through the debris toward a rotten wooden door frame (no door, just a frame) midway along the single remaining interior dividing wall. It's pitch black on the other side, and I stop, refusing to go any farther.

"Whatever you've got in there, just bring it out into the open. This place is about to collapse."

"It's a lot stronger than it looks. I used to work in construction and I've checked it all out. Anyway, most of the building's buried."

His assurances don't make me feel any better, but I continue to follow him into the darkness. I grab onto the back of his coat with one hand, my knife still held ready in the other.

"Careful here," he says, dragging his feet along the ground. He inches forward slowly, then seems to suddenly drop down a few inches.

I instinctively try to steady him, but he's okay. "Staircase," he tells me. "Five steps down."

I follow blind down the steep and narrow stairs, my shoulders brushing against walls that have suddenly closed in on either side. At the bottom of the steps Sutton stops and I walk into the back of him, unable to see anything. He gently pushes me over to one side, and I stand next to him in a narrow alcove of space.

"What is this place?" I ask, whispering because I'm worried if I speak too loud I'll cause a cave-in.

"Just give me a second . . ."

He drags one of his feet along the ground again and makes contact with something heavy. I can't see anything, but I hear it scrape along the floor. Almost completely blind, I stretch my arms out in front of me and feel my way along a cold, damp wall until the surface under my fingertips changes from brick to metal. I stop and feel back to the point where the change occurs and run my fingers down an uneven edge, eventually reaching something that feels like a hinge. Another door?

Sutton pushes me out of the way again. I'm not expecting it, and I stagger back a couple of paces and tense up, ready for him if he comes for me. My eyes are adjusting to the dark a little and I can just about make out his shape as he bends down to pick something up. Is it some kind of weapon? If he wanted to kill me (and I don't know why he would) then surely he'd have done it back at the house and spared us both this damn day trip to the farm? Sutton lifts what looks like a length of metal pipe, then bangs it against the door three times. The sound of metal on metal reverberates loudly around this small enclosed space, filling my head.

"What the hell are you doing?"

"Shh . . ."

He leans forward to listen, and the silence when the noise finally fades is all-consuming. Is he crazy? Nothing happens for an age. I'm about to turn and get out when I hear it—a steady *thump, thump, thump* coming from the other side of the wall. Shit, there's someone in there. I have a sudden deluge of questions poised on the very tip of my tongue, but I don't ask anything because Sutton starts banging again.

Five times, this time. I stay silent and wait. Then I hear five knocks back in quick reply.

"Sutton, what—"

"Shh," he hisses at me, resting a hand on my shoulder. He waits, and I eventually hear a single knock coming from the other side. He hits the door once more with the metal pipe, then carefully drops it down and shuffles back out of the way.

"Who is it?" I ask. He doesn't answer. "Sutton, who's in there?"

I hear another series of sounds now: metal scraping on metal, bolts and latches being undone. Then, with a groan and the high-pitched squeak of stiff hinges, the door slowly opens inward. There's light in there. Faint, artificial light, visible only because everything else is so dark.

Before going through, Sutton stops and positions himself directly between me and the door. His face is slightly illuminated now and I can see his eyes behind the lenses of his glasses, searching my face and try-ing to gauge my reaction. He seems suddenly anxious again, like he was when he arrived at the house first thing this morning. Christ alone knows what he's got himself mixed up with here. He looks over his shoulder, then back at me again. I try to push past him, but he's fast and he blocks me.

"Just be calm and be patient," he whispers ominously. "Like I said, this changes everything."

"Spare me the bullshit, you overdramatic prick."

Sick of all the waiting, I push forward again, and this time he stands aside to let me through. I find myself in the middle of a room no more than a couple of yards square, much more solid and secure look-ing than the rest of this place, whatever this place actually is. There is a load of empty boxes and crates scattered around, and the light comes from a single dull lamp resting on a wooden trestle table on the other side of the room. From the very little I can see, this looks like a bun-ker of some kind. A remnant from World War II, perhaps? A forgot-ten relic of the Cold War, from those times when paranoid government departments and local councils drew up pointless plans and contin-gencies for running the charred remains of the country from numerous ill-equipped underground sites like this one, out in the middle of nowhere. For a moment I'm gone, transfixed by my bizarre surroundings, staring at the pale gray walls mottled with mildew and remembering a time when it was countries and superpowers that fought each other, not individuals . . .

The door we came through slams shut behind me and I spin around quickly. Then I see him. There's an Unchanged man holding a rifle, aiming it straight into my face. In spite of everything that's happened, the unexpected sight of one of them is too much to stand. I draw my knife and run toward him with an instinctive speed and ferocity that surprises even me, knocking the barrel of the gun away and lunging at him, focusing on the thought of smashing his head in and leaving him lying dead at my feet.

"McCoyne, don't!"

Sutton throws himself at me, slamming me against the side wall. I slide down to the floor and immediately try to scramble back onto my feet. The Unchanged man stands over me, his rifle pointing down into my face, ready to fire.

"Thought you said he was okay," he says to Sutton, his voice filled with nervous anger.

"He is okay," Sutton says, helping me up but still keeping me at a distance. I try to lunge for the Unchanged again, but Sutton anticipates my movements and pushes me back against the wall. "Control yourself," he warns.

"Unchanged, Sutton? What the fuck are you doing?"

Before he can answer, another door opens, opposite to the one we came in through. Another Unchanged man appears. Both of them are desperately thin, their tired faces drawn and hollow, skin pale and covered with sores, eyes black and wide. How long have they been hiding down here?

"Who the hell's this?" the second Unchanged asks.

"It's okay, Parker," Sutton tells him. "He's with me."

"Fucker went for me," the first one sneers, rifle still just inches from my face.

"That was my fault. I didn't tell him about you. I didn't want to risk it until I'd got him down here."

Sutton's still pushing me back. I start to relax slightly, and I feel him loosen his grip. The initial shock's fading, and my self-control is beginning to return. *Don't lose your head,* I tell myself. I need to stay calm, stay in control, then get the fuck back to Lowestoft and tell Hinchcliffe about this place.

"What's going on?" I ask. Sutton takes a cautious step away from me, and the first Unchanged man panics again. He pushes me back, jabbing the barrel of the gun hard into my chest. I raise my hands.

"Don't," Sutton says, trying to move the Unchanged away. "If he was going to kill you he'd have done it by now, believe me. Like I said, it was just the shock of seeing you. He had no idea."

"So why is he here?" the one called Parker asks, not taking his eyes off me. The other Unchanged stands his ground, refusing to lower his weapon.

"You know why," Sutton answers. "I told you I needed help. I can't do this on my own anymore. McCoyne was my only option. Without him we're all screwed."

"You should have warned us."

"You should have warned *me,*" I say, wincing as the rifle roughly probes my delicate gut.

"I knew," the gunman tells Parker, clearly enjoying the discomfort he's causing me.

"I had to keep it quiet in case things didn't work out," Sutton continues. "Dean needed to know because I knew it'd be him who opened the door and I didn't want him panicking and shooting us both. It was the only way. I didn't want the others to get concerned."

"Others?" I interrupt, feeling my skin prickling with unease. "There are *others?*"

Sutton finally manages to get the armed man to lower his rifle. I'm still thinking constantly about killing these evil bastards, but my control is continuing to return. Like Sutton said, it was the shock of finding myself face-to-face with these people that made me react so immediately, so viciously. I'd be stupid to try anything. I'm outnumbered and they're armed, and at this moment in time I don't know whether Sutton would fight with me or against me.

"Get rid of him," Parker says. "You shouldn't have brought him here, Pete."

Sutton stands in the very center of the room, separating me from the Unchanged like a referee at a boxing match.

"I had to bring him, you know I did. We talked about this."

"What the hell are you doing?" I demand, ignoring their inconsequential conversation. "If Hinchcliffe or anyone else finds out what's down here, they'll kill you as well as these two."

"If it wasn't for Pete we'd be dead anyway," Dean, the gunman, says. I don't react. It's one thing finding myself shut underground with two Unchanged scum; acknowledging either of them is another matter altogether.

"Do you really think I'm that stupid?" Sutton sighs. "Do you think I'd let any of them know about this place?"

"You told me."

"Yes, but you're different from the rest of them, I keep telling you. You're like me. You can help these people. I can't do this on my own anymore."

"Do what? I don't understand. I'm not going to help Unchanged, and neither should you. Just kill them and walk away."

"I can't."

"But they're just *Unchanged*, Sutton, probably the last of their kind. Things are hard enough up there without all of this."

"Looks like he's going to be a real help," Parker sighs sarcastically, leaning back against the wall and staring straight at me. "Bad move bringing him here. We should kill him."

"You couldn't do it," I spit at him. "And that's why you're down here and I'm up there."

"I'll do it," Dean says menacingly, raising the rifle and taking a step forward. I lunge forward to defend myself, but Sutton blocks me, wedging himself between us again. He now has me on one side and the barrel of the rifle on the other. With surprising calm and self-assurance, he pushes us both away to our respective corners.

"And how will that help anyone?" he asks, his voice terse, clearly not impressed. "It's that kind of bullshit that got us all into this mess. Like I said, Dean, I didn't have any choice. You know how hard this is getting. I can't do everything on my own anymore, and if I can't do it, we're all history."

I grab Sutton's shoulder and turn him around to face me. "Will you just tell me what's going on?"

He gestures for Parker to open the door opposite the entrance we came through. Parker's still hesitant.

"Don't," Dean says, the rifle still raised.

"It's okay," Sutton calmly replies. "Like I said, Dean, he'd have killed you by now if he was going to. He's like me. Just give him a little time to get used to the situation."

"Keep him under control, then," he orders nervously, "because I'll shoot you both if I have to."

Parker rests his hands on the door, then pauses again.

"You're completely sure about this, Pete?"

Sutton nods again. "We don't have any choice."

Parker opens the door. It's heavy like a safe door, and he needs to use all his weight to push it fully open. He blocks my way forward, still unsure, and I recoil when I accidentally brush against him. Sutton squeezes between us, and Parker reluctantly moves to one side to let him through. I feel the barrel of the rifle resting between my shoulder blades.

"Keep yourself under control, Danny," Sutton whispers as I follow him. "Don't do anything stupid."

We enter another room. The lighting's marginally better in here, but the shape of the space is very different and I'm still not able to see much. I can just about make out enough of the walls and ceiling to see that this looks like some kind of long, sloping access corridor. Sutton slows and grabs my arm again, obviously expecting me to react. As my eyes become used to the light levels I see that there are more

Unchanged in here at the farthest end of the corridor. I count another four of them sitting on the floor, leaning up against the walls. I stare at each one of them as I pass. They look like famine victims from old TV news reports, limbs like sticks. Two of them are too weak to even lift their heads. One glares at me, a mix of hate and horror on her face. The fourth scuttles away along the floor, hurriedly moving back in the direction from which we've just come to get out of the way. They are broken, empty people. Do they know what I am? I know I should be killing them or at least finding a way to get someone here to do it for me. The fact I'm doing neither is adding to the nausea I'm already feeling. These pathetic fuckers make me feel physically sick.

"I don't understand," I say to Sutton, keeping my voice deliberately low, still conscious of the rifle aimed at my back. "Why? Why risk so much for a handful of Unchanged? Why risk so much for *any* Unchanged? You should have killed them."

We reach the end of the corridor, just me and Sutton now. I glance back and see that Dean and Parker have stopped following, but they're still watching closely. A lamp hanging on the wall illuminates another metal door. Sutton sighs and takes off his glasses and rubs his eyes.

"Sometimes you just don't have any choice. Sometimes decisions are made for you. Things happen, and you just have to deal with them as best you can. The right option isn't always the easiest one to take."

I'm still trying to decipher his bullshit when he leans forward and opens the next door. He gently pushes it and it swings open wide, revealing a much larger space that's filled with light. For a few blissfully ignorant seconds I'm distracted trying to work out why there's such a vast construction as this buried deep under a farmer's field in Suffolk, and the full enormity of what I'm seeing doesn't immediately hit home.

Then it does, and I can hardly stand.

This place is full of people. I can see their faces and hear their voices and smell them and . . . and Christ, there must be more than twenty Unchanged in here.

23

SUTTON LEADS ME DEEPER into the large room, and I'm struggling to cope with what I'm seeing. For a couple of seconds all I can make out is an unholy mass of people filling the space in front of me. I've only managed to take a few steps forward when my dazed and confused brain switches back into gear and the full implication of what's around us hits home. I take hold of Sutton's arm, spin him around, and slam him back against the nearest wall. I focus all my attention on him, but I'm aware of terrified Unchanged scattering all around us, fleeing like cockroaches about to be crushed under a boot. Do they know what I am? They're all watching me, desperately trying not to let me catch them staring. With frightening ease Sutton shifts his balance and reverses our positions, and now I'm the one up against the wall. I feel my strength drain away as a wave of sickness washes over me. Sutton pushes me through another doorway, grabbing a lamp as we disappear into the darkness.

Disoriented, I lose my footing and stumble. Sutton shuts the door and I look up and suddenly I'm aware of figures all around me. I lunge for the nearest one and it simply collapses under my weight. It's a bloody mannequin. We're in a room full of fucking store window dummies. None of this makes any sense. I slump down to the floor, pulse pounding, sweat pouring off me, trying to work out how I'm going to get back out and kill those fuckers on the other side of the door.

"What the fuck's going on, Sutton?" I demand, panting.

He stands over me, looking down. Behind the thick lenses of his glasses, his eyes dart anxiously around my face. "You're really not well, are you?"

"Don't change the subject. What's going on?" I ask again.

"It's okay."

"Okay? How can it be okay?"

He stares at me again, trying to work out what I'm thinking. Truth is, even I don't know what I'm thinking right now. Finding so many Unchanged like this has left me with a gut-full of bitter, conflicting emotions. I know I should have already killed them, but I don't know if I can do it. I don't know if I have the strength, and there are too many of them. I wish someone else had found them and could do it for me. They need to be killed because, as I've been telling myself for months, the sooner the last Unchanged has been wiped off the face of the planet, the sooner this pointless, bloody war will finally be over. I was starting to think it already was.

"Sorry about the bullshit about Southwold's supplies, you'd never have come if I'd told you," Sutton says, his voice echoing around the room.

"Damn right I wouldn't have come. For crying out loud, what were you thinking?"

"I said you were like me, didn't I? I know you won't hurt these people. I knew the moment I saw you."

"Being with these people will bring you nothing but grief. You should get rid of them now. If you can't do that, you should just get away and not come back."

"I can't do that," he says, "and I think you're wrong. Just let me explain—"

"There's nothing to explain."

"It's not what you think."

I try to stand but I can't get up, another crippling wave of nausea making it almost impossible for me to move. It's a combination of nerves and the airless, sweaty stench of this badly ventilated and over-crowded hideout. My head's thumping. Sutton helps me to my feet, and I lean back against the wall.

"What is this place?" I ask him, looking around at the emotionless painted faces of the mannequins that surround us. Some of them are dressed in old-fashioned army uniforms.

"A nuclear bunker," he announces. "It was operational until the end of the Cold War. Then they decommissioned it and turned it into a tourist attraction. Hence the dummies."

His words just bounce off me, barely sinking in. I should probably ask him a load of other questions, but my brain is still struggling to make sense of any of this. Stupidly, all I can think right now is how much I hate Hinchcliffe. If it hadn't been for him then I wouldn't have gone to Southwold and if I hadn't been in Southwold, I wouldn't have met Peter Sutton, and if I hadn't met Sutton I wouldn't know anything about this damn place or the Unchanged hiding down here. Thinking about Hinchcliffe makes me remember what he forced me to do with that woman yesterday afternoon . . . and then part of me starts wondering whether I should just stay down here in the dark and never put my head above ground again. Nothing makes sense any more. Whenever I think I'm starting to come to terms with the way this dys-functional new world works, something always happens that leaves me feeling as confused and disoriented as I did when I killed Lizzie's dad, Harry. Right back to square one again. Life feels like a game of Snakes and Ladders, but without any ladders.

Sutton waits, then cautiously edges nearer. "I told you this place changes everything."

"And I told you you were an overdramatic prick. This changes nothing."

"Well, it's changed everything for me," he says. "Before I found these people I was lost."

"You've lost your fucking mind, that's about all."

"I knew you'd feel this way at first, but just stop and think for a minute, Danny."

"Think about what? About the fact that you're a traitor? About what Hinchcliffe's going to do to you when he finds out about this place?"

"No, I want you to think about yourself. Think about what you've had to do over the last year. Think about how much you've lost."

"And how much I've gained."

"Have you gained anything?"

"My freedom. This time last year I was at a dead end."

"Things are better for you today because . . . ?" He waits for me to answer, and the silence is deafening. "You're alone, your health's deteriorating, you're living by yourself in a freezing-cold house in an otherwise empty housing development—doesn't look so great to me."

"Are things any better for you?"

"Not really," he answers. "Truth be told, life's shit for all of us now. You, me, these Unchanged. Killing them won't make any difference."

"That's not the point."

"There's something else I want you to see," he says, supporting my weight and gently leading me back toward the door. More Unchanged scatter when it opens, their wiry limbs and sudden movements making them appear unnervingly insectlike. We go back out into the main area of this part of the bunker. Some sections of the odd-shaped space are dimly illuminated by dull lamps; other corners remain shrouded in darkness. The walls that I can see are covered in old photographs, maps, and other paraphernalia, making the room appear smaller than it actually is.

"Just look at them, Danny," he says, shuffling me around and gesturing over to where a group of them are sitting at a mess table, watching us nervously. "These people didn't do anything wrong. They didn't deserve any of what happened to them."

"Neither did I. Neither did you. This war wasn't anyone's fault, it just happened."

"But the fact the war's dragged on *is* our fault. We have to stop the fighting."

"The fighting will end when all the Unchanged are gone."

"Do you really still believe that?"

"Yes," I answer quickly, even though I don't. It's an instinctive reaction. Sometimes I think I say these things just because I'm used to saying them, like I've been conditioned to react. "You know as well as I do that we were all forced into this, forced to take sides and fight."

"Maybe that's where we're still going wrong," he says, starting to sound suspiciously like people I heard talking way back in the summer, just before I lost my daughter forever and half the country disappeared in a white-hot nuclear haze. "Look at what happened in Southwold," he continues unnecessarily.

"This isn't right, though. You shouldn't be doing this."

"Not helping these people wouldn't be right either."

One of the Unchanged closest to me shuffles his legs suddenly, and I almost overreact at the completely innocent movement.

"But you're not helping them, are you? Can't you see that? All you're doing is delaying the inevitable. They'll have to leave here eventually, and the second they do, they'll be killed. Christ alone knows how you've managed to keep them alive down here for so long anyway."

He gestures for me to keep my voice down, but I'm past caring.

"I did it because I had to," he says. "Come on, Danny, these people have got nothing to do with the fighting. They're just like you and me. You've got more in common with them than with Hinchcliffe and his fighters."

There's no point arguing, this deluded idiot isn't going to listen. I look around this dank, claustrophobic bunker in disbelief. I've risked and lost everything to help wipe these bastards out, and all the time Peter fucking Sutton was sheltering them. *Protecting them.* I'm filled with anger, and all I want to do is kill the lot of them, Sutton included— but I know I won't. I don't even know if I can. I've killed hundreds of refugees like this, but I'm outnumbered now and in no state to fight today. Or am I just making excuses? I watch an Unchanged man sitting on the edge of a thin mattress on the floor, comforting a woman and holding her close. Despite the fact they both look skeletal and close to death, the way they are together reminds me how I used to hold Lizzie before all of this began.

Don't be such a fucking idiot. You're nothing like them and you had no choice. You did what you had to do. They are the enemy.

Is that really true? Did I have a choice?

"Just tell me why?" I ask, surprising myself by asking the question I'd been thinking out loud. I'm hoping Sutton will say something profound that will help make sense of this sudden madness.

"I'll show you," he answers, beckoning me to follow him deeper into the bunker. He gently pushes past an elderly Unchanged woman, acknowledging her by name as if she matters, then takes me down another short corridor and into a large L-shaped space. We have to step over and around even more people to get through. One man is badly burned, his face heavily scarred, but his wounds are clean and have been obviously been treated. "See that?"

"See what?"

"The kids. Right over on the far side, there's a couple of kids playing."

I follow the line of his gaze and quickly spot the children. For a few seconds I'm transfixed. They're *playing*. These are the first kids I've seen since the start of the war who aren't fighting or screaming, or throwing themselves at me and attacking, or standing swaying in a dark corner in a catatonic haze . . . these children are actually *playing*. They're laughing and talking and interacting with each other. They're pushing each other around and picking themselves back up and . . . and it's hard to come to terms with what I'm seeing. This behavior—so normal and innocent—now seems strange and unnatural. It's hard to believe that even now, even after being buried underground in this cold, damp, dark armpit of a place for who knows how long, they're still managing to find something positive in their dire and hopeless situation. For the briefest of moments I almost feel a sense of regret. How many people like this have I killed?

FOCUS!

"What about them?" I ask.

"See the older girl with the boy on her knee? Sitting just over from the others?"

I immediately see who he's talking about. Separated slightly from the rest of the young group and sitting in the soft circle of light coming from another lamp, a girl is holding a toddler. She looks like an underage mom, probably in her late teens, and he's no older than two years old, three at the most. He sits on her knee and she holds him tight, arms wrapped around him, gently bouncing him up and down. She probably doesn't even realize she's doing it. It's an instinctive, settling, protecting movement.

"That boy," he says, his voice suddenly lower and the tone noticeably different, "is my grandson."

"Your grandson? But how . . . ?"

He moves me away, turning me around so I'm not staring. I can't help looking back.

"Please . . . they don't know. None of them know."

"I don't understand. How?"

"I don't know what it was like for you, Danny, but I had my doubts about the war from the very beginning. I kept fighting because I thought I had to, because I thought I had to choose a side and if I didn't kill them they'd kill me, but I didn't get swept up on the wave of it all like everybody else did. I started to wonder whether there really was a difference between us at all, or whether the Hate and the Change were just the results of some massive, manufactured social paranoia."

"You think? After all that's happened?"

"Why not? How many people did you know who were religious? There used to be thousands of religions with barely a shred of evidence between the lot of them, all of them the product of overactive imaginations, superstitions, and fear. People used to kill each other because they believed in different versions of stories that could never be proved or disproved, used to let themselves die because some book said they shouldn't have blood transfusions, used to cut their hair a certain way or grow their hair or cut off their foreskins or abstain from sex . . . None of the divisions between them were a million miles from what happened with the Hate, were they? Intangible. Inexplicable. Pointless."

I don't bother to reply. This isn't the time for theological debate. If there ever was a God, he's long since packed his bags and moved on.

"After a few weeks," he continues, rant over, "I ended up back around the area where I used to live and where what was left of my family still were. That was where I fell in with Simon Penkridge and Selena, and they helped me learn how to hold the Hate. It was a logical progression. It felt natural and right."

"But you didn't get sent into the cities?"

"Like I said, I didn't buy into the fighting like everyone else. I got out before it was too late. I don't know, maybe people like you and me have got some predetermined setting that's different from the rest. I think more people could have learned to hold the Hate if they'd stopped fighting long enough to be shown how. Maybe not the worst of the fighters, but the rest of them."

"The underclass?"

"Yes. The people who only fight when they absolutely have to, not because they want to. Problem is, most people like that have been crushed or killed and all we're left with now are dumb feral bastards like this guy Hinchcliffe and his crew. You and me, Danny, we can see beyond the battle and look toward other things, bigger things . . ."

I agree with him to an extent, but right now all I'm trying to do is look beyond being trapped in this bunker. Regardless of anything Sutton might say (and he hasn't actually said a lot so far), I still want out of here. I don't need any of this. It's another dangerous and unnecessary complication I could do without. I've only been here a few minutes and already I feel like I'm caught between Sutton trying to pull me in one direction and Hinchcliffe the other. If I don't do something about it fast I'll be torn in half: ripped straight down the middle.

"I found an Unchanged camp and I was scavenging food from them," Sutton continues. "I watched them from a distance for days, scared to get too close. I didn't trust myself, didn't know what I'd do. All I knew was that there were faces there I recognized . . . friends, people I used to see in the street . . . and then I saw Jodie with little Andrew."

"Andrew?"

He nods back across the shelter again.

"My grandson. Jodie was my daughter-in-law. My son was already long gone, either dead or lost fighting somewhere, but those two were both Unchanged. Eventually they were picked up by the military. They were being evacuated to one of the refugee camps when the convoy they were traveling in was attacked. I'd been following them because I didn't know what else to do. Jodie was killed, but some of the others managed to get away, and they took Andrew with them. I waited until I was completely sure of myself, until I knew I could definitely control myself and not attack, then I helped them and hid them. Only Parker and Dean and a couple of others really know what I am."

"What about the rest of them?"

"They think I'm like them. They think I'm one of the Unchanged who can fake the Hate."

"And what about me?"

"They'll assume you're the same."

Even now, after all this time, the very notion of being thought of as Unchanged still stirs up some deep-rooted emotion inside me. It's an uncomfortable, disproportionate reaction that's hard to keep swallowed down. It's even more difficult to suppress my feelings when I start to wonder if they might be right. Could that be what we both really are?

"So how did you end up here?" I ask, suddenly desperate for a distraction.

"Long story . . . maybe I'll have time to tell you one day. Believe it or not, I figure this is probably the safest part of the country, geographically, that is. And when I found this bunker . . ."

"How did you find it?"

"I had a friend who used to visit decommissioned bunkers. A weird hobby, I know, but there you go. I remembered him telling me about a few places down in this neck of the woods."

"Very convenient."

He shrugs his shoulders. "Well, that's how it is."

"So if it's your grandson you're worried about," I ask, "why not just get him out of here and leave the rest of this bunch behind?"

He shakes his head and leads me back to a slightly quieter part of the room.

"You're the only person who knows about Andrew. I didn't used to see him that often. He was barely a year old when the war started. He hardly even knew me."

"But you haven't answered my question."

"Apart from the fact he'll never survive anywhere else, I don't think I'd be any good for him. I'm not getting any younger, and I was a crap parent anyway. My son didn't want anything to do with me."

"Are these people going to be any better?"

"Take a look around you, Danny. Just look at them. Look at how they talk to each other and how they interact. Listen to them. It's a million miles removed from what we're seeing in places like Lowestoft. This is how the world used to be. This is what we really lost because of the fighting."

"Bullshit."

"Is it? You saw what happened in Southwold. That's as good as it's going to get up there. Do you think it's ever going to stop? Look at what's happening. The human race is regressing. It's like some kind of de-evolution. Take the Brutes, for example—you saw that poor bitch by the farm. They're incapable of functioning anymore. Kids are the same. Have you seen how wild they've become?"

I don't bother telling him about the things I've seen.

"And the fighters," he continues, "for Christ's sake, they're in charge now. People have stopped thinking. Violence has taken the place of discussions and negotiations. Day by day what's left of civilization is becoming less and less civilized. Where's it going to end? Those stupid fuckers ruling the roost are never going to relinquish the power they've suddenly been given, are they? Things will get far, far worse before they get any better."

"So? There's nothing anyone can do about it. How is keeping a bunker full of Unchanged alive going to make any difference?"

"Don't you see? These people are constant. They're normal, and we're the freaks. This was all about keeping Andrew safe to begin with, but I've come to realize now that these people are all that's left of the human race. We've just got to hope there comes a time when they'll be able to go back aboveground and start again."

Fuck. Sutton has truly lost his mind.

"Are you out of your fucking mind? You've got to face facts, these people are history and all we've got left now is cunts like Hinchcliffe and places like Lowestoft."

"You're wrong," he protests. "Help me keep them safe, Danny. All's not yet lost."

I'm not listening to any more of this bullshit. "All *is* lost," I tell him as I shove him out of the way and try to find my way back to the exit. I can't take any more of this today. Has Sutton been driven crazy by months of fighting? Whatever's behind this madness, it's not my problem. I'm going to do what I promised myself I'd do last night—leave Lowestoft and get away from everything and everybody. I sidestep the man and woman I watched earlier, now lying together, their bodies still locked in an embrace, and all I can think about suddenly is being shut in that damn hotel room yesterday and that rough, loveless sex and how empty and vile it made me feel . . . The only person I want to be with now is me. I don't need anyone else. Maybe I'll go tell Hinchcliffe about this place, then leave them all to fight out their futures between them.

Desperate to get out, I turn to go through the door into the corridor and walk straight into Joseph Mallon coming the other way.

24

DANNY?" HE SAYS, HIS voice trembling with uncertainty and surprise. "Danny McCoyne, is that really you?"

"Joseph?"

Is it him, or have I finally lost my mind? Am I so sick I've started hallucinating now? His voice is unmistakable, but he looks literally half the man he used to be. His face, broad and beaming when he held me captive in the convent, is now distressingly gaunt. His cheeks are sunken and hollow, the whites of his eyes as yellow as his teeth. He wears a grubby woolen sweater that hangs off him like it's several sizes too big.

"I thought you were dead."

"I thought *you* were dead," I answer, slumping back against the wall in disbelief. This can't be happening. I feel like I'm about to pass out, my hands and feet suddenly numb and heavy, fingertips tingling, eyes not focusing properly . . . I *must* be hallucinating.

"You two know each other?" Sutton asks, chasing after me, sounding as shocked as I am. Mallon nods his head vigorously and stares at me, his rasping breathing sounding uncomfortably erratic. He's in worse shape than me. He grabs my hand and shakes it furiously, grinning like a madman.

"Did you know about this?" I ask Sutton. I look straight at him, demanding an explanation, but he doesn't answer. I can't tell whether he's genuinely shocked or if he orchestrated this whole situation just to try to keep me down here.

"I had no idea . . ."

"What happened to you, Danny?" Mallon says as he looks me up and down. "You look like shit, man." I don't have a chance to respond before he speaks again, turning to talk to Sutton this time. "Danny was one of the ones I told you about, back in the city with Sahota."

"But how did you . . . ?"

I'm unable to finish my question, not even sure what it is I'm trying to ask. He might look like a shadow of the man he was, but Mallon still manages to seem infinitely more composed than I feel. He's acting like he's found a long-lost friend, not someone he kept locked in a cell for days on end, chained to a piss-soaked bed—someone who wanted to kill him. I focus on that thought for a second. There's a part of me that still thinks I should do it.

"Back at the convent," he begins, in that instantly familiar, rich accent, "there was a lot of bullshit flying about." He looks at Sutton. "I told you about Sahota . . . the guy pulling the strings there? I figured out what he was, what he was all about, and how he was training up people like Danny here for some crazy last crusade. I knew he was bad news, but I didn't let on. I acted dumb and played along with it 'cause I didn't have any choice—I knew he'd kill me if I stepped out of line. He gave me food and he kept me safe from all the chaos outside, so I put up with it, but I knew it wouldn't last, and I was ready. The moment he packed up and disappeared, I knew something bad was coming."

"Wait," I interrupt, "he *disappeared?*"

"It was like someone flicked a switch, Danny. One minute he's sitting in his office, giving out his orders, the next he's loading up a car, clearing out the supplies, getting his people together, and getting the hell out of there. They killed the rest of us before they left, but I was one step ahead of the game. Locked myself in your old room, as it happens. Hid under the bed and waited there until I was sure they'd all gone."

"But the bomb . . . how did you get away?"

"A combination of good luck and common sense," he answers. "The area around the convent was empty, not a single person left there but me. Then, next day, crack of dawn, everything goes crazy. I hear fighting, then there's this unbelievable noise and the army starts racing away from the middle of town. Didn't take a genius to work out that the shit was about to hit the fan big-time. Sahota's people had left a couple of cars behind. I had one of them ready, and I joined the convoy out of the city. I saw the explosion in the distance, but I was far enough away by then. I dug in with the military until they were attacked. Me and a couple of others managed to get away, and that was when we ran into Peter here and his people. 'Cause he's like you he was able to keep up all the bullshit and pretense and keep us hidden. Now here we are, several months and several stops farther down the line. And here you are, too. Jesus Christ, Danny McCoyne, it's good to see you! I can't believe it's you!"

I can't believe it's him, either. I try again to make sense of everything I've heard today, to unweave the stories Mallon and Sutton have told me and try to find a logical explanation as to why I'm in a bunker buried under a farm with a bunch of foul Unchanged, but I can't. It's as impossible as it sounds. My overriding emotion right now, stronger even than anything I feel for either Mallon or the Unchanged, is anger toward Hinchcliffe and Sutton. Now, if what Mallon's just said is true, then that anger spreads to Sahota, too, because after dispatching me and many others into the city to fight and sacrifice ourselves in the name of *the cause,* he turned tail and ran. Cowardly fucker.

"I need help to look after these people," Sutton says. I look into his face, but in the half-light his expression is impossible to read. Is he genuine, or is he just another manipulative shyster, out to use me and exploit me like everyone else? "This is their only chance. This is *our* only chance."

"You shouldn't have brought me here."

"Yes I should. Please stay, Danny, I need your help. I can't do this on my own anymore."

"Can't do what exactly? You keep saying that."

"I can't provide for all these people by myself. I was working in Southwold to try to get food and water, but there wasn't enough, and . . ."

The penny drops.

"So that's it? That's why you really wanted me here? You think because of my connections with Hinchcliffe I'll be able to sort everything out for you and keep you stocked up with supplies? Fuck off, Sutton. Go hijack one of those trucks you saw in Southwold."

"No, it's nothing like that," he backpedals quickly. "I didn't even know you were connected to Hinchcliffe. If I had, then maybe I wouldn't have asked you."

"I wish you hadn't."

"Take a look around you," he says, his voice intentionally louder, wanting to be heard now. "These people deserve more than this."

"Not my responsibility."

"Yes it is," he shouts, loud enough to fill the whole shelter and stop all other conversations dead. "It's *our* responsibility."

I shake my head with despair. What do I have to do to make this dumb fucker understand?

"Not *my* responsibility," I shout back equally loudly, then lower my voice again. "I'm not interested. What's to stop me bringing Hinchcliffe's fighters here and ending this bullshit today?"

"You won't do that, Danny," Mallon says. "I know you're better than that. I know what kind of a man you are. I saw it."

"You saw nothing."

"Yes I did. Back at the convent I saw a man who still had his priorities straight, even after all that had happened. You were still thinking about your family when all that everyone else like you wanted to do was kill. Tell me, did you ever find your daughter?"

"What was left of her."

"Sorry, man. Was she . . . ?"

I shake my head, but I can't bring myself to explain. It hurts too much. I look deep into Mallon's dark, staring eyes and wish with every fiber of my being that I'd never met either him or Sutton. Then again, I remind myself, without Mallon I'd never have been able to get back into the city and I'd never have found Ellis and shared those last few moments with Lizzie. They'd have died together in the bomb blast, and I'd have been none the wiser. Strange how important, in retrospect, those last few seconds we had together were. I think about them every day. Lizzie gave up everything she had left for Ellis. The memories of what happened to her and what my daughter became still fill me with unbearable pain.

I can't take this.

I can't do it.

I push past both of them and run for the exit. Mallon tries to hold me back, but I shrug him off and keep moving.

25

THE COLD AIR OUTSIDE hits my chest like a hammer blow, but I keep moving. I run back toward the farm, but I've scarcely made it to the top of the rise before I'm doubled over with pain, coughing so violently I can hardly breathe, making so much foul noise that the solitary cow bolts and runs for cover again. I make it back to the buildings, stumbling down the slope. In a momentary gap between painful convulsions I manage to suck in a lungful of air and spit a lump of sticky, dribbling phlegm against a wall. I watch it as it slowly drips down to the ground. My spit is red-brown and streaked with blood, and there's a foul metallic aftertaste in my mouth. Fuck. What's happening to me? I'm falling apart, physically and mentally. I slump back against the wall of the burned-out farmhouse, too weak to stay standing, sobbing with the pain. Christ, it hurts.

Peter Sutton slowly approaches. I wish he'd fuck off and leave me alone, but I'm too tired to fight or argue.

"I'm sorry," he says pathetically. "There was no other way."

"You should never have brought me here," I tell him again, still wheezing badly.

"I didn't know what else to do. I'm desperate, Danny. I didn't have any choice. When I saw you in Southwold and realized you were like me . . ."

I slide farther down the wall and land hard on my backside on the ice-cold dirt.

"You *did* have a choice. You still do. You can just walk away from this place right now and not look back. Just forget about them."

"Is that what you're going to do?"

"That's exactly what I'm going to do," I tell him, pausing midsentence to clutch my chest as another wave of cramping pain takes hold. It's snowing hard now, and I can feel my face and hands starting to freeze.

"You know I can't do that," he says, standing over me and looking down. He helps me sit up straight again.

"Why not? What's stopping you? Why not just leave them down there to starve to death? It'll be easier on them in the long run. Better than being forced out into the open and killed, and that's what's going to happen eventually. They can't stay down there forever."

"Those people down there are more human than most of what's up here."

"Then maybe it's time to redefine 'human.'"

He shakes his head and crouches down in front of me. I gasp for breath as the painful cramps return yet again. I'm shivering now. Shaking. Freezing cold. Sutton continues to watch me, but I can't read his expression. Can barely even focus on his face through the snow.

"You're in a bad way. Listen, there's a doctor here. One of the women back there, Tracey, she used to be a GP. She might be able to do something to help you."

"You think I'm going to let one of the Unchanged touch me? Jesus Christ—"

"Come on, rise above this, Danny. I really need your help."

"The best way I can help is to bring Hinchcliffe here and finish this today."

"You won't do that, I know you won't. I understand why you're feeling this way, and I've listened to everything you said, but you know as well as I do that I can't just abandon these people. I can't give up on my own flesh and blood."

I have to tell him. Have to try to make him see.

"After I met Mallon," I explain, speaking slowly, trying to conserve energy, "I went into one of their refugee camps. We were sent there to kill, but I was looking for my family. I needed to find out what had happened to my daughter 'cause I knew she was like us."

He looks confused.

"But if she was like us . . . ?"

"I knew her mother would have done everything she could to try to keep the kids together. I managed to track her down, and I was right. She had Ellis drugged and locked up."

There's an awkward silence. He's knows there's no happy ending to my story because of the comment I made to Mallon earlier, and because there are no happy endings anymore.

"I tried to take her with me and get out of the city, but it was impossible. She wasn't my little girl anymore. There was nothing left of her but Hate. Christ, Peter, you should have seen her. She didn't even know me. I had to fight with her just to try to get her to safety. The city was tearing itself apart all around us, but all she wanted to do was keep killing. I managed to get us just out of range of the bomb blast, but even then, even after what had happened and what we'd been through, she still kept on fighting. Her Hate wasn't like the Hate that made you and me fight, it was a thousand times worse than that. It had poisoned her to the core."

"So where is she now?"

"Dead, probably."

"Why are you telling me this?"

I slowly manage to drag myself back up onto my feet, my legs heavy. I clear my throat, spit again, and take a few slow, painful steps.

"You need to understand that you're not helping anybody by doing this. I've come to a conclusion, and I think you need to do the same. This world is dying. It's sick to the core and there's no hope left. You and me, we'll grow old and die or we'll get ourselves killed, and in the end there will only be people like Hinchcliffe, his fighters, and the worst of the children left. If you'd seen the things I'd seen, then you'd know that your grandson back there doesn't stand a chance. None of the kids do, and without kids, there's no future. You should just block the bunker door and bury the lot of them. Now get me back to Lowestoft."

I start to walk away but stop again, sensing that he hasn't followed. Every extra movement takes ten times the effort it should, but I slowly turn back around.

"I think you're wrong," he says.

"Well, I know I'm right."

"Just answer one question for me, Danny. Why did you bother?"

"What?"

"Looking for your daughter and wife . . . why did you bother?"

"Because I didn't know what Ellis had become. Because I had this fucking stupid idea in my head that she'd be just as I left her and we'd stay fighting side by side together until the war was over. I thought some kind of normality might eventually return, but it won't. The world is dead."

"Not yet it isn't."

"Jesus, Peter, my own daughter didn't even recognize me."

"You said you had other kids. What happened to them?"

"Ellis killed them."

"How many?"

"Two boys."

"Both Unchanged?"

"Yes."

I go on walking back to the car. He goes on talking.

"So tell me," he shouts after me, "knowing what you know now, if I'd taken you down into that bunker today and you'd seen that one of your Unchanged sons had survived, would you still be turning your back on them?"

26

SUTTON DROVE ME BACK to the house. True to his word, he left me there with barely any protest. He started to talk about ways I could find him again if I changed my mind, but I told him not to bother. I told him I didn't want to see him again, and that if I did, I'd kill him. I told him I'd have to tell Hinchcliffe. He said it didn't make any difference because the bunker's secure. Unless Hinchcliffe's got a few oxyacetylene burners or a tank lying around, he said, it doesn't matter. No one's getting in, and the Unchanged aren't about to come out.

The house wasn't where I needed to be, though. I waited there for a couple of hours longer and tried to pull myself together, hoping that the constant thumping in my head would stop and I'd start to feel better. I'd been telling myself it was just the aftereffects of the beer from last night, or the food I'd eaten yesterday, or the dog the day before that, or whatever I'd done the previous day or last week, but I knew it wasn't.

This is serious. I can't go on like this. I'm getting worse every day. I'm back inside the compound now, walking toward Hinchcliffe's factory, about to do something I should have done a long time ago. I need help.

The snow's stopped and it's pissing down with rain now, adding to the misery. The late afternoon sky is filled with endless black clouds. The guard on the approach road recognizes me and lets me through. Other than him I see only one more guard. He's standing just inside the entrance door at the end of the factory where the Unchanged kids are held, sheltering from the rain. I'm scared, and I lose my nerve before I get too close and walk straight past, heading instead toward the enormous, useless wind turbine that towers over everything. It's a symbol of what this place once was and what it'll never be again; the ultimate physical manifestation of all Hinchcliffe's bullshit.

It's no good. I can't put this off any longer.

I walk back the other way, and this time the guard in the doorway sees me and yells at me to either "get over here or fuck off." He's wrapped up against the bitter cold, wearing so many layers that he looks grossly overweight. His mouth is hidden by a scarf and his upturned collar, and he has ski goggles covering his eyes. He has a rifle slung over his shoulder. I presume it's there to stop escapees rather than to prevent anyone breaking in.

"What do you want?" he demands, his voice muffled.

"Rona Scott," I answer. "I need to see her."

"Says who?"

"Says Hinchcliffe."

He lifts up his goggles and eyes me up and down, then pulls his scarf down a couple of inches, just enough to clear his mouth, making it easier to speak.

"I've seen you before, haven't I?"

"Have you?"

"Yeah . . . ain't you the one what finds the Unchanged?"

"That's me," I answer quickly, desperate to get out of the cold. It's raining even harder now, the water bouncing back up off the pavement. "Look, is the doctor here? I need to see her."

He stops to think again. This guy's not the smartest, and that's probably why he drew the short straw and ended up being posted out here on his own. I can't tell whether he's trying to psych me out with these long, silent pauses or if he's just slow. I reach inside my coat, and he reacts to my sudden movement, swinging his rifle around.

"Don't," I tell him, raising my hands to show I don't want any trouble. When he relaxes I take out a can of beer from my pocket, hoping to speed up this painfully drawn-out encounter with a little bribery. He halfheartedly tries to remain impassive and hard, but I can see a sudden glint in his eye. He's like a kid looking in a toy store window.

"Inside," he says as he takes the can from me. He glances from side to side before moving out of the way to let me pass. As if anyone else is going to have followed me out here. Fucking idiot.

The building is oppressively quiet save for a few muffled sounds in the distance, and it's no warmer indoors than out. I've never made it this far in before. This end of the complex looks like it was mostly office space. I'm in an open-plan reception area, which has been turned into a checkpoint by Hinchcliffe's guard, and it reminds me of the reception desk back at the housing project where I used to work. There are a couple of rooms filled with rubbish leading off from here, and a wide staircase that goes up to the second floor. There's also another door into a corridor, long and straight and dark, which I presume leads into the rest of the factory. Curious, I walk toward it and try to peer in through a porthole-shaped safety glass window.

"Not that way," the guard says, making me jump.

"Where, then?"

No response. He looks at me expectantly. I dig down into the pockets of my coat again and this time bring out a packet of sweets. I don't know where they came from or why I've got them. I found them in the house before I came out and thought they might be useful.

"This is all I've got," I tell him, talking to him like I used to talk to my children. "Where's the doctor?"

He points up the stairs.

"Up there there's a load of offices. She's in one of them. Second or third floor, don't know which."

"Thanks for your help," I say sarcastically as I chuck him his sweets.

Dripping wet and exhausted, I start to climb up the metal steps, my boots clanging and filling the building with noise. At the top of the first flight of stairs is an open door and, beyond it, another narrow corridor with three doors along one side and one at the far end. Fortunately there are long rectangular windows in each of the doors that allow me to see inside. Rona Scott is sitting in the first room, slouched in a chair, staring straight ahead. This must have been some kind of meeting room or training area once. There's no other furniture now except for a long gray desk beside her that's covered with rubbish and clutter. I pause before trying to attract her attention, feeling undeniably nervous. Wait. She's talking. Is someone in there with her?

Scott looks exhausted. Her face is flustered, her cheeks bloodred, and she's smoking a cigarette, flicking ash onto the dirty terra-cotta-colored carpet. I've spoken to her (rather, she's spoken *at* me) on a few occasions before today, and I don't relish the prospect of having to talk to her again. She's a foul-tempered woman at the best of times, and I'm tempted just to turn around now and go back to the house rather than face her. She suddenly gets up, moving unexpectedly quickly, and I step back to stay in the shadows, keeping out of sight but still able to see her through the glass. From my new position I can see that the room is actually double length, and the far end is in almost total darkness. There's a concertina-like folding wall across the middle, which has been left half open. Scott strides purposefully through the gap and disappears out of view.

"Do something, you useless little prick!" she yells at someone unseen, her bellowing voice muffled but still clearly audible even through the closed door. "For god's sake, come on!"

The hostility in her voice is unnerving, and I actually start to edge back toward the stairs before telling myself to get a grip. She reappears again and mooches through the clutter on the table. She picks something up—looks like an open glass jar—then moves back into the shadows.

"You know you want it," I hear her shout. "Come on, react! Don't just sit there, you pathetic piece of shit."

She walks back this way, the jar held out in front of her; then she looks around. Damn, she's seen me. I try to get out of the way but it's too late. No backing out now. She angrily yanks the door open.

"What the fuck do you want?"

"Sorry," I stammer, immediately on the wrong foot. "I didn't mean to disturb you—"

"Yes you did," she bawls at me. "No one ever comes here unless they don't have any choice. You didn't come here by accident, so you *did* mean to disturb me."

"Hinchcliffe said I should—"

"You McCoyne?"

"Yes, I—"

"He said you'd probably turn up at some point. Give me a couple of minutes and I'll be with you."

When she stops talking I become aware of a faint whimpering noise coming from elsewhere in the room. Scott moves away from the door, and I follow her inside. At the far end, strapped to a chair by ropes tied across her tiny torso and around her ankles and wrists, is an Unchanged child. It's one of the kids from the council depot nest we cleared out earlier this week, I'm sure it is. When she sees that someone else is in the room, she starts moaning in fear, tugging at her restraints to try to get free. The effort's too much, though, and she gives up and slumps forward sobbing, letting her bonds take her weight, her long, greasy hair hanging down and covering her dirty face. Poor little shit. What the hell has Scott been doing to her?

"Interesting," Scott says, watching both the girl and me, her eyes flicking between us.

"What is?"

"The way she reacted when you appeared," she says.

"She recognizes me, that's all. I helped catch her."

"I just need one of these little cunts to show a bit of backbone and start fighting. Get Hinchcliffe off my back for a while. It wasn't so bad when Thacker was in charge. Hinchcliffe's got no patience. He wants results or he wants them dead."

The little girl, shaking with cold, cries out again. In a sudden fit of rage that takes both me and the child by surprise, the doctor spins around and hurls the glass jar at her. It hits the wall just above her head and explodes, showering her with sharp shards of glass and sticky globules of food.

"Jesus, what the fuck are you doing?" I shout, forgetting myself.

Rona Scott leans back and looks at me disapprovingly. "Looks like someone's been spending too much time around these things."

"It's not that. I just—"

Scott's not interested. She runs toward the girl again, grabs her shoulders, and yells into her face. The child screams back at the top of her voice, tied tight but still straining to get away. "That's better," Scott says, taunting the kid, slapping her cheek. "Now that's more like it." She turns her back on the still-screaming child and looks at me. "Right this way."

She shoves me out of the room and locks the door, muffling the little girl's cries but not blocking them out completely. She stops in the middle of the corridor, preventing me from going any farther, waiting expectantly. I realize what she's waiting for and reach into my inside pocket and pull out a half-full packet of cigarettes I've been holding on to for a while. She studies the packet for a moment, checks how many smokes are inside, then grunts her approval and heads for the staircase.

We climb another flight of steps up to the third floor, which looks identical in layout to the second. She takes me into the room at the far end of the corridor, double the size of the others. There's a wide window on one wall that gives Scott a virtually uninterrupted view out across Hinchcliffe's compound. On the opposite wall, a smaller window overlooks the sea. Driving rain clatters constantly against the glass. There's more light in here than in any other part of the building I've been in so far, but that's not a good thing. This is Rona Scott's clinic–cum–living-quarters, and I'd have preferred not to be able to see anything.

"Over there," she grunts at me, pointing across the room. I walk across the cluttered space, picking my way through the rubbish that covers the floor. There are unpleasant stains and used swabs and dressings everywhere, crusted hard and brown. Discarded strips of bandage lie around the place like gruesome, blood-soaked paper-chain decorations. This place makes me realize just how much the role of a doctor (if Rona Scott ever really was a doctor) has changed. No longer concerned with the ongoing well-being and general health of their patients, they're now here just to patch people up and keep them fighting as hard as possible for as long as they can. As with any war, countless numbers of people have suffered horrific injuries over the last year. Fortunately for them, most died quickly on the battlefield or later as a result of radiation sickness, infection, or malnutrition. Doctors like Rona Scott are rarely bothered by people like me, and it shows. This room, although still having the faintest smell of antiseptic, now has all the dignity and class of a back-street vehicle repair shop.

Scott walks over to where I'm standing, drops her cigarette, and stubs it out on the carpet. I've never been this close to her before, and I pray I never am again. She looks even worse than I do, as if she's been personally collecting samples of all the diseases and conditions she might still have to treat. Her breath is foul. The bottom of one of her earlobes is missing and has been patched up with adhesive tape that's covered with blood. I hope that little girl downstairs did it.

"Okay, make it quick. What's wrong with you?"

"Where do I start?"

"What hurts most?"

"Everything hurts," I answer honestly. "No appetite, lost a load of weight, fucking awful cough, sometimes there's blood when I piss . . ."

"You look bad."

"Thanks."

She picks up a flashlight and shines it into my eyes, sighing with effort every time she moves. I don't know whether she's as unfit as I feel or whether she just resents every second of time she's wasting on me. Is she like this with everyone? Is it because I'm not a battle-scarred soldier or one of Hinchcliffe's precious fighters?

"Strip to the waist," she orders, and I immediately do as I'm told, starting to shiver even before I'm done. I catch a brief glimpse of myself in a full-length mirror in the corner, and I have to look twice to be sure it's really me. I stare at my skeletal reflection. Christ, I can see every individual rib. I'm hollow chested. My chest goes in instead of out like it used to . . .

"Stand still," she says but I can't stop shaking. She peels off her grubby fingerless woolen gloves and starts touching me. I recoil from her unforgiving, icelike fingers. She roughly pushes and prods at my skin, working her way around my kidneys and belly with the bedside manner of a butcher working in an abattoir. I wince when she jabs her fingers into me, just below my rib cage, then wince again when she pinches my gut. Is she actually doing anything or just using me for stress relief? Finally she unearths a stethoscope from under a pile of papers and used dressings on a window ledge and presses it against various different parts of my back and front. Examination over, she tells me to get dressed.

"Well?" I ask as I quickly pull my clothes back on again.

"Not a lot to say, really."

"So what's wrong with me?"

She groans and plumps her heavy frame down into a chair, which creaks with surprise under her sudden weight. She rummages around on top of a desk and fishes out a half-smoked cigarette, then spends a few seconds picking dirt off the filter and flicking ash off the end before lighting up. Bitch is doing this on purpose, I'm sure of it. She's tormenting me, dragging this out unnecessarily. She's probably enjoying the feeling of power. She's probably heard what I can do with the Hate, and now she's showing me who's in charge.

"Were you close to any of the bombs?" she eventually asks.

"Which bombs?" I answer stupidly.

"*The* bombs. Remember? Great big friggin' explosions? Bright light? Mushroom clouds?"

"I was about ten miles from one of them. Might have been farther. Why?"

"Don't suppose it matters really, but it probably didn't help. We've probably all had enough of a dose by now. How long were you exposed for?"

"Exposed?"

"How long were you out there?"

"I don't know. I passed out for a while. I was picked up on the highway, but I don't know how long."

"Wouldn't have made much difference anyway," she says, drawing on her cigarette and looking past me at the rain running down the window. "No doubt we'll all end up going the same way in the end. Christ, they threw enough of that shit up into the atmosphere to do us all in."

"So what's wrong with me?" I ask again, although I think I already know the answer. I think I knew it before I came here. I've suspected for a while, but I didn't want to accept it.

"Cancer," she finally says, before adding a disclaimer, "probably."

For a second all I can think about is the way she said "probably," as if we're still in the old world and she's covering her back in case she's made a misdiagnosis and I sue. The fact she's just confirmed my worst fear goes almost unnoticed at first, but then it slowly starts to sink in. *Cancer.*

"Where?"

"What?"

"The cancer, where is it?"

"I'd do an MRI scan, but the power's down," she says sarcastically. "Hard to say for certain," she finally answers. "You've got something big in your gut, probably in your stomach, too, but there are bound to be more. Those are secondaries, I think, but I'm no expert. Truth is you're probably riddled with it by now."

I stare at her, my mouth hanging open, knowing what I want to ask next but not knowing if I can. She looks up at me, makes fleeting eye contact, then looks away again, anticipating the question that's inevitably coming.

"How long?"

There, I finally managed to spit the words out. Scott smokes again and pauses before answering.

"Don't know. No accurate way of telling anymore. Could be weeks, could be months. Maybe a year at the absolute outside if you're lucky."

"If I'm *lucky*?"

"Figure of speech."

"But isn't there anything you can do?"

"Like what? The National Health Service is falling apart at the seams, in case you hadn't noticed. There are no spare beds anywhere. Come to think of it, there are no beds."

"There must be something."

"You know the score, McCoyne. You've been around here long enough to know what it's like. There probably used to be a cure, or some surgical procedure that might have given you a little more time, but things have changed. If there was a drug, your chances of finding a good enough supply now are pretty much zero, and even if you did, it'd probably be contaminated and you wouldn't know how to administer it. No point wasting the little time you've got left worrying about it, if you ask me. And you did ask me, so I think you should listen."

"But there must be *something*," I say again.

She shakes her head. "Only thing you can do," she starts, giving me hope for that briefest of moments, "is take control and finish it sooner rather than later. Save yourself the pain."

"You're joking," I hear myself instinctively say, my brain completely failing to process everything I'm being told. "Tell me you're joking."

She just looks at me with disdain, then gets up and walks toward the door. She holds it open and waits for me to leave.

"Do I look like I'm joking? When was the last time you heard me laughing? When was the last time you heard anyone laughing? Tell you what, here's a good one for you: Find yourself a gun and shove it in your mouth. Take one bullet tonight before bedtime. Caution, may cause headaches and drowsiness."

Her insensitive comment goes unanswered. Suddenly the room is painfully quiet and empty, the only noise is the rain as it continues to hammer against the windows.

"Just go," she says. "There's nothing I can do for you. There's nothing anyone can do. Live with it till you die from it."

27

I'**M ON THE EDGE** of the empty development, almost back at the house. The thought of being shut away in the dark there again makes my heart sink, but it's the only place I've got left to go. Don't remember how I got here. Don't even remember leaving the factory.

Take a couple of days off, Hinchcliffe told me. Relax and straighten yourself out, he said. That was a fucking joke. Relax? Since when has anyone been able to relax in this vile, fucked-up world? Straighten myself out? Jesus, that's equally impossible. In the space of a day everything has become infinitely more complicated and yet immeasurably simpler at the same time: more to think about, but less time to do it. My mind flits constantly as I walk through the torrential rain, never settling on any one thing long enough to give me time to work anything out. If I'm not thinking about the fact I'm dying, I'm thinking about Peter Sutton, Joseph Mallon, and the crowd of Unchanged buried underground. And if I'm not thinking about them, I'm thinking about the little girl strapped to the chair in Rona Scott's fucking torture chamber. I can't get her out of my head, poor little cow. And if I'm not thinking about her, I'm thinking about my own kids, and that's never a good sign. Under it all there's just one main thought I keep coming back to: *I have a terminal disease.*

If this had happened to me in my old life, I'd be panicking now, and so would everyone else. I'd be thinking about the kids and Lizzie, checking whether I had any insurance coverage, avoiding all the difficult but necessary practical conversations that Liz would be having with me about the future I wasn't going to have . . . but today there's no panic and no noise, just a strange, uneasy calm—an empty black hole where my life used to be. I knew I wasn't well, and nothing the doctor said came as a great surprise, but at least until I'd spoken to her there was still an element of uncertainty and doubt, and I could still think I might wake up tomorrow and feel better. Now that's gone, and the only thing I know for sure is that I'm well and truly fucked. There was a guy at work who got cancer. We all had half a day off for his funeral, and the crematorium was packed. There were hundreds of people there—hundreds of lives affected by one death. Christ, no one will even notice when I go. If I die alone at the house, my body will just be left there to rot. No one gives a shit about me. They all just take what they need from me, then dump me.

I trudge slowly through the housing development, soaked through, laughing to myself at the bloody irony of it all. I've survived the war—countless attacks, battles, and fights, a gas chamber, bombings, a nuclear blast even—and yet it's my own flesh and bone that's finally going to finish me off as my body eats itself from the inside out.

I remember Adam, the crippled fighter I spent a few days with last summer, when the war was close to reaching its peak and the killing still felt brave and righteous. I often think about him. In constant pain and barely able to move without help, all he wanted to do was fight. In spite of his obvious physical limitations, the only thing that mattered to him was killing—wiping out the last of the Unchanged before they could get to him. It's not his determination or his aggression I remember most, though. It's his attitude to death. I sat with him as his body shut itself down, and I listened to him still talking about the next fight and the next kill as if he was going to go on forever. He was like an animal, blissfully unaware of his own mortality, living for each moment, not wallowing in self-pity and waiting for his life to reach its inevitably anticlimactic ending.

What I've learned today has forced me into a position that is almost the exact opposite of Adam's. He felt free and uninhibited; I'm restricted and trapped. His death meant nothing to him; mine is all I can think about. I'm already consumed by it; damned to spend my last days, weeks, and months (if I'm *lucky*) wondering how many more times I'll wake up and see the sun rise, how many more times I'll fall asleep, how many more fights I'll have or avoid, how many books I'll read or how many more times I'll go to certain places or see certain people . . .

I'm between a rock and a hard place—Hinchcliffe on one side, Peter Sutton on the other—and I know I have to either do something about it or take Rona Scott's advice and finish things right now. Last night I was on the verge of packing up and getting out of here for good, and Christ, I wish I had. Apart from suicide, leaving here is my only remaining option.

There's a light up ahead. Someone with a flashlight is coming toward me, a coat over his head. Even from this distance I can tell by his height and the way he's moving that it's Rufus. What the fuck does he want now? Why can't everyone just fuck off and leave me alone? There's always someone looking for me, and they all want something. None of them ever wants to do anything for me. Well, they can all go to hell. I've got nothing left to give.

"Danny," he yells as he flags me down, his voice sounding even more tense and unsure than usual. "Thank God I found you. Hinchcliffe wants to see you."

"Hinchcliffe can fuck off," I tell him, pushing past and continuing on toward the house. Rufus scurries after me, again overtaking and getting in my way, desperately trying to stop me.

"Where have you been?"

"Leave me alone, Rufus."

"I've been looking for you all day."

"Now you've found me."

"You have to come—"

"I don't *have* to do anything," I tell him. "You can tell Hinchcliffe to go fuck himself. I'm through running around after him. I quit."

"No, Danny," he says, beginning to sob, "you can't. Please. If I go back without you again he'll kill me."

"Then don't go back. Make a stand. Let someone else deal with him."

"I've never seen him like this before. Please, Danny, you've got to come."

Decision time. How much longer do I keep putting up with all this crap? I don't enjoy seeing Rufus like this, but at least he's still got a choice. My hand has been forced.

"Listen," I tell him, a hand on either shoulder, standing him upright and looking into his face, "I'm not going back. I'm finished with this place and with Hinchcliffe. I'm going to pack my stuff and get out of here, and if you've got any sense, I think you should do the same."

He just looks at me pathetically, dumbstruck and terrified. What he does next is up to him, but my mind's made up.

"You can't . . . I can't . . ."

"Yes you can, Rufus. Hinchcliffe is an evil cunt, and the only hold he's got over you is fear. Don't go back. Walk out of here tonight and find somewhere else. That's what I'm doing."

"But there is nowhere else. I—"

"Good luck, pal. I hope everything works out for you."

With that I force myself to move and sidestep him. When I look back I see he's still standing in the pouring rain in the middle of the street, just watching me go.

28

KNOW I'VE MADE a rod for my own back, but that's just how it is. Once Rufus plucks up the courage to go back and face Hinchcliffe (and I know he will—he'll be too scared not to, and he doesn't have the strength to walk away from this place), then the shit will hit the fan. He'll probably send Llewellyn or one of the others out here to find me. I know I'm doing the right thing, but I've managed to put myself under a whole load of pressure I didn't need. Well, you have to go with your gut feeling, I guess, even when your gut is apparently stuffed full of tumors.

The day has evaporated and it's late now, but I force myself to keep working, packing up as much stuff as I can carry before word filters down to Hinchcliffe that I'm no longer playing ball. The fucker is going to explode. I'll get as much together as I can, then maybe move it to another house nearby, just to get it away from here. I'll find a way of getting a car, and once I've done that, I'm gone. Good-bye Hinchcliffe and good-bye Lowestoft. Good-bye Rufus, too. I feel bad for him, but he has to make a stand. He doesn't even have to fight, just walk.

I've packed almost everything except for the food under the floor-boards. I head upstairs to see if there's anything of any worth left in the bedrooms. I rarely ever come up here because all I've ever needed to use in this house has been the living room and kitchen, so these upstairs rooms are just as the previous occupants left them, and it freaks me out. I spent a few nights up here when I first started using the house, but I couldn't sleep among the memories. Coming upstairs is like stepping back in time a year into a dust-covered reminder of the pre-war world. It's like the people who lived here just got up one morning and never came back, and that's probably exactly what happened. There's a pile of laundry still waiting to be put away on the end of an unmade double bed, and a board game on a kid's bedroom floor, abandoned before the last game was ever finished. There are pictures of the people who lived here on the wall, and I try not to look at them. I feel like their eyes are following me as I walk around what's left of their home.

The only things I keep up here are a few weapons. A pistol, a handful of bullets, and a grenade, all hidden in the dried-up water tank. The grenade's a souvenir. It came from the final battle in my hometown. Julia gave it to me before I—

What was that?

Shit. A car.

I run to the front bedroom window and look down. I can hear it but I can't see it. I strain to see and then pull my head back as it screeches around the corner at the end of the road. It overshoots the house; then the driver slams on the brakes and reverses back, wheels skidding on the icy road. Fuck, it's Hinchcliffe. What's he doing here? This is bad news. He must be extremely pissed off to have dragged himself out of the courthouse and come here. I stand to the side of the window and press myself back against the wall, trying to work out how I'm going to get out without him seeing me. I lean forward slightly and look out again. Rufus gets out of the car but tries to hang back, cowering away. Hinchcliffe grabs him, then marches up the drive, dragging him behind. He kicks the front door, then yells through the mail slot.

"Open up, McCoyne. Open this fucking door right now!"

What do I do? I press myself back against the wall again, too scared to go down but also too scared not to. I could try the attic, but I don't know if there's a ladder to get up, and even if there is, I'd be backing myself into a corner with no way out. Downstairs I hear the door begin to splinter and crack as Hinchcliffe boots it again and again. What the hell did Rufus say to him? I told him to stand up for himself when he came around here earlier, and is that what he's done? Or has he betrayed me so that Hinchcliffe would go easy on him? My fear suddenly increases massively—Christ, what if he had me followed earlier? What if he knows about Peter Sutton and the Unchanged? Worse still, what if I was wrong about Sutton? What if he's double-crossed me and told Hinchcliffe I'm the one harboring Unchanged to get himself off the hook?

"Open this fucking door, McCoyne!" Hinchcliffe yells again, and I know my best option is to get out through the back of the house. I'll go down and slip out, then come back later as I'd planned and fetch my stuff. I check around the edge of the window frame again. There's only Hinchcliffe and Rufus here, no other fighters. I could hide in any one of the hundreds of other empty houses around this estate and they'd be none the wiser.

On the street below, poor old Rufus tries to make a run for it. Hinchcliffe knows what he's up to and he's having none of it. He turns on him in a heartbeat and kicks his legs out from under him. Rufus crashes down on his back on the driveway with a heavy thump and a horrible yelp of pain. Hinchcliffe kicks him in the kidney, screaming at him that he's not going anywhere until they've found me, then takes another run at the door.

Got to move fast.

I start to run through the house, but I'm not even halfway down the stairs when the door flies open, finally giving way under the force of Hinchcliffe's boot. I try to turn back but trip and land on my backside on the bottom step as splinters of broken wood and shards of glass go flying in all directions around me.

"McCoyne," he yells when he sees me. "Where the fuck have you been?"

"Upstairs. I was asleep," I tell him, trying to lie my way out of trouble. "I'm sick, Hinchcliffe. I didn't know you were here."

I can't tell whether or not he believes me. He turns and grabs hold of Rufus, then hauls him into the house. Rufus stands and stares at me with a petrified expression on his face. He's been badly beaten. His right eye is swollen shut, and there's blood running down his chin. At least he's managing to hold my gaze. That's a good sign, I hope. I don't think he'd be able to look at me if he'd told Hinchcliffe what I said earlier. Poor bastard's no good at handling situations like this.

"Where have you been?" Hinchcliffe asks again.

"I already told you, asleep upstairs."

"No, earlier. I sent Rufus to find you and you weren't here."

"When?" I ask, deliberately acting dumb, hoping he'll give me some details to help flesh out my story. "I'm not well. I had a few drinks and I took some stuff to help me sleep . . ."

Hinchcliffe glares at me, the shadows and darkness making his face look uncomfortably angular and fierce, accentuating his anger. "What time was that?"

"What?"

"You heard me."

"I don't know, honest. I don't wear a watch. It was dark and—"

"What about earlier? Where were you this afternoon?"

"I went to see Rona Scott."

"I know about that, she told me. I'm talking about before then."

I can't risk telling him anything. "I don't know. Look, Hinchcliffe, I'm sorry if I wasn't around. Did Scott tell you what she told me? Thing is, I'm dying. I've just been walking around, trying to get my head together so I could—"

"We're all dying," he interrupts. "Now stop pissing around and tell me where you were when the plane flew over."

"Plane? What plane?"

What the hell is he talking about now? The skies are empty, have been for months. Even the birds are dying out. The last thing I saw flying was the missile carrying the warhead that destroyed my home-town. I don't feel any less nervous now, but suddenly the pressure is fractionally reduced. Is this the reason he's come out here? Unless he thinks I was flying this plane (which would be impossible), then maybe I'm not the real focus of his fury tonight.

"Just before midday," he explains slowly, virtually spitting each word at me, "a plane flew over the town."

"And you think I've got something to do with it?"

"Don't be so fucking stupid," he snaps (confirming my suspicions), "of course I don't think that. I don't know what you do out here on your own, but I know you're not flying fucking airplanes."

"What, then?"

Frustrated, Hinchcliffe turns his back on me and kicks what's left of the door shut. Rufus flinches at the noise, then shuffles farther away, trying to move deeper into the house and hoping neither of us will notice. I start to feel marginally more confident, as it seems I'm not the problem here. Someone else has pissed him off.

"*I* run this place," he says, turning around and advancing toward me menacingly, pointing his finger into my face. I take a step back to get out of his way and trip and fall back onto the stairs again. I've never seen him like this before. He's incensed, barely able to keep his anger suppressed. I need to watch my step here and choose my next words carefully. Don't want to do anything that's going to push him over the edge.

"I know you run Lowestoft. Everyone here knows it."

"Yes, but those fuckers up there don't," he yells, jabbing his finger skyward.

"Yes, but—"

"But nothing. I need to keep control here. I need to know exactly what's going on. I can't have people doing things that I can't control, you understand?"

I'm not sure I do.

"So did they just fly over? Just happen to come across the town by chance?"

He shakes his head and massages his temples. "No, they flew circuits. Put on a proper fucking show. They might have found us by chance, but they definitely checked everything out properly before they left."

"So what type of plane was it?"

"What?" he asks, confused.

"What type of plane? Military? A jet or bomber?"

He shakes his head again. "No, nothing like that."

"What, then?"

"Just a little plane. Two- or four-seater, something like that."

"So what's the problem? Someone probably just got lucky and managed to get a plane up and—"

"What's the problem?!" he screams at me, storming forward again, now so close that I can feel his hot, booze-tinged breath on my face. "What's the problem? The problem is that they're doing something I can't. I can't allow anyone to have that kind of advantage over me."

"A little plane? Is that really such an advantage?"

"Well, if you'd been here like you should have been, McCoyne, you'd have seen the effect it had. *That's* what I'm talking about. When that plane flew over, every single fucker in Lowestoft stopped what they were doing and looked up at it. My fighters, the underclass—all of them."

"Yes, but a two-seater plane . . . Come on, what are they going to do?"

"Nothing right now, but it's what they *could* do that's important. They've got one plane today, they could have two tomorrow. They could train pilots and have a whole goddamn fleet up in the air before we know it. Now they know we're here they'll be back. They could drop bombs on us and there'd be nothing we could do."

"That's not likely to happen, is it? Like I said, it's probably just someone who got lucky."

"I know that and you know that, McCoyne, but the hundreds of dumb bastards lining the streets of this town don't."

"So hunt them out. Try to get whoever it was on the team."

For a moment he's quiet. He leans back against the wall and runs his fingers through his hair, then massages his temples. I'm sure he's already thought of that. He's probably already sent his fighters out there hunting the plane and its pilot—and if and when he finds them, I know he'll leave them with no choice but to work with him.

"Thing is," he says, sounding marginally calmer again, "seeing people flying around affects what the people here think about me. They know I don't have any planes, so they automatically assume those bastards up there are superior. This is eroding my authority and putting unnecessary strain on the control I've got here. I can't let that happen, you understand?"

"Yes, but—"

He holds up his hand and stops me talking.

"There's also the very real possibility that they *might* attack from the skies. What would I do then? Have people standing on rooftops chucking stones back at them if they fly low enough?"

"The chances of them attacking are remote—"

"How do you know that? Anyway, a chance is a chance. It gives them a tactical advantage, and we have to do something about it."

"We?" I say stupidly. Hinchcliffe glares at me again, then starts pacing around the living room. Rufus scuttles out of the way as he moves toward him. Hinchcliffe spots the wrench I leave lying around for self-defense. He picks it up and starts swinging it, passing it from hand to hand and feeling its weight.

"Here's what's going to happen," he announces. "I'm sending Llewellyn and a few others out at first light to find those bastards. Llewellyn thinks he's worked out where they're likely to have come from. He'll find them and either bring them back to me or get rid of them. And you're going with them."

"Me? Why?"

"Don't pretend you don't fucking know. Same reason I always send you. You're so fucking insignificant that no one gives you a second glance. You can assess the situation better than most, and if you can't assess it, you can at least spy on the fuckers and tell me what's going on."

"But I'm sick."

"So? I'm not asking you to run a fucking marathon."

I try to think of a valid reason that'll make him change his mind, but I can't.

"Okay," I say, desperate to pacify him but already trying to think of ways to get away from this mess once and for all. I'm relieved when he starts walking back toward the door. Rufus hesitates, then follows in his footsteps, unsure what to do next. Clumsy bastard knocks another stack of books over, then walks into Hinchcliffe when he stops suddenly.

"Sorry, Hinchcliffe," he mumbles pathetically, cowering back. Hinchcliffe ignores him and slowly turns back around to face me.

"Where were you, Danny?"

"What?"

"When the plane flew over, where were you? You still haven't told me."

"I don't know when that was. Like I said, I'm sick. I went for a walk to try to clear my head, and when I got back I went to see your doctor."

"Does it affect your hearing?"

"What?"

"This 'sickness' of yours, makes you deaf, does it?"

"No."

"So how come you didn't hear anything? They were circling Lowestoft for almost an hour, maybe even longer. How could you not have heard it?"

"I don't know. How am I supposed to answer that? I've had things on my mind. Like I said, I could have been asleep or down by the beach . . ."

"It's all a bit convenient, isn't it?"

"Is it?"

He stares at me, unblinking. Does he know more than he's letting on? My pulse is racing, but I hold his gaze. He finally breaks eye contact and looks away, and the relief is immense.

"No, probably not."

"What, then? What are you saying?"

"You talk the talk, Danny, but do you really understand how important this might be?"

"Yes, you've just explained."

"So you understand that it's crucial for me to keep control of this place?"

"Yes."

"So why weren't you here?"

"You said to take some time off. You said you didn't need me."

"I thought you were smarter than that."

"What?"

"I might have told you I didn't have anything I needed you to do for a couple of days, but I didn't say you could go away on a fucking vacation."

"I didn't go on vacation, I just—"

He holds up his hand (and my wrench) again to silence me. Arrogant bastard.

"In future you'll be here exactly when I want you to be. Understand?"

"Have I ever not been? Have I ever—"

"I need to know who I can trust, Danny."

"You can trust me. You know you can."

"You let me down today. Llewellyn could have been on his way by now. If you'd been there he could have followed the damn plane out of town. Now we've given them a head start and they could be anywhere."

"They're flying, Hinchcliffe. They could be anywhere anyway."

He takes another couple of steps closer, and I freeze. *Keep your fucking mouth shut, you idiot*, I scream to myself.

"When you get back with Llewellyn," he seethes, "you're going to collect all your shit from this house and find somewhere to stay in the middle of town, closer to the courthouse."

"But—"

"I'm not asking, I'm telling."

"What difference does it make?" I protest, desperate not to give up my privacy, remembering too late that I'm not planning on hanging around. Hinchcliffe moves closer still, and I immediately shut up, regretting my outburst. Then, with a grunt of sudden, unexpected anger, he spins around and smashes the wrench into Rufus's face. Rufus immediately drops to the ground, and I stare at him, stunned. He lies on his back, arms and legs still moving, face covered with blood, whimpering through broken teeth. Hinchcliffe leans down and smacks him in the head again, finishing him off. He stands up, one foot either side of the now motionless body, and thrusts the bloody wrench at me.

"Don't ever give me any reason not to trust you again."

"I won't . . ."

"I don't know where the fuck you were today, but from now on you do exactly what you're told. You don't ask questions, you just do what I tell you. Understand?"

"I understand," I say quietly, looking down at the battered body of my friend.

"Get the stuff you need together. We're heading back into town. And don't ever fuck with me again, Danny, because you *will* regret it."

29

I'M IN THE BACK of an armor-plated van with Llewellyn and three other fighters, scared shitless. This is my worst nightmare. Llewellyn's never trusted me, and he's been waiting for a chance to get me away from Lowestoft on my own. There's something different about the way he's acting toward me today, and the longer this journey lasts, the more convinced I am that he's probably the one who persuaded Hinchcliffe I should be part of this pointless expedition so he could get rid of me. Fucker's going to kill me and concoct some bullshit story to explain to Hinchcliffe why his prize pet is dead.

The four members of my armed guard talk to each other in secretive whispers, deliberately excluding me. I'm used to it. I've felt like an outsider for as long as I've been in Lowestoft. No matter how I look at it, I seem to have a foot in neither camp. I'm neither fighter nor underclass; not like the rest of them, but not Unchanged either, just an unwanted, mixed-breed outcast. Today my paranoia has been ramped up by several hundred percent. Whatever the intentions of these men are, I won't know for sure what they're planning until they make their move. I have to try to stay one step ahead of the game, like I learned to do with the Unchanged. I have to hope that, wherever we end up, I'll be able to find a way of giving them the slip and getting away. What I'll do after I've broken cover is anyone's guess. I don't suppose it matters anymore. I'm not eating, hardly drinking . . . I'll just find a rock to crawl under and sit it out. I can't waste any more time thinking about it. I might not have any time left.

Llewellyn sits up front next to the driver, Ben Healey. In the back with me are two other men, handpicked for their aggression and strength: Chandra—the disfigured guard I saw outside Hinchcliffe's hotel breeding center—and Swales, a cocky and aggressive young bastard I've had little to do with until today.

We're in radio contact with Hinchcliffe, but communications with Lowestoft have been brief and infrequent. I'm not going to risk saying anything, but they surely must realize we're never going to find that plane today. Christ, it could have come from anywhere. Overseas, even. No one knows for sure what's happening in other countries (it's hard enough finding out what's going on here), but I'm guessing everywhere else must be in as dire and desperate a state as this place is. Regardless, the fact remains: Looking for the plane and its pilot is going to be like looking for a needle in a pile of a thousand massive haystacks. What if it came from somewhere on the other side of the huge radioactive scar that now stretches much of the length of the country? There's no point trying to tell Llewellyn; he's never going listen to me. Instead he'll just concentrate on his impossible task and won't question anything. If Hinchcliffe told these morons to kill themselves I think most of them probably would, but it's more likely they're going to kill me.

Llewellyn glances over his shoulder and makes eye contact with me, and my blood runs cold. This bastard seems to be enjoying himself. He can't wait to be shot of me. The longer I'm around, the more he resents the fact that I'm useful to Hinchcliffe. Fighters can be replaced, but me . . . I'm unique (unfortunately), and Llewellyn doesn't like it.

I peer out of the wire-mesh-covered window to my side and see that we've entered the outskirts of what used to be the city of Norwich. It's an empty, lifeless place now, nothing more than a desolate shell. I don't know what happened here during the war, but it obviously wasn't a big enough concern to warrant being nuked. Over the last few months it's been systematically stripped clean, first by Thacker, then Hinchcliffe. Too large and unwieldy a place to be governed effectively, and not as geographically well placed as the port of Lowestoft, it's just been abandoned, left to decay.

A sudden sharp crackle of static comes from the radio. Llewellyn grabs it quickly and talks. I strain to hear what he's saying, but it's impossible. He turns around and glances back at me again, and his expression says more than a thousand words ever would. He looks on edge, nervous almost. Now I'm certain that he's going to try to get rid of me—but why now? Why all the way out here?

I'm stuck in this van until we stop moving. *Stick to the plan,* I tell myself repeatedly. *Wait until they let you out, then fight, keep fighting, and if and when you get the chance, run like fuck.*

30

THE VAN GRINDS TO a sudden, shuddering halt alongside a ruined department store. Its front wall has collapsed, spilling rubble out onto the street and leaving every individual level of the building open to the elements. We're parked up on the pavement, hidden by a mountain of fallen masonry, well out of sight. Across the way there's a road sign pointing back toward Lowestoft, and for the first time ever I almost wish I was back there. Anywhere but here.

"Out," Llewellyn orders from the front seat. Chandra grabs my arm. I panic and try to fight him off, but he's stronger than me, and all my struggling does is encourage his buddy Swales to take hold of my other arm. Llewellyn runs around to the back of the van and yanks the door open, and between them they frog-march me out onto the street, picking me up as if I'm made of paper. Llewellyn has a pistol in his hand, and I don't doubt for a second that he'll use it. I force myself not to try to fight just yet, remembering how I used to be able to swallow down the Hate and remain in control even when I was neck deep in vile Unchanged. I did it yesterday, and I can do it now. The element of surprise is all I have left. I have to bide my time and catch these bastards off guard.

"Llewellyn, I just—"

"Don't talk, just move," he says, throwing my backpack at me, then shoving me hard between the shoulder blades. "We don't have long. You're an unnecessary complication, McCoyne."

What the hell did he mean by that? I try to ask, but no one's listening. With Llewellyn behind me, Healey in front, and the other two on either side, they've got me boxed in. I don't understand why they needed to bring me all this distance just to put a bullet in my head. The four men march at a speed I find difficult to match, but Llewellyn keeps me moving, pushing me in the back whenever I slow down. I want to fight. For the first time in weeks, I want to attack and fight back, but all the anger and aggression I used to have, the fury and the rage that used to burn inside me, are gone now and there's nothing left. Before today there was always a way out, but I can't see one today. My only option now is to try to break free and run, and I know I probably don't have either the strength or the speed to outrun one of these fighters, let alone all of them. It's the four of them against me, and in my heart I know that this time I'm finally fucked.

We stop at a traffic island, and Healey consults a folded-up map, checking our location against what's left of our surroundings. "Not far now," he says, filling me with the same cloying sense of dread I remember feeling when I was being led blindfolded through the convent with Joseph Mallon. Now, just for a single dangerous second, I'm distracted thinking about him again. I almost envy him and the rest of the Unchanged, buried in their bunker beneath the farm, isolated from the alien world above them. Maybe some of what Peter Sutton said yesterday was right. They're safe, I'm screwed. Who's the most sensible?

"You nervous, McCoyne?" Llewellyn asks, breaking ranks and catching my eye. I try to play it cool but fail completely, and my terror must be obvious. His face remains passive and unemotional at first, but then he can't help himself and breaks into a wide, sadistic smile. He's actually enjoying this. Evil motherfucker. "Do you think we're going to find any airplanes today?" he sneers. Chandra sniggers and tightens his grip on my arm when I try to react. This isn't right. If they knew how sick I am, would they let me go? Maybe I can persuade them to free me because I'll probably be dead soon anyway and no one will know any different. It's not like I'm going to go back to Lowestoft and tell Hinchcliffe what they've done. Who the hell am I kidding? Do I really expect hard, emotionless fuckers like this to show any compassion? I don't even bother trying to fight, saving my energy instead so I can make my final break for freedom when the moment comes. By the look of things, that's not going to be long. We duck down through a hole in a chain-link fence, then cross a patch of scrubland. My nerves increase with every step. I can't help myself . . .

"Whatever you're going to do to me, just do it."

Llewellyn looks at me, puzzled. "What makes you think we're going to do anything to you? You're paranoid, man." He turns to the others. "This it?" he asks.

Healey nods. Chandra lets go of me and I try to run. They're too damn fast for me. Llewellyn shoots out his arm, grabs me, and pulls me back into line.

"Don't," he warns ominously.

The area of town we've reached seems to have suffered slightly less damage than elsewhere, and most of the buildings around us are still largely intact. Following some predetermined plan, my four-fighter guard suddenly disperses. Healey and Swales go one way; Chandra stops walking and takes a radio out from his backpack. Llewellyn still has ahold of me, and he keeps me moving forward. I try to pry his fingers off my arm, but he's having none of it. He tightens his grip.

"Just do it," I beg pathetically, "please . . ."

"Pull yourself together, you miserable dick," he says as he drags me toward a wide-fronted, Gothic-looking building. What the hell is this place? It's too big to be a church. Was it some kind of school? A prison, city hall, or some other public office before the war? He opens the arch-shaped white wooden door, looks around, then pushes me inside. He shuts it behind us and finally lets me go. "Listen, I'm not going to kill you. I've got better things to do today."

"Then why did you—"

"You shouldn't even be here. Fucking Hinchcliffe. Don't know why he sent you out with us."

It takes my eyes a few seconds to become accustomed to the light indoors. We're standing in the entrance hall of some kind of museum. It has the unmistakable air of the past about it; a bubble of the old, old world, trapped here in the rubble of the new.

"What are we doing here?"

"It's funny how things work out sometimes," Llewellyn says, although from where I'm standing there's nothing funny about it at all. "You never know what you're going to find around the corner these days."

I follow him up several flights of a wide marble staircase, legs weak with effort and relief, to the third floor of the building. We pass glass cabinets filled with remnants of long-dead people and long-lost things. This place is remarkably ornate and well preserved, and I find myself remembering a time when there was more to life than just hunting and killing and fighting to stay alive. There's some damage here (there's some damage everywhere), but many of the paintings, statues, and displays remain virtually untouched. None of this is important now. What's happened to us all has made who we used to be completely irrelevant. No one's interested in art, nor in any other aspect of the world before the war. It's strange to think that you could be the owner of an original Picasso, Rembrandt, or Van Gogh but it wouldn't matter a damn if no one would trade it with you for food. It's bizarre to think that all the paint-covered canvases around the world that used to command obscene, almost unimaginable prices are worth less in real terms now than a single can of beans.

I'm allowing myself to become distracted by my surroundings, and I can't afford to be. Llewellyn's radio crackles again, and he holds it up to his ear, taking a few steps away from me as he does so. A tinny voice bursts from the speaker, but I can't make out what it's saying. Llewellyn seems to understand perfectly.

"We're ready out here. Healey's on the ground for you. We'll be waiting in the museum."

"What's this all about, Llewellyn? Why are we here?"

"You'll see," he says, enjoying making me squirm. "You've got about fifteen minutes to wait. Have a wander around, but don't try and get out, 'cause Healey's guarding the door downstairs and I've told him to break your legs if you try anything." He laughs. "Relax and enjoy the exhibits! Soak up the atmosphere."

Fifteen minutes feels like fifteen hours. Llewellyn watches me continually. Eventually something distracts him outside and his expression immediately changes and becomes more serious. He beckons me over and I stand next to him in front of a tall, floor-to-ceiling window and look down over the patch of sloping, overgrown grassland we walked across to get here.

"Your friend Hinchcliffe," he finally says, "isn't quite as smart and all-powerful as he thinks he is."

"He's not my friend" is my immediate reaction.

"Figure of speech. You know what I mean." He seems about to tell me more when there's another ugly burst of noise from the radio. "Got it," he says after listening to another indecipherable transmission. He calls down to Healey, who I can see on the ground below us. Healey looks up, radio in hand. "They're here," Llewellyn tells him.

"Who's here?" I ask, confused.

"I fucking hate Hinchcliffe," Llewellyn says. "I know it's not about who you like or don't like anymore, but I fucking hate him with his stupid long hair and his fucking attitude."

"So why have you stuck by him?"

"Same reason you have. Like it or not, the bastard has influence and he's hard as nails. It's better to have him on your side than end up fighting against him."

"So is that what you're planning? Some kind of rebellion? An uprising in Lowestoft?"

"It's not about what *I'm* planning, but you're not a million miles off the mark."

"What, then?"

Llewellyn looks as if he's about to answer, but then he stops. He stares out of the window into the distance again, then presses his ear against it. He lifts his head from the glass, then taps it with his finger. For a few seconds I hear nothing, and I'm starting to wonder if my hearing is as screwed as the rest of my worn-out body, but then I gradually become aware of a deep, low rumbling noise. It quickly gets louder, and it's soon so deep and so loud that the window starts to rattle and shake in its frame. Then I see a tank appear. Belching black exhaust fumes into the air, it bulldozes its way across the grassland, caterpillar tracks churning the ground, and stops directly below us. There's a crudely painted red and white circular insignia on its front and its side. I've seen those markings before . . . I look up again and see that the tank was just the first of several vehicles now moving toward the museum in convoy. Christ, what is this? Most of the advancing machines are clearly military (although there are several civilian cars and bikes here, too, bulked up with improvised armor plating and other defenses), and all of them are decorated with the same red and white concentric circles as the trucks I saw in Southwold. Nestled right in the middle of it all are two heavily armored troop carriers. Where the hell did this bunch come from? The traffic fans out, leaving a space for the first troop carrier to drive closer to the museum. It stops a short distance from the entrance, brakes hissing.

"Bang on time."

"Llewellyn, what is this?"

"You ever heard that expression, keep your friends close and your enemies closer?"

"Yes, but—"

"Well, get ready to meet your friends. Word to the wise, McCoyne: Doesn't matter who you are or what you can do, these days all that matters is staying on the team with the fuckers who've got the most muscle and the biggest guns, and that's this crowd. This is just the advance party."

The door of the troop carrier slides open, and somewhere between ten and fifteen figures quickly emerge, all of them wearing similarly colored clothing—a very basic, improvised uniform of sorts. The troops form a loose protective guard of two roughly parallel lines that stretch from the vehicle right up to the door of the museum. A number of other people follow them out of the transport and walk through the gap that's opened up between them. I see two men, then a woman, then a small, white-haired man who walks with a stick . . .

"Who are they?" I ask.

"See the old guy?" Llewellyn says, with something approximating pride and genuine emotion in his voice. "That's Chris Ankin."

I can't believe what I'm hearing.

"Chris Ankin? *The* Chris Ankin?"

"Mind your p's and q's," he says as he tugs my arm and leads me back down the stairs. "Prime Minister, President, Commander in Chief, Sir, Your Highness—call him what you like, he's the Boss Man now."

31

LEWELLYN AND CHANDRA ARE whisked away, and Healey returns to the van. I'm left alone with Swales. He seems almost as bemused by events as I am, and I get the distinct impression he's here just to make up the numbers. We watch from a ground-floor window as the new arrivals quickly set up camp. Some build fires and erect temporary shelters. Others are dispatched into what's left of Norwich, presumably to look for fuel and supplies and anything else of value. They're working *together*, no hint of aggression or any pecking order.

Swales notices a line forming outside a mess tent. He heads straight for it, and I follow him. We're given a little food without question—some kind of bland, rice-based paste and a few thin crackers—and a mug of coffee each and left to our own devices again. It's not great tasting, but it's not half-cooked dog, either, and I manage to swallow a few mouthfuls. We sit on a bench in a sheltered alcove just outside the museum building, out of the way of everyone else but still close enough to watch. It's funny, less than an hour ago Swales was definitely one of "them," but now we're thick as thieves, relatively comfortable in each other's company because there's someone new in town, neither of us having any immediate desire to mix with these strangers.

There's controlled activity all around us still as these people, whoever they are, continue to establish their makeshift base. Each person is carrying out their allotted task without question or complaint, people who were obviously fighters working alongside people who obviously weren't . . . it's a pale imitation, but it's almost like things used to be. This is like what I saw in Southwold, albeit on a much grander scale. So what's the connection? Are they all stealing from Hinchcliffe?

"You gonna eat that?" Swales asks, nudging me with his elbow and nodding at my practically untouched food.

"You want it?"

He snatches the plate and starts scooping up the rice paste with clumsy fingers, smearing nearly as much of it over his face as he manages to get into his mouth.

"Good?"

"Good," he answers, wolfing down a cracker. "I'll eat anything, me," he continues, showering me with crumbs.

"So I can see."

Swales obviously isn't the sharpest tool in the box, but his strength and size (and no doubt his track record and ongoing appetite for violence) have helped him become one of Hinchcliffe's "elite." He's strong, impressionable, and, I expect, easily manipulated—perfect fighter fodder.

"So what do you think about all this, then?" he asks.

That's a surprisingly difficult question to answer. These days it seems that something happens every few minutes that skews my perspective on everything again. Everything feels fluid. Nothing sits still.

"Depends what 'all this' is, doesn't it?"

"Don't get you."

"First I thought we were out plane spotting, then I thought Llewellyn was going to kill me, and now I'm sitting having lunch with half an army. I'll be honest with you, Swales, I don't have a fucking clue what's going on anymore."

"I got told nothing. Llewellyn said he'd got a job for me, that's all. Didn't know nothing about all this."

"So what do you think about it all?"

Swales has a naïveté and innocence that may well prove to be his undoing. He talks candidly, barely even thinking about what he's saying. Still, that probably makes him more honest and reliable than most of the backstabbing bastards Hinchcliffe surrounds himself with.

"Got to be a good thing, ain't it?"

"Suppose."

"This is like things used to be."

"I guess."

He pauses to eat more food. Then, when his second plate's almost clear, he speaks again.

"You know what I used to do for a job, Danny?"

"No."

"I used to flip burgers 'cause that was the only job I could find. There's plenty about the old times I miss—"

"But not flipping burgers?"

"Definitely *not* flipping burgers!" He laughs. "I miss my mom and my brother, even though he turned out to be one of them. Miss my buddies . . . Don't get me wrong, I wouldn't go back for any money, but I wouldn't say I'm happy with the way everything is, you know?"

"Like what?"

"Like the fighting. You do it 'cause you have to, but that don't make it right. You can't just kick back and relax like you used to. You've always got to be on the lookout. Llewellyn says you got to stay one step ahead of everybody else, 'cause the one guy you're not watching is the one who'll creep up behind you and kill you."

"So what do you think about that? Is he right?"

"Suppose. I'm just tired of it, that's all. But what's happening here, what that Chris Ankin guy's doing, that sounds like a better option to me. Llewellyn says Ankin's gonna see all of us right in the end."

Poor bastard, he really does believe everything he's told. Then again, I think to myself as I look around this place, maybe I'm the one who's wrong. He may have been a long way from the front line of battle, but

Ankin, more than anyone else, has been in control from the start. He's not like Hinchcliffe. Hinchcliffe was just someone who just happened to be in the right place at the right time and took advantage of what he found to force himself into power. Ankin is different. And to have kept control for so long through so much, he must have done the right thing by his people. There's a world of difference between the organized, uniformed people here and Hinchcliffe's army of a couple of hundred individual fighters. Johannson, Thacker, and many others have proved how tenuous positions of power have become, and yet this weak-looking, white-haired politician has outlasted them all.

Maybe Peter Sutton was wrong and our species *can* take a step back from the abyss? Who the hell am I kidding? I'll believe it when I see it.

"It'll take more than this bunch to make everything right again."

"That's the best part," Swales says excitedly, "there *is* more than this bunch. That's what Llewellyn thinks, anyway. He says there's thousands more of them on the way to Norwich. Thousands of them!"

AN UNEXPECTEDLY COMFORTABLE NIGHT'S sleep on the floor in a quiet corner of the museum is rudely interrupted at first light. Despite the fact that the first thing I see is Llewellyn's foul, scowling face glaring down at me, I immediately feel different today. Optimism is too strong a word, but there's no denying that, unexpectedly, things look more hopeful this morning than they have in months. The illusion doesn't last long, when I start coughing my guts up and I remember what Rona Scott told me. If really this does turn out to be the dawn of a brave new world, I'm probably not going to get to see very much of it.

Llewellyn is chaperoning me this morning. I manage to get outside to take a piss in the half inch of snow that's fallen overnight, but before I've even finished shaking myself dry, he's already dragging me back indoors. He seems uncharacteristically anxious as he herds me into a large, busy room on the ground floor of the museum and tells me to sit down and wait. I don't have to wait long to find out why.

In a week that has been crammed with bizarre events, this takes the cake. The events of the last few days in particular have been unbelievably surreal, like a crazy, barely controlled chain reaction, and it feels like the more I try to shut myself off and pull away from the madness, the worse it gets. Being forced to contribute to Hinchcliffe's fucked-up breeding program was bad enough, but even that paled into insignificance alongside the unspeakable things that Peter Sutton showed me underground. In the space of a couple of days I've been told I'm dying; I've watched Rufus, the closest thing I had to a friend, be killed in front of me for no reason other than Hinchcliffe's spite and frustration; I've convinced myself I was going to be executed . . . and now this? Here I am, in a dust-covered museum café, sitting across a table from Chris Ankin. *The* Chris Ankin. The ex–government official who broadcast that message I heard so long ago: the call to arms for all us fighters who, until he dared to speak out, had felt persecuted and alone. The man whose face I saw on a computer screen in the back of a van when my life changed direction again. The man who, by word of mouth alone it seemed, managed to coordinate an invisible army that marched into Unchanged settlements and stirred them up so much that they imploded and tore themselves apart. *The* Chris Ankin. The closest thing to a true leader we've had. Until now I'd never actually stopped to think about how much I owe this man. Without his words I'd have remained alone and unprepared for the onset of war. Without his planning and foresight I'd never have made it back into the city, I'd probably never have learned to hold the Hate, and, most importantly, I would never have shared those last few precious minutes with Lizzie and Ellis. It seems that whenever I cross paths with Ankin, everything changes. Today that makes me feel nervous. Why is he here, and why does he suddenly want to talk to me?

As usual I'm like a fifth wheel and the longer I have to wait, the worse I feel. Right now Ankin is busy talking to someone. The guy crouching down next to him is clean-shaven and relatively smartly dressed. It's strange; I look around at the people who arrived here with Ankin and in some ways it's almost as if I'm looking at another race, another species even. Without realizing I'm doing it I make a pathetic attempt to straighten my long, straggly hair with the tips of my fingers, as if it's going to make a difference. These people are far better organized than anyone else I've seen since the war ended, better fed and fitter, too. Most of them wear something resembling a uniform, they have a clear command structure that appears to work, they are regimented and controlled, and they each have clearly defined jobs to do. In comparison to the military forces I remember from before the war, even the Unchanged, they're still amateurish and ill disciplined, but they appear so much more capable than anyone else I've come across since the bombs were dropped. I thought that what I'd seen in Lowestoft was as close to civilization as we were ever going to get, but these people are on another level altogether. They remind me of the ragtag, cobbled-together armies I used to see in TV footage from war-torn African and Middle Eastern conflicts a long time ago: the warlord ruled militias that used to butcher, rape, and pillage their way through starving, nomadic populations, diverting aid cash and using drug money to keep themselves stocked up with weapons. Except, incredibly, these people seem *less* aggressive. They're armed to the teeth, and each person here (me included) has probably carried out more killings and been involved in more atrocities than any of those so-called freedom fighters I remember, but now they seem calm, assured, and in complete control.

The man talking to Ankin stands up and disappears, and Ankin finally turns his attention to me. I feel my pulse quicken.

"Danny McCoyne," he says. "Llewellyn's told me a lot about you."

"Has he?" I reply quickly, silently hoping that the bit he *hasn't* heard about me includes the time I spent underground with more than thirty Unchanged recently without killing them.

"He says you're a useful man to have around."

"He's got a strange way of showing it. I thought he was going to kill me yesterday."

Ankin smiles broadly. "We all have to keep our cards close to our vests these days, Danny. Your friend Hinchcliffe wouldn't have taken it well if he knew Llewellyn was working for me."

"You don't know the half of it," I tell him, "and by the way, in spite of what you might have heard, Hinchcliffe's definitely no friend of mine."

"You know him well, though."

"Better than most, I suppose. Not through choice."

"I understand that. Kind of an awkward character, by all accounts."

"Kind of a cunt, actually."

"Indeed. Anyway, back to you. I'm sure you've got more than a few questions you'd like to ask about what you've seen."

He smiles at me—a glimpse of an obviously fake and well-rehearsed politician's smile from way back—and he studies my face intently. The power of his stare and his undeniably authoritarian presence is such that everything else seems to fade away and lose focus until it feels like we're the only people left in the room.

"I'd like to know where you came from and where you've been. Why's it taken you so long to get here?"

He thinks before answering, still staring at me, still smiling. "Tell me, Danny," he finally says, leaning forward and, again like an old-time politician, avoiding answering my question by asking another of his own, "how much do you know about this strange new world of ours?"

"Not a lot. I know some of what's happening around Lowestoft, not much else."

"That's about as much as I'd expect. Don't you think it's strange how much things have changed over the last year or so? I'm guessing that this time last year you were probably stuck in a rut like most of the rest of us, just going through the motions and getting through life as best you could, one day at a time."

How right he is . . .

"Now you can do pretty much what you want, when you want, can't you? Your priorities have completely changed, of course, and you have to work harder to get the basics like food and water and such stuff, but you're your own master now. You're less restricted and held back than you used to be."

Apart from the specter of Hinchcliffe that looms over me constantly, he's right again, although he's not telling me anything I don't already know.

"But there's an obvious paradox here, isn't there?" he announces.

"Is there?"

"Yes. Your world's suddenly gotten a lot smaller, hasn't it? A year ago you could switch on your TV or go online and you could find out in seconds what was happening pretty much anywhere around the world. You could send an e-mail or pick up the phone and talk instantly to people in other countries."

"Right, and now we only know what's happening immediately around us," I interrupt, anticipating what I think he's going to say next. "Anything could be happening elsewhere, but if we can't see it or hear it and we can't walk there or drive to it, we probably wouldn't ever know anything about it. All the borders and barriers have been broken down, but we can't get close enough to them to get over to the other side."

"Exactly," he says, leaning back in his chair, wagging his finger at me. "Llewellyn was right about you. You really do get it!"

That makes me feel uneasy again. I've forgotten how I'm supposed to respond to compliments. These days, on the very rare occasions someone says something positive about you, it's inevitably followed by either a request for help or an attempt on your life. I'm hoping Ankin's going to ask me to help him, because if things get heavy around here, I'm fucked.

"What point are you making?" I ask.

"Tell me how you got here," he replies, still managing to avoid my questions.

"What, how I got to Norwich?" I ask stupidly. He shakes his head.

"No, how you got through the war. How you managed to survive for this long."

"Just did what I had to, I guess. I just kept fighting."

"There are plenty of people who just kept fighting, and most of them are dead. What makes you any different?"

"Luck of the draw," I answer, not sure I want to give anything else away.

"I don't believe you. There's got to be more to it than that. Look at what happened to the Brutes—now that's the result of just fighting, and you're clearly no Brute, Danny."

"I caught a few breaks, had some close calls . . ."

Ankin's clearly growing tired of my bullshit.

"Llewellyn says you can hold the Hate."

"For what it's worth," I answer. "Not much call for it these days, now the Unchanged are gone."

"True, but having that ability says something about the kind of person you are. It shows that you're less impulsive than most, that you've got self-control and willpower. Tell me, Danny, where did you learn to do it?"

"Came across a guy called Sahota. Or rather, he came across me."

"Ahh . . . Sahota! I had a feeling you were one of his."

"One of his?"

"From his 'reeducation' programs."

"Is that what he called them?"

"So you were sent into one of the refugee camps?"

My mind suddenly fills with unwanted memories of those nightmare days last summer.

"I've never been through anything like it," I tell him. "It was incredible . . . horrific . . ."

"Even so, you did it," he says, "and you survived it. No matter how bad an ordeal it was, you managed to get through it and come out the other side, and in relatively decent shape, too, considering what happened. Seems to me, Danny, that if you managed to get out of that almighty mess in one piece, then Llewellyn's right, you're definitely someone worth having on our side."

His smooth talk is really starting to unnerve me.

"Look, just cut the crap, what do you want?"

Ankin grins at me and avoids answering yet another question.

"We were just talking about how much the world's changed, and how it feels like everything's become smaller and more confined. Our needs and priorities have changed, too. I think that as a race we've reached a pivotal point in our development and—"

"Spare me the bullshit and get to the point."

He sighs. "I think we've reached a make-or-break moment. You told me that all you know now is Lowestoft. Well, let me broaden your horizons a little."

"Go on."

"When the enemy refugee camps imploded, then exploded, much of the country became uninhabitable. Virtually every major city center was destroyed, most of them completely vaporized, some by us, some by them. As you'd expect, the radiation and pollution have spread since then. Even more people have died, and even more of the land has been contaminated. I've been trying to coordinate what's left and ascertain how much of the country is actually still inhabitable."

"And how much is that?"

"Less than you might have thought. It's pretty much just the extremities now. Apart from Edinburgh and Glasgow, much of Scotland escaped the worst of it, and parts of North Wales, too. Cornwall and some parts of Devon are livable, but pretty much everything else, from Leeds and Manchester down all the way to the south coast, is dead. Now, all that might not be as big a problem as it sounds, because as you've probably noticed, there aren't that many of us left alive. There's no way of knowing exactly how many, but our best estimations are a million at most, maybe only half that number. So what I'm trying to do is unify the remaining population and bring it together."

"Good luck with that." I laugh, not even bothering to try to hide my skepticism. "You'd be the first person in history to manage it."

He ignores me and continues. "The radiation makes travel difficult at best, and getting cross-country is next to impossible. You either need to fly, go the long way around, or choose one of the less polluted regions and move through it damn fast. Sahota's actually over on the west coast as we speak, negotiating with the Welsh."

"Negotiating with the Welsh! Christ, it all sounds a bit tribal."

"Yes, that's exactly how things will be if we don't do something about it. Someone needs to make a stand and try to bring some order to what's left before we completely lose control, and that's why I'm here. London and the southeast is dead, but where we are now, from the outermost edge of the East Midlands across to the east coast, and from Hull right down to Cambridge, is one of the largest inhabitable areas remaining. We're in control of most of it now."

"Try telling that to Hinchcliffe."

"Exactly, and that's my problem. We've known about him for a

while and we've been happy to let him get on with what he's been doing. He's managed to build up quite a little empire for himself."

"He has, and he's not about to let anyone come in and take it over.
You do realize that, don't you?"

"Of course I do, and I wouldn't expect any different. A man in his
position is naturally going to want to protect his investment and not
give up power. Which is why I didn't actually say anything about taking over. The best option for all concerned would be to get him on
our side."

"I can tell you now, that's never going to happen. Hinchcliffe's not
much of a team player."

"I get that impression, and ultimately it'll be his decision. People
who've taken charge of places like he has don't usually tend to give a
damn about anyone or anything else. I'm not that naive, Danny. I know
what I'm dealing with here."

"Are you sure?"

"I've done this before. We used to call them dictators. Anyway, my
focus is the people, not Hinchcliffe. From what I've heard, there are a
lot of people in and around Lowestoft who need help. We are thousands strong, with more firepower than—"

"I know you used to be in government, but that doesn't mean anything now. I know exactly how Hinchcliffe will react when you turn up.
He won't ever recognize any authority but his own. He's only out for
himself. You turn up and you'll just be walking into a fight to the
death, no matter how many soldiers or guns you've got."

"You're probably right," Ankin says nonchalantly. "Like I said,
though, situations like this have been successfully dealt with before.
Hinchcliffe isn't the only person trying to carve out a place in the history books for himself. We have to start somewhere, and we have to
make a stand."

History books—now there's a quaint, old-fashioned notion. People
don't bother with *any* books these days, much less those that are concerned with our irrelevant lives before the war. Ankin just told me he
wasn't naive, but I can't help wondering if he really does appreciate
how deep-rooted the damage inflicted on the population as a whole

has been. I look at him across the table. His face is frustratingly difficult to read.

"Was that your plane that flew over Lowestoft?"

"Yes."

"What exactly was the point of that?"

"Threefold, I suppose. First, it was a signal for Llewellyn, and his excuse if you like, to come to Norwich and rendezvous with us. We've had to carefully coordinate our arrival here."

"Coordinate with who?"

"Llewellyn for a start, and various other people, too. The plane was the easiest way of letting him know it was time. Second, I wanted to stir up the people of Lowestoft and get them thinking. I thought a flyover by a small, unarmed plane would be enough of a distraction to make them ask questions, but not enough for them to misconstrue it as a threat. I didn't want to bring out the big guns just yet."

"And the third reason?"

"To get Hinchcliffe thinking, too."

"You certainly managed that. Fucker was livid."

"That really wasn't my intention. I just wanted him to realize he's not the only one left with any influence around here."

"He's the only one with any influence in Lowestoft."

"At the moment, yes, and we can both say what we like about him, but the fact remains, he's managed to turn the town into the largest and most established community we've yet come across."

"It's hardly a community. It's just several thousand people who happen to be in the same place, nothing more."

"Okay, wrong choice of word perhaps. Settlement, then. Whatever you want to call it, he's managed to keep a lot of people in order."

"The fighters are scared of him, and everyone else is scared of the fighters, that's all."

"What about you?"

"I'd be lying if I said I wasn't scared of what Hinchcliffe might do. I've seen him in action. He genuinely doesn't give a shit about anyone else, and he'll do whatever he thinks he needs to do to make his point. He says everything boils down to the two *f*'s—food and fear."

"I don't necessarily agree with that, but I know where he's coming from."

"So how come you know so much about Lowestoft?"

"We've had people in and around the place for a while. Llewellyn risked a hell of a lot for us, and there were several others. Do you know Neil Casey?"

"I thought he was dead," I tell him, remembering the day I spent gravedigging, desperately trying to see if one of the bodies I was helping to bury was Hinchcliffe's missing foot soldier.

"He wasn't this morning." Ankin chuckles to himself. "Last time I spoke to him he was still very much alive."

"Hinchcliffe sent me to look for him in Southwold. Was that place your doing, too?"

"What had been happening in Southwold was initially because of John Warner, nothing to do with us. I'd been talking to John for some time. He shared a lot of our ideals, and we were doing what we could to help. He was definitely on the right track."

"I assume you know what happened there?"

"What Hinchcliffe did to Southwold was unforgivable. We were hoping to use the place as a staging post instead of here. It was a difficult one to call, and I got it wrong. I didn't intend for John and his people to get dragged in like that. Hinchcliffe was obviously under the impression that Southwold was a threat."

"He saw it as a threat to his authority, nothing more than that."

I keep my mouth shut about the part I played in Warner's downfall. Even though Hinchcliffe maneuvered me into that position, I still feel partially responsible for what happened.

"The thing is, Danny," he continues, the tone of his voice suddenly changing, "what Hinchcliffe's doing won't last. He's going to run out of supplies and ideas eventually. Then he's screwed."

"I know. I've tried talking to him about it."

"When people like Hinchcliffe realize their number's up, they never go quietly. What happens next in Lowestoft is crucial, and we can't afford to fail. We're in danger of losing so much of what we used to have, you know? All that knowledge, technology, and experience . . .

it's too important just to throw it all away. We'll end up living in caves again."

"So what exactly are you planning, and why are you talking to me?"

"I honestly didn't know anything about you until we arrived here. You're an unexpected bonus, Danny. You're someone who's had unprecedented access to Hinchcliffe. You know how he thinks and how he works. Long and short of it, I want your help. Because, in answer to your first question, as soon as all my people are in position, we're heading for Lowestoft. There are thousands of people there who are suffering, and I've got a duty to try to help them."

"What about Hinchcliffe?"

"Well, that's the million-dollar question, isn't it? If I'm honest, we'd been planning to infiltrate and get rid of him."

"That's what he did to Thacker, the guy who was in charge before him."

"I know."

"If you do that, you'll be operating down at his level. That makes you no better than him."

"I'm well aware of that, too, and it was a price I was willing to pay—but it doesn't have to be that way now."

"Why not?"

"Because we're going to give Hinchcliffe a choice and make him think he's still in control. Who knows, if he plays ball with us, he still could be."

"What if he tells you to fuck off?"

"Then that's up to him. Like I said, we're going to give him a choice. He can let us in to help strengthen and support the town . . ."

"Or . . ." I press when Ankin pauses.

"Or he can get out and leave running the place to me and my people."

"That's never going to happen."

"It will if we handle him right. That's why I'm so pleased that Llewellyn introduced me to you." He pauses ominously, but I already know what's coming next. "I want you to go back into Lowestoft and make sure Hinchcliffe is aware of all his options. Make him see the bigger picture."

"No way. You're out of your fucking mind if you think I'm going to be the one who goes back there to tell him to pack his bags and get out."

"No, no," Ankin says, holding up his hands defensively, "that's not what I'm asking at all. I want you to go back there as someone who knows him, not as a messenger from me. Just tell him about us. Give him a chance to get used to the idea before we arrive. Come on, Danny, can't you see how much easier that'll be? I've got thousands of people waiting to march into Lowestoft, and when they see us, most of the people who are already there will immediately switch sides. It'll be Hinchcliffe and a few hundred fighters against everybody else; they won't stand a chance in battle. So let's you and me do all we can to try to stop that battle from ever starting."

SINCE MY MEETING WITH Ankin first thing this morning, I've been kept under close watch. I was taken into a small office on the second floor of the museum under the pretense of waiting to see the main man again a few hours ago, but the longer I've been here, the more obvious it's become that this is just a holding cell. It's getting dark now, and I don't think they're going to let me out until it's time to go back. The door's not locked, but every time I look out I see people swarming around on the landing, usually Chandra or Swales taking turns standing watch.

Llewellyn says that Ankin is expecting to rendezvous with thousands more of his people outside Lowestoft, and from what I've already seen I have no doubt it'll happen. As soon as they're in position, Llewellyn said, Ankin is also expecting me to trot off into town and explain to Hinchcliffe that he needs to step aside and let someone else take over the place. Like fuck. Hinchcliffe's not going to play ball, and neither am I. They don't really need me, and I definitely don't need them. It's time to get out of here.

My body clock is ticking fast, and I can't afford to waste any more time. My days are numbered, and I really couldn't give a damn about any of these people and their stupid, pointless power struggles. It's exactly the same bullshit politics I used to try to avoid getting tangled up in at work, but here the stakes are immeasurably higher. Except for me. My fate is already sealed. Nothing any of them do will make any difference to me now, so why should I care? What does it matter to me who's left running Lowestoft, or the whole damn country, for that matter? Sitting here alone in the dark over the last couple of hours, I've reached an important conclusion: I'm not going to waste the little time I have left on anyone else—Hinchcliffe, Ankin, Llewellyn, Peter Sutton, Joseph Mallon . . . fuck the lot of them. I don't care where I end up, I'm just going to get as far away from everyone and everything else as I possibly can.

I've waited hours for a chance to make my move, and now it's time. Both Chandra and Swales have gone, and the landing is clear. Shivering with cold, I button up my coat and swing my backpack onto my shoulders. I carefully push the door open just a crack, suddenly feeling like a character in one of those old spy movies I'd forgotten about until now. When I'm sure the corridor outside is empty, I take a few tentative steps out of the room, then stop and listen. I can hear a myriad of muffled noises coming from outside and below, but up here it's silent and I keep going.

A sudden movement out of the corner of my eye makes me freeze. At the end of the short landing, where this stunted corridor opens out into the main part of the museum viewing area, a lone boot is sticking out from behind a wall. I creep closer until I'm near enough to peer around the corner, and I see that it's Swales. The dumb bastard is fast asleep on guard duty, and there's no one else on the rest of this level. It's almost dark—the only illumination coming from the very last light of day seeping in through grimy glass panels in the ceiling high above my head. I stick close to the wall, clinging to the shadows, and cautiously edge along, aiming for the staircase I climbed with Llewellyn when we first got here. I'll go down to the ground floor, then try to find another way out. Hardly any of these people know me, so it shouldn't be too hard to slip past them. Hinchcliffe always says I have a face that's easy to forget, but that doesn't stop me feeling like the center of attention the farther I manage to get from where I'm supposed to be. There's bound to be a window I can climb through somewhere. Failing that, there'll be emergency exits and fire escapes I can use. If I can retrace my steps through the dead streets of Norwich, I'll be able to find somewhere to shelter and hide until it's safe. Ankin's march into Lowestoft is going to happen with or without me, so by this time tomorrow, this ruin of a city should be deserted again. If I stay off the roads and vary my route, I'll be as hard to find as Ankin's damn airplane.

I reach the top of the stairs and peer down over the ornately carved balustrade. I can hear voices below, but it's hard to be sure exactly where they're coming from. I take a few hesitant steps down, then stop to listen again. The voices are moving away and getting quieter. I think my way is clear. I start moving again, concentrating on trying to get to—

"Where the fuck d'you think you're going?"

The wide staircase makes the voice sound directionless, and it's impossible to see much in the gloom. I look around me and see nothing and no one, but then the thump of heavily booted feet thundering down the steps after me makes me look up. Shit, it's Healey, Llewellyn's driver. I try to make a run for it, but he's faster than me and he anticipates my movements. He stretches out his long, muscular arm and grabs my backpack. I try to slip out of it, figuring I'll be faster without it anyway, but he yanks me back before I can get my arms out of the straps and I fall backward, my head cracking against the marble steps.

"Llewellyn!" Healey shouts, his booming voice filling the whole building. "Get up here!"

He starts dragging me back up. His strength is immense, and he pulls me up the stairs like I'm a rag doll. I kick my legs and try to grab hold of the handrail, but everything's happening too fast, and I can barely get back up onto my feet. Llewellyn pounds up the stairs toward me, emerging from the darkness like a wild animal charging, face full of fury and rage.

"Who was on guard?" he yells as he thunders past me, grabbing one of my bag straps and helping Healey haul me up.

"Swales," Healey immediately answers, not about to take any of the flack.

We reach the top of the stairs, and I finally get my feet back down and stand up straight. Llewellyn lets go, but Healey keeps hold of me and throws me back toward my cell. Swales lumbers towards us, a panicked expression on his still half-asleep face.

"Sorry, Llewellyn," he says, "I couldn't help it. I didn't mean to—"

Llewellyn doesn't let him finish his sentence. He punches him in the mouth—a short, sharp, stinging jab—and then, when he hits the deck, starts repeatedly kicking him in the belly, sending him sliding farther back across the floor each time his boot makes contact.

"You useless fucker," he screams at him as the pounding continues. "They'll have our balls if he gets away."

Healey pushes me back into the office again and slams the door shut. I try to open it, but he's holding it from the other side. I can hear Llewellyn yelling orders, but his words are drowned out by the noise of someone dragging furniture across the landing to block me in. When the noise finally stops I can hear him again.

"Go get Ankin. He needs to talk to this freak and put the little bastard straight."

TRAPPED. I'VE BEEN OVER every inch of this damn room, and there's no way out other than the door I came in through and the window, which is bolted shut. Desperate, I grab the heaviest thing I can find—a fire extinguisher—and throw it at the glass. It shatters, filling the room with noise and allowing the bitter wind to gust in, immediately sending the already low temperature plummeting farther. I knock out the last shards of glass and lean out, but it's too big a fall; a sheer drop onto concrete, not even any drainpipes, gutters, or ledges to use to help me climb down.

More voices. Fast-approaching footsteps.

I grip my knife tight and stand ready to fight. The office door is yanked open and Chris Ankin storms in. He's carrying a bright lamp that burns my eyes, and I catch a glimpse of Llewellyn and several others outside before the door's slammed shut again. The harsh illumination makes Ankin's weathered face look severe and intense. He's much older than me and physically smaller, but the sheer force of his angry entrance makes me cower back until I can't get any farther away.

"Put that knife down, you useless fucker," he spits at me. No more smooth talk. He puts the lamp down on the edge of a desk, then leans on his walking stick and glares across the room at me, breathing hard. "I don't think you quite understand," he says, pointing accusingly. "I might not have made myself completely clear earlier. Whether you like it or not, one way or another you're going back to Lowestoft to deliver my message to Hinchcliffe."

All the vote-winning pretense has been dropped now, and for the first time I'm seeing the real Ankin. I've never been good at dealing with people in positions of authority, and I feel as anxious now as I do when I'm with Hinchcliffe—but there's an important difference here that I'm quick to remember: Ankin has no hold over me. He needs me more than I need him.

"Why should I help you? What are you going to do if I don't do what you say? Kill me?"

He moves toward me again menacingly.

"I understand your position, McCoyne," he says, virtually spitting out each word, "but here's mine. Everything hinges on us getting into Lowestoft and keeping the structure of the town intact. You'll help because I've told you you'll help, and if I have to march you in there with a loaded gun held to your head, then that's what I'll do."

This isn't the way I wanted it to be, but so be it. Other than a little time in this grubby world I have nothing left. No family, no friends, no life, hardly any possessions ... I can't be bothered arguing any more. The harder I try to fight, the more I always seem to lose.

"Kill me now, then."

"What?"

"I won't do it, Ankin. I'm tired of fuckers like you pushing me around and telling me what to do. You're going to have to kill me, because I'm not going back to Lowestoft."

"Don't be so stupid," he says. "What's that going to achieve?"

"Absolutely nothing. Then again, that's exactly what me talking to Hinchcliffe will achieve also. In case you hadn't heard, the man's a complete fucking psychopath. Like I told you earlier, if you think he's going to shuffle off into the distance and let you take over everything he's built up in Lowestoft, you're very much mistaken."

Ankin's a sensible man, I'm sure he is. Regardless of the games he plays and the outdated political interests he still seems to nurture, I know he's no fool. He looks straight at me, and I can see him silently weighing up his limited options. He's in a crap position to try to bargain with me, and he knows it.

"Hinchcliffe relies on you, doesn't he?"

"He's a nasty, resourceful bastard. He doesn't rely on anyone. He uses people, that's all. If I'm not around, he'll just find someone else."

"You think? That's not the impression I get from Llewellyn. He seems to think you're different. Tell me, how long have you been there?"

"A few months."

"And how did you come to Hinchcliffe's attention?"

"I led him to the Unchanged nests, helped him to hunt them out and get rid of them."

"So you've been pretty valuable to him?"

"I wouldn't go that far. Definitely not now the Unchanged are gone."

"Well, he obviously still needs you. Otherwise he wouldn't have sent you out here with Llewellyn. No offense, but you're not the strongest-looking fighter."

"None taken."

"Look," he says, sounding weary, "I'm going to lay things on the line for you. You're going back into Lowestoft tomorrow, whether you like it or not."

"Like fuck I am—"

"You don't have any choice. Like I said, taking the town is of paramount importance."

"Spare me the rhetoric. I won't go."

"You will. This is bigger than you and me, Danny, much bigger."

Ankin starts pacing the small room, running his fingers through his shock of white hair, seething with anger and frustration. The strangest thing is that, suddenly, I feel nothing. No fear or apprehension . . .

absolutely nothing. I'm still curious, though. Something doesn't ring true.

"I don't get it."

"Don't get what?" he asks, barely able to look in my direction.

"Why you think you need Lowestoft so badly. It's just a modest little town, for crying out loud. Why not just move on to the next place?"

Ankin walks to the broken window. It's pitch black outside, and I doubt he can see anything, but still he stares out for an uncomfortably long time.

"Okay, here's the score," he finally says. "I'll level with you. The stuff I told you earlier, I didn't give you the full picture."

I'm not surprised. I try to guess what he's going to say next. That there are no reenforcements, perhaps? That there's an even bigger army out there somewhere hunting *him* down?

"Go on . . ."

"It's the politician in me—I can't help trying to give everything the right spin to help get my point across. It's hard to break the habits of a lifetime, you know?"

"Try."

He sits down on the edge of the desk, leaning on his stick for support.

"Things are worse than I said earlier. I just didn't want to put too much pressure on you at once."

"Worse? How could things be any worse?"

"Sahota's not negotiating in Wales. Last I heard he was fighting there, trying to get a foothold in the north of the country. We haven't had any contact from him for a while."

"How long?"

"About three months."

"Jesus."

"I told you that Devon and Cornwall were probably livable, but the fact is the contamination's so bad we haven't even been able to get down there. Truth is we don't hold out much hope of anyone being left alive there now. You know how it all happened, the refugee camps drew people into the cities, and where the Unchanged went . . ."

"We followed."

"Exactly. Most of our people were drawn inland toward the fighting. Up north, Glasgow and Edinburgh were taken out with two bombs within hours of each other, and the cumulative effect of that was devastating. Much of Scotland is uninhabitable now. In fact, the only parts of Scotland we think are still livable are the places where hardly anyone lived anyway—and out in those extreme parts of the country, if there is anyone left alive, they're going to have a hell of a job living through the winter."

"So what exactly are you saying to me? That the whole country is dead?"

"I'm saying that this area is far more important than I originally led you to believe."

"Wait, are you saying that this is it?"

He pauses before answering. "Pretty much. There were other towns, other outposts, but not anymore. It's all so fragile, Danny. All it takes is for a few cracks to show and they fall apart."

"Jesus Christ."

"So you can understand why I need to get into Lowestoft, can't you? It's the largest center of population there is."

"On this side of the country?"

"No, in the whole country."

"Fuck me. You are joking, aren't you? Lowestoft?"

I can tell from the expression on his face that joking is the very last thing on his mind.

"I'm sure there are more people left alive than there are just in Lowestoft, but they're scattered over massive areas. There's nowhere else left like this right now. Lowestoft is unique, probably the biggest concentration of people there still is, we think—and as I said, any people who are left out on their own through the next few months are going to find it awfully hard to survive. No regular food supplies, an extreme winter because of the bombs . . ."

"But if you're as well supported as you say you are, why not just take Hinchcliffe out and take the damn place by force?"

"It's an option, and I haven't ruled it out, but it might not be as easy as it sounds. Thing is, like anybody else, Hinchcliffe and his fighters will do all they can to protect themselves. Remove him and some other tough bastard will just rise up and take his place. If we were to go in heavy-handed, there's a real danger we could bring the whole damn place crashing down around us, and then what? Having you here has given us an unexpected opportunity to try to negotiate and break this cycle of violence. We all need Lowestoft intact. We need the people to survive, the buildings to survive, Hinchcliffe's food stocks to survive—"

"He won't tell you where the food is. No one knows but him."

"I'm sure he won't, but that just further underlines my point. This is our very last chance."

Ankin's words have become a blur of noise. I'm still struggling to grasp the concept that the small, run-down port on the east coast where I've been trapped for the last few months has, by default, become the most important place in the country. The new capital, even.

"So what about you?" I ask him. "Why are you here now?"

"We've been on the road for most of the time."

"On the road?"

"We were originally based around Hull, but that wasn't an ideal location. The pollution levels up there became too dangerous, and with the numbers of people we've been trying to coordinate, it just became impractical. We needed to find somewhere safer and more central, and that's Lowestoft."

"So that's your real reason for coming here, isn't it? You're a king without a kingdom."

"Not at all, though I suppose you could look at it like that. The fact is, it's less about the kingdom and more about the subjects. We need numbers to get this country functioning again. If we're going to be able to salvage anything from the ruins of what we've all lost, we need to get people together in decent numbers. We can criticize his methods, but Hinchcliffe's managed to do just that. From what I've heard, though, he's only interested in feathering his own nest and everyone else can go to hell."

"That's pretty much it."

Ankin looks down at his boots. He seems defeated and lost, all the bullshit and spin suddenly knocked out of him.

"We have to do this, Danny. This might look like a minor skirmish in comparison to the things we've all seen and done over the last year, like two tribes scrapping over a strip of land, but it isn't, it's much more than that. Everything I'm hearing tells me Lowestoft can't continue to survive how it is right now, and at the same time my people can't survive without Lowestoft. If we don't make this happen, then this country will die. This is our very last chance. The pressure's not just on your shoulders, but you can make a crucial difference here. You're in a unique position to help stop our slide back into anarchy."

"I think you might be too late."

"Well, I don't, and while there's breath in my body and even the slightest of chances, I'm going to do what I can to make it happen."

I have to give him his due, he's good. For a fraction of a second I almost buy into his story, but it's all irrelevant to me now. None of it matters. Everything I ever cared about is gone. Ankin seems to know that and anticipates it.

"I assume you don't owe Hinchcliffe anything," he says, his voice flat and unemotional now, "so what could I do to make you help me?"

"There's nothing. All I have now is time, and I'm rapidly running out of that. I just want to spend the days and weeks I've got left on my own. No more fighting, no more bullshit politics and exploitation, no pressure . . . No offense, Ankin, but you can fight your own battle with Hinchcliffe tomorrow."

I try to walk away, wanting to end this pointless conversation, but there's nowhere left to go. A gust of cold air and the sudden movement catch me by surprise, and before I know it I'm doubled over coughing. I lean on the back of a chair for support, hacking my guts up. I manage to turn away and avoid the embarrassment of showering Ankin with bloody spittle.

"You don't sound so good," he says. "Come to mention it, you don't look so good either."

"I'm sick."

"You don't say. Been suffering long?"

"Since the bombs."

"What, some sort of cancer, is it?"

"That's what I'm told."

"What are you doing about it?"

I manage to stop coughing temporarily. I collapse into the chair, panting hard.

"What can I do? Live with it till you die from it, that's the advice the doctor gave me."

"Must frustrate you, though, knowing that before all this happened, there might have been some drugs you could have taken or something else you could have done."

"It breaks my fucking heart. It's this goddamn war that's made me sick."

"I agree, and that just reinforces everything I've been trying to say to you. It's so important we finish the work we've started here and try to put what's left of this broken country back together. I don't suppose medical care is very high up on Hinchcliffe's list of priorities, is it?"

"He doesn't give a shit unless he's the one who's hurting."

Ankin stops and thinks for a moment longer, watching me as I cough again, then wipe my mouth. I instinctively hide the smear of blood on the back of my hand.

"This country needs you, Danny."

"Well, I don't need it."

"Look, I'm not promising anything, but I could have a word with a few people we've got here with us. Most of my medics are elsewhere right now, but we do have a doctor on-site. He won't be able to operate or come up with a cure or anything like that, but I'm guessing you're probably well past that stage anyway. He might be able to make the time you've got left a little easier."

"Are you bribing me now?"

He grins. "Suppose I am. Still, it's a genuine offer, Danny. You help me, and I'll help you."

"And you think your people *can* help me?"

"Like I said, I doubt we can save you, but I'm sure we can make things a little easier. We could either give you a while longer or make the wait a little shorter, whichever you choose. You interested?"

"Not really."

"Come on, Danny," he says, his frustration clear. "Just talk to Hinchcliffe for me. They say he listens to you."

"Hinchcliffe doesn't listen to anyone."

"You underestimate yourself."

"No, you overestimate me."

"That's not what I'm hearing. Look, there's nothing you can do or say to change the fact that we're marching on Lowestoft tomorrow, you included. Go on ahead and talk to him for me, pave the way for us, and I'll guarantee your safety."

"Just how are you going to do that?"

"Leave it to me. Llewellyn will travel with you. He'll get you in, then he'll get you out again. After that, the time you have left is your own, I promise. A few more hours, one meeting with Hinchcliffe, then I swear you're free to go."

35

IT'S PITCH BLACK AND rain is coming in through the broken window when Llewellyn barges into my freezing-cold room and hauls me up onto my feet. Christ, it must be the middle of the night. He drags me downstairs, ignoring my protests and hardly saying a word, then shoves me out through the museum door. With my right arm held in his viselike grip, he leads me through the muddy quagmire outside.

"Time for your checkup," he says, virtually throwing me into the back of a long red and white truck, then slamming and locking the door behind me. It's as dark inside the truck as it is outside, and I work my way along its length looking for another way out. It's some kind of medical vehicle, laid out like a makeshift mobile clinic. On closer inspection, it looks like one of those blood donation units that used to come to the offices back home every so often. I used to give blood just for the free cup of tea and an hour off work.

I'm drenched and shivering. The windows are welded shut, and there's no other obvious way out. There's a skylight above me, and that looks like my only viable means of escape. Groaning with effort, I manage to drag a metal box across the floor and try to get up, but it's not high enough and the tips of my fingers barely reach the ceiling. I'm looking around for something else to stand on when the door flies open again. The noise startles me, and I look around to see a balding, willow-framed man climbing the steps up into the back of the unit, using the handrail to both support himself and haul himself up. He looks at me with a mix of bewilderment and disinterest, then calmly closes the door again and hangs his light from a hook on the ceiling.

"Danny McCoyne?" he asks as he removes a scarf and two outdoor jackets, then puts on a heavily stained white overcoat.

"Yes."

"Sit down, please, Mr. McCoyne, and stop trying to escape. There's really no need; I'm actually trying to help you. It's bad enough that I have to come here at this hour, so let's not make things any harder than they need be."

With little other option, I do as he says, taken aback for a moment by being called Mr. McCoyne for the first time in as long as I can remember. He takes off his half-moon glasses, which have steamed up, and cleans them on his grubby lapel. He's tall and thin, and something about his manner and the way he carries himself suggests he's well educated. In comparison to Rona Scott he's a bloody angel. That foul woman is a butcher: brutal and rough. I visualize this man standing amid the carnage on the battlefield, carefully dissecting Unchanged rather than just hacking them apart like everyone else.

"Mr. Ankin has asked me to have a look and see if there's anything we can do for you. How long have you been sick?"

"I don't know when it started. It's only over the last few weeks that things have gotten really bad."

He nods thoughtfully, then starts to carry out a very brief physical examination. He checks the same things Rona Scott checked, but he makes me feel like a patient, not a slab of meat. He checks my pulse, listens to my heart, looks into my eyes, asks me about allergies and medication and all the other questions doctors used to ask back in the day. I'm feeling nervous suddenly, and without thinking I start asking questions back—pointless small talk to calm myself down.

"Have you been with Ankin long?"

"Several months."

"Where have you been based?"

"In this unit, mostly," he answers as he prods and pokes at my gut with freezing, spindly fingers.

"Have you seen much of the rest of the country?"

"Too much," he says, obviously in no mood to chat.

"Ankin was telling me about Hull. Were you there?"

"For a while, until the fighting."

"What fighting? Ankin said—"

"Look, I know you're anxious, Mr. McCoyne, but I'm trying to work. Please shut up and stop asking questions."

The doctor shoves his hand down the neck of his sweater and pulls out a bunch of keys on a chain. He studies them carefully, holding them closer to the light, then picks one and unlocks a metal cabinet. He mooches through the contents of various shelves filled with clinking glass bottles and vials before selecting one and peering at its label through his glasses, which are now perched perilously close to the end of his nose.

"You're obviously very important to Mr. Ankin," he says, rejecting one bottle and choosing another.

"You think?"

"Absolutely. Believe me, they don't just dish this stuff out to every Tom, Dick, or Harry who needs it. Do you have any idea how many people are walking around out there in the same kind of condition as you are?"

"I don't know how many people are walking around out there pe-riod," I answer quickly.

"Fewer than you'd expect," he says. "Now, I'm no expert, but I've seen an abnormal level of cancers and deaths from—"

"Wait a second. Go back a step. What do you mean, you're no ex-pert?"

He finally settles on a third bottle half-filled with clear liquid and draws a syringe-full from it.

"I'm no expert, but I'm no idiot, either. Truth is, there aren't any experts left. This time last year I was researching genetics at Birmingham University, cutting up fruit flies, writing papers, and delivering lectures to students who couldn't have been any less interested if they'd tried. I'd originally planned to go into medicine, and I did my basic training before I specialized, so I'm not a complete novice if that's what you're worried about. You know how these things have a habit of turning out. Since the war started I've spent most of my time patching up soldiers so they can keep fighting, learning on the job. It makes a change to be asked to do something different."

"But you do know what you're doing?"

"I know enough. Listen, I may not be formally qualified, but you're not going to find anyone better to help you today. Anyway, no one's forcing you to have this treatment. Just go if you want to and we'll say no more about it. I would offer to get you a second opinion, but mine's the only opinion left!"

He chuckles to himself. I don't see the funny side.

"It's okay. Just do it."

"You're a lucky boy," he says, patronizing me.

"I don't feel lucky. What is that stuff, anyway?"

"Steroids. Keep you going for a while longer. It won't do anything to fight the disease, but it'll mask the symptoms for a time."

"How long?"

"A day, maybe two."

There's a lull in the conversation as I peel back various layers of sodden clothing to expose the top of my right arm.

"What about me?"

"What about you?"

"How long do you think I've got left?"

I've asked the question before I've realized what I'm saying, and I immediately wish I could rewind time and retract it. Too late. He looks down at me again and frowns, then returns his attention to preparing the drugs for injection.

"Bear in mind," he says, hunting for a swab and a reasonably clean dressing, "that I don't have any medical records for you, not that anyone has any records anymore. So my estimations could be way off. This is based purely on my gut instinct and several other recent cases I've seen, nothing else, and you also have to remember that we're about to reach the coldest part of winter, and I doubt any of us are eating properly, so we're all going to be more susceptible to—"

"I understand all of that," I interrupt, "just tell me what you think."

"I don't think you have long, Mr. McCoyne, I don't think you have long at all. From what I can see, the disease looks pretty well advanced."

He shoves the needle into my skin, but I don't feel a thing. He drops the syringe into a plastic bin, then picks up another. He grips the same arm tight, then injects me again. This time it hurts.

"What the hell's that? Jesus, how much of that stuff are you putting into me?"

"Not steroids this time," he says, his voice beginning to fade. "This one's a special request from Messrs. Ankin and Llewellyn."

MOVING. DRIVING. ROAD'S UNEVEN. Being thrown from side to side.

I open my eyes and look around. It's light, and I'm in the front passenger seat of a van—the same one that brought me to Norwich, I think. Llewellyn's next to me. I pretend to still be asleep while I try to work out what's going on. Now I'm fully awake I realize I feel less ill than usual. Could it be that the drugs Ankin's doctor gave me are actually having a positive effect? I feel stronger today, and this sudden, drug-fueled change in my health makes me realize how sick I really have become. A hole in the road causes the van to lurch. I hit my head against the window and sit up. Llewellyn looks across and sees that I'm awake.

"Fuck me, you took your time coming around," he says. "I was starting to get worried. Thought Ankin's quack had given you an overdose."

The doctor. Injections. It starts coming back to me. I sit up and try to rub my eyes, but my wrist hurts and my hand is yanked back when I try to lift it. Fuckers have handcuffed me to the van door.

"What's this for?"

"Precaution," Llewellyn says. "I didn't want you running off on me. Now shut up, wake up, and get ready."

"Why, where are we?"

"About five miles out of Lowestoft."

I sit up quickly in panic and look around. He's right, we're on the A146 heading back toward Lowestoft, and we're not alone. There are several of Ankin's vehicles ahead of us and many more behind, all easily identified by the circular red and white insignia daubed in paint. The crude designs vary in size and shape from machine to machine, but their simple aim is achieved—these markings exist to clearly differentiate them from us.

"So what's the plan?" I ask. "I assume there is a plan."

"Ankin's troops are already in place," he explains, "split between the north and south entrances to town."

"Already?"

"They're on the outskirts, thousands of them by all accounts, drawing the crowds away from Hinchcliffe's compound. It's called tactics, you see, McCoyne. These people are smart, and well tooled. They'll get the locals on their side, and that'll leave just Hinchcliffe and the rest of the men for Ankin and us to deal with. I'll get you in, and while you're talking to Hinchcliffe, I'll tell the others what's going on."

"How am I supposed to let Ankin know what he says?"

"Christ, you're bloody naive. Ankin doesn't give a shit what he says. We can all guess what Hinchcliffe's reaction's going to be."

"So why are we even bothering?"

"To keep him busy. To distract him from what's actually happening."

"You mean I'm a decoy?"

"That's about it."

"Shit. Forget it. I won't do it."

"Listen, friend, you're handcuffed to this van and we're not stopping until we're outside Hinchcliffe's front door. I'm delivering you personally. You don't have a lot of choice. Do what you've got to do, and if you behave yourself and Hinchcliffe doesn't do you in, I'll come back and get you out of there."

"You bastard. I'll tell him what's happening. I'll tell him what you did."

"Do you think I care? Hinchcliffe will be finished before nightfall. You, too, if you're not careful."

"What about Curtis and the rest of them? You think they're all going to swap sides just like that because you tell them to?"

"Well, that's up to them, isn't it? But wouldn't you? Let's face it, with Ankin and all this crew on one side, and a shit like Hinchcliffe standing on his own on the other, there's no contest, is there?"

THE A46 SPLITS AND we head south, down toward the bottom edge of Lowestoft, passing close to the housing development where I've been living. The van is still wedged between Ankin's trucks and other vehicles, with a tank leading the way. Just over a mile now.

We're soon passing through the familiar shanty-town surroundings, but the scene is very different from what I've seen here before. More of Ankin's troops are up ahead, forming a blockade on the A12 just prior to where the first of the underclass hordes are gathered. I understand that this is just one section of this so-called army, but there are far fewer of them than I'd imagined. I'd pictured endless columns of uniformed soldiers, armed to the teeth, backed up with huge amounts of firepower. The reality is unsettling. There are just hundreds where I expected to see thousands. Two or three tanks where I expected to see twenty or thirty. One small airplane . . .

"Where's everybody else?"

"I think this *is* everybody else," Llewellyn replies under his breath, sounding as surprised as me.

There are several lines of these so-called soldiers blocking the road ahead, each of them carrying a makeshift riot shield. Coming the other way are the first of the underclass, and I can see a bizarre range of reactions taking place wherever the two sides collide. Some remain in their shelters, seemingly too afraid to move, while others grab whatever they can use as weapons, determined to protect themselves at all costs from these perceived invaders. Some immediately capitulate; others fight like they've just uncovered an Unchanged nest. The vehicle leading the convoy begins to slow.

"What the fuck . . . ?" Llewellyn mumbles, as shocked by what he's seeing as I am.

We're about two-thirds of a mile from the compound, just on the edge of the bulk of the underclass settlements. The convoy stops well behind the line of shielded soldiers, and I sit up in my seat to try to get a better view of what's happening. Again and again, the range of reactions I've already seen is being repeated. Some people are throwing themselves at the feet of Ankin's troops as if they're their saviors, about to pluck them up and whisk them away from the unending hell their lives have become. Others attack the soldiers, perhaps driven by some deranged desire to defend the little they have here because it's all they have left. Deeper in, pockets of underclass are beginning to turn against each other now as rifts appear between groups of people and individuals. Some want to fight, some want to surrender. There's no consensus.

Llewellyn stops just short of the soldiers. Ankin's transport behind us has stopped, too. I look around and see one of Ankin's lackeys running toward the van. Llewellyn opens the door and leans out to speak to him.

"What the fuck's going on?" he demands, but he doesn't get an answer.

"Ankin says you're to keep moving. The rest of us will hold position here until this has died down and we've had word that McCoyne's inside. We'll start our advance in about an hour. Same goes for the columns waiting by the north gates."

Columns? Christ, that's an overly ambitious military term to be using. What I'm seeing around me now is hardly a column of soldiers. From where I'm sitting, apart from the color of their shirts there doesn't seem a huge amount of difference between Ankin's people moving one way and the ever-increasing crowds of underclass coming the other. In fact, the similarities are frightening.

The lackey disappears quickly, and Llewellyn slams the door. Conversation over.

"Well?"

He doesn't answer me. Instead he just swerves around the back of the vehicle in front and drives on down the road. He blasts the horn as we approach the human blockade, and a ragged split appears. We accelerate and drive through, narrowly avoiding a bunch of desperate underclass running the other way. A lump of concrete smashes against the window I'm staring out through, the glass protected by a layer of heavy-duty wire mesh, and I jump back with surprise.

The last half mile to the compound is easier. Here word of the approaching army hasn't yet reached the population, and most of them go about their business (or lack of business) as normal. They barely bat an eyelid as we drive past. It's early, and many are still in their shelters, delaying the start of yet another day for as long as they can. Ahead of us a group of scavengers pick their way through a mountain of frost-covered refuse—an unplanned landfill site where a children's play area used to be—looking for scraps of food in the fermenting rubbish. Others crowd around fires. Almost all of them ignore us.

We eventually reach the south gate across the bridge. Llewellyn glances across at me, then blasts the horn. A pair of eyes appear at a wire-mesh observation slot. They disappear again quickly, and the gate is opened.

"Don't fuck this up," he tells me. "All you have to do is keep him busy. I'll give you an hour maximum. Just get this straight, freak, if you try anything stupid I'll kill you. Ankin says you want out of here, so just do what you've been told and your freedom's yours."

I don't respond. I barely even hear him. It's partially because I'm too scared to care, but also because something's not right here. The very center of Lowestoft feels different this morning. There are more fighters on the streets than usual, and some of the Switchbacks are unexpectedly armed. The place appears otherwise empty. Llewellyn tosses a set of keys over to me as we near the center of the compound. I drop them in the footwell and have to duck down and stretch to reach them, my wrist still attached to the door. I eventually manage to unlock the handcuffs. Do I make a run for it now? For a moment I consider it until I catch a glimpse in the side mirror of a mob of people in the street behind us. I look up again and see even more of them on either side of the road up ahead.

"I'm going to leave you just short of the courthouse, okay?" Llewellyn asks, focused and oblivious. "Just do what you've been told and you'll be okay. Understand?"

"I understand."

He throws the van around a sharp right-hand turn.

"We both want the same thing, McCoyne, we both want to get rid of Hinchcliffe. But I swear, if you—"

He stops talking abruptly, and I look up to see what's wrong. The road ahead is blocked. Familiar-looking fighters advance toward us and surround the van. Curtis, Llewellyn's deputy, hammers on the glass, and Llewellyn winds his window down.

"Hinchcliffe wants to see both of you," he says. Llewellyn looks across at me, a hint of nervousness in his eyes.

"Doesn't change anything. Just makes things a little more complicated. I'll square things with this bunch. You go in there and feed him as much bullshit as you can."

Before I can argue he's out of the van. Patterson opens my door and pulls me out. Llewellyn tries to speak to Curtis.

"We need to talk."

"Not interested. Get moving."

"But Curtis—"

"If you've got a problem, tell Hinchcliffe."

Llewellyn tries to struggle but stops when the stunted barrel of a shotgun is shoved into his ribs. With that we're led toward the courthouse, surrounded by a phalanx of fighters.

"Good morning," someone shouts. I glance around, but I can't see who's speaking; then I look up and see Hinchcliffe standing on the roof of the courthouse. "Bring them straight up here, boys," he orders. "I've been looking forward to this."

WE'RE ESCORTED QUICKLY THROUGH the building. Llewellyn is in front, marching with an arrogance that belies the nerves I know he must be feeling. The place is almost completely deserted. The corridors are empty, and there's no one in the usually busy courtroom hub. We continue through Hinchcliffe's personal quarters. Most of the fighters don't follow us, and I can't help thinking that, in spite of everything, there are some places that are still sacrosanct. No matter what happens, Hinchcliffe's ivory tower remains intact. His rooms are in as bad a state as ever, like a particularly rebellious teenage boy's bedroom. There's a woman lying on the floor, sprawled out on her back. I only notice her when Curtis treads on her outstretched hand and she yelps with pain. Her face is drugged, expressionless and blank. Another private extension of Hinchcliffe's foul breeding program, no doubt.

Past the conference room, through another door I haven't been through before, and we reach a dark staircase. I climb the first flight, Llewellyn right in front of me now, then turn through one hundred and eighty degrees and climb a shorter second flight up. Out through a final door where Hinchcliffe is waiting for us, and I find myself standing in the middle of an area of flat roof. Curtis goes back down, and suddenly I only have Hinchcliffe and Llewellyn for company. Hinchcliffe pushes the door shut.

The roof is completely clear except for a deckchair and a pile of half-used supplies. An empty beer can rolls into a dirty puddle, blown across the asphalt by a gust of wind. It's damn cold up here, and it's starting to snow again. Llewellyn tries to talk to Hinchcliffe, jabbering like a nervous kid, but the KC's not listening. He just walks away, then stops and turns back to face us both.

"Find the plane?" he asks casually.

"I—" I start to answer, trying to remember what my story's supposed to be.

"Not you," he interrupts. He points directly at Llewellyn. "You."

"Listen, Hinchcliffe," Llewellyn begins, "I just—"

"Wait a second," he says, cutting across him. "Before you start, do me a favor and spare me the bullshit, okay? Honesty only on my rooftop, right?" He winks at me like a psychotic, old-school serial killer, playing with his victims and taunting them before going in for the kill. Crazy bastard. He takes a sudden step forward and I take half a step back, not sure how much space there is between me and the edge of the roof.

"Hinchcliffe, you really need to listen," Llewellyn says again.

"Do I? And why would that be, Llewellyn?"

His once-loyal fighter swallows hard and anxiously shifts his weight from foot to foot.

"There's an army coming," he says, quickly changing his story to try to dig himself out of the hell-sized abyss he's suddenly gazing down into. "Look, there was nothing I could do. They found us and—"

I'd like to have heard the rest of his bullshit and lies, but Llewellyn isn't even allowed to get to the end of his sentence, let alone finish his story. In a movement so sudden and unexpected that I don't realize what's happening until it's done, Hinchcliffe drops his shoulder and charges into him, sending him flying over the edge of the roof. There's a moment of complete silence—everything everywhere seems to stop suddenly—then I hear him hit the ground. There's no need to look, but I don't have any choice. Hinchcliffe puts one hand around my shoulder, grabs hold of my arm with his other hand, and pushes me toward the edge. Below us, Llewellyn's body lies impaled on a spiked metal railing, dangling down by its legs, head cracked open on the concrete like an egg. "Nasty," Hinchcliffe says. Bastard. Llewellyn was supposed to be getting me out of here, but at this moment in time I don't give a shit about him, I'm more concerned about what Hinchcliffe's going to do next. The tightness of his hold on me increases. I start to struggle, but he's far stronger than I am and there's nothing I can do. I try to dig my feet in, hoping I can get a grip and overbalance him, because if I'm going down, this fucker's going with me. He moves a hand and grasps the back of my neck and pushes my head farther forward until I'm leaning right over.

"Hinchcliffe, I . . . ," I start, not knowing what I'm trying to say, fighting to keep my balance and not fall. He suddenly pulls me back, spins me around, pushes me away, and laughs at me.

"Just playing with you!"

"What? But I . . ." I stagger away from him, trying to quickly put maximum distance between us.

"Don't worry, son," he says, "I know the score."

"Do you?" Fuck, I wish I did. I move away from the edge of the roof, still backing away, and he follows me toward the door that leads back down into the building.

"I knew that fucker was up to something," he explains. "I'd had my suspicions for a while, but all that business with the plane really sealed it for me. Did he think I was stupid? Llewellyn was a hard bastard and he had his uses, but he wasn't nearly as smart as he liked to think he was. Honestly, did he really think I'd buy all that bullshit about piling a few pals into a van and driving off to find that fucking airplane? Come on, give me some credit. That was one of the reasons I sent you along, too, to screw things up for him and complicate whatever it was he was actually trying to do."

"*One* of the reasons?"

"Yeah, that and the fact I knew there was a good chance you'd end up back here again. I knew you'd help me fill in the blanks. Our pal Llewellyn and whoever he was working for, they're not the only people who like to indulge in the odd spot of subterfuge and double-crossing. When I sent you all out the other day, I sent Curtis after you. He followed you into Norwich, stuck around long enough to see this so-called army that's supposed to be coming, then came back and told me all about it."

"What he saw was only part of the army. There are reinforcements coming. Thousands of them."

"Do you believe that?"

"Why shouldn't I?"

"Because I've seen them, Danny. I've got people out there watching. They've told you thousands, but there are just a few hundred of them loitering at either end of town. Ask yourself, if they were as all-powerful and all-conquering as they'd have you believe, wouldn't they have conquered already?"

"I suppose, but—"

"It's all spin, trying to make themselves seem more impressive than they actually are. Who's behind all this?"

"Remember Chris Ankin?"

"Chris who?"

"He used to be in the government."

Hinchcliffe thinks for a second. "Ahh . . . I've got him. Works and Pensions minister before the war, wasn't he? Just another mouthpiece in a gray pinstripe suit. All talk and no balls. Pathetic. Thing about people like that," he continues, "is that you should never believe *anything* they tell you. There's always a hidden agenda."

"Ankin was the one who spread the messages, though, remember? The one who coordinated the attacks on the cities."

"There you go, my point exactly. He's got you completely suckered in. I thought you were smarter than that, Dan. Nobody really coordinated those attacks, they occurred naturally. What happened in the cities was inevitable, and only someone who had either something to prove or something to hide would try to take credit for them."

"Does that really matter now? Fact is, they're marching on Lowestoft."

Hinchcliffe walks away, shaking his head. He sits down in his deck-chair in the center of the roof and starts scanning the horizon through a pair of binoculars.

"So do you think I should be worried?"

"What kind of a question is that? Of course you should be worried. Haven't you been listening to anything I said, there's a fucking army marching on Lowestoft and they want you out. Doesn't matter how big it is, it's a fucking army!"

He continues to stare into the distance, looking back now in the direction from which Llewellyn and I approached a short while ago. Even from up here I can see signs of activity in the streets around the compound.

"Are they well armed?"

"They've got more than you have. Tanks and all sorts . . ."

"Probably haven't got a lot of ammo, though."

"So? A tank's a tank. They'll drive straight through the gates, Hinchcliffe."

"And what's been the reaction of the good folk of Lowestoft so far?"

"I've seen some trying to fight, some just keeping out of the way. Most seem to be doing whatever they're told to do. You know the score, Hinchcliffe. It's like Llewellyn used to say, always get in good with the person with the biggest gun."

"So why here?"

"What?"

"That's the thing I don't understand. Why are they so interested in Lowestoft?" he asks. He genuinely has no idea. "Surely someone who's as powerful as this Ankin guy claims to be could take their pick of anywhere. Why here? Are they just trying to prove a point?"

"They're here because this place is all that's left. Ankin figures this is pretty much the population center of the country now."

For a few seconds Hinchcliffe is quiet. He has a bemused expression on his face, and I can see him trying to come to terms with what I've just told him.

"Fuck me . . ."

"That's what I said when I found out—but I think it's true, Hinchcliffe, everywhere else is dead."

"So why did you come back here, Danny? It's out of the frying pan, into the fire for you, isn't it?"

"Because they made me" is my immediate answer. "When I refused, the bastards drugged me and chained me up inside a van. I didn't have any choice. Believe me, I'd rather be anywhere but here."

He looks puzzled. "Strange. Why go to all that effort?"

"Because I'm supposed to be a decoy. I was supposed to keep you busy while Llewellyn spread the word around town that you were under attack."

"And he thought that was going to work? Jesus Christ, Llewellyn was more of an idiot than I thought. My fighters might be hard as nails, but they'll run like everybody else if their necks are on the line."

"I tried to tell him. I said you wouldn't listen."

He pauses to think again. I'm numb with cold and I want to get off this roof, but Hinchcliffe hasn't finished with me yet.

"Tell me, Dan," he continues, "what would you do? If you were standing in my shoes right now, what would you do?"

"For a start, I would never be in your shoes," I answer quickly, deciding that there's no point being anything other than honest with him. "I'm not like you. It's stupid bastards like you who caused all this mess."

"Now, now," he says, remaining unsettlingly calm, "no need for name-calling."

"I'm through with fighting, and I'm through with you, Hinchcliffe. I'd have turned my back on this place and all the grief that goes with it a long time ago, but if I really was in your position right now, I'd be seriously thinking about slipping out through the back door and letting Ankin get on with it."

Hinchcliffe nods thoughtfully. "So you think I should give up control of Lowestoft just like that?"

"I don't know. To be honest, I don't care. The way I see it, the whole world has been destroyed by this war, Hinchcliffe. I don't know whether this place is the beginning of something new or the very end of everything. Either way, it's not looking good."

I start moving toward the door. I'm freezing and tired of wasting my breath. Hinchcliffe won't listen to anything I've got to say. I'm about to open it when he speaks again.

"You've met this Ankin," he says, getting up and walking toward me. "Tell me, Danny, would things be any different if he was in charge here?"

"I can't answer that. What does it matter, Hinchcliffe?"

I reach down for the handle again. He grabs my wrist and won't let go.

"Don't," he says. "You're staying with me, Danny. I still need you. You're not going anywhere."

39

THE LONGER HINCHCLIFFE WAITS and does nothing, the more likely it is that Ankin will be forced to make a move. Maybe that's what he's hoping?

Hinchcliffe's tactics—if any of what's happening now is actually planned—are strange, almost unreadable. Unable to get out of the building, I head up onto the roof of the courthouse again and use the binoculars he's left up there to scan the streets below. They're virtually deserted. Most of Hinchcliffe's remaining fighters have been ordered to either congregate around this building or guard the gates and the food stores. There are about a hundred of them downstairs, armed with every last weapon they can lay their hands on. Is he really planning to defend his territory like this? Sticks and stones against tanks and guns?

There's a quiet buzzing sound that steadily increases in volume. I can see Ankin's plane in the distance now, approaching quickly from the general direction of Norwich, here to report back to Ankin and to whip the crowds around town into a nervous frenzy. There's no doubt it'll work. The noise coming from the fighters below me begins to grow louder and more fractious. These men want to fight, but what can they do when their perceived enemy is out of reach a couple of thousand feet above them?

I feel exposed up here. I go back inside through Hinchcliffe's chamber, then look for him in the courtroom. I hear his voice echoing through the otherwise empty corridors as he barks orders at his fighters, suddenly sending groups of them off in different directions. I creep closer to the main entrance and peer outside, and there I see him, right out in front of the building, coordinating the chaos.

As I watch, a car screeches around the corner and pulls up in front of the courthouse. Curtis gets out.

"The whole fucking place is surrounded, Hinchcliffe," he says. Hinchcliffe says nothing, but plenty of other questions come from elsewhere in the crowd.

"Surrounded by what? How many are there?"

"Someone said tanks. Have those fuckers got tanks?"

"Should have stuck with Llewellyn—"

"Defend the positions I've told you to defend," Hinchcliffe says, his voice suddenly louder than the rest. "Food stocks, the gates, this building."

"What's the fucking point?" someone stupidly asks. "We're outnumbered. There's ten times as many people on the other side of the barrier, and that's before—"

The fighter doesn't finish making his point. I watch from around the side of the door as Curtis drags him out into the open and attacks him with his machete. Taken by surprise, the other fighter drops to the ground. He raises his arm to protect himself, but Curtis keeps chopping down regardless, slicing his flesh and virtually removing the man's arm, then rams his boot down onto his chest and starts to hack at his head and neck. I step back into the shadows and disappear into a room off the main entrance corridor. There's a street-level window, and I watch as a range of reactions spreads through the fighters with lightning speed. Someone jumps Curtis, smacking him across the back of the legs with a metal bar and dropping him to his knees. Someone else then attacks Curtis's attacker. Then another fighter wades through the crowd to get to Curtis's car. Someone else cuts him off and tries to take the car for himself. Others turn and run for cover—

I press myself flat against the wall as I see Hinchcliffe start to slowly slip back into the courthouse. As the chaos outside quickly increases in ferocity, spreading like a brush fire, he quietly reenters the building and shuts and bolts the door behind him. I hold my breath and stay perfectly still, listening to his footsteps moving along the corridor outside this room, waiting until I'm sure he's gone.

Time to get out of here.

This is my last chance.

I need to get to the house, get whatever stuff I can, then leave here and never look back.

40

A **T THE END OF** another corridor, a broken sign hanging from the ceiling points toward a fire exit hidden behind an untidy stack of boxes and crates, most of them empty. I fight my way through the rubbish, then force the door open and get out of the building, desperate to disappear before Hinchcliffe comes looking for me or the sudden violence outside escalates further. I follow the metal railings around the side of the courthouse, passing Llewellyn's impaled corpse, running through the massive puddle of blood that's seeped out of his body and not giving the stupid fucker a second glance. I pause at the back of the building to check that no one's around, then sprint away. Once again I'm thankful for the steroids that Ankin's doctor pumped me full of earlier today. If I hadn't been drugged up, I'd never have been able to run like this. No doubt I'll pay for it eventually when the effects wear off, but right now it doesn't matter.

I try to follow the main road down toward the south gate, keeping the ocean to my left, but another sudden swell of trouble in a side street forces me to change direction. I'm close to the redbrick shopping center, one of the sites where Hinchcliffe stockpiles food and supplies. It's in the process of being ransacked. Fighters scramble through debris, desperate to get their hands on whatever they can before someone else takes it. Some of them are attacked as they fight their way back out into the open. A gang of Switchbacks corner one. He manages to batter one of them, but three more take him down, blades flashing in the early morning light, bludgeons pounding him into a pulp. Men still loyal to Hinchcliffe try for a while to stop the looting, but they're soon overcome and are either battered into submission or forced to switch sides. I get a glimpse inside one of the food buildings through an open door as I run past. It's virtually empty now. Has everything already been taken, or was there never anything there?

Lowestoft is falling apart around me—splintering and fragmenting as I watch. Until now the specter of Hinchcliffe has loomed large over this place, and everyone has been in his shadow, too afraid to do anything that might risk incurring his wrath. Today his dominance has been challenged without even a single shot being fired between the fighters in the compound and Ankin's army outside the town, and everything is rapidly beginning to fall apart. The ease with which it's happened is terrifying. It's almost as if Ankin wanted it to be this way.

Another left turn leads me back toward the coast and the main road again. The streets are filling with activity, and word of what's happening seems to have spread with lightning speed. The people I see are uniformly panicked and scared, unsure what they should do. Some are simply barricading themselves into the buildings where they live, blocking up those doors and windows that are still accessible from outside. Others are preparing to defend themselves. Most have resorted to the language of the moment: violence and hate. More small mobs have appeared on street corners armed with clubs and blades and whatever else they can find. Some of these groups of people merge; others turn on each other in sudden, desperate fights over territory and weapons.

I can finally see the south gate up ahead, but there's already a large crowd there trying to get out. A couple of fighters still loyal to Hinchcliffe try to push the bulk of the people back into the compound, but several more of them are doing the exact opposite—frantically trying to get the gate open. A couple of smaller, more athletic-looking people are scrambling up the sides of the trucks that form the barrier and are throwing themselves over.

A fight breaks out in the middle of the crowd in front of the gate. One man—a young, aggressive bastard I've taken a beating from before now—is warding off several others with a pistol and a knife. He's gesturing desperately toward the metal barrier, but his words are being drowned out by increasing levels of noise coming from the other side. He lashes out at the one-legged guard, who can't get away, slashing a line across his chest with the tip of his blade. He then fires his pistol several times, killing two more, before throwing it into the crowd when he's out of ammunition. The gunshots are enough to force the people to scatter momentarily, and the brief distraction gives him enough time to get the access door in the gate open and get out. I can't see much—several other fighters race to the barrier and close it again within a few seconds—but I see enough, and so does much of the rest of the crowd. The young fighter runs down the road, arms held high in surrender. Coming toward him, coming toward the heart of Lowestoft, is one of Ankin's tanks. Behind it, for as far as I can see, the road is filled with more people and vehicles. As the gate slams shut again the crowd on this side reacts with increased anger and fear, and another fight erupts, which spreads rapidly.

I need to find another way out of town. If Ankin's this close and he has anything like the manpower he's boasted of having, then the entire compound must surely have been surrounded by now. I double back, now running away from the ever-expanding riot and moving back toward Hinchcliffe and the courthouse again, seriously lacking anything resembling a coherent plan of action. In the space of just a few minutes the streets have begun to fill with even more chaos and confusion, wanton violence flooding the entire compound.

I've run out of options. All the major routes north and south are blocked now, and everything to the west will be impassable before long if the panic and rioting continue to increase. The beach is the only sensible route left to take. It'll take me much longer to get away, but at least it should be clear. Providing the tides are kind and the violence here is contained to the half-mile square around Hinchcliffe's base, I should be able to follow the shingle and sand until I'm level with the development, then get back up onto the roads again and reach the house.

I turn and head down toward the ocean, my body still fooled into thinking it's healthy by the drugs. I know I can keep running at this speed if I don't push too hard. The noise of the waves increases steadily as I approach the sea, but then I become aware of another, even louder noise. Ankin's plane again? I look up and see a helicopter flying low and fast toward the town. For a second I stop dead in my tracks, transfixed as I watch the machine crawl along under the dark gray clouds, taillights blinking through the gloom. It's been so long since I've seen anything like this . . . and now it's directly over the center of Lowestoft, flying this way toward the ocean. My brain is screaming at me, trying to make me understand that whoever's flying the chopper isn't interested in me or even capable of attack, but common sense has gone out of the window and now I'm running like I think the pilot's about to machine-gun me down. It seems that everyone else feels the same level of paranoia, because the arrival of the helicopter has whipped the crowds behind me into an unpredictable frenzy, herding many of them in this direction. Fuck, are we being rounded up? I've almost reached the beach now, but there are other people swarming nearby, and with the perceived threat of attacks from the air it suddenly seems a dangerously exposed place to be. I need an alternative. I look up again and then I see it: a place that's out on a limb, isolated and alone; a place where I can shelter until the chaos dies down; a place where no fucker in their right mind would go.

I put my head down and start sprinting toward Hinchcliffe's factory.

41

THE PLACE IS DESERTED. Hinchcliffe's guards are gone, and there are no signs of life around the outside of this vast, ugly building. Everything looks featureless and black in the late morning gloom. I plan to head straight for the entrance I used to get inside when I saw Rona Scott, but I'm disoriented and I end up at the wrong end of the site, outside the metal industrial units Hinchcliffe bought me to before. The doors of several of the small buildings are open, and I panic and freeze, thinking I'm about to be surrounded by a pack of feral kids, working together like starving hyenas. The helicopter flies off toward the other end of the compound, and as the noise of its engine finally fades I realize this place is silent. The children are long gone, probably released by the kid-wrangler. There's only one of them left here. It's the older boy I saw previously. I see him sitting in the corner of his cell, covering his head.

"Get out of here," I shout at him. "Run!"

He doesn't move, doesn't even react. The kid's catatonic, and I know I can't waste any more time here. I double back and head straight for the entrance I used to get to Rona Scott's office previously, figuring that's as good a place as any to shelter. The main door has been left unlocked, and I slip into the building unseen. I close it behind me, then lean up against it, panting hard and listening for sounds of movement, conscious that my noise is now filling this otherwise empty place.

The guard's station in the reception area has been abandoned. The desk is empty, and behind it I find a dirty sleeping bag lying among crushed soda cans, food wrappers, and an empty liquor bottle. The scavenger in me takes over and I quickly check through the mess, but the only things I find of any value are a pathetically weak long-handled flashlight, some scraps of clothing, and half of the packet of candy I used to bribe the guard with the other day. Looks like he was rationing himself and he didn't get to finish them before either duty called or he fled.

I shout out just in case I'm not alone.

"Hello. Is anybody there?"

I'm relieved when no one answers. The last thing I want is to be trapped here with Rona Scott or any of Hinchcliffe's other cronies. I do hear something in another part of the building, and I remain still as I try to make it out. It's a quiet, indistinct scurrying noise, and I lose track of it when Ankin's helicopter returns and flies overhead again. It was probably just rats. Vermin have learned to hide in places like this where they're away from the bulk of the population but still close enough to hunt for scraps. Back in the main part of town and the surrounding areas, rodents are often hunted out for food. It's as if our places on the lower levels of the food chain have become interchangeable.

This place will have to do. With a little luck I can hide out here until the situation outside either blows over or comes to a head when Ankin's army inevitably breaches the gates. I can bide my time, then get out of town along the beach as I'd originally planned.

I retrace my steps up to where I found Rona Scott when I was last here, back toward the room where she confirmed my death sentence a few days ago. Christ, is that all it's been, a few days? So much has happened that it feels like a lifetime ago now. That thought makes each step I climb feel like it takes ten times the effort. How much closer am I to my inevitable end now than when I was last here? Is this what it's going to be like from now on? Constantly wondering how long is left?

I check the room where I found Scott before. It's dark, the blinds half drawn, and to my relief she's not here. I go inside and look through the clutter on the table for food, pausing when I hear muffled shouting in the far distance, followed by gunfire and a high-pitched scream, sounding like a lynch mob catching up with its target. I turn around and jump with shock and surprise when I see the little girl I saw here previously. She's still strapped to her seat, sitting bolt upright and staring at me in abject terror.

"I'm not going to hurt you," I tell her, and even though she probably doesn't believe me, I mean it. She doesn't react, too scared even to move. I approach her cautiously, not wanting her to panic or start screaming or do anything that might alert people to the fact I'm here. She doesn't flinch as I kneel down in front of her. "You need to go. There are people outside who'll hurt you. When you get out there, just run."

I touch her wrist to undo the first of the bindings that hold her to the chair, and she doesn't even move when I brush against her skin. She's as cold as the room we're in. I look into her face again. Her eyes are still focused on the same point in the distance. I shake her shoulder and wave my hand in front of her face, but it's no use. By the looks of things she's been dead for a while.

Upstairs, Rona Scott's "clinic" is also empty. I have a quick, half-hearted search around for vials of drugs that look anything like the steroids Ankin's doctor gave me, but I know I'm wasting my time. I find a two-thirds-full bottle of aspirin tablets and I shove them into my coat pocket. Maybe I'll take a couple if the pain gets too bad. Then again, if the pain gets that bad maybe I'll just take the whole damn lot.

The view from the window up here is unobstructed virtually all the way back into the very heart of Hinchcliffe's compound. The helicopter buzzes overhead, and I think the south gate is open now. There's a crowd on this side of the barrier trying to get out, and an army on the other side trying to get in, their numbers swollen by huge waves of underclass looking for food or vengeance or both. The same thing's surely happening at the other end of town, and at any other potential access points. I stand and watch as the people of Lowestoft collide head-on and begin to tear themselves apart.

Is this what happened in Hull, and in all those other places where I'm sure that similar communities must have sprung up around the country? And was Lowestoft really the last of them? If Ankin's right and this place is the only place left, then the chain reaction that's spreading through this town now truly is the beginning of the end of everything.

42

THE STREETS THAT I can see from this window are constantly filled with movement now, frantic and uncontrollable, and I wonder: Where in all that chaos out there is Hinchcliffe?

The overwhelming uncertainty consuming this place and my frustrating inability to be able to do anything are affecting my concept of time now. I don't know whether I've been here for one hour or four. It's ice cold in this building, and the rain outside has turned to sleet. Everything looks relentlessly gray out there. My head is pounding. Are the effects of the drugs already fading?

I'm leaning up against the glass, staring at a street fight in the distance, numb to the bloody violence, when there's a series of sudden bright flashes around Hinchcliffe's courthouse building. Were they explosions? Now there are flames in the windows, and from what I can see the police station barracks used by most of his fighters is also under attack. A flood of people—fighters and Switchbacks alike—run from the scene. They've barely made any progress when they collide with an equally large surge of people coming from the opposite direction.

What the hell's going on? I keep watching long enough to see several of Ankin's tanks rolling slowly toward the burning courthouse, converging on it from different directions.

The center of Lowestoft is a damned war zone. There are an incalculable number of people in there now, far more than there were originally. It's the cumulative effect of Ankin's invading army and the hordes of underclass all descending on the place at the same time. There are other buildings on fire, too. Before long the whole town will be in flames.

I need to move. The fighting is still a distraction at the moment, drawing people into the dying center of town, but it's only a matter of time before they come looking around here. I should act now, and take advantage of the effects of Ankin's drugs before they completely wear off.

I have one last quick search around the doctor's room, then head back down to the guard station. I'm about to leave, but I stop myself. This building is huge and relatively inaccessible. For the most part people were too scared to come here. Knowing that the population would probably stay away and there'd be plenty of secure space here, wouldn't this have made a perfect store for Hinchcliffe? For the sake of a few more minutes, I decide to scout around a little more of the place. I need to try to eat now and cram my body full of as much nutrition as possible while I still can. It scares me to think about how I'm going to feel again when the drugs wear off. Feeling better has made me realize how ill I've really become.

Opposite the main door is the entrance to a long, dark corridor I remember seeing when I was here before. Grabbing the flashlight I found earlier (the light it gives off is poor, but at least it's heavy enough to make a decent club), I start moving along it. I stop when I reach a second door at the far end of the corridor, and peer through a round porthole window. I'm looking out over a vast, mostly empty, hangarlike space. There are large clear panels in the high, corrugated metal ceiling that diffuse the light, and it's hard to make out much detail. The door's stiff and it sticks at first, but I shove it open and go through, then immediately stop and cover my mouth and try not to gag. The smell in here is appalling and instantly recognizable. The unmistakable stench of death.

There's a raised metal gantry running around the edge of this cavernous room about a yard off the ground. I walk along it slowly, my footsteps echoing around the building. There's a huge amount of industrial pipework hanging down that obscures much of my view, and for a second I wonder whether this was another of those gas chamber killing sites from the beginning of the war. I stop walking, and just for a second I think I can hear something in here with me. It's a quiet, scrambling sound that comes from the far side of this large space and echoes off the walls—the vermin I heard when I first arrived here, perhaps? Thinking about it, the combination of the dead flesh I can smell and the fact that so few people ever came to this place would make this a prime site for a nest of rats or other scavenging creatures. It's weird, in spite of everything that's happened to me recently and all that's going on less than a mile away in the center of Lowestoft, the idea of stumbling blind into a horde of starving rodents is more frightening than anything else. There's more light the farther I go into the room, and I jog along the gantry to get out of the shadows.

Bizarre. At the far end of this open space the floor has been divided up with metal barriers into a number of pens, maybe as many as twenty altogether. It looks like a cattle market, but didn't Hinchcliffe tell me this place was originally used to process seafood? Then I remember what he was using this factory for, and even though I don't want to look, I climb down to check the nearest of the pens.

The metal divides have created spaces that are each approximately six feet square. The floor of the pen closest to me is covered with what looks like hay and scraps of clothing, but otherwise it's empty. In the one next to it, however, there's something else. It's oddly shaped, and it's hard to make out what it is. I lean down over the railings to reach it or at least get a better look, and I immediately wish I hadn't. Lying slumped in the corner of the cage with its back to me, one arm stretched up and shackled by the wrist to the highest of the metal rungs, is the emaciated body of an Unchanged child. It's so badly decayed and the light's so dull that I can barely make out enough detail to estimate either its sex or its age. There are more of them, too. I start walking again, and I see that there are bodies in most of the pens. Most are little more than withered, bony husks now, while a few clearly died more recently and are less decayed.

There's a yard-wide pathway that runs right through the middle of the pens, and I follow it, looking from side to side and struggling to come to terms with what I see around me. I've seen more horrific sights in the last year than I ever thought possible—images I still see when I close my eyes each night—but I've never come across anything like this before. Regardless of the fact that these children were, as far as I can tell, all Unchanged, the wanton cruelty and neglect that they've been subjected to in this place is unimaginable. For a second I think about Hinchcliffe again, and I hope the fucker is burning in his courthouse palace right now. To have tried to turn a couple of children and have failed is one thing. To just have killed them would have been understandable in the circumstances, but this? To have continued to repeatedly abuse child after child is another matter altogether. Hinchcliffe and Rona Scott must have derived some sick, sadistic pleasure from this appalling torture. Evil fuckers.

I crouch down and look between the metal rungs into another pen, where there's a small boy about the age my youngest son was before he was killed. I shine the miserable light from my flashlight into his face and bang it against the railings to try to get a reaction from him. Nothing happens. I stare at the corpse a while longer and realize the boy was probably older than he looked. His limbs are long, but his body appears collapsed and shrunken by decay. He died lying flat on his back, his arms and legs unchained. Couldn't he have at least tried to get away? Maybe he knew it would have been futile, or maybe he no longer had the strength or desire to escape. I shine the light around the pen and see that there are chains in here after all. Then I look at his withered right wrist and I realize his shrunken hand just slipped out from his shackles.

In every subsequent pen I pass, I see something horrific. I thought that nothing could hurt like this anymore, but I'm struggling to comprehend what I'm seeing. In one cage is the body of a girl—ten or eleven years old, perhaps—and her chains have been wrapped around her neck several times. Did someone do this to her, or did she do it to herself?

Is this the great victory we've been fighting for? Am I a part of this? Am I responsible for it? I helped bring many of these children here, so is what happened to them my fault? But what was the alternative? If they hadn't died here, they'd have died somewhere else. A year ago people were flying around the world, sending probes out into space, eradicating diseases, firing atoms around underground tunnels to find out how the universe was created . . . and look at us now. If Lowestoft truly is the last best hope for this country, and if this kind of atrocity is at its very heart, then what hope do we have? Is this Hinchcliffe's great plan for the future? Is Chris Ankin's vision any different?

I stagger back across the pathway and collide with the barrier around another pen. The vile noise of metal on metal seems to take forever to fade away into silence. I know I should keep moving, but I'm lost again, staring into the cage I've just disturbed, unable to look away. Here there are two bodies, and for a moment I'm struggling to work out why they were being doubled up when there was clearly more than enough space here for them to be separated. They were chained by their necks to diagonally opposite corners, and even though they're heavily discolored by rot, I can see that both of their small bodies are covered in scratches and marks. Had they been fighting each other? Fuck . . . had these kids been forced to fight each other to the death like caged dogs? Was Hinchcliffe using them for sport?

There's another sudden noise, much closer this time, too loud for a rat. I spin around quickly, but I can't see anything.

"Who's there?"

I freeze, figuring that it'll either be one of Hinchcliffe's fighters or Ankin's soldiers, and trying to work out my story for being here. No one answers. I keep walking, then stop when I hear the noise again, even closer now. I'm almost on top of it—a frantic shuffling and scurrying as something does its best not to be seen. Then there's the faintest chink of metal on metal, like chains being rattled. I glance down into the nearest few pens, but I can't see anything. Wait! There, just for a second, in the farthest corner of the cage behind the one I'm standing right in front of, I see something. I clumsily climb over the barriers to get closer, almost falling when one of my boots gets tangled up, and my sudden movements unleash a wave of panic in the shadows. Now I can see it. One of the children is still alive! An Unchanged boy tries to climb out of his pen and into another in desperation, but there's a chain wrapped around his ankle. He's weak and terrified and yanks at the chain to free himself but falls back and smashes down onto his face, yelping with pain when he hits the ground. I climb into his pen, and he continues to back away from me, pushing himself along the floor until he can go no farther back. About the same age as my son Edward was, he's barely clothed and is blue with cold. He's in worse physical condition than I am.

"Don't fight," I tell him. "I won't hurt you."

He just stares at me, too afraid even to blink, and I don't know what to do. Every time I move he flinches. I climb back out of his pen and into another to put some space between us, hoping he'll see that I'm not going to kill him.

"Are there any more of you?"

The boy doesn't answer. His face looks familiar. He's the lad from the last Unchanged nest I helped clear out, I'm sure he is. I lean forward and he spits at me, and now I know I'm right.

"Are there any more of you?" I ask again. I give him a few seconds to answer, but he remains silent. I wait a moment longer, but I know I have to go. I can't afford to waste any more time here. I climb back over the barriers until I reach the walkway, then start walking. This catatonic kid is lost anyway. There's nothing I can do for him.

"Wait," a quiet and unexpectedly fragile voice says from behind me. I turn back around and see that he's at the front of his cage now, leaning against the barrier. I keep walking, determined now to get away from Lowestoft and everyone and everything in it. "Please," he says, "let us out."

I keep moving but then stop and turn back again when he rattles his chains against the barrier in protest.

"Shh," I say to him, "they'll hear you if you—"

I shut up when I realize he's not the one making the noise. It's coming from another pen on the same side of the walkway, a little farther back. I can see another Unchanged face looking back at me now; small, round, and ghostly pale. It's a little girl. Dressed only in a grubby ripped T-shirt several sizes too big, she's standing on tiptoes to look at me over the top of the metal divide. When I take a step toward her she takes several panicked steps back, almost tripping over her own chained feet.

"You're the one who told them where we were," the boy says accusingly, his voice now stronger.

"What?"

"We were hiding and you told them where we were. It's all your fault."

"I had to do it," I say without thinking. Then I curse myself—what the hell am I apologizing for? Why am I explaining myself to him? Why am I explaining myself to one of the Unchanged?

"No you didn't. They wouldn't have found us if you hadn't told them. It's your fault."

Arrogant little bastard. The way he's shouting now reminds me of the way I used to argue with Ed. I start walking again, and the girl starts to cry.

"Let us out," the boy demands. I ignore him and keep going, then stop again because my head is suddenly full of stupid, dangerous thoughts. He's right, isn't he? It *is* my fault they're here. But what else could I have done? It was them or me, and these days you have to look after yourself 'cause no other fucker's going to help. Anyway, they'd have had to come out of their shelter eventually. All I did was make things happen faster than they would otherwise have. I'm saving them pain in the long run, or at least I would have if they hadn't ended up in here.

"Please!" he shouts as I try to walk on, but this time I stop because I know I'm wrong. No matter how I try to dress it up and justify what I did, these kids are only in the position they are today because of me. It doesn't matter what they are or what I am or what we're supposed to do to each other, I can't just leave them to die here. Lowestoft is burning around us, for Christ's sake. Well, maybe I can leave them, but the point is, I realize, I don't want to. The very least they deserve is a chance, no matter how slight. I can't deny them that.

I walk back toward the little girl and check her chains, which are held in position with a padlock.

"Don't hurt her," the boy shouts as the girl squirms to get away. "I'll get you if you hurt her."

"I'm not going to hurt anyone," I answer, testing the strength of the lock and the clasp around her bony ankle. "I'll be back. I'll see what I can do."

The noise of battle outside is increasing in volume. Even through the walls of this huge place, I can hear occasional bangs and screams, the helicopter flying overhead, guns and shells being fired, and the constant noise of engines. I try to block it all from my mind as I look for something to free the children with. *All I need to do*, I tell myself, *is let them go.*

In the farthest corner of this dank, foul-smelling place, I find a bloodstained workbench that's covered in lengths of chains, discarded locks, bits of bone, small teeth, and other, less easily identifiable things. There's a huge bunch of keys hung on a metal hoop on the wall, but there are too many to go through and I can't waste time checking each one of them. Instead I opt for a set of heavy, long-handled metal cutters I find leaning against the side of the bench. I head back to the pens, and the girl screams as I advance toward her with the cutters held high. Her helpless sobbing is heartbreaking.

"I'm not going to hurt you," I tell her, desperate for her to understand. "Look."

I climb over to the boy. He continues to recoil from me. I pull him closer, dragging him back across the floor, then use the cutters to snap the loop of the padlock that holds his chains in place. He removes his shackles, then clambers out of the pen after me, his movements stilted and clumsy after being restricted for so long. This time when I approach the girl she's a little quieter—still sobbing, but not screaming. I carefully ease the blade of the cutters over the loop of her padlock, then press down hard. It takes more effort this time (and I can feel my energy levels really starting to fade), but the lock eventually gives. I unravel her chains, and then, when she can't get over the barrier, I reach down and lift her up. There's nothing to her, absolutely no weight at all. She holds on to me, her tiny arms tight around my shoulders, her legs wrapped around my waist. I try to put her down, but I can't. She won't let go. This reminds me how it used to be when I held Ellis and the boys, feeling them close against you, hearing their breathing, reacting to their every movement . . .

Put the fucking kid down and get out of here.

I try to lower her, but she still won't let go. When another loud explosion rocks the building, she grips me even tighter, her fingers digging into my back.

Put the fucking kid down!

This time I peel her off me, prying off her fingers and unraveling her legs, then putting her down and backing up to put some distance between us. She just stands there looking up at me, not saying anything but asking a thousand questions with those huge, innocent eyes.

"Where's Charlie?"

"Who?"

"Charlie," she says. "You know, Charlotte. She came here with us."

She's talking about the dead girl upstairs. I try to tell her the truth, but I can't.

"She's already gone," I lie. "Now you need to do the same. Get out of here. There's trouble coming."

"Where?" the boy asks, shivering. He's dressing himself in rags he's stripped from another child's corpse.

"What?"

"Where do we go?"

"How am I supposed to know? Just stay away from the town. Get onto the beach and follow it south as far as you can."

"Which way's south?"

"That way," I tell him, pointing and backing away from them both again.

"But the people out there," he continues, his voice unsure, "the Haters . . . they'll find us, won't they? They'll kill us . . ."

The girl starts to cry again, and I struggle to shut the noise out. What do these children think I am? I spent a couple of days in their shelter with them, but surely they must know I'm not like them. Then again, they also know I'm not acting like any of the other people they've seen since they've been here.

"Can't you take us back?" the girl asks, her voice barely audible. Her bottom lip quivers and tears roll down her cheeks.

"Back where?"

"Back to where we were before. With Sally and Mr. Greene. Where all those cones and traffic signs were."

She's talking about the storage depot where I found them. "You can't go back there," I answer quickly, not thinking about the effect my words will have on her. "That place is gone now, and all the people who were there are gone, too."

She just nods, her tiny body shuddering as she sobs, her tear-streaked face filled with resignation.

"You got any food?" the boy asks. "Really hungry."

I check my bag and my pockets. All I find is the half-finished packet of sweets, which I hand over.

"My daddy says—" the girl begins.

"That you shouldn't take sweets from strangers," I say, finishing her sentence for her, immediately slipping back into parent mode even after all this time. "Your daddy was right, but things are a bit different now, aren't they?"

She doesn't answer, too busy cramming several of the sweets into her mouth. Strings of sticky dribble are running down her chin. This is probably the first thing these kids have eaten in days. The roar of another engine outside snaps me out of my dangerous malaise. I jog toward the nearest door.

"You can't leave us," the boy shouts after me.

"Yes I can."

"But they'll kill us . . ."

"It's probably for the best."

I know I should just keep moving and not look back again, but I can't. Standing behind me, their mouths full of sugar, faces streaked with dirt, are two kids. Two normal, rational kids behaving like normal, rational human beings, not like the hundreds of blood-crazed, mad bastards fighting to the death outside this place. Kids like the children in the family I used to be a part of before the Hate tore everything apart and left my world in ruins, not like the barely controlled, feral creatures Hinchcliffe held captive elsewhere on this site. This innocent, completely helpless boy and girl deserve better than this, but what else can I do? They're dead already. The second they're outside this place they'll be torn to pieces... My head fills with images of them being attacked by a pack of people like me, being ripped apart just because they're not like us. It's inevitable—just the way the world is now—but the idea of them being hunted down and killed suddenly feels abhorrent.

There is an answer. It's obvious, but I don't want to accept it.

"Please," the boy says, his eyes scanning my face, desperately searching for even the faintest flicker of hope, "just help us to get away."

"Okay," I say, cursing my stupidity as soon as I've spoken. "I'll take you somewhere there are other people like you."

43

THIS IS THE VAN they used to bring me and these kids back here after the nest had been cleared out. I find it parked in another part of the factory, left abandoned in an area of open space next to a roller-shutter door, the keys still in the ignition. I open up the back and try to get the kids inside, but neither of them will move. They stare at the metal cage bolted to the wall, no doubt remembering the last time.

"Get in," I tell them, gently pushing the girl forward. She doesn't move. The boy holds her hand. "What's your name, son?"

"Jake."

"And what about you?"

"Chloe."

"Listen, we don't have a lot of time. There's a lot of fighting going on outside, so we need to move fast. I know you're scared, but if you don't get into the van, you're not going to make it. You don't have to get into the cage, just get into the damn van."

Chloe looks at Jake. He scowls, thinks for a second longer, then nods. I help them up, shut the door, then head over toward the roller-shutter. It won't move. Another fucking padlock. I fetch the metal cutters and try to get it open. It eventually gives, but not without an unexpected amount of effort. I'm soaked with sweat now, and I can feel the sickness returning.

The engine starts on the third try. I watch the fuel gauge climb. I will it to keep moving, but it barely manages to reach a quarter full. That should be enough to get us out of Lowestoft and clear of the fighting; then it's just a question of finding Peter Sutton and the Unchanged bunker, dumping these kids, and disappearing. I try to visualize the route to the bunker, remembering how long and featureless the roads around here are. One wrong turn and I could end up back in the center of Lowestoft before I've even realized I've gone the wrong way.

"Hold on," I shout to the kids as I turn the van around and pull away. I watch them in the rearview mirror, huddled together in the corner, freezing cold and terrified but relieved to be free. "Keep your heads down. Don't let anyone see you, okay?"

"Where are we going?" Jake asks as I steer through the open door and onto the road, out into the gray light of day.

"There's a place I know. Someone showed it to me a few days ago. There are people like you there."

"Like the old place?" Chloe asks.

"Better than that," I tell her.

The engine splutters and almost dies, and I remember how unreliable this heap of a van is. I drive away from the factory, accelerating hard, then stop.

"What's the matter?" Jake asks, his voice suddenly sounding nervous again.

"Nothing. Just trying to decide which way's best."

Fuck. I didn't think this through. Truth is, there is no best way out of here. Heading north around the top of the compound would probably be easiest, but that's going in completely the wrong direction, and I'd have to drive a huge loop around to get anywhere near the bunker. The best—the only—option is to try to head south and get out over the bridge. For a fraction of a second I consider either dumping the kids altogether or trying to run with them along the beach, but I know both those choices are useless, too. All I can do is start driving and hope for the best.

I accelerate again, and for the first few yards it's easy. The roads are still swarming with people, but they're more interested in surviving now than in anything I'm doing. *All I need to do is get over the bridge*, I keep telling myself. *Once I'm on the other side of the water everything will be easier.*

The people here are herding along the streets like sheep, some moving toward the fires still burning around the courthouse, others heading out of town. The massive column of people and vehicles I saw coming through the gate across the bridge earlier seems now to have reduced to a slow trickle. The air is filled with drifting smoke, and the figures on the road move to either side as I drive toward them. It's less than half a mile to the gate. A couple of minutes and we'll be out of here. I swerve around a fight that spills out of a building, and when I look back in my mirror I see that Jake has his face pressed against the glass.

"Get your fucking head down!" I scream at him. He does as I say, but it's too late, he's been seen. Perhaps because no one's able to process the bizarre reality of the appearance of an Unchanged child in the middle of the crumbling chaos of Lowestoft, there's the slightest delay before I'm aware of any real reaction. But then, when I brake hard to avoid a collision with some kind of armored truck coming the other way, a horde of people begin throwing themselves at the sides of the van. The engine almost dies, and they hammer against the glass and try to grab at the doors. The children sink down and cover their heads in terror, and I accelerate again, barely managing to keep the van on the road.

I follow the bend in the road around to the left, and I can see the bridge ahead of me now. The gates are open, but there's still a heavy military presence here. Ankin's troops are blocking the way in and out of town, doing all they can to keep the trouble contained. I can already see several of them moving toward me, weapons raised.

"Stay down!" I yell again at the kids. I jam my foot down on the accelerator pedal, sink back into my seat, and grip the steering wheel tight as we race toward the blockade. Over the top of the dashboard I see sudden, frantic movement as we hurtle toward the troops and they dive away in either direction as I smash through them. Shots ring out and bullets thud into the side of the van. The back windows shatter, showering Jake and Chloe with glass.

"Who's shooting?" Jake asks. He crawls along the length of the van, then gets up and hangs over the seat next to me, blocking my view behind.

"Get out of the way," I yell at him, trying to push him away and still keep control. He fights to stay where he is, but I manage to shove him hard out of the way, and in the suddenly clear rearview mirror I see headlights behind us. The fuckers are following.

"Someone's coming," Chloe wails, looking out through a bullet hole. "I can see motorbikes."

I look up again. There are two bikes and a jeep in pursuit now. We're on the A12, and although littered with debris, the road is virtually clear of other traffic. Sticking to the main road is the safest option. If I try to find an alternative route I could end up driving down a road that's blocked or doubling back and going the wrong way. I need to keep going until we reach Wrentham. Once we're there I'll know we're not far from the bunker. Just got to keep moving . . .

The miles flash past quickly, the road straight and uninterrupted. Our pursuers are gaining fast, but that's inevitable given the dilapidated state of this van. Being caught is an obvious concern, but I know I have an even bigger problem to deal with. Assuming we make it to the bunker, how do we get in without leading Ankin's soldiers straight to it?

"Are we nearly there?" Chloe shouts at me from the back of the van, her innocent comment striking an immediately familiar chord. I instinctively react like I always used to.

"We'll get there when we get there."

"They're coming," Jake says. "Drive faster."

"I can't."

One of the bikes accelerates, and within a few seconds it's up alongside us. I try to ram it off the road, but the driver anticipates my clumsy maneuver and drops back out of the way, and it's me that almost loses control. I clip the curb, then steer hard and overcompensate, caught out by the camber of the road and almost hitting the curb on the other side. The second bike passes us now, squeezing through the gap, and I'm starting to wish I'd stayed hidden in Rona Scott's office and never bothered trying to get out.

Wrentham. We enter the village at speed, sandwiched between the bikes, with the jeep gaining steadily. Now the dumb bastard on the bike ahead of me is regretting being in front. He looks back over his shoulder, trying to work out which way I'm going to go as we race toward the crossroads, then chooses the wrong option and continues toward Southwold. I steer right to take the road that leads to the bunker, and I shove my foot down hard on the accelerator pedal again to get to maximum speed and take advantage of this moment of clear road ahead. The van's struggling to keep going, and it's just a matter of seconds before both of the bikes are swarming around the back again. Fortunately the road here narrows slightly, and I weave from side to side. There's no way either of them is getting past.

I catch a glimpse of something through the bare-branched trees. It's gone again in a heartbeat, and I think I must have been mistaken, but then there's another gap in the hedgerow and I look across and see the remains of the battlefield I remember seeing when Sutton brought me out here.

We're close now. Very close.

Wait. This must be it. I'm sure I can see the outline of the farm buildings in the near distance up ahead. I swerve hard to block one of the bikes from trying to pass again, and Chloe screams with pain as she's thrown across the back of the van and hits the side of her head against the metal cage. Her piercing scream cuts right through me, but it helps me focus, too. It's like when Ellis and Josh used to fight in the backseat of my car.

"Hold on," I tell them both, as much for my benefit as theirs, quickly checking over my shoulder that they're both braced for impact. I let one of the bikes slip past, then slam on the brakes. The first rider races ahead, at first not even noticing I've stopped. The second driver pulls up hard to avoid a collision and loses balance, the bike kicking out from under him. I accelerate again, but the engine doesn't react. It threatens to stall, and I will it to keep ticking over. Our speed finally begins to increase, and I steer hard right through the open gateway into the dilapidated farm, a few precious seconds of space behind us.

The well-worn wheels of the van struggle to get a grip on the mud- and ice-covered track. The back end swings out violently as I turn, and I feel it smack against one of the gateposts, but I manage to keep control and keep my speed up, trying to remember the exact layout of the farm as I career toward the collection of dark, empty buildings, desperate to get out of sight before any of our pursuers catch up. Directly ahead now is the derelict cowshed where Peter Sutton left his car when he brought me here. I look back and see the jeep just turning into the farm. I drive into the shed, then slam on the brakes and kill the engine.

"Keep your damn heads down," I yell at the kids again, hoping I've done enough to keep us hidden. I can hear the jeep approaching. "Don't move a muscle! If they see either of you, we've all had it."

I sink down into my seat and watch in the mirrors, completely still, moving only my eyes. Within a few seconds the jeep appears in the muddy yard behind us and skids to an abrupt halt. Moments later the two bikes arrive. With the bike riders, at least one other soldier in the jeep, probably more . . . the odds aren't looking good. I could try to take them by surprise, start the engine again, drive away and hope to get enough of a head start on them, then hide out and come back here later, but what's that going to achieve? I'm low on fuel, and the bunker is the only place I can take these kids.

"Head hurts," Chloe whimpers.

"Shut up," I hiss at her. "They'll hear you."

Jake reaches across and covers her mouth with his hand. In the middle of the yard behind us, two more of Ankin's soldiers get out of the back of the jeep, then split up, the driver ordering them away in different directions. Along with the two motorcyclists they fan out across the farm, and I watch in the rearview mirror as one of them starts walking directly toward the cowshed, no doubt following the fresh tracks we've left in the mud and ice. Moving as little as possible, I reach across to the passenger seat and grab the metal cutters I brought with me from the factory.

I can hear the soldier approaching, boots crunching louder with every advancing step. It's a woman, her face smeared with the grime of battle, and she's carrying a pistol. She peers into the shed, then edges into the darkness cautiously, not about to take any chances. She moves slowly, inching ever closer to the back of this still-warm bullet-riddled wreck of a van. For a fraction of a second our eyes seem to meet in the rearview mirror, but I don't think she's yet sure what she saw. She takes another step forward, then stops and spins around on the spot. The silence is interrupted by a single gunshot. The back of her skull explodes out over the back of the van and I hear her dead body slam against the vehicle before she drops to the ground. I can't see anything, but I guess there's someone standing on the other side of the farm with a rifle. There's a second shot—I can't see if it hits anyone—then there's a third, and I'm pretty sure that one's from another direction entirely. I'm trying to work out what's going on from my pitifully small viewpoint while still keeping low in the driver's seat; I don't want any of Sutton's people taking me out before they realize who I am and what— *who*—I've brought them.

I can see two soldiers crouched down on my side of the jeep, using the car for cover. They begin to return fire, single shots, and almost instantly a hail of gunfire ricochets around the farm. It reminds me of a Western gunfight, one of those old Saturday afternoon films I used to watch when I was a kid. Then the windshield of the jeep is shattered by a bullet and I only realize the driver was still inside when his now-dead body half-falls out of the door. One of the others runs for cover, but he's shot as he sprints towards this dilapidated shed. The last soldier scrambles up and runs back to the nearest bike. He drags it upright and jumps on, showering his fallen comrades with mud as he hauls it around in a tight circle and aims at the farmyard gate.

I get out of the van, run round to the back, and help the children climb out. Holding Chloe's hand tight in one hand, Jake by the other, I wait just inside the shed door where I can still see out. In the distance, at the highest point of the dirt track before it drops down toward the bunker, a lone figure is frantically waving at me.

"Okay, now we've got to run," I tell the children, and as we pound across the churned-up farmyard, Jake pulls free and sprints ahead. Now I can see the man waving us on is Dean. Last time I saw him, that rifle was aimed at me.

"Behind you!" he shouts. I turn around and see a man, gaining on me fast. I must have lost track in the confusion; I didn't think there were any left.

"Keep running and don't stop," I tell Chloe, shoving her away, and I turn around to try to fend off Ankin's soldier, but I've misjudged his speed and he's on top of me before I can do anything to defend myself. He's got a riot baton, which he swings around and thumps into my gut. The incredible pain immediately makes me fold in two and I'm flat on my back in the mud before I know what's happened. He drops down hard on my chest, forcing every scrap of oxygen from my lungs.

"What the fuck are you doing?" he screams into my face. "They're Unchanged, you fucking traitor!"

My arms are pinned down by his knees, and there's nothing I can do to protect myself when he punches me in the face. He spits in my eye, blinding me for an instant, and I don't see his fist coming until he smacks me in the mouth again. My lip is split, and the pain is intense. Killing the Unchanged is more important to him than dealing with me. He springs up again and runs after them, but, more through luck than judgment, I manage to stretch out an arm behind me and catch hold of one of his feet. He trips and slams down face-first into the dirt. He's far faster and far stronger than I am and he's back up in seconds, shaking me off with ease but turning back and booting me in the right kidney for my troubles. I'm enough of a distraction to give Dean a chance to get closer. He steps forward and fires into the soldier's face from point-blank range. The corpse drops on top of me, what's left of his dead head smacking hard against mine, and I fight to stay focused and keep breathing through the sudden, all-consuming darkness.

44

SIT UP QUICKLY, but the pain's too much and I immediately drop down again, my skull cracking back against the hard concrete floor. I open my eyes, but it's dark and everything's blurred. I can see someone standing over me, looking down. Unchanged. Something inside me instinctively makes me try to get up and fight before I remember what happened. I try to move again, but I can't. Hurts too much. I can tell from the position of the light and the damp smell in here that this is the small room at the entrance to the Unchanged bunker. The person looking down at me moves closer, his features slowly becoming more distinct. Is that Joseph Mallon?

"Joseph?"

"Lie still, Danny," he says, his face distressingly haggard and hollow but his voice immediately recognizable. He gently rests his hand on my shoulder. "Tracey's done what she could for you."

"Tracey?"

"Our doctor. She's cleaned your wounds as best she can, but you're in a bad way."

I try to get up again, this time managing to prop myself up on my elbows. I slowly shuffle my broken body around and lean back against a wall. I lift my hands to my swollen face and pick dry blood from my eyes. I don't know whether it's the beating I've just taken, the drugs finally wearing off, or a combination of both, but I feel bad. Really bad. Worse than ever. There's a woman watching me. Tracey, I presume. She storms out of the room.

"If the stupid bastard won't listen, there's nothing I can do to help him."

Joseph acknowledges her, but I ignore her.

"What happened?" I ask him, having to concentrate hard to make each word.

"Peter knew something was going on out there. He heard all the engines and the planes and helicopters and saw the fighting in the distance. He'd been staying aboveground in the old farmhouse since yesterday, keeping a lookout. Then you showed up here, and all hell broke loose."

"The children. I had two kids with me . . ."

"They're safe in the back rooms with the others. Where did you find them, Danny? Are there more?"

"It's a long story that you really don't want to hear," I answer, catching my breath as a wave of pain washes over me. "And no, they're the last."

"Well, maybe I would like to hear that story one day, but not today. Today we have problems to solve first. Really big problems."

"Where's Peter?"

Joseph moves to one side. Lying on the floor on the opposite side of the room is a body under a bloodstained sheet.

"Shit."

"Poor bastard got caught in all that shooting. They got him before Dean could get them."

Mallon passes me a bottle of water. I swill some around in my mouth, then spit it out to clear the blood. I drink a little, and its icy temperature seems to wake my body and makes me feel slightly more alive. I try to focus on my surroundings. The boy Jake is standing in the doorway watching me, hiding behind Parker.

"What's happening out there, Danny?" Mallon asks.

I look straight at him. "I didn't tell anyone about you, if that's what you think."

"I didn't say that."

"It's nothing you haven't heard before," I tell him. "Just the same old same old."

"What?"

"You were right, you know, back then at the convent. All those things you used to say about not fighting and making a stand and trying to break the cycle. I thought you were a fucking crank at the time, but you were right."

"I don't follow. What's that got to do with today?"

"We're imploding. What's left of the human race is tearing itself apart up there, and there's nothing anyone can do to stop it. The last army in the country is marching on the last town in the country, and there's probably very little of either of them left by now. It's like you said, every man for himself. The thing is, the less there is left to fight for, the higher the stakes seem to get."

"That still doesn't explain what you're doing out here, or how you came to have these children with you."

"I made a decision a while back, before I knew you were here in this place, in fact. I decided I'd had enough of fighting, had enough of everything. I was trying to get away. The kids were just a complication."

"I don't believe that."

"Believe what you like. I couldn't leave them out there on their own, so I was just delivering them to you before I fucked off for good. That's what I'm still planning to do."

"Well, that might not be so easy now."

"Why not?"

"Because of our position. They know where we are now, Danny. They've seen us here. We're up shit creek without a paddle, and we need your help."

Why can't everybody just leave me be?

"I'm past helping. I'm tired of being used. It just gets me deeper and deeper into the mire and doesn't do anyone any good. I'm sick and I'm dying, Joseph, and I just want to be left alone. There are enough of you here to be able to look after yourselves."

"You know that's not true. We can't do it without help, and it's up to you now that Peter's gone. Jesus, Danny, if millions of us were wiped out by your kind, what chance do less than thirty of us have?"

"No chance at all," I tell him, keeping my voice low so that Jake doesn't hear.

"We've been down here for months. We're weak and we're tired and we know that everything's stacked against us, but we're not just going to give up."

"You've got weapons, and it's chaos up there. You might still have a slight chance."

"We've got a handful of guns," he corrects me, "but we've just used most of our ammunition saving your backside."

"Then maybe you shouldn't have bothered."

"Maybe you're right," he says angrily. "Okay, I'll rephrase that. We just used up half our ammunition helping Peter Sutton and saving the life of those two kids. Anyway, whatever we did and whatever we did it for, we need your help now. We've hardly got any supplies left. We'll starve if we don't—"

"You want supplies? I can tell you where to find supplies, but I'm not—"

"Listen, those fuckers up there are going to come back, Danny. Dean says at least one of them got away, and there are still bodies out there, remember? They've seen us. They saw Dean and they know we're here. Even if they can't get into the bunker, they'll be waiting for us when we eventually come out. You think they're just going to forget about us? Forget about you?"

"I'm nothing to them."

"That's not what I'd heard. That's not what Peter told me."

"With all due respect, maybe you shouldn't have listened to everything Peter said."

"He was a good man. He kept us alive, and I trusted him."

"You call this living? Look around, Joseph. This place is no different from the mass graves I saw outside the gas chambers. You're all just waiting to die."

"What about you?"

"Me, too. You'll probably all outlast me. I don't have long left."

"So why let it end this way? Do something with the little time you have, Danny. After all you came through to get here, how hard you fought to find your daughter, the things you managed to survive . . . I can't believe you're talking like this now."

"Sorry if I've let you down," I sneer, concentrating on another sudden cramping pain in my gut rather than anything Mallon has to say.

"It's not just me, though, is it?" he continues, not giving up on the guilt trip. "It's the rest of them. It's everyone down here. You're our last chance."

"That's bullshit."

"Is it? Way I see it, even if everything else has fallen apart up there, you can still help us. You, me, and everyone else down here, we might be all there is left now."

45

AN HOUR PASSES, MAYBE longer. The pain gradually subsides as long as I stay still, but I know the bastard who attacked me aboveground has done some serious damage to my already seriously damaged insides. The temporary relief the drugs gave me from the pain is definitely over. I can feel my body giving up and breaking down.

The Unchanged have left me alone in here. I don't know whether they're maintaining a respectful distance from the dead and dying (my only company is Peter Sutton's corpse) or if they're just afraid of me.

The door to the corridor that leads down into the main part of the bunker is open, and I can hear Joseph talking, addressing the group. Christ alone knows what he's telling them. My guess is he's trying to get them ready to leave, but doesn't the dumb bastard realize what it's like up there now? Surely Sutton would have told him? These people are almost certainly the last Unchanged left alive, and as soon as they put their heads above the surface they'll be hunted down and killed. They might last a few hours or days, maybe a week if they're lucky, but sooner or later they'll be destroyed. Their fates are as certain as

mine. Poor fuckers. My mind—tired and confused—fills with base-
less, nightmare images of the girl Chloe being tracked and killed by
my dead daughter Ellis.

The voices down the corridor are becoming raised, and I try to sit
up to listen closer. The pain in my gut is too severe, and I have to lie back
down and stretch out again. I roll over onto my front and gradually
manage to lift myself up onto all fours, then slowly climb the wall
until I'm standing up straight. I edge toward the door, then take a few
unsteady steps farther down the sloping corridor, dragging my heavy
feet. By the time I get close to the other end, Joseph's in full flow again.

"We've talked about this before. We knew this day would come
eventually."

"We have to stay down here," someone protests. "They'll never find
this place."

"You think so? They know where we are now, that's the difference,
and they'll keep on looking until they find us. We've all seen what
they're like. They won't stop until they've forced us out into the open
and killed us all, because in their stupid, misguided minds they still
believe it's them or us. That's why we need to move from here now while
we've still got a chance, before they come looking."

"It's suicide."

"No it isn't. Sitting down here in the dark, slowly starving to death,
is suicidal. I agree it's not much, but at least we do have *some* chance up
there."

"Where are we supposed to go? They're everywhere," Tracey, the
doctor, asks, her voice full of anger. I can see her standing opposite
Joseph, arms crossed, body language uncomfortably confrontational.
I keep walking, gravity and the incline helping me to move. Almost at
the far door now.

"Peter and I discussed that. You are right, but they've been hit almost as hard by this war as we have. Their numbers are massively reduced. Peter had a plan. He said we should head straight for the ocean,
get on a boat, and get off the mainland. Doesn't matter where we go
after that, we just have to—"

"Where exactly do you think you're going to get a boat from?" I ask, staggering a little closer, leaning up against the door frame for support, dripping with sweat.

Joseph turns around and shrugs. "We're on the coast. There will be something somewhere."

"You're hoping. You're going to need a better plan than that. There's not much left undamaged up there, you know."

"I didn't think there would be."

"So what are you going to do exactly? Just walk around all the boatyards together until you find something, all of you wearing hats and dark glasses, hoping no one notices you? Get real."

A ripple of nervous conversation spreads quickly through the group. I can see them all for the first time now.

"Why don't you just fuck off," Tracey says. "Go back and—"

"We'll manage," Joseph insists, interrupting and trying to defuse her anger. "We have so far."

"It's thanks to him that Peter's dead," a badly burned man yells, gesturing at me accusingly.

"It's thanks to Danny these two children are alive, Gary," Joseph counters.

"There's nothing left of most of the towns around here," I tell them, feeling strangely obliged to be honest and let these people know exactly what's what aboveground. "I was told that Lowestoft was the only place left, and that's being torn to pieces as we speak. As far as finding a boat goes, you'll be lucky to find anything still floating, never mind anything big enough to carry all of you."

"Peter told me about a couple of places. Oulton Broad, does that sound familiar?"

I know the place he's talking about. From what I understand, it was a base for pleasure cruising and family boating vacations in the days before the war. It's close to Lowestoft, but far enough away from the very center of town to have remained relatively overlooked and ignored. It's weeks since I've been anywhere near the water there.

"Oulton Broad's a possibility, but even if you managed to find a big enough boat, you've still got a massive problem to deal with before you start."

"Such as?"

"It's inland. If you're planning on heading for the ocean, you're going to have to sail right through Lowestoft to get there. Oh, and I might not have mentioned," I add sarcastically, "there's a bit of a war going on up there right now."

"Well, that could work in our favor," Joseph says optimistically. "A distraction."

"You think? I'll tell you something, fight or no fight, if anyone gets so much as a sniff of just one of you, then everything else will be forgotten and the hunt will be back on. All the infighting will stop and you'll be the only targets again."

Another frightened murmur spreads quickly through the group. Many of the Unchanged are staring at me now. I make momentary eye contact with Chloe. Perhaps she doesn't fully follow the conversation, but I can tell from the expression on her face that the implications of what she's hearing are clearly understood. Jake, sitting on a desk and swinging his legs, lifts his hand and points a finger at me.

"I bet he can show us a better place to find a boat," he says, his voice initially quiet but steadily gaining in confidence. "He knows where to go," he tells the others.

"He's already told us he's not interested in helping," Tracey says.

Jake's not listening. "Then make him do it."

"We can't."

"You can show us, can't you?" he says again, looking straight at me. "We were by the sea when you found us. You must know where the boats are."

Joseph looks back at me again. "Well?"

"I know of a couple of places, but you're not listening to me, are you? It's going to be hard enough for any of you to get anywhere near Lowestoft. Then, if by some chance you do manage to find a boat, there's the little question of getting it going. I don't know anything about boats or engines—"

"We do," he interrupts. "You think we haven't planned for something like this? Do you think we've just been sitting down here twiddling our thumbs and staring into space for weeks on end feeling sorry for ourselves? We knew this day would come eventually. As good as it was, this place was never going to last. Where's Todd?"

A man emerges from the gloom at the back of the group. A gangly, awkward-looking guy with an Einstein-like shock of gray-white hair, he acknowledges Joseph and nods at me.

"Who's this?"

"My name's Todd Weston," he answers, stepping over and around people to get closer to the front. "I know my way around boats. You get me to it, I'll sail it."

I lean back against the wall and look up at the ceiling. How the hell am I going to get through to these people?

"Do you really think you're just going to trot along to Lowestoft, pick yourselves up a boat, and sail it away into the sunset? Didn't you hear me, the place isn't full of tourists anymore, it's a fucking war zone. Plus there's so much smoke and shit in the air that you can't see the fucking sunset anymore, never mind sail away into it."

"Where exactly is the fighting?" Joseph asks.

"Want me to draw you a fucking map?"

"Don't be facetious. I just want to know if the fighting's near the boatyards," he says, his voice annoyingly calm, bordering on patronizing.

"I don't know for sure. It seemed to be concentrated in and around the compound in the center of town from what I saw of it, but—"

"So theoretically we could get in and out again without anyone noticing?"

"Hardly. What are you planning? Are you going to bus people in?"

"Lose the sarcasm and change your attitude, Danny," he snaps, his voice suddenly harder. "We're talking about people's lives here. Stop looking for excuses and try to find a way out. That's what the old Danny McCoyne would have done."

"Yeah, and the new Danny McCoyne wouldn't bother at all. Look at me, for Christ's sake. I'm a dead man walking. I'm riddled with cancer, I've just had seven shades of shit kicked out of me, and—"

"And you're still going. You're standing here helping, whether you realize it or not. You continually underestimate yourself. Don't forget,

Danny, you're the man who managed to find the proverbial needle in the haystack. When the whole country was falling apart and going to hell around you, you were the one who managed to find his daughter and save her. I don't know of any other father who could have done that. If it wasn't for you, she'd have been——"

"I didn't save her," I interrupt angrily, doing all I can not to think about Ellis.

"What your daughter became and what happened to her wasn't your fault. You did all you could, more than most. You fought your way into the heart of the biggest fucking battle of all, then managed to get yourself and your girl back out again before it was too late. I don't know anyone else who's done anything near comparable. Peter Sutton was in awe of you, you damn fool."

"Then he was the fool, not me."

"Can't you see, you're our only option, Danny. Without you we're screwed."

"I'm screwed anyway."

"I know that, and I'm truly sorry, but what else are you going to do with the time you have left? You're not the kind of man who'll just crawl under a rock and wait there to die, are you? You're better than that. Go out with a purpose. Give people something to remember you by."

I know he's being deliberately overdramatic and playing to his captive audience, but the thing is, there's a part of me that knows he might be right. I *am* different from the rest of the useless, brain-dead fucks that inhabit this poisoned, dying country. My problem is I've always struggled to accept responsibility, and I don't see why I should start trying to change things now. Surely it's too late? Joseph looks at me expectantly for an answer, and I do all I can to look anywhere else. Tracey glares at me. Parker and Todd are a little less vicious but no less hopeful. Dean holds his rifle, looking like he's about to point it at me to try to force me to help. I look from face to face, then find myself looking straight at Chloe and Jake again.

Deep breath.

"Okay, I'll ask you once more, how do you think you're going to get everyone onto a boat? Assuming you can find one, that is."

"No one said that was what we were planning," Todd says. "When Pete, Joseph, and me first started talking about this, we ruled that out right away. We knew that if we had to get away fast, we'd end up bringing the boat to the people, not trying to take the people to the boat."

"What, here? Are we close to a river or . . . ?"

He's shaking his head at me. Joseph explains.

"We were going to split up. Peter and I were going to find the boat with Todd. Everyone else was going to head to a prearranged point farther down the coast and wait for us."

"What prearranged point?"

"We hadn't got that far," he admits.

"Great."

Every nerve in my body that still feels anything is screaming at me to shut up and get out of here, but there's something screaming equally loud at me not to. As hard as it is for me to accept, Joseph's right. When I think about everything I've seen and been a part of in Lowestoft these last few days, I know I can't just turn my back on these people. There's more decency and civility here in this cramped bunker than there is in the rest of the country combined. Besides, I'm just fooling myself if I think I'm going to get far on my own. My body is well and truly fucked, and I'm living on borrowed time. My choice now is simple and stark: Whether I'm left down here or I manage to crawl back up to the surface, I can either die alone or try to do the right thing by these Unchanged. The last Unchanged.

There's a hushed, expectant silence throughout the bunker.

"Southwold," I eventually say.

"What?" Joseph asks, looking confused.

"That's where you need to go. That's your ideal meeting point, ten miles south of Lowestoft. Get everyone down there, then get a boat from one of the yards in town and sail it down the coast. With a little luck you'll find something near the ocean. Southwold is a dead place now. It's your best option. Probably your only option."

"So will you help us?"

I pause again. Am I completely sure about this? *Think carefully.*

"I'll do what I can," I hear myself answer, regretting the words before they've even left my mouth.

"We'll need supplies. We've got nothing."

"There's a house I was using. It's more than a mile outside Lowestoft. I've got a load of stuff there I'm never going to need. If we're careful we can collect it on the way through to the boatyard."

"We need to get moving, then," he says. "Let's clear this place out and be ready to get out by morning. We should move fast, while they're still distracted with their damn infighting and before they start looking for those corpses up there."

46

THEY WERE BETTER PREPARED for this day than I'd expected, but Peter Sutton's death and my unannounced arrival at the bunker have forced the Unchanged to drastically alter their plans. We left as dawn broke. Using the van I brought the children here in and the delivery truck that Sutton already had hidden in the cowshed (it's obvious now that he had it ready for a day like today), Joseph and Parker are driving the bulk of the group down to Southwold, where they'll wait at the lighthouse, if it's still standing. I'm on the way back into Lowestoft with Todd and Dean in the dead soldiers' jeep. We're going to clear out the stash of supplies from the house I was using, then load the whole lot into the biggest boat we can find that's still seaworthy. Then, if by some miracle we manage to sail through Lowestoft and out the other side, we'll rendezvous with the others at Southwold. I hold out very little hope of ever getting there, and it's becoming increasingly difficult to hide my pessimism.

It's another icy-cold day, and the fact that the windshield of this jeep was shot out in the fighting yesterday isn't helping. Everywhere is covered with a half inch of snow this morning, the white on the ground making the sky look dirtier than usual, and there's been a severe frost. The bodies of Ankin's soldiers were frozen solid when a couple of the men tried to shift them earlier. The layer of snow makes it easy for anyone to follow our tracks, but we don't have any option. Although the three sets of tire marks led away from the farm in the same direction initially, they split at Wrentham. With a little luck anyone trying to track our movements will follow the jeep back toward Lowestoft and leave the others alone.

I'm still in constant pain, but I have to drive. Dean and Todd are in the back of the jeep, both of them armed and ready to fight if they have to, but remaining hidden under blankets because if anyone sees them, we're all dead. I keep telling myself that I must be out of my fucking mind to be a part of this madness. At least the fact we're in one of Ankin's vehicles with its unsubtle red and white circle markings should make us appear less conspicuous if we're spotted. Unless Hinchcliffe somehow won yesterday's battle royal, that is. If he's still in charge, the paint job will literally become a target.

It's not long before I can see Lowestoft up ahead. I can't make out any of the buildings yet, rather just a dark haze where the gray smoke of battle is still drifting up into the sky, and the faint orange glow of several fires lighting up the underside of the heavy cloud cover. Is there anything left of the damn place? Even today, months after everything began to fall apart, after all the endless killing and bombing and wanton destruction I've witnessed, the sight of the dying town in the near distance makes my cold heart sink like a stone. It might make our mission simpler, but it was all so fucking pointless. I don't even know who fired the first metaphorical shot yesterday, and I doubt Ankin or Hinchcliffe does either.

I drive back down the A12 toward Lowestoft. I'll turn off shortly, about a mile and a half before we get anywhere near the center of town, then I'll use back roads to get into the development. Wait. There's movement on the road up ahead. I slow down, and Dean immediately reacts behind me.

"What's wrong?" he asks, starting to shuffle nervously under the blanket.

"Now's not the time to be looking up," I tell him. "There are people coming."

"What kind of people?"

"What do you think?"

Stupid question—but who the hell are they? They're as drab and gray as everything else, and they blend colorlessly into their surroundings, making it hard to accurately gauge their numbers. I can see perhaps as many as twenty of them now, dragging themselves wearily away from Lowestoft, carrying their few remaining belongings in bags and boxes, moving alone or in pairs, large gaps opening up between them. They don't even look up when I pass, instead keeping their heads bowed with either exhaustion or fear, maybe both. They look like refugees. That would make sense, I suppose, as much as anything makes sense today. If the fighting continued after I got away yesterday, there's probably hardly anything of the town left, and therefore no point staying anywhere near Lowestoft anymore. This may well be the beginning of an exodus. Or maybe it's the tail end of one? Are these few people all that's left?

"Who is it?" Dean asks, only daring to speak when I change direction and pull off the main road, then accelerate again toward the development.

"Refugees. As lost as the rest of us."

The house looks just as I left it as I pull up outside, the remains of the door that Hinchcliffe kicked in still swinging to and fro in the wind. I reverse down the drive and park next to the side door, then get out and peer in through the living room window, shielding my eyes from the snow's glare. Doesn't look like anything's been disturbed. Place looks like a fucking bomb site, but it's the same bomb site I left earlier in the week. There are no footprints in the snow but mine. I check up and down the road, and then, once I'm sure it's safe, I open the back of the jeep and pull the blankets off Dean and Todd.

"In there," I tell them, pushing them toward the front of the house, terrified that someone's going to see them. "Move!"

I follow them in, then walk straight into Todd's back. Both he and Dean have stopped dead and are staring into the living room. I push past them to see what's wrong. It's Rufus's body. I forgot about him, poor bastard. I grab my dead friend's ankles and try to drag him out of the way.

"This is the kind of thing you're up against," I tell them, struggling to move Rufus because he's frozen to the ground. "This guy was a friend of mine who fucked up."

Still struggling with the corpse, I glance up and see them both staring back at me in horror.

"Your friend, but why . . . ?" Todd starts to ask.

"Not me," I quickly interrupt, setting him straight. "I didn't do it."

I don't know if they believe me or not; it doesn't make any difference. I pick up my sleeping bag that's still draped over the back of my chair and use it to cover Rufus up. There's nothing worth salvaging in this room. My pile of books and some of my other belongings lie scattered all around the place, and that's where they'll stay now. I don't need them anymore. Even if I started reading another book today, the way I'm feeling I doubt I'd last long enough to finish it. I go through into the kitchen, beckoning the men to follow, then peel up the linoleum and lift up the floorboards.

"Start with all of this," I tell them, crouching down and showing them where my food store is. "Then open the cupboards and take what you can from them, too. I'll have a look and see if there's anything useful upstairs."

I remove the padlock and chain from the side door so they can easily load up the back of the jeep, then throw Dean the keys and leave them both to it. I climb the steps to the mausoleum-like rooms on the second floor, heading straight for the dried-up water tank where I keep my pathetic weapons cache: a pistol, some ammunition, and a grenade.

Last time I was here—last time I was trying to leave Lowestoft—I was working alone and intending to travel alone, too. Things are different now. The Unchanged need to get enough stuff together for at least thirty people. Bedding, clothes, furniture for firewood, everything counts today. Between us we need to completely empty this place and leave nothing behind. Maybe we should check a few of the nearest houses, too, if we have time. We should fill the car to capacity and take as much stuff as possible with us to the boatyard.

The noises downstairs have stopped. By the sound of things they're done loading the jeep. I've been watching the road outside from an upstairs window, making sure no one comes snooping around. The people we saw as we were driving back here were a concern. If any of them drift off the main road and end up around this place we could be in trouble. My body hurts, and it's hard to concentrate. Every movement is an effort, and I lean against the windowsill and stare out, my eyes drawn to the drifting black smoke rising up over what's left of Lowestoft in the distance.

I throw a couple of sheets and blankets down the stairs, then empty out a chest of drawers and chuck a load of clothing and underwear down, too. In the bathroom there's a little soap and shampoo and a few other things in a mirrored cabinet on the wall. We had one like that in the apartment back home. I used to shave in front of it, but the man I see when I look in the mirror today is nothing like the man I used to be. Today I look like the life has been sucked out of me, and I'm thankful for the mess of hair and the straggly beard that hide the full extent of my physical deterioration. The longer I look, the more frightened I get. If someone cut me open, they'd find more cancer than man now, I think.

I pause to catch my breath again in the back bedroom, the child's room with the abandoned board game on the floor. I used to avoid coming in here before, but things feel different today. It's not much of a gesture, but I pick up a couple of small teddy bears and shove them in my pocket along with the grenade and gun. I bet that kid Chloe will like them. She deserves to have something like—

"What's going on, Danny?"

I freeze and stand perfectly still, unable to move, staring at the wall dead ahead, gripping another toy tight in my hand. I know that voice. It's neither Todd nor Dean. Too calm. Too composed. Too confident. It can't be, can it? I slowly turn around, and there, standing in the doorway in front of me, his clothes glistening with streaks of freshly spilled blood, is Hinchcliffe. My mouth's dry and I can't speak. How can this be happening?

"Found two Unchanged downstairs, helping themselves to your stuff. What's that all about? Don't worry, by the way, Danny, I straightened them out for you. Stopped them stealing anything. Killed both of the fuckers before they even knew I was watching."

"I can explain, Hinchcliffe . . ."

"I doubt you can."

He takes a step toward me, and I move back until I hit the wall and I can't go any farther.

"It's not what you think."

"How would you know? You don't know what I think. I don't know how you think, either. I thought I was starting to understand, but you keep surprising me, Danny McCoyne."

"Why are you here?"

"Because I knew you'd come back. You're so fucking naive. You've got no idea, have you?"

"I don't know what you're talking about."

He walks forward again, and I've got nowhere left to go. He leans over me, an arm on either side of my shoulders, pinning me down without even having to touch me. He checks my pockets, taking my grenade, my pistol, and one of my knives. He digs the tip of the knife into the wall, level with my eyeline. He twists the blade around and makes a hole, plaster dust drifting down and landing on my boot.

"Why do you think I've kept hold of you for so long, Danny?" he asks. "Is it because of your dynamic personality? Your sparkling wit? Your remarkable strength?"

Sarcastic bastard.

"Because I'm useful to you? Because I can hold the Hate? Because I can hunt out the Unchanged?"

"Right on all three counts," he says, "but you still don't completely get it."

I can't think straight, and I doubt I'd be able to understand what he's talking about even if I could. He pushes himself away from the wall and walks away. I have two more knives on me; should I just try to attack and get this over with? The temptation's strong, but I don't think I can. Even if I did, Hinchcliffe's always been far more powerful than me. He's just killed two Unchanged men without breaking a sweat. I wouldn't stand a chance.

"You, Danny," he explains, pointing at me with my blade, "are unique. Didn't you ever wonder why I gave you so many chances?"

"To be honest, I was just relieved you weren't kicking the shit out of me. Anything else was a bonus."

He laughs and sits down on the end of the narrow single bed on one side of this room. He picks up a small metal toy—looks like a music box—from a bedside table, then puts down his knife and turns a key to wind it up. When he lets it go it starts to play a tune. A lullaby. Can't remember the name of it. Makes me want to cry.

"The reality, Danny," he says, talking over the beautiful noise, "is that you're different. I told you before that I liked the way you could take a step back from everything, remember? You've always been able to look beyond the fighting and see the bigger picture. Most people think you're a useless coward, and to an extent you are, but there's more to you than that."

"So how is a useless coward supposed to help the all-powerful Hinchcliffe?"

"Simple, you're always looking for the way out. You come at problems from a different perspective that no one else sees. We're all focused on the kill, but not you. I came back here for you, Danny, because I knew you'd be trying to get away from the fighting, not running toward it like the rest of them, and I knew you'd end up here again eventually. I'm not stupid, I know how much stuff you've got hidden away here. Christ, I've been giving you extra rations for weeks, and I know you haven't been eating any of it. It was pretty damn obvious you'd been stashing it away somewhere. Close enough to Lowestoft for you to get to, far enough away to avoid any fallout, so to speak."

"Take everything."

"I don't want your food, you moron."

"What, then?"

"I want to know where you were going. I knew you'd have a plan to get away, Dan, I just didn't think it would involve Unchanged."

"It doesn't now you've killed them."

"For fuck's sake, what else was I going to do? They were Unchanged, Danny."

"They hadn't done anything wrong."

"They were still breathing, that's wrong in my book."

"Then maybe you need a new book."

He gets up fast and charges across the room, slamming into me before I have a chance to react, shoving me hard against the wall, his hand wrapped around my throat.

"Don't push me," he hisses in my face, tightening his grip. "I'm really not in the mood. I've had a bad couple of days."

"It didn't have to be like this."

"Like what?"

"You could have talked to Ankin. You could have tried to find some common ground."

"I didn't get the chance. Anyway, the Unchanged are our common ground, or at least they were. Now it's just every man for himself. It wouldn't have mattered if I'd talked to Ankin for six fucking months and agreed with him on everything, the end result would have been the same."

"No it wouldn't. There was no need for what you did."

He lets me go and takes a step back.

"What *I* did? You fuckwit, Danny, I didn't do anything. For the record, neither did Ankin. Lowestoft is dead today because Ankin's appearance gave people a choice."

"What?"

"I watched the whole thing from up on the roof once it kicked off. I always knew there was a chance it was going to happen. That was why I came down so hard on John Warner in Southwold last week. People always think the grass is greener on the other side, but it's not. You have to take away the temptation. Everywhere you look now, everything is fucked. Word got around that Ankin had surrounded the town. Half the people panicked and tried to fight them off because they thought they were coming in to raid Lowestoft like we've raided everywhere else. The other half were throwing themselves at their mercy, thinking these assholes in their fucking uniforms with their fucking tanks were bringing them some kind of salvation. The people destroyed Lowestoft, not me and not Ankin. Granted, it would have been better if the stupid fucker hadn't turned up like that, but that's how it goes."

"I don't understand. You just walked away from it all?"

"From what? From a few hundred fighters who couldn't take a shit without checking with me first? From a couple of thousand underclass who could barely function? Do you think any of that actually mattered?"

"What about your breeding plan? The stuff that was going on at the factory? All the food you'd been storing?"

"The storerooms were almost empty, and the factory was just a remnant from Thacker's day, something to keep Rona Scott entertained and out of my hair. As for the hotel...that was just a way to keep people quiet and keep them occupied. You know, all that stuff you said after you came back from Southwold that time, you were absolutely right. The world is well and truly fucked, and the only thing that matters now is looking after number one. No amount of farming, fucking, or fighting is going to change anything, I've come to realize that. I stayed in Lowestoft because it was my best option until now, but it was never anything worth fighting for. I knew it wouldn't last."

"What about your fighters?"

"What about them? They can make their own choices. They've got brains—some of them, anyway. Those who haven't will just go the way of the Brutes."

"What about you? What do you do now?"

"Well, that's the million-dollar question, isn't it? And it depends on you. Like I said, I always knew something like this was probably going to happen sooner or later. Didn't think it would be quite so fast, though."

"Wait, wait . . . what do you mean, it depends on me? What have I got to do with anything?"

"You've got a plan, haven't you? You weren't just showing those foul fuckers downstairs around your house, were you? You must have had a damn good reason to risk bringing them here."

"I was giving them the food. I don't need it."

"Bullshit. Where were they going to take it?"

"How am I supposed to know?"

He shoots out his arm and slams me back against the wall again, winding me.

"Pissing me off is *not* a good idea, McCoyne. Tell me what you were planning."

"I'm not telling you anything. Listen, just kill me if it'll make you feel better. I'll be dead soon anyway."

He screws up his fist and pulls it back, and for a moment I brace myself, but he doesn't hit me. In frustration, he turns around and kicks the abandoned board game across the room.

"You're probably right," he says. "You can't talk if you're dead."

"I'm not going to talk."

"You don't have to. I'm getting to know you too well. I can tell when you're lying."

"Why would I bother lying now? What's the point?"

"Depends how many more Unchanged you're hiding."

"I'm not hiding any Unchanged. Come on, Hinchcliffe—"

"Deny it all you like, I know you're helping more of them."

"Think what you want."

"The taller guy downstairs," he says, "just before I killed him, I heard him say something about a boat, and something about a guy called Joseph."

I try bullshitting my way out of trouble. "The name means nothing to me. All I know is they were going to try to take a boat from one of the boatyards in town."

"They'd never have made it."

"That's what I told them."

"I still don't believe you."

"I still don't care."

He stands across the room and glares at me, and I can see him thinking, working through the options.

"So where is this Joseph?"

"I told you, I've never heard of him."

"And I told you, I can tell when you're lying. So if the Unchanged were trying to get onto a boat, it's safe to assume this mystery man Joseph and his pals are close to water."

"Hinchcliffe, I'm not going to tell you anything."

"They're not going to want to travel any farther inland, so the coast would have been the best option—and as the bulk of Ankin's forces came from Norwich to the north, I'm guessing they'll have wanted to travel south. Am I getting close now?"

My silence gives him all the answers he needs. He grabs my arm and drags me downstairs.

47

HINCHCLIFFE KNOWS HIS WAY around this place far better than I do. Bastard's obviously had his escape routes planned for some time. He drives the fully loaded jeep at a frantic speed along back roads and side streets I didn't even know existed, frequently skidding in the ice and snow, obviously as eager to get away from Lowestoft as I am.

The nauseous panic I've felt since he appeared in the house has finally started to reduce. I've spent weeks focusing on myself, my every decision made at the potential expense of everyone and everything else. Hinchcliffe is still doing exactly that, but now I find that I can't. I know that the fate of Joseph Mallon and the rest of the Unchanged now rests squarely on my shoulders, and suddenly it matters. Peter Sutton told me they were all that was left of the human race, and I'm starting to think he might be right. If I don't get to Southwold, they're fucked. I might not have the boat we promised them, but this jeep full of supplies is their lifeline. This food will buy them a little time, and with all that's happening in and around Lowestoft, that time might be enough for them to find another way of getting away. Then again, if I turn up there with Hinchcliffe, they won't have a hope in hell anyway. I have to get as close as I can, then get rid of him.

"All this was inevitable," he says as he swings the jeep around another corner, sliding across the road and just missing hitting a lone vagrant who scrambles for cover. Hinchcliffe doesn't even flinch.

"What are you talking about?"

"The war, them and us—the human race has been on a downward spiral since the first caveman killed the fucker living in the cave next door because he'd stolen his woman or his dinner."

"We were better than that. It didn't have to be this way."

"Yes it did. We're all hardwired to want to survive, and when push comes to shove, we'll do it at the expense of everyone else. I worked in the City, remember? I used to shaft people for a living. The Change came, and the war that followed was inevitable. There was nothing any of us could have done to stop it. We just did what we had to do, you included."

"We've all played our part, I don't deny that—but trying to rebuild a society based on power and fear? How was that ever going to be anything but a failure?"

"I was never trying to rebuild a society, you idiot. Don't you listen? I was just trying to survive. This day has been a long time coming," he continues, swerving around a traffic circle the wrong way and joining the A12. "Thing is, Danny, people have *always* been out for themselves, even when they made it look like they were cooperating. Look at this Ankin guy and all those other politicians you remember—elected into power to serve the people, but all they were doing was making sure their own backsides were comfortable and safe, lining their own nests. All the Hate did was accelerate things and help us all cut through some of the bullshit. Look back and you'll see that everything's always been built on power and fear. Think back to any story you remember from the news before all of this began, and you'll be able to trace it back to someone, somewhere who wasn't prepared to be fucked over by someone else."

I don't do what he says, because I'm sure he's probably right to an extent. What's gone is gone. The fact remains, though, I think he's wrong, and that a small group of Unchanged has survived against the odds is proof positive. We pass a couple more people on the side of the road, fighters and underclass. They all look the same now— pathetically lost and alone, with nothing left to fight for. Hinchcliffe doesn't even look at them. The bastard truly doesn't give a damn about anyone but himself.

"It can't all be as simple as you try to make it sound. Fighting doesn't solve everything."

"I never said it did," he says, struggling for a moment to keep control of the jeep in the slushlike snow.

"That's what you implied."

"You can get people to do what you want without hitting them."

"But it's easier if you do hit them? Or just let them think they're going to get the shit kicked out of them?"

"Something like that. Look, it's survival of the fittest, that's all I'm saying, and I'm damn sure I'm going to be the one who survives."

"What for?"

"What kind of a question's that? It's obvious."

"Is it? Spell it out to me, Hinchcliffe, because I don't get it. If you're the only one left standing after all of this, how exactly will you be feeling? You'll be a lonely fucking despot with nothing to do and no one left to order around. There's a cost to everything, and the more you take, the more you destroy. The last man standing in this world will inherit a fucking empty ruin."

"You've been spending too much time around Unchanged," he sneers at me. It's snowing hard again now, a sudden blizzard, and it blows in through the broken windshield, making it hard to see exactly where we are. I'm aware of the snow-covered shapes of several buildings on either side, and I realize we must have reached Wrentham, just past the midpoint between Lowestoft and Southwold. If I'm going to try to get out of this mess, I need to act fast.

"Just let me go, Hinchcliffe. Keep the jeep and all the food, just let me go."

"Why should I?"

"Because I'm dying. I'm not like you, I don't want to fight anymore.

I just want to go somewhere quiet. Somewhere I'm not going to be surrounded by people taking from me. I've got nothing left to give."

"My heart bleeds," he says, clearly not giving a shit. We're approaching the junction in the road now. He brakes hard and almost loses control of the jeep again, skidding to a slow stop and nudging up against the curb. "But we both know that's not true, don't we. We need to find this guy Joseph, remember? So which way now?"

"You choose," I say, determined not to help. We're barely two miles from Southwold, three at the most.

"Interesting," he mumbles, opening his window and looking down at the road. Some of the earlier snow has thawed and then frozen again. "Lots of tire tracks here. I'm guessing this was you earlier?"

I don't bother answering. He drives forward again, following the tracks he can see, and I slump back into my seat with relief. He's taken the wrong route and we're heading toward the bunker now. If he keeps going this way we'll end up back at the farm, and I'll make a break for it once we're there. There's a motorbike still lying in the yard, I think, and Peter Sutton's car is probably hidden somewhere nearby. Or maybe I can just trick Hinchcliffe into going inside the bunker, then shut him in? I like the idea of burying the bastard alive down there.

"Wait a minute," he says suddenly, "this isn't right. This road leads inland. You might have come *from* this direction, but this wasn't the way you were planning to go back, was it, Danny?"

My lack of response seems to answer his question. He pulls hard on the handbrake and spins the jeep around through one hundred and eighty degrees, sliding through the ice and slush until we're facing back the way we came. This time, when we reach the junction again, he looks more carefully at the tracks. I'm hoping enough fresh snow has fallen to make things less obvious, but it hasn't. He spots the wide sets of tracks left by the van and the delivery truck heading toward Southwold. The fucker is frustratingly smart. The tone of his voice changes as he accelerates toward the coast. He sounds excited, his mouth virtually salivating at the thought of killing Unchanged again.

"How many of them are there? There's at least two sets of tracks here, so we must be talking more than five. Ten? Honestly, Danny, you should have known better than anyone that we'd find them eventually."

"Just leave them alone, Hinchcliffe. Let them be."

He shoots a quick glance in my direction, letting me know in no uncertain terms what he thinks of that idea.

"You must be sicker than I thought. Leave Unchanged alive? For fuck's sake, I can't believe I'm hearing this."

He's riled, and I sense an opportunity to distract him. His temper and aggression might be his undoing. About a mile and a half to go now. Need to act fast.

"They're not a threat to you, and just about everybody else worth worrying about is dead. You should just get over yourself, Hinchcliffe. Just fuck off and get on with what's left of your own life and leave the Unchanged alone."

"Listen to what you're saying, McCoyne. This is Unchanged we're talking about. They were the cause of this fucking mess, and you want to let them live?"

"What difference does it make? There's hardly anyone left alive now. Just go your own way."

"You fucking moron! I should kill you!"

I know where I am now. I can see the snow-covered roofs of the business park where I left the car when Hinchcliffe sent me to Southwold before. Got to do it. Do it now.

"I'd rather spend the little time I've got left with the Unchanged than you, Hinchcliffe," I tell him, sneering and deliberately antagonizing him now. "It's fuckers like you who caused this war. At least they're—"

He snaps and lunges across the car at me. I duck under his flailing arms and grab the steering wheel from under him, turning it hard right. He tries to shove me back out of the way, but I've caught him off guard and I won't let go. His balance is off center and his reaction is too little, too late. He finally manages to push me away, then looks back out front and tries to steer in the opposite direction, but we're going too fast and the ground is covered with ice. The jeep skids, lifting up onto two wheels, then overturns and flips over. I tense my body and brace myself as we roll over and over, stopping with a sudden jolt as we hit the side of a building, thumping back down onto four wheels. My head snaps back on my shoulders with the sudden impact, and there's an immediate sharp, jabbing pain in my right ankle, but I stay conscious. Hinchcliffe is thrown forward, his head smacking hard against the wheel with a sickening crunch. He drops back into his seat and doesn't move, blood pouring down his face.

For a moment I just sit there, numb with the shock of the crash, watching Hinchcliffe and waiting for any sign of movement. He's completely still, not a flicker of life. I unstrap myself and force myself closer, desperate to make sure. I put my ear next to his mouth, terrified he's about to wake up and lunge forward. Nothing. No sound. I try to feel for a pulse with ice-cold, numb hands, but I can't feel anything.

This is it.

I'm still alive, and what's left of me is in one piece. The passenger door's buckled and won't open, so I have to scramble out through the broken windshield. I look back, once, then I start down the road, wishing I could move faster.

It's about a mile to Southwold.

48

I CAN TASTE BLOOD in my mouth, and I'm dragging my right foot now more than walking on it, but I'm almost there. I followed the intermittent tire tracks left by the others for as long as I could, then took a shortcut across the fields I worked in when I was last here.

The ice-cold air seems to numb the pain. The falling snow reminds me of ash drifting down, and I feel a sense of déjà vu, remembering walking along the highway just after the bomb. I remember lying on my back on the warm, sticky asphalt, watching Ellis as she disappeared alone into the radioactive gloom. The memory of everything I lost that day is enough to keep me moving toward the center of Southwold. I might still be able to help the rest of the Unchanged get away. More than that, I don't want to die out here on my own.

I stagger into the village, feeling myself fading with every slow step I take forward. Everything looks different here today, so much so that I'm not entirely sure this is Southwold at all. The dusting of snow makes everything look featureless and plain, but that's not the real reason for my confusion. The tips of the wreckage of those buildings destroyed by Hinchcliffe's fighters peek out through the ice, almost as if they're ashamed to be seen, and the pointless devastation is incredible and heartbreaking. Parts of the village have been virtually demolished; all of it now appears uninhabitable. There are row after row of burned houses, almost every building ruined, and my disorientation continues to increase until, at last, the distinctive outline of the lighthouse appears up ahead of me. Perhaps one of the only buildings left undamaged, its outline is blurred by another flurry of snow. Using its tall, tapering shape as a marker, I head straight for it, alternately looking up at its unlit light, then down at the undisturbed snow lying all around me, desperate to find more tire tracks or footprints. They'll be hiding inside. No Unchanged with any sense would risk being caught out in the open.

I cross the intersection and walk past the ruins of the hotel from where John Warner used to run this place. The building has been completely gutted by fire, as have many of the surrounding buildings. There's a mound of charred, snow-covered corpses in the middle of the village square, blackened limbs entwined, burned faces staring into space. I force myself to look away, and I remember this place as it was when I was last here. John Warner had genuinely good intentions, but he was wasting his time, I realize that now. What's left of my side of the human race is fucked: doomed to repeatedly beat itself into oblivion until there's nothing left of it but ashes and a handful of empty, hollow men like me.

I take a wrong turn through the side streets and have to double back and follow my own footprints to get back on track again. Exhausted, I eventually reach the lighthouse and lean up against the curved outside wall of the building for support, slowly sliding around it until I find the door. I half step, half fall inside, relieved to finally be out of the biting wind. The building is silent like a tomb, and I catch my breath with surprise when I step back and trip over the outstretched arm of a corpse. I look down, and, bizarrely, I feel real relief that it's someone like me and not one of the Unchanged. Judging from the stink and the discoloration of his skin, this guy's been dead for a while. Probably one of Warner's lookouts killed by Hinchcliffe's men.

I stagger to the foot of the stairs that spiral up inside the lighthouse and listen hopefully, but I don't hear anything other than my own labored, panting breaths. Maybe they're hiding at the top of the tower?

"Joseph," I shout, my voice echoing around the confined space. I wait for an answer, but none comes. "Joseph, it's Danny."

Still nothing.

I start to climb, knowing I have no choice but to check every inch of the building to be sure, and wishing we'd agreed on a meeting place with fewer stairs. I have to stop after every third or fourth step, and psych myself up to climb higher. I crane my neck upward, searching for movement in the shadows way above me. Where the hell are they? With each step I take, the more obvious it becomes that Joseph and the others never made it to Southwold. Anything could have happened to them once they'd left the bunker. Those tracks in the snow, they could have been made by anybody. With Lowestoft imploding and much of its surviving population leaving the town, this area might well have been crawling with people who would have killed the Unchanged in a heartbeat—massacred every last one of them before they'd even stopped to question why they were there or how they'd managed to survive for so long—and if the refugees didn't get them, it was even more likely that Ankin's troops would have. With hindsight, trying to get away from the bunker now seems the most stupid and sacrificial of moves. Even so, they had to try. They couldn't just sit there and wait to die. I shout out a couple more times as I continue to climb, but each time the only audible reply comes from my own voice echoing back at me.

Finally, legs trembling with effort, virtually having to crawl the last few steps on my hands and knees, I reach the top of the lighthouse. I use a rail to haul myself upright, then push myself through the door and out onto the observation platform. The wind's even stronger and colder up here, and I have to hold on tight just to stay standing. I lean back against the glass that surrounds the huge, useless lamp and stare out toward the sea, barely able to support my own weight any longer. I'm filled with an overwhelming, crushing sense of disappointment that they're not here, and it's all I can do to keep myself upright. Looking out into the nothingness of the gray clouds and falling snow, I find myself imagining how the Unchanged might have been caught. I picture Joseph trying hopelessly to reason with Hinchcliffe's Neanderthal fuckers or Ankin's troops, whichever found them first. I picture the little girl Chloe trying to run from them, bare feet crunching through the snow as she's chased down by a pack of the foul bastards . . .

I've had enough.

The more effort I put in, the less I achieve. It's time to stop. Maybe I should just go back inside, drag up a chair, then sit back and watch the sun rise as many more times as I can before I go. No one will disturb me up here. No one will know where I am. More to the point, no one will care.

Is this the moment where my life starts flashing before my eyes? Isn't that what's supposed to happen now? Just for a second I allow myself to drift back and remember things as they used to be before the war: the hellhole of an apartment I used to live in with Lizzie and the kids, doing a mindless job for a pittance pay, barely making ends meet, the endless arguing and struggling with the kids, all the grief I used to get from Harry . . . but I'd still rather be there than here today. Christ, I spent so much time focusing on the negatives that I completely missed the positives, which were there in abundance. The security, the relationships, being safe within the four walls of our home, the closeness I had with Lizzie and the children . . . It's an old cliché, but it's so true: You never realize what you've got until you lose it. I remember the war and all the killing—the joy and euphoria I used to feel whenever I ended an Unchanged life. To think, for a time I was thankful for the Hate and the freedom I thought it gave me. Now, even though I try hard not to, I find myself thinking about Ellis again, remembering what the Hate did to her and what she became. What it did to all of us . . .

It must be time now.

I lean back against the window and look out to sea, numb with cold, weak with effort, and hollow with disappointment. I'd go back inside, but I'm too tired to move. Everything's too much effort. Maybe I'll just sit here and—

Wait.

What's that?

It's probably just the snow or my eyes playing tricks on me, but I swear I just saw something moving down at street level. I lean forward over the edge of the lighthouse railings and look down, struggling to focus through the blizzard. Then I see it again . . . a brief flash of movement between two buildings, someone running from right to left. I shield my eyes from the white glare and look out along the seafront, but I can hardly see anything through the haze. I follow the line of the promenade from level with the center of the village all the way out toward the half-collapsed pier. What was it I saw? Scavengers? More refugees from Lowestoft? Or did I just imagine it? Am I going out of my mind and hallucinating now too? Maybe that'd be a good thing . . .

I look out toward the remains of the pier in the distance, then fix my eyes on a long strip of virtually empty parking lot that begins outside its dilapidated frontage and stretches away into the distance. I can see the shapes of several long-abandoned vehicles, and a couple nearer the entrance to the pier that aren't covered in snow. Wait a second . . . could it be? I lean out over the edge of the lighthouse railings as far as I dare, knowing another few inches won't make a scrap of difference but praying it will, desperately trying to make out more detail. It looks like a van and a truck. Through a momentary break in the snow I see the side of the truck. Although I can't distinguish any real level of detail from back here, I'm sure I can make out the outline of the picture of the woman's face I remember, staring at the truck parked in the cowshed before Peter Sutton showed me the bunker. That's definitely the van I drove away from Hinchcliffe's factory yesterday. Jesus Christ, they must have made it. Joseph and the others made it to Southwold! I quickly scan the length of the pier again, this time focusing on the collection of ramshackle wooden buildings on the walkways that stretch out over the ocean—and there, some sheltering from the blizzard in empty gift shops and cafés, others hanging out over the railings, waiting to catch sight of the boat that's never going to come, I see them. The last of the Unchanged. I make myself move again. Got to get down there.

Heading down the tightly spiraling steps is infinitely easier than climbing up. I stumble down quickly and trip out of the door, then start moving toward the pier, wishing I could go faster but knowing I can't. Not much energy left, now. Not much time left, either. I head directly for the ocean, moving in a straight line down through the ruins until I reach the promenade, then start the long walk up toward the pier, the bitter wind feeling like it's knocking me two steps sideways for every step I manage to take forward. The snow is like a dense fog again now, and I'm walking blind, but eventually the building at the shore end of the pier looms large ahead of me, a once proud and grand facade that's now as crumbling and worn as everything else.

"McCoyne," a voice shouts at me, and I look around for whoever's yelling. Can't tell where it came from or who it was. Didn't sound like Joseph. Was it Parker or one of the others? The noise of the wind and the waves just adds to the confusion, and I keep moving forward. I stop when I reach the van and the truck and look back. Someone's walking toward me, following me from the town. Can't make out who it is. He starts to speed up, but whoever it is, he's clearly struggling. Is he injured? I take a couple of steps back toward him, then stop. Fuck, it's Hinchcliffe. I try to get away, but despite his injuries he's still too fast for me, his hate and anger driving him on, oblivious to his pain. He reaches out and grabs my shoulder, then spins me around and throws me back against the side of the van. The noise echoes through the air like a gunshot, and I bounce back off the metal toward him, straight into his fist. He catches me hard on the chin, and I slam back against the van again, then drop to the ground, face numb, head filled with blinding pain. He picks me up by the collar again, lifting me until our faces are just inches apart. My feet are off the ground, toes barely scraping the slush.

"Hinchcliffe, I—"

"What the hell are you trying to do? I should kill you right now."

"That's your answer to everything."

He throws me back against the van again, and I drop to my knees. I watch him as he comes toward me, drenched with his own blood, fist raised ready to strike again and finish me off. I don't have the strength to defend myself anymore. Just let it happen . . .

"I don't understand," he says. "Why, Danny? You could've had it all."

"What, like you?" I manage to spit at him, my mouth filled with blood. "We've all lost everything, you stupid bastard, and it's all thanks to people like you. The more you try to take, the more stuff slips through your fingers, didn't you realize that? You started with a whole town and ended up barricaded into one corner of it. Even then you were a virtual prisoner in the courthouse. You've lost that now and there's nothing left. It's over. It's all gone. Just leave me alone, Hinchcliffe."

Still staring down at me and breathing hard, he takes a step back, then runs forward and punches his fist into the side of the van. I slowly pick myself up, dribbling red into the snow around my feet.

"Just kill me if you're going to. Why don't you just get it over with?"

"Because you're still useful. Look around you, Danny. The fact you're here at all just proves my point. There are people still fighting and dying in Lowestoft, but you're safe. *We're* safe. It's like you've been observing the rest of us, only getting involved and getting your hands dirty when you absolutely have to."

"Or when you forced me to."

"Look what you achieved—"

"I've achieved nothing, Hinchcliffe. I've lost everything, same as you."

"But you're the man who walked free from a gas chamber. You told me stories about how you talked your way out of Unchanged traps. For Christ's sake, you were almost right under one of the bombs but you managed to get away."

"Right place, right time . . ."

"It's more than that. It has to be."

"Empty words, Hinchcliffe."

"No, I swear. Listen to me, we can get out of this mess and start again. I know where we can find food, and there's a place—"

"You're out of your fucking mind. You just don't get it, do you? All you know now is fighting. You won't ever change. It doesn't matter where you go or what you do, the end result will always be the same. You don't need me to help you fuck things up."

Hinchcliffe walks away, and I can see that he's losing a lot of blood from his left leg. He's limping badly. I push myself off the side of the van and try to slip past and get to the front of the pier entrance building, but I've barely taken a couple of steps before he sees me. He lunges for me, and I lose my already unsteady footing and hit the deck. I'm on my back looking up at him leaning down over me. He draws a holstered machete.

"Maybe you're right—"

"Leave him alone, you bastard," another voice shouts. I lean my head back and see that it's Parker. He's aiming a rifle directly at Hinchcliffe, and behind him Joseph Mallon is standing in an open doorway. Hinchcliffe stares at the Unchanged in disbelief, then dives at Parker, unable to suppress his instinctive hatred of the Unchanged. Scrambling back out of the way, Parker fires the rifle but misses as Hinchcliffe anticipates and drops to the ground. Seemingly oblivious to any pain he must be feeling, he immediately gets up again and flashes his blade at Parker. The Unchanged man's rifle and his severed right arm fall into the snow just a short distance from where I'm lying. Hinchcliffe drags him down and drops onto his stomach, then plunges the machete down again and again into his flesh, totally consumed with Hate, everything else temporarily forgotten. I drag myself back up and push Joseph away.

"Get out of here," I yell into his face as I shove him back through the door, then pull it shut again. I watch him as he watches me through the glass, then starts to back away because Hinchcliffe is close again. I catch a brief reflection of his movement and spin around to face him. I catch him as he throws himself at the door like a vicious, hunting animal. It takes all my remaining strength to hold him back.

"Unchanged," he hisses, trying to fight his way past me. "We have to kill them!"

He tries to throw me to one side, but I've got hold of him and I won't let go. We spin around through almost a full three hundred and sixty degrees together and he smashes me against the door again. I feel every bone in my body rattle, but I still won't let go.

"Just leave them, Hinchcliffe," I plead with him, our faces just inches apart.

"Leave them? Are you out of your fucking mind? Listen to yourself. You know this will never be over until they're all dead and—"

"You know as well as I do that this is never going to end. If we're not fighting Unchanged we're fighting each other. It's like you said, we're on a downward spiral, and this is rock bottom."

"You're farther down than me," he says, and he lifts up his knee and thuds it into my balls. A wave of nauseating pain shoots through me, and I let him go. Another Unchanged man bursts out through the door to the pier and tries to rush him. He hits Hinchcliffe at full speed, and the two of them smack into the side of the delivery truck. For a second it looks like he's been overpowered, but Hinchcliffe's aggression and rage are remarkable and unmatched. He pushes the malnourished Unchanged man away with barely any effort, then snatches up Parker's rifle from the ground and, holding it by the barrel, smacks him around the head repeatedly with its wooden butt.

"Come on," a desperate voice whispers in my ear. It's Joseph. He puts his hands under my shoulders, lifts me back up, and drags me toward the pier door. Hinchcliffe doesn't even notice. He's totally focused on the kill, venting all his anger, hatred, and frustration on the poor blood-soaked bastard who lies dying at his feet.

WE MOVE QUICKLY THROUGH a musty amusement arcade, Joseph having to support me as we stagger along the gaps between rows of silent gaming machines. He ducks and weaves around one-armed bandits and video-game cabinets with smashed screens, trying to keep us moving at a speed I can barely match. He heads for another open door at the far end of this large, high-ceilinged room and I follow him through, out onto the pier. The wind out here over the sea is ferocious. The slatted wooden walkways are slippery as grease, the snow and ice turned to slush by the salt spray from the water below. There are several narrow buildings up ahead, stretching up along the center of the pier. A door at the front of the third one along is being held open.

"Get inside," Joseph says, shoving me into what used to be a gift shop. There are still rows of dust-covered souvenirs on shelves on the walls. The Unchanged are cowering in every available space. Wherever I look I see their frightened faces staring back at me, most of them desperate for help and reassurance. I'm in no position to provide either. Others of them are armed and ready to fight.

"Where are Parker and Charlie?" a man crouching down next to me asks. Joseph shakes his head.

"They didn't stand a chance," I tell him. "None of you do."

"What the hell happened, Danny?" Joseph asks. "What about Todd and Dean? The boat?"

"We never made it as far as the boatyard," I explain. "He was waiting for me back at the house when we got there. He waited until they'd loaded up the jeep, then killed them both while I was out of the way. I didn't know he was going to be there, Joseph, I swear. Fucker was on to me."

"Who is he?" someone else asks.

"Hinchcliffe."

"Peter told me about him," Joseph says. "Said he was the worst of the worst."

"That's about right."

"But there must be something we can do?"

Tracey, the doctor, gets to her feet. "I know exactly what we can do," she says, picking up a bludgeon. "We kill the fucker." She has to get past me to get out. She tries to push me aside, but the shack's so narrow and tightly packed that she can't get through. I try to hold her back, but she shoves me away.

"You don't understand—"

"No, *you* don't understand," she yells at me. "There are almost thirty of us and just one of him. We get out there now and we kill him."

"Then that will make you just as bad as him."

"So? It's a necessity, McCoyne. We have to do it to survive. There's a world of difference between killing just one man to save us and all the thousands of innocent deaths that people like him are responsible for."

"Is there?"

"Of course there is."

"So what do you think I am?"

"What?"

"Me and Peter Sutton, how do you think we managed to survive aboveground for so long?"

"Peter told us," she answers. "He said he could fake the anger and make them think he was like them. He said you were the same. Peter risked everything for us."

"There's no disputing that, but he wasn't completely honest with any of you."

There's a ripple of discontent when I dare say something negative about Sutton.

"What are you talking about?"

"We're like them," I tell her. "Me and Peter, we're the Haters, just like Hinchcliffe out there, and all those other bastards that have hounded you and made your lives hell for the last year."

"I don't believe you."

"It's true," Joseph says. "I saw it for myself before I found Peter. I knew Danny from way back. He was a killer. He learned how to suppress the urge to fight."

The space around me grows in size, and I sense people pushing themselves back against the walls to put the maximum possible distance between us.

"Then as soon as we've finished with this Hinchcliffe, we'll come back for you," Tracey sneers.

"Probably not worth the effort. I'll be dead soon anyway."

"Good."

I'm about to speak again when someone screams. I turn around and look back along the pier toward the shore. I can see Hinchcliffe just inside the arcade building now, coming this way.

"Thing is," I tell them, "whatever it was that caused the divide between us, it doesn't matter now. I don't know why it happened, and I doubt any of us ever will. All that matters now is what happens next. We've got to abandon all this us-and-them bullshit, because we're all that's left of the human race. You can either put a stop to the killing today or keep going at it until we're all dead."

"Which part of this don't you understand, you fucking moron?" Tracey asks. "If we don't kill him, he'll kill us."

Farther down the pier, Hinchcliffe is checking each of the wooden buildings in turn, kicking down doors and hunting for the Unchanged.

"The first person I killed," I tell all of them, shouting to make myself heard over their nervous voices and the sound of the wind battering this exposed shack, "was my father-in-law. And do you know why I did it? You want to know what made me kill Harry and the hundreds of other people I went on to kill after him? I killed them all because I thought that if I didn't, they'd kill me. Do you understand that? People like me killed people like you because we thought we had to do it before you killed us. Does that make any sense? It doesn't to me. Almost a year further on and I still don't understand why. But does it sound familiar? It should, because you're saying exactly the same thing now. Kill him before he kills us. It doesn't have to be this way. You can put an end to it today."

The door at the other end of this narrow building flies open, and Gary, the badly scarred man, rushes outside, armed with a length of metal tubing. He runs back toward Hinchcliffe to try to head him off, but the poor naive bastard is still shackled with the uncertainty of being Unchanged. Instead of immediately attacking, he stops short and wildly swings at Hinchcliffe, who deflects one glancing blow, then catches the end of the pipe as it comes toward him again. Even injured he has more strength than this single, malnourished Unchanged. With each of them holding on to one end of the metal tubing, Hinchcliffe uses his weight and power advantage to swing Gary around into the railings along the edge of the pier. His body visibly rattles, and he screams with agony, then drops to his knees. Before anyone else can react, Hinchcliffe lays into him, beating him to a bloody pulp with ferocious speed, then lifting up his battered frame and pushing it over the side of the pier, down into the freezing waves below.

"Get them out of here, Joseph," I yell as panic spreads quickly through the group. He does as I say, herding the rest of the Unchanged as a single mass out through the door at the far end of this narrow space, then trying to usher them back down along the other side of the wooden buildings. I instinctively check that the children are safe. A woman is carrying Peter Sutton's grandson, and someone else has got Chloe on his back. I see the boy Jake's head deep in the middle of the throng.

"Keep moving and keep safe," I yell after them. They're all that's left now.

I exit through the other door. Hinchcliffe's staggering toward this building. I block his way forward, hoping to buy the others a little time. He stops and rocks back on his heels, panting hard.

"Just let them go, Hinchcliffe," I tell him, knowing my words will probably have little effect. "What difference does it make to you whether they live or die? There are so few of them left. There are so few of *us* left. Just let them go."

"You know I can't do that," he says, lurching closer. "You shouldn't be able to, either."

He clumsily tries to sidestep me, but I move, too, and he just slumps against me, exhausted, his sudden weight almost knocking me over. He tries to push past, but I won't let go.

"Are you scared of them? Do you think a few starved Unchanged are that much of a threat to you? Christ, Hinchcliffe, some of them are just kids."

"It makes no difference."

"Just walk away. I'll come with you. We'll go wherever you want. Start again somewhere like you said. Let's just end this today."

"I'll end it, Danny, and I don't need your help anymore."

"But can't you see? The fighting is the cause of all of this, not the solution."

Hinchcliffe grabs at my collar and flips me over, slamming me down onto my back and winding me. I can hardly breathe. He starts to move away, and I roll over and reach out to try to catch him but I'm too slow and I watch helplessly as he strides farther down the pier. I crawl over to the handrail and pull myself back up onto my feet. Up ahead, Hinchcliffe takes my pistol from his pocket and starts firing indiscriminately at the Unchanged. Two shots go nowhere; the third hits one of them in the leg. A woman collapses in agony. Suddenly inspired, he surges toward her without mercy. She's still alive when he reaches her, but within seconds she's dead, finished by the remaining bullets and a volley of savage kicks to the side of her head.

Through the snow I see the Unchanged group has split. Most have continued to move back toward the shore with Joseph, but several others have panicked and gone the other way and are now hopelessly isolated. In confusion they run toward the far end of the pier, and Hinchcliffe heads after them, half staggering, half sprinting, unbelievably managing to somehow find enough energy to keep moving. He tackles the closest of them, an elderly man with long yellow-white hair, pulling his legs out from under him. He smashes his face repeatedly into the metal base of an observation point, continuing long after he's dead.

I drag myself along the railings toward him. There are massive holes in the decking here—huge chunks missing like they've been bitten away by some enormous creature—and I can hear the pier creaking and groaning beneath me, its weakened metal struts straining the farther we get from the shore. By the time I've managed to make it across, Hinchcliffe is already attacking another man, smothering his screaming face with his hand. He's distracted by the intensity of the kill, and I throw myself at him. He lets go of the man's corpse and turns on me, using his bulk to force me back into the farthest corner of the pier, then tightening his grasp around my throat. My feet slip and slide on the wet boards and I can't get a grip. I can hardly breathe. His eyes lock onto mine.

"I've had enough of you, you useless cunt. You're worse than they are."

"I'm *the same* as them. We both are."

Hinchcliffe shoves me back, an expression of utter disgust and contempt on his hate-filled, blood-streaked face. He raises his hand and screws up his fist, but my eyes focus on something happening behind him. He sees that I'm distracted and looks back over his shoulder. The Unchanged are returning. A group of four of them is advancing toward him. Tracey, the doctor, is at the front of the group, her bludgeon held high, ready to strike. I'm forgotten in a heartbeat, immediately dismissed. Hinchcliffe turns and throws himself at them. Tracey lashes out, but he ducks under her weapon and grabs the man immediately to her right instead, catching him completely off guard, twisting his outstretched arm around and forcing the knife he's carrying up into his own gut. Tracey spins around and smacks the bludgeon down across his back, and he drops to his knees. Another man comes at him with a block of wood, and the two of them rain down a barrage of blows. Still he keeps fighting. The fucker's on his knees, but he won't give up. He tries to stand, blood pouring from gashed skin, matting his long, sweat-soaked hair. He manages to raise himself up onto one foot, but before he can stand fully upright the fourth Unchanged comes at him and plunges a serrated blade deep into his belly. He drops onto his back, skull cracking against the deck, and this time he doesn't move.

I lean back against the edge of the pier, too exhausted to do any-thing. The three remaining Unchanged stand over Hinchcliffe's corpse, then turn to face me.

"Now you," Tracey says.

"Just leave me. I helped you."

"You're one of them, McCoyne. As long as there are any of your kind left alive, we're all still in danger."

"You're wrong. It's over now."

"It will be once you're dead."

The three of them come at me like a pack with a speed and anger I can't match. I try to squirm past, but one of them trips me up. He rolls me over onto my back, then stamps his boot into my groin.

"Kill him," another one of them shouts, yelling into the wind. "Finish it!"

I try to get up, but I'm kicked right back down again. I land on top of Hinchcliffe's bloody corpse. His eyes flicker open. The bastard is still alive.

"You were wrong," he says, gurgling blood, his voice barely audible. "You should have listened to me . . ."

"Fucker's got a grenade!" Tracey shouts.

Rough hands grab me under my shoulders and drag me off Hinch-cliffe. I'm dropped on my back again. I look across and see that Hinch-cliffe has the grenade he took from me earlier. The Unchanged try to pry it out of his hands, but it's too late. The pin's out. One of them stamps on his wrist, and his fingers instinctively open, letting it go. I see it roll away from him, rattling along the woodwork. The Unchanged scatter, but there's no time. They run past me screaming, but there's nothing they can do. They can't—

Seven Minutes Later

THEY DRAGGED THE BODIES they could find from the surf beneath the collapsed pier, most of them dead, some injured, one of them dying. They carried the dying man to safety and hid him in an empty building along with the others who'd managed to get back to shore. They made him as comfortable and warm as they could. There was nothing more they could do for him than that.

They stayed there for more than half a day.

When they were finally ready to move, Danny McCoyne briefly regained consciousness but quickly slipped away again. He drifted in and out of darkness for a couple of minutes longer, enough time to know that the Unchanged were carrying him. He could hear the snow crunching beneath their feet. Or was it shingle? He looked up, and between flashes of brightness, he saw a face he recognized. The man put a reassuring hand on his shoulder and spoke to him.

"Not long now, Danny. Almost there."

Two Days Later

THE NEXT TIME HE woke for anything more than a couple of minutes, the whole world felt like it was moving. The ground was shifting and rolling beneath him. He felt the same hand on the same shoulder, gently shaking him awake this time. He tried to sit up but he couldn't. No strength left.

When Joseph saw that he was awake, he called for help. Two men wrapped Danny up in blankets and helped carry him outside. The brightness hurt his eyes and his vision was blurred, but he could see and feel enough to know they were at sea. They sat him down in a chair, and Joseph sat next to him. Danny looked around and, very slowly, his eyes began to adjust to the daylight. At first all he could see was the gray above and the blue-green around them, but soon he saw distant browns and blacks, too. The world slowly began to come into focus. He was looking back toward the land and the blackened, smoldering ruins of yet another dead town.

"We've been out here for the best part of two days," Joseph said quietly. "Found this boat just outside Southwold and managed to get it going. I just wanted you to know that we made it. Thought you'd like to see what you did before . . ."

He didn't need to finish his sentence. Danny knew what he was avoiding saying, and he was right, he didn't have long. He was surprised he was still here. Maybe he was dead already? He didn't think that was the case. He could still feel his body running down. Parts of him ached; other parts he couldn't feel at all. He hurt less than he had before, but he knew that wasn't a good thing.

The boat slowly turned through the water, lazily sailing back toward the shore. The sun was right above them now, hazy yellow, just about visible through the wispy cloud cover. It hurt Danny to look, but it was too beautiful not to.

"This is what's left of Felixstowe, I think," Joseph said. "We've stopped a few times to look for supplies, but everywhere has been pretty much the same as this. Everywhere is dead. Not a soul left alive. Oh, we found your jeep before we left Southwold, by the way. Got all the supplies you brought with you. Quite a hoard you had there, Danny."

Joseph waited for a response, but none came.

"We're going to keep heading down this way. My guess—my hope—is that if we can get south of what's left of London, we might find somewhere. Kent, maybe. Dungeness."

"Isle of Wight," Danny managed to say, his weak voice sounding like someone else's. "It's supposed to be nice there."

"I'll bear that in mind," Joseph said.

Danny said nothing else. He just sat back and listened to the normality of the moment. The waves lapping against the bow of the boat, the engine chugging contentedly, people talking, kids playing . . .

"You still here, Danny?" Joseph asked, startling him. "I was hoping you were going to stay with us a while longer."

"Don't know if I can."

He rested his hand on Danny's arm. "You should try. You deserve it. You did a good thing, you know."

"I did more bad things than good. We all did."

Danny looked across the deck of the boat. He saw people standing out in the open with each other, surveying the dead town they were approaching. Just a couple of days ago, they'd been trapped underground with little realistic prospect of ever seeing daylight again. He watched as Chloe played with Peter Sutton's grandson, both of them wrapped up in as many layers of clothing as they could comfortably wear. At the bow of the boat, a man and a woman stood together, locked in a passionate embrace, wind blowing the woman's hair, the two of them looking like characters from some film.

"You want a drink?"

"No. Save it."

"You should try to have something."

"No point. Just want to rest now."

Danny closed his eyes, the brightness finally too much to stand. In the darkness he thought back and remembered the people he'd lost. He wished that Lizzie and their three children were on this boat now instead of him. Or maybe here with him . . .

A few seconds passed. Or had it been minutes? The dead town seemed closer than when he'd last looked.

"You still with us, friend?"

Danny's eyes flickered open again. "Very tired, Joe."

Joseph wrapped another blanket around his shoulders. Danny let his head loll forward, but then snapped it back again quickly when he heard a child yelp with pain. The noise startled him. It made him panic, made him remember.

"Don't worry, it's nothing," Joseph said, immediately sensing his dying friend's unease. "Just kids being kids, that's all."

Danny watched as a woman separated Jake and Chloe, both of them bickering over half a can of soda.

"She stole it off me," Jake protested. He yanked Chloe's hair, then grabbed the can from her and knocked the rest of it back in one gulp.

"That was mine!" Chloe screamed, lunging for him again. "I'll get you for that," she sobbed.

Exhausted, Danny's eyes flickered shut.